THE LOST PRINCE OF CADIRA

STEPHANIE ANNE

THE SHADOWLAND SAGA BOOK 1

THE

LOST

PRINCE

OF

CADIRA

STEPHANIE ANNE

THE LOST PRINCE OF CADIRA
Copyright © 2020 by Stephanie Anne

For information contact :
https://www.stephanieanneauthor.com/

Cover design by Celin Graphics
Edited by Chloe Hodge
Book Formatting by Derek Murphy @Creativindie
ISBN: 978-0-6488520-0-1 (paperback)
ISBN: 978-0-6488520-1-8 (e-book)
ISBN: 978-0-6488520-2-5 (hardcover)
FIRST EDITION: OCTOBER 2020

TO MY MUM, JENNIFER, FOR
INTRODUCING ME TO THE WORLD OF YA
AND LETTING ME FIND MY PASSION AND
PURPOSE THERE.

1

NEW ORLEANS

The hairs on the back of Eliza's neck bristled as she crept through the night. Barbs of ancient magic prickled her skin; it danced across the night with the power of a thousand stars, pulsing throughout the New Orleans cemetery like a dazzling conduit of enchantments and curses. The whispers of the dead were carried on the chilling autumn breeze, brushing over her skin like phantom fingers, sending a course of shivers up her spine.

The prickling sensation did not cease as her own magic formed a living barrier around her. It speared out into the night like creeping vines, connecting her with the essence of New Orleans and its dead, who lay in the maze of stone tombs around her.

Eyes followed her, their gaze watchful. Keys clutched between her steady fingers, Eliza stepped around cement blocks and withered flower bouquets, stopping before a towering white mausoleum, heart pounding in her chest.

In the branches, she heard the screeching caw of crows. They sat perched in the skeletal limbs of the dilapidated tree to her right, their beady eyes as bright as the stars that glared down at her from the sky. They continued their dangerous song, even as she glared from the shadows, but they were the only thing she could hear in the endless night.

She still felt it, though, that sense of not quite being alone. Despite the precautions she had taken to protect herself—charms sewn into the hems of her jeans, the iron ring on her pinkie finger—it did not stop the shiver of doubt that coursed down her spine. The sensation of being followed had sent her careening into the cemetery. The familiarity of the cemetery steadied her racing heart, but not by much.

Eliza's green eyes flickered over the shadows, searching the cracks in the mausoleums. They darted down the small alleys between the white stone structures that usually housed spirits who had been forgotten, bound to the land and not their resting places. Despite that knowledge, she let herself imagine she was completely alone with the dead. But even the dead weren't that quiet.

As if summoned by the deep entanglement of power, Eliza's magic rose and swelled until it surrounded her like a protective shield. A flash of silver caught her eye, and drawing in a shuddering breath, Eliza looked up to the space above the white marble mausoleum.

The air continued to pulse with that strange and dangerous magic; its ancient thrum drew her out of the darkness, sent her own magic spiralling back to her out of fear. In the back of her mind, she felt that ageless power whisper to her, a tangle of raw energy. The iron on her finger heated. Something told her to run.

Her blood ran cold, fear rearing its head. She wanted to turn around and run, but she was caught between terror and stupid curiosity.

Silver moonlight reflected off a drawn sword; Eliza's gaze travelled up the shining blade to the armoured hand that held it. Even in the dark, with the dim light of the city illuminating the cemetery, she couldn't mistake what she saw as she continued eyeing him— pointed ears and piercing green eyes. *Faery*. Lithe and tall, his silhouette stood out against the blankets of light that made up the New Orleans skyline. Only one thought entered her head as she took him in: *I am in deep, deep shit.*

Sitting on his shoulder, with irises of molten gold, was a raven with the darkest feathers. The ancient power she had sensed thrummed from that being, Eliza realised, as she took a hesitant step back. *A Changed One*. That deceptive power of Shifting radiated from the gold-eyed raven.

They were not of the mortal realm, where magic was squashed, and darkness lay in the hands of humans with power. Nothing as ancient as the Changed One, with its immeasurable power and immortal status, would be caught dead wandering through the mortal realm, or following Eliza through a New Orleans cemetery. And she knew they had not been banished to this world, either. Not in the same way she had, not like Kay.

They were something else entirely. They did not belong here.

Eliza ran.

Mausoleums and graves stretched out around her, filling her senses and her vision, until all she could see was death—perhaps even her death, too.

A Faery Knight and a Changed One. She snorted, even with the fear drumming deep in her bones. Never in her life had she felt such power, and never before had she imagined it would be directed at *her*. It both terrified her and excited her. But she knew to run first and ask questions later.

I'm terrified of a freaking bird, she thought. Eliza skidded to a halt and swore. Standing by the exit, the Knight waited, his ancient sword still drawn. His back was to her, and despite her situation, Eliza poked out her tongue before turning away. She eyed the mausoleums with frustration before running once again.

She knew the place better than the reapers who guarded it. And she should have been able to get herself out. Overhead, the caw of crows signalled her appearance. But her gut told her it wasn't the mortal creatures who dwelled in New Orleans who gave her away.

Twigs snapped beneath her feet, and though she stayed upright, every so often her feet would snag on a piece of loose rubble or slip on stray flowers that had blown off the mausoleum doors. Eliza's breath turned to ice in her lungs as she continued her sprint through the darkness, only stopping when she slammed into the side of a soot-stained mausoleum, shaking free the dried flowers and layer of wet leaves that cascaded down her back.

"Shit." She hated the feeling of wet leaves clinging to her neck. They reminded her too much of slimy bugs.

Swinging around, she ploughed straight through the half-visible silhouette of a spirit.

Walking through a spirit was not like walking through air, especially when she—and she alone—could see them. For a regular mortal, or her grandfather or Kay, a spirit felt like a cold patch of air. For Eliza, it felt like stepping through a wall of jelly and coming out the other side unscathed.

The spirit in question took a dignified step away, her loud, "Excuse you!" filling the air. Eliza flinched and stepped into the safety of the darkness behind a mausoleum, though for the most part, she knew the Faery Knight and his raven could not possibly be able to hear the two-hundred-year-old ghost standing in the light of the waning moon.

"Hush up," Eliza said, forced to keep her voice low. They might not be able to hear Miranda, but they certainly could hear *her*. "Something is following me, and I need you to be *quiet*."

Eliza had met Miranda years ago by chance—the spirit had been newly awakened in modern day New Orleans after being dug up in light of an old murder investigation... Or so Eliza had been informed by the young woman's spirit. Miranda had been shot in the chest, the bullet recovered—and matching that of a recent murder victim. It had been Eliza's first—and only—attempt in helping the spirits. At the time, it had been exciting, but Eliza had quickly learned how dangerous her magic could be in the eyes of mortals. It had been enough for her to be discrete with the power that came so naturally to her.

The spirit's gaze followed Eliza's; together, they half-heartedly searched the darkness between the mausoleums, even the rooves, but everywhere Eliza looked, she could not spot that flash of silver or the golden glare of the raven. That ageless magic still thrummed through her, though she couldn't feel the full extent of it anymore.

"Ahem." Miranda coughed, drawing Eliza's attention back to where they stood, back to the soot-covered mausoleum and the fences to her right. "What is following you? And will it cause *me* any harm?"

Eliza rolled her eyes, though her heart still raced in her chest— from the sprint and from fear. "I thought I was being followed by something..." *By a Faery Knight and a creature changed by ancient magic. Because, yeah, that'll go over well with the traditionalist.* She grimaced. Miranda knew nothing of the magical realm and its otherworldly occupants. Eliza wanted to keep it that way.

"Looked like a Knight," Eliza continued. "Maybe." She felt a pang of guilt lying to Miranda, but Eliza doubted she'd handle questions about her world, even if the questions came from a curious spirit.

Miranda followed at a distance as Eliza walked up to the fence and checked both avenues before setting herself up to climb.

"I do not believe I have ever seen a Knight here before," the ghost mused, her gloved hands resting over the top of her bloodied chest. "Was he handsome, like the Knights in Momma's fairy-tales?"

Eliza hesitated halfway over the top of the crumbling wall surrounding the cemetery. Below her, on the other side, the streets were nearly empty, as if the people of New Orleans knew to fear the cemeteries at night. She grunted, swinging her other leg over. "I was a little distracted," she said, sparing the spirit one last look. "I'll see you tomorrow, Miranda."

The spirit merely looked up at the wall indignantly, arms crossed tightly over her bloodied chest. "Good night, Miss Elizabeth. I do hope the bed bugs eat you."

Eliza laughed. Jumping from the top of the fence, she landed silently on the balls of her feet, and rose.

Just as quickly as she appeared, Eliza made sure she disappeared. Knowing that she wasn't alone, that she was being followed, only made her move faster. Even in the swallowing quiet of the street and the enveloping darkness, Eliza felt eyes on her; eyes that did not belong to anything from this world.

Eliza shoved her hands into the pockets of her hoody and started for the road home.

Despite the darkness—the shadows that seemed to devour the light and feast on the stars—Eliza could find her way. Ever since she could remember, the streets of New Orleans' French Quarter was her backyard. The metropolis of light and colour, of people and customs, had swaddled the scared five-year-old when she had first appeared in the mortal world. And since then, she had sworn to care for them in the way they had her.

The old building Eliza called home appeared before her, sitting between two larger, modern blocks of wrought iron and red bricks. It had two storeys with a red-brick exterior and wraparound balconies, with rooms that held artefacts from another world and a courtyard filled to the brim with magic. Eliza couldn't imagine herself living anywhere else. Not in the mortal world, and certainly not in the world she had been born in.

Sometimes, she forgot that she was not entirely from Earth.

Sometimes, she wished forgetting were the easy part.

Standing across from the house, Eliza hesitated. Still, that feeling of being followed did not leave her. Had she been wrong to come straight home? *No*, she thought. Her grandfather would know what to do, surely.

She bit her lip and looked back down the street towards the cemetery. She thought the Knight would be there, watching her from the other side of the road. But there was nothing.

A light flickered on in one of the front rooms, then another in the courtyard. Pursing her lips, Eliza already knew what trouble would be coming for her, especially if her grandfather *and* Kay had sensed her arrival, and knew that midnight had already clicked over without so much as a word from her.

With a sigh, Eliza crossed the street, shoulders hunched. She stopped at the dotted line in the centre of the road, brows furrowed. The hairs on the back of her neck prickled once again, and her gaze darted behind her shoulder. She searched the dimly lit street for that flash of silver or the golden irises of the raven but found nothing. Not even a blip on her radar.

Nevertheless, she sprinted the rest of the way, skidding to a stop once inside of the wrought iron doors, then slammed them shut.

If they followed her home, they'd be pissed to know how fortified the house was. Magic protected them there, though it was only a whisper of what belonged in the other world. It was that sense of safety that calmed her racing heart.

Swallowing the lump in her throat, Eliza slowly uncoiled herself.

"Elizabeth." The darkness that surrounded the entryway receded as the courtyard lit up, revealing not only herself, but her grandfather, who stood in the doorway with his arms crossed. At his side, their flat-nosed cat, Odin, paced, copper tail twitching, one blue-green eye blinking up at her. Both, unsurprisingly, looked disappointed.

She stood at her full height—nearly as tall as her grandfather—and spoke. "I can explain, please."

Fortunately, her grandfather, Davis, was a forgiving man, but with his arms crossed and thin lips pursed, Eliza could not help but wonder if perhaps she was slowly destroying that trust he had in her. She had promised to be home by eleven, and yet the large grandfather clock in the courtyard continued to tick past midnight, until it was closer to the witching hour than her curfew.

"Something was following me," she said, releasing a heavy breath.

Almost like breaking a trance, her grandfather sighed and shook his head, silver hair mussed. Odin ran into the courtyard situated at the centre of their house and beckoned them to follow. At a distance, Eliza walked behind her grandfather as he said, "Something is always following you." His voice was soft, not reprimanding, but not forgiving either. Tired. "What was it today?"

At seven, she had constructed an elaborate story about how she had become friends with the gnome who walked her to the babysitter's on Fridays, and at age ten, Eliza had claimed an ogre had been following her home from the park one day. Saying something was following her wasn't a surprise, and she knew that. It didn't stop her heart from dropping; the lack of faith she felt from her grandfather stung.

But Eliza hesitated nonetheless, biting down on her bottom lip. It wasn't that he would not *believe* her, but Eliza knew the story of the boy who cried wolf too many times. But still, she tried. "I'm not lying," she said, following him into the courtyard. Sitting at a wrought iron table and chairs, Kay poured three cups of tea. "Or joking. Something is *out there,* and it was following me."

Kay, who had been in her life since Eliza first entered New Orleans, sat with her thin arms crossed over her chest. Eliza's first memory of her was bright and magical; the New Orleans city park and the Botanical Gardens; willow trees with limbs reaching for the grass, children running through the gardens. Eliza had been five. Kay had told Eliza about her own world, of a girl lost to her people for a crime she did not commit.

Eliza's grandfather did not turn around as he said, "I did not say that you were." His voice took on a softer tenor as he pointed to one of the faded, paint-chipped chairs. "Sit."

The inner courtyard of their home was decorated like that of a movie set, Eliza thought, like something a Hollywood director imagined up about how Witches or faeries lived in their enchanted homes. Creeping vines dressed in white, black, and red roses climbed up the walls and over into the balconies, creating a wall of flowers. It was like nature was slowly reclaiming the foundations of her home. Taking up one side of the courtyard was a garden, tended to by Kay, and in it grew plants that would not usually survive the New Orleans climate, or the mortal world's limited magic.

At the other end of the yard was the grand, mahogany grandfather clock her grandfather had brought from their world, and it, too, had been overtaken by the creeping vines that filled their home.

Kay slid her the cup of steaming peppermint tea with a tight-lipped smile; the older woman withheld her disappointment, but Eliza could see it sparking in her violet eyes. "Took you long enough to get home," she said.

Eliza merely shook her head, exasperated. "Like I said, I can explain." Her guardians remained silent as they watched her. Davis had finally taken his seat at the table and sipped slowly at the cooling tea in his withered hands, while Kay stretched her arms out. Odin, too, joined them, sitting at his own place on the fourth chair.

A strange sense of foreboding settled over her, like the other shoe was about to drop. Almost like a snap, and it was gone. It left her feeling somewhat apprehensive, anxious as she stared down at the swirling mint tea. But she could not shake that feeling of being watched, of being observed by the raven and the Knight.

Fae, she reminded herself, rolling her eyes. *Fae were following me.* She couldn't be sure if that had anything to do with the blood-relation she had with the immortal creatures, but she wasn't entirely sure if she wanted to find out. Eliza knew little of her heritage, other than that her parents had been close with Kay and Davis, and that any blood relations she had were long dead by the time she had stumbled out of the portal and onto the streets of New Orleans.

Some nights, that lack of knowledge—the unanswered questions and the forgotten memories—left her feeling hollow, like a large part of herself was missing.

For the most part, she played it off. Her family—the only one she had and the only one that cared—were in New Orleans, in the world she'd been exiled to. But she feared asking questions would separate her from the only family she had.

In the twelve years she had lived here, Eliza had never felt so alone as she did when trying to explain herself to her guardians. It twisted in her gut as she looked at them, and she knew it didn't really have anything to do with the fact that she claimed to have been followed—it had everything to do with how she didn't belong to the world she loved.

Eliza met Kay's stare, then Davis's, and cleared her throat. "The museum had some late visitors, out-of-towners who clearly could not read our closing times. There was a creep who wouldn't leave too." Her boss had let her leave through the back, but she didn't mention that, nor that the creep had made more eye-contact than Eliza deemed appropriate. "I got out at about eleven, and I felt *something* following me. I decided to cut through the cemetery, and I saw them."

Kay's brows shot up, but those violet eyes of hers remained unworried. "Who?"

8

"Ghosts follow you all the time, dear," her grandfather reasoned, reaching a weathered hand towards her. Something in his eyes darkened, and for a moment she thought she saw recognition flare in his silver eyes. "Most of the time, you do not notice them. Perhaps these ones realised you could sense them and took to following you to get your attention."

Heat flooded her cheeks, but she shook her head. "It wasn't spirits! I can tell the difference," she said, a bit indignantly. "Anyway, I doubt *Fae* spirits wander around New Orleans like a bad smell."

If she had wanted a reaction from her guardians, Eliza did not get it. Kay's eyes darkened, while Davis's lips thinned, but neither of them said a word.

Eliza looked between them. "I'm not making this up," she said, slumping in her seat. In the chair beside hers, Odin meowed loudly. She ignored him with a twist of her lips. "There is a Faery in New Orleans, or is that something you won't believe?" Despite herself, anger thrummed deep in Eliza's bones, making her fingers clench and her heart beat erratically in her chest.

The grandfather clock struck one, and the courtyard filled with a twinkling faery song to announce the hour, almost like it was mocking Eliza and her fear. But fear of what? The truth of it brought her stomach into her throat.

Faeries are tricksters, Kay had told her once, years ago. *But they are ancient, and they are deadly.*

Eliza wasn't even sure *where* she fit on the mortal spectrum, what with the traces of Faery blood and magic pumping through her veins. That uncertainty left her feeling alone, *different*. Would she master immortality like Kay and Davis? Or would she wither and die while her family lived on?

Davis cleared his throat and pushed his tea aside. Her grandfather locked eyes with her, a white envelope now tucked into his hands. "I cannot believe that you are almost ready."

Curiosity swelled within her, despite the anger and indignation she'd been feeling moments before. Almost like a switch had been flipped, Eliza focused on him rather than the Fae. "Ready for what?" she asked quizzically. Her eyes dropped down to the envelope.

Davis slid the paper to her, though did not release his grip. His fingers shook. "There is much that you have not been allowed to know up until this point. What I am about to give you will change your life, but it does not have to change you."

Eliza cocked a brow; her whole life, she had known there was something more to her training, more to the reasons why she was forced from her home world of Cadira and into the throng of the mortal realm. Though she dreamt of the life she could have had in Cadira, she had grown to love New Orleans, for the city and its people had raised her as one of their own. Perhaps she was going back—back to the world that had thrown her away, back to the world she had no memory of, other than the copper scent of blood mixed with crisp air and death. Perhaps her grandfather was ready to send her away, or at least tell her *why* she was even in New Orleans in the first place.

But... Eliza shook her head, something deep within her revolting at the idea of going back. A sudden seed of fear wedged itself in her gut at the thought. *No,* she thought, swallowing thickly, *I'll never go back. Not if I have anything to do with it.* She wanted to know about her past, about her life before New Orleans, but not at the expense of losing everything she already had and loved.

As if sensing the fear Eliza tried to withhold, her two guardians shared a look of despair and worry.

Eliza clenched her teeth and slowly dragged the envelope towards herself. "Is it from Cadira?"

"Yes, it is," Davis said quietly, folding his hands together. Eliza noticed the small tremor in his fingers. Did he know? Was he aware of what was written within the letter? "I never thought it would come this soon. I honestly thought there would be more time."

Her heart pounded as she slid her nail beneath the envelope's seal. With every movement, her hands shook from trepidation. What was it? She wondered if the letters contents would change everything.

First, she noticed the smell of ink that bled through the parchment, strong and sharp against the perfumed smell of roses that wafted from the paper. Roses made her think of a woman, perhaps a relative of hers, but she couldn't dredge up a memory. Was one of them contacting her at long last? Eliza tried to think of the possibility, and realised if it were a Cadiran relative, then they had probably learnt of Eliza's upcoming eighteenth birthday, though it was still at least five months away. Based on what she'd learnt of Cadiran politics and customs, Eliza would be preparing for her entrance into society, if she still lived there, that was.

No, she thought, with an inner shake of her head. Her hands shook as she held the letter, unable to open it. Maybe she was to be drafted in some war for the king; she was technically still a citizen of Cadira, and there were whispers that a war was brewing on the horizon. Perhaps she was to fight with her magic.

Or...

Eliza slammed down those thoughts and pulled the parchment apart to read the bleeding, inked words:

> *Elizabeth Kindall, daughter of the mountain tribes, apprentice of Portal Keeper Davis Kindall.*
> *By request of King Bastian III, you are hereby invited to the Winter Palace to stand before His Majesty to honour the agreement held between your guardian, Keeper Davis, and His Majesty, the king. For reasons best kept secret for your safety and the kingdom's, you will be expected by the entrance of the closest wards by sunrise, one week from receiving this letter in your realm.*
> *In the name of the King and his followers,*
> *His Royal Attendant.*

A breath escaped her dry lips as confusion swelled within her. *An audience with the king?* Either she royally screwed up or there was more to her past than she expected. Best case scenario, it could be a royal pardon for whatever crime had sent her to Cadira. She wasn't sure, not when she had no memories of her time in Cadira. Worst case, a claiming or an arranged marriage. *Don't rule out the possibilities yet*, she thought, biting her lip, *the king could want anything.*

The only thing she cared about, however, was if she'd be back in New Orleans by the end of that day.

The king... It had to be a joke. Eliza searched her guardians' faces for an answer, but they were closed off from her.

Catching her stare, Kay sighed. "Kid..."

That fear she had almost forgotten gripped her tightly as she gazed upon her two guardians. Even her grandfather had tears pooling in his dark eyes. Their pale faces seemed to crumple at the sight of the letter.

Eliza knew little about her king. The line of Cadiran royals ended with him, though there were rumours of an illegitimate child hidden somewhere and a hope that the son stolen from him, his true heir, was still alive.

The first time Eliza had heard about the legendary attack on the king, she'd been twelve. Kay had described the brutality of the event; the dead queen and princess, the prince stolen from his crib, the mass murder of every soldier and staff member who happened to get in the way of the intruders.

A shiver danced down Eliza's spine.

"What does this mean?" she asked, pushing back a tangle of hair that had fallen over her face. Only moments ago, she had been worrying about a *Faery* in New Orleans following her. "Do the Fae have anything to do with this?" She *was* distantly related to the immortal creatures that dwelled beyond the Willican Forest, and they were following her.

Davis frowned, shaking his head, but Eliza saw something flash in his eyes. "Let King Bastian explain it all to you."

Outside their home, Eliza could hear the distinct song that was New Orleans; late night jazz music drifting up from Bourbon Street, muffled rumbles of traffic, the occasional wail of a siren, and the cheers that sporadically arose down the street.

Everything that made New Orleans home, she realised, would be taken from her. The king wanted her to go to Cadira for an audience. Would she ever return?

Eliza tried not to let *that* fear shine too brightly in her eyes.

"Let the king explain," Kay said finally, eyes still glistening with tears. "Out of respect to him, let him explain."

Eliza shook her head, clenching her trembling hands into fists, feeling the sharpness of her nails bite into the soft flesh of her palms. "Fine." She slid out of her chair, sighing deeply.

Kay reached out a hand but stopped. "Eliza..."

Eliza merely shook her head. "I'm going to bed." A single tear slipped down her flushed cheek. "I'll talk to you in the morning."

Without another thought about the king's mysterious summons, Eliza shuffled into the parlour of the house and up the heavy wood stairs towards her bedroom. She passed collections of odds and ends, things that made her home magical and brilliant and exciting, things she knew would not go with her to Cadira.

Would she have to pack? Eliza considered the old, worn duffel she had shoved under her bed, the one with the hole in the side that Kay had patched with pretty satin from Cadira. She thought about her *Game of Thrones* t-shirts and *Marvel* socks and realised that none of those things had any place in that world.

To go to Cadira, she realised she would have to give up a critical part of herself; the normal, home schooled, museum worker, who listened to indie jazz bands in her spare time and had too many piercings in her ears.

The things she cared about... they didn't belong in Cadira; her smart-mouth and ripped jeans certainly didn't belong amongst the ruffles and tiaras of court. *She* didn't belong amongst the dazzling creatures of her birth world, no matter how much she'd once tried. She'd given up when she realised the reality of her situation—she wasn't sure if she fit there, and now she didn't fit in New Orleans either.

She released a breath; she was *meeting* with the king in his Winter Palace. That did not mean she had to stay there, right?

Eliza flipped the light-switch of her room; above her, constellations appeared so bright they lit up the ceiling; a legendary queen pointing towards the west, her crown pointing north, and in the other corner of her room, the Goddess Azula looking over her. Eliza's room was her only true connection to her birthplace, the closest she had ever let herself get.

The open window across from Eliza revealed the eeriness of the streets of New Orleans; the streetlights flickered on and off, and the buzz of electricity echoed in Eliza's ears.

Suddenly, underneath the floodlight, a form shrouded in shadows, appeared, his silver armour reflecting the light at odd angles.

Eliza took a hesitant step forward.

The Knight raised his head and met Eliza's stare. The gold-eyed raven, perched on his shoulder, cawed, as if calling for her to join them.

For some reason, Eliza deeply considered jumping from her window and disappearing into the night, leaving behind the worries of a desperate king and the expectations that were suddenly thrust upon her.

Before she could take another step, the light flickered again, and they were gone.

2

BLOOD & NECROMANCY

I could be sleeping...

Eliza pulled her dark hair back, scrunching her nose up as she gazed in the mirror. While her eyes weren't her most favourable feature, she couldn't help but notice the dullness that had entered them since reading the king's letter.

Honestly, she thought, frowning at herself. Moss green eyes stared back. The thought of being drawn into the politics of royalty made her heart thunder.

"You okay in there?" Kay asked, knocking on the door. Eliza stiffened. She looked herself over once more, from her black jeans to the plain black t-shirt she'd thrown on. Simple, but only for training.

Eliza sighed and touched the golden doorknob. *Stop being so worried*, she chided herself, gnawing on her bottom lip. Light-headed, she pulled the door open and stepped out into the hall.

Kay leaned against the wall by the bathroom door, wrapped in a cosy, rainbow-coloured shawl. Her silver-white hair was pulled back in a bun, frizzy-strands hanging out at odd angles. Her lined face was creased in worry, and her thin lips pursed as she looked Eliza over. She reached out a hand and touched Eliza's shoulder. "You okay, kid?"

Bile rose in Eliza's throat as she leaned back against the door-jam. "Honestly? I feel like shit."

Had it been her grandfather, she wouldn't have said anything; she'd have sucked it up and went along with whatever was in store for her. However, the knot in her stomach tightened until all she could feel was that growing sense of worry and doubt. It had been eating at her since she'd gone to bed, and hadn't receded when she'd awoken, either.

If only I could read minds, she thought, *or see the future*. But she couldn't; her affinity lay in death and necromancy, bound to the land as much as spirits were. Her whole life, she had trained, but never with her necromancy, not with the darkness that dwelled within her.

Eliza released a heavy breath, closing in on herself. "I just... I don't get why, you know?"

Kay gave her shoulder a gentle squeeze. "What's really worrying you?"

Everything? She bit her lip. "I don't know." She couldn't deny the excitement that coursed through her, of the possibilities being presented to her by the king. *My heritage, Cadira... everything I've wanted...* And never asked for.

Head cocked; Kay looked down at her. "You think it's all too good to be true, don't you?" Her brows furrowed, cheeks burning red.

The air in Eliza's lungs left her quickly. *Yes.* "What if it's not what I imagined? What if the king just locks me up and throws away the key?"

"Why would you think that?" Kay asked, straightening.

Eliza shrugged and looked away, biting down on her lip. "I don't even know why I'm here, Kay. What happened before all this?"

Something about what she said changed Kay's demeanour.

Heat flooded through Eliza as she stared down her guardian. Kay, who had lived most of her life in Cadira, had left the world she'd been born of for crimes she hadn't committed. And now, she could never return.

"Would you go back?" Eliza asked, breaking the silence. "Would you go back to Cadira, if the courts granted it?"

Because Kay belonged to a different ruler and to a different kingdom, Eliza couldn't begin to *imagine* what lengths Kay would have to go through to be allowed entry into the magical realm. Even with her power, entering Cadira—even going *near* the courts that exiled her—could mean certain death.

What Eliza knew about Kay's situation in Cadira, in the Courts of Light in the south, was little, and depended mostly on stolen moments and whispers heard in the darkness.

Kay's eyes softened, tears glistening. "If it meant giving up New Orleans and you, no."

"Then why do you expect me to do the same?" *Why do you expect me to go along with this and risk never coming back?*

Somewhere in the darkness of Eliza's mind, a memory clawed to the surface. *Ice. Snow. A blizzard wrecking the land.* She remembered white trees and glistening stars. Harsh yet beautiful. Consuming. Cadira. But she shook the memory from her mind.

"This is a meeting with the king," Kay said. She reached a hand up and cupped Eliza's face. "You don't even know what he's going to say. Stop worrying about what *might* happen and focus on what is happening now."

She patted Eliza's cheek; soft hands comfortingly warm. "You will see the king; you will hear what he has to say. And whatever happens next, you know your grandfather and I will always, *always* be proud of you."

Tears burned behind Eliza's eyes. Taking in a shuddering breath, she forced the swelling fear back. What did she have to be afraid of? She wondered. Yet, she couldn't deny the inkling of doubt—doubt in herself, in her abilities, her worth—that bubbled deep within her.

Or the strange shiver that crawled over her skin, like a warning.

Kay's hand dropped, and as she took a step back, the feeling disappeared completely. "Now. Don't we have lessons?"

Eliza rolled her eyes and fell back into the familiar guise of intolerable teen, if not for Kay's sake, but for her own. Normality, and the consistency that came with keeping to routine should have been enough to keep her mind off the looming event.

While their house was large, as the only *living* occupants of the household, many of the rooms were vacant. Other rooms were stored with her grandfather's odd collections of Cadiran relics, amassed over his years of training and becoming a Keeper.

Keepers were the protectors of the wards between the two realms. Earth, with its limited magic and knowledge, needed protection from the magic of Cadira. And Cadira needed to stay a secret. For over a thousand years, that had been her grandfather's job.

Most doors in their home remained locked, *especially* if the rooms were being used to house ancient artefacts. Eliza recalled a rather vague memory of accidentally summoning an Igiulon demon one night while *exploring*—she'd been nine, and it had been directly after her grandfather had warned her *not* to step foot in any of the rooms. She'd picked the lock, completely dismissing his warning, and touched a rather old staff.

A smile twitched at her lips as she passed the door now, and she could almost see the singes by the doorknob from when she'd tried to escape. In her head, she could still see the claw marks on the other side, close to where her head had been.

The training room came into view; closed off by a simple white door. The room held all the instruments her guardians used in order to teach her magic. Eliza had learnt at a young age that the room itself was protected with boundary spells in case she lost control of her magic.

For as long as she could remember, the room smelt of sulphur and sage. Eliza sucked in a breath as she entered. She faced the room she'd spent almost twelve years in—learning, practicing, training. Eliza had been taught how to read and write and enchant at the small table under the large iron-latticed window that looked out over the courtyard. Mounted bookshelves took up the longest wall, full of texts about the world Eliza was born into. At a young age, she'd craved all the knowledge she possibly could about that world, and had managed to get through so many, but it had never quenched her thirst.

Kay walked in next and went to the table, shrugging off her shawl. She draped it over the back of a chair and turned to Eliza with a smile. "Defence magic today, I think. Since you seem to be so determined to think Faeries are following you."

Eliza huffed, puffing out her bottom lip. "Why don't you ever believe me?"

"Remember the boy who cried wolf?" Kay asked, leaning back. She crossed her arms over her chest. "You're the girl who cried ogre one too many times. When you get eaten, *then* I'll believe you." Her smile *looked* sweet, but Eliza could read the message beneath it: *you either have proof, or you have nothing. Especially in this world.*

"Why don't we ever practice with my *other* abilities?" Eliza asked, staying by the door.

Kay pursed her lips. "Whatever do you mean?" Her hand dropped from one of the titles, and when she turned around, Eliza got her full attention.

The room took on a warmth Eliza couldn't escape. She rolled her sleeves up before crossing her arms.

"I know how to summon flames, and create tornados, and find water. I think I'm adept enough with elemental magic, but I can see *ghosts*. Why don't we ever talk about it?" Her heart thundered wildly in her chest as she waited.

She could see the thoughts ticking over in Kay's mind—the contemplation in the set of her lips, the answer in the slow tilt of her head. Kay was either an open book, or a box of mysteries, wrapped in colourful shawls with secret-keeping eyes that watched *everything*.

Kay tapped a violet-painted nail to her lips. "Because that isn't my place."

Why am I not surprised? "Why doesn't Grandpa?" Eliza asked. Adrenaline rushed through her. Rarely did she talk back to her guardians; she never needed to. But she felt a desperation within her that gnawed at the fears she'd tried so hard to keep bundled up within her. "He's a Keeper of the Wards."

"It is something *neither* of us can teach you, Eliza. And it is not the place of *either* of us to do so."

"Why?" Her arms dropped to her sides, and a dull ache thrummed at her temples.

With her head cocked, Kay watched her with a keenness that made Eliza shudder. "Why are you suddenly so interested?" Kay asked, voice low. Her grey brows furrowed. "What's gotten into you?"

Eliza swallowed the lump in her throat. "Maybe the uncertain future is bringing out my need for answers?"

"Well, it's certainly bringing out an attitude I don't quite appreciate," Kay said.

Eliza couldn't help flinching, curling in on herself. *Why is this getting to me?* She thought back to the whimsical stories Kay and her grandfather told her about ancient queens who defeated spreading darkness, and dragon-riders who won battles. If the king wanted to see her, it had to have something to do with magic: she wasn't special beyond the fact that her grandfather raised her.

Raised her to take his place, one day. Was that day coming so soon?

Kay's eyes softened, and she walked to where Eliza leaned against the door. She reached a hand up and touched Eliza's hot cheek. "Is this meeting with the king *really* bothering you so much?" Kay asked softly.

Eliza released a shaky breath. "Yes," she replied honestly.

Kay gave her a soft smile, tipping her chin up so their gazes met. "Eliza, where is your sense of adventure?"

Eliza barked a strangled laugh, covering her mouth. "I dropped it in the cemetery last night while running away from the Faery Knight who *suddenly appeared* the same night as that stupid letter."

Kay pursed her lips, unamused. "*That* could just be a coincidence."

Eliza eyed her warily, then, hackles rising. "Why is it suddenly just a coincidence?" she asked. Kay took a step back, and whatever progress they'd made disappeared. "Why don't you and grandpa want me to do *more* with my magic?"

"Because what you can do is *dangerous*," Kay hissed. The room became abnormally silent. "You do not speak about it, you tell no one, *especially* in Cadira. Do you understand me? Centuries ago, they hunted Witches with your kind of magic and butchered them. Even the Blood Witches were targeted."

Blood Witches. Eliza's heart stopped at the name; what she knew about the illusive tribe of Witches came only from the stories Kay or her grandfather told her. They were powerful, they were deadly, and they protected only their own. Guarded by immortal warriors, the Witches were hidden from the rest of Cadira in the Labyrinth Mountains, never heard from, never seen. If even *they* had been targeted...

Eliza swallowed down the bile that rose in her throat. She wracked her memory for any mention of necromancy in any of the texts she'd studied but found none in the recesses of her mind. *None.* She went cold. She hadn't even stopped to *consider* what her magic might mean in Cadira—it hadn't even crossed her mind.

She did not ask any more questions, couldn't find her voice to do so. She merely nodded in acceptance, not voicing the question that nagged at the back of her mind:

What am I stepping into?

~

Eliza bit down on the inside of her cheek as she ran her hand over the line of old leather-bound books in the training room. Her finger came back, caked in dust. When had she last looked at these books?

She could almost feel the excitement of the world electrifying in her veins. The little girl in Eliza lived off the thrill of learning about the world she'd been born to, of understanding the way magic worked, how heroes were born, and if evil had truly been defeated.

But in all her years of excitedly reading and researching that world, she hadn't come across anything that could explain *her*. No entry, no mention. If she thought hard enough, she could have sworn she might have read about the witch burnings and massacres for any who could see, speak, and listen to the dead. It came to her almost like an afterthought since Kay had mentioned it.

It nagged at her, though, knowing that there had been others like her in that world. Part of her couldn't help but wonder if *that* had been the reason for her being exiled from Cadira. She shook her head. *If that were it,* she thought, *I'd be dead.*

The realisation sent a shiver down her spine.

Black leather adorned with gold and silver caught her attention. Eliza pulled the volume down from a shelf above her head and ran her fingers over the soft cover. Engraved into it, a golden Ouroboros stared back at her—the snake eating its own tail glimmered with symbols of magic; fire, earth, air, water, healing, and... by the head, beneath its eye, Eliza spotted the upside-down crescent-moon symbol for necromancy.

The book had no index. She scanned the pages for any mention of necromancy, too afraid to use a spell, if only because the thought of leaving a magical trace sent her stomach turning.

She skimmed the pages as she went, occasionally stopping at passages she vaguely remembered.

Magic is the essence that makes up the world; it flows through the land and connects each and every living being to one another. Magic is a lifeline, centring the land and its inhabitants. It does not belong to every human and creature, but those who do have an affinity to use the magic offered to them are presented with a connection to the land that others will not feel.

Magic cannot be learnt; it is an affinity that one is born with. It cannot be created, and it cannot be destroyed, as it is a power that is given by the land.

However, should the land be destroyed, then magic could potentially disappear. Many Witches and Warlocks have argued the depth magic runs in our land. From the Courts of Light to the Fae Territories, all the way to the dragon riders of Laziroth, magic is heavily debated.

If one should take this into consideration...

Eliza heaved a sigh, skimming the rest. She knew that much—*common knowledge*, she thought, especially in Cadira. Kay had described the sensation to her long ago as like having a sixth sense—the connection to the land had given her an *edge*. Eliza had yet to have that feeling, and sometimes yearned for it, deep within herself, where her magic dwelled. That connection she had lost so long ago felt like a phantom limb now.

The thin pages felt fragile between her fingers, like dry leaves in autumn, ready to crumble. She flicked through them carefully, keeping an eye out for the simple word that held enough meaning to dictate whether or not she would survive in that world.

But she pushed through that inkling of fear. *It won't help me in the end,* she thought with a heavy sigh.

Eliza's fingers shook as she flipped through the pages; the longer she skimmed passages about dragon riding and elemental magic, illusion work and healing, the quicker the words started to blur together until...

Necromancy is the ability to commune with the dead. Amongst the Blood Witch tribes, it is considered a sacred art in foretelling the future. In other sects of magic users, communing with the dead is considered dark and evil magic. While magic is generally a sacred art connected to the land and drawn from it, necromancy is considered a darker form of manipulation. Those who find an affinity to the darker magic are said to conspire with darkness, that they plan on taking the light from Cadira, and drown the land in absolute darkness. Necromancers are not natural.

For several hundred years, known necromancers were hunted down for their dark use of magic. Since the initial massacres and trials, necromancy—and those associated with it—have gone into hiding.

Eliza closed the book, face pale. Her heart hammered in her chest, and she could hear nothing over the pounding of blood in her ears.

Not me, she thought, hands shaking. *I don't want that.*

But what could she do? The danger was there, written in swirling black ink—any with her power were dangerous. Maybe Kay *was* right.

But if she was, then *why* was Eliza being thrown into that world once again?

Fear—undeniable and heavy—dropped into the pit of her stomach. Every part of her went cold. If it were a crime to have her power, then what would Eliza face as punishment? If there had been trials and *massacres*, then what would happen to her if the king knew?

She swallowed the lump in her throat. It made sense, she thought, as to why they wouldn't tell her anything. Either they were sworn to secrecy or they were trying to protect her from something.

With a flick of her wrist, the book slid back into place on the shelf above her head. Heart pounding, she left the training room behind and didn't fully comprehend where she was going until she was out on the street, facing what would normally be a welcome sight.

Instead, chills shuddered through her, cold and exhausting.

I don't need to go. Eliza stepped out and crossed the street, wrapping her arms around herself as she did. *I don't need to see Cadira. Can't I just say no?*

She shook her head and sighed loudly, stepping into the quiet comfort of the cemetery.

In the reflection of a plaque, Eliza rolled her eyes at herself. *Stop being such a Gods-damned coward, Eliza!* It didn't stop the small pang of fear that had nestled itself in her gut. She wasn't even sure if it *was* fear she felt anymore; every lesson she'd had on trusting her instincts, on listening to the sixth-sense that connected her to the magic of her world, told her there was more to the meeting than her guardians let on.

It's not fear, she thought, stopping abruptly by a set of identical mausoleums. *It's a warning. And anyway, I'm not being a coward. It's called self-preservation.*

"Necromancy is going to get me killed," she said aloud, shaking her head. "Seeing the dead isn't that evil anyway." She kicked a loose stone out of her way. She collapsed to the ground, leaning her head back against the warm stone of the mausoleum.

"The living shouldn't wallow amongst the dead."

She started, leaning away from the sound of the voice. Eliza looked up into a withered, almost translucent face, and startling blue eyes.

Standing over her, the old man leaned a white, bony shoulder against the stained stone wall. He looked like he might have died during the 1920's; he wore a three-piece blue pin-stripe suit and a bowler hat. His dark brows knitted together as he looked down at her.

He nodded towards a gaggle of tourists that walked past and eyed them with a smile.

"Death is just another *thing* that happens." The old spirit spared her a knowing look. "Don't let it fool you; it *pretends* to be the end, but it's just another stop on the long train to immortality. For people like you, death shouldn't even be a fear."

Eliza shivered, wrapping her arms around herself. "Why?"

"Well," he said, laughing softly, "you might very well be the only person *alive* who can answer all those damned '*what if*' questions about what happens after death. You might very well be like a God in their eyes."

"What if I don't want to be? What if even I fear death?" she asked.

He smiled. "Then it must be an awfully tragic affair if that's how you see it. To fear death is to fear immortality, and to fear that means to fear eternity. Is that so bad?"

Spirits were always sprouting some kind of bullshit from their old lives in her opinion; it used to confuse her as a child, but now she ignored it. *Life lessons*, they called it, but Kay had always called it mumbo-jumbo.

She ground her teeth together and pushed off the side of the mausoleum. His laugh grated on her as she left the shadows and entered the bright, New Orleans day. The sounds of the city washed over her; the rumble of cars paired with the soft chatter of tourists. Eliza could feel the excitement of the people, feel their racing hearts as if she herself was experiencing the same sensation.

Life: that's what she felt twisting its way through the winding streets of the French Quarter. Not death or darkness, but pure, undiluted life. It coursed through her like a pulse, one she couldn't ignore.

3

DEMONS

Eliza awoke from her fitful sleep with crusty eyes and a blaring headache. Dreams of sword-wielding Fae and gold-eyed ravens, bloody crowns and massacred Necromancers had plagued her, leaving her more exhausted than when she'd gone to bed.

While she hadn't been entirely afraid of the king before, now she couldn't stop jumping to conclusions about what the letter might really mean—her death, and maybe the deaths of Kay and her grandfather, too.

She rolled over with a tired sigh, her bleary eyes barely taking in her grandfather standing in the doorway. With a start, she threw her legs over the side of the bed.

His silver eyes conveyed nothing. He merely beckoned her with a gloved hand, as if to say, "Come," and like a good ward, she did as she was told.

Eliza knew well enough that the simple command couldn't mean anything good. Dressing quickly, Eliza ignored the shiver of wrongness that danced down her spine. Almost uncertainly, she reached for her magic, for that connection to the land. But she couldn't mistake the brush of ancient power that made her heart accelerate, or the strange flare in Cadiran magic that rose in response.

Was she really as 'unnatural' as the book had made her out to be? She shook her head and looked herself over in the mirror; at her dark-brown hair, pulled into a messy bun, never quite straight or just a little too tangled for curly. Not to mention the dark bags under her dull-green eyes.

She quickly pulled on a pair of jeans and a simple grey t-shirt, donned her worn Docs, and exited her room without looking in the mirror. She already knew what she would see: a 5'7" girl with a bit of curve, olive skin that was officially pale because of autumn, and messy hair from a lack of sleep.

The red, white, and black roses that grew along the creeping vines seemed to brighten as she passed, and she breathed in their sweet scents as she walked. Sitting at the wrought iron table, Kay quietly sipped her tea, Odin sitting on her lap, purring in contentment as Kay's fingers brushed through his long fur.

Kay didn't look up as she murmured, "He's waiting by the car."

Again, no acknowledgement, no gleam in her violet eyes concerning the king's letter and the revelation of the Faery Knight who followed her... or of their talk yesterday about necromancy.

Eliza's palms turned sweaty as she left the cover of the house; the streets were already alive and boisterous, and she found her grandfather leaning against their old BMW, parked on the street and covered in dust.

"What's going on?" she asked, slipping into the passenger seat as her grandfather rounded the front of the car. When he finally started the engine, Eliza clicked her seatbelt into place and turned to him. She didn't need to mention the strange rise in Cadiran magic—his worry was written clearly in the lines of his face.

With his brow furrowed in concentration, Eliza could clearly see his age written across his face; from the deep lines of his forehead, to the paleness of his lips, sometimes she forgot that her grandfather was hundreds of years old—and not the seventy-five he pretended to be.

He did not speak straight away, and instead drove for two miles before saying, "A breach in the warding, nothing too serious yet. But it is a good learning opportunity for you."

Eliza's heart skipped a beat in excitement; rarely did she get to see the wards that acted as the barrier between her world and Cadira. Keepers like her grandfather were spread all over the mortal world, protecting and caring for the portals, taking positions that would allow them to serve at all times. Her whole life, Eliza thought she was learning to take her grandfather's place or be his partner on the other side of the portal. There were always two Keepers standing guard, one on either side, and she'd hoped to be next.

She didn't bother trying to hide her excitement as she asked, "Am I going to handle this breech on my own?"

Davis gave her a silent nod, sparing her a single, unreadable look. For the remainder of the car ride, they spoke only to ask and answer questions; *How does one close a breach?* he'd asked, and she had answered dutifully, *by winding the threads of our worlds separately, and as one, to create a wall rather than a doorway.*

Finally, they drew closer to the decrepit dirt track that lead to the small, warded temple where the barrier of Cadira was safely hidden. "Did you get a sense of what was trying to get through?" she asked.

Davis glanced at her, face shadowed, but turned back to the road a moment later as if her question was something as simple as 'How is the weather?' When he refused to reply, she hunkered down in her seat and crossed her arms over her chest. "I thought this was supposed to be a learning point."

Her grandfather reached out and patted her leg. "Whatever is trying to get through will be easy enough for you to handle."

"That doesn't answer my question," she pointed out.

He sighed, retracting his hand. "I know. Perhaps you should feel for it yourself?"

This is progress, she thought, closing her eyes. Eliza reached for the threads of magic that bound the lands together. *He trusts me enough with the wards.*

As her magic touched those threads of power, the car slowly pulled to a stop in the humid marshlands that made up the Louisiana bayou, outside of what looked like a crumbling hunting cabin. Rotten wood made up the exterior, covered in moss and vines that crept over fallen trees and large stones that were piled up to one side. Darkness wound through the light like smoke around stars, greeting her with force. She recoiled and opened her eyes with a shudder.

A frown drew across her brows as Eliza craned her neck to get a better look inside of the cabin, but from what she could tell—based on the warding put in place and maintained by her grandfather—the interior was still shrouded in darkness, which meant that whatever was trying to get *through* hadn't broken past the gates yet.

Mud squelched beneath the heels of her boots as she stepped out of the car. A shiver danced up the length of her spine, like a warning shot being fired, and carefully, Eliza looked around. Part of her expected to see the unsettling vision of a lost spirit, one who wandered the bayou searching for their grave or their murderer.

Another part of her searched for gold eyes and a silver sword.

She tried to lock that part of her away before it could do any more damage to her already precarious psyche.

The old cabin-façade did not have a front door. When Davis waved his hand, the stacked boulders shimmered to reveal the interior of the secluded, Cadiran temple: white marble walls with veins of gold and silver running through the stone. In the very centre was a pillar that reached Eliza's waist. It held a golden bowl, holding a flame that did not extinguish.

And across from the entrance was a wall made entirely of glass.

Eliza could not see her reflection in the glass; only shadows and swirling figures—a darkness so deep it never ended. She knew the process of opening the gateway like she knew her times tables, and although the wards across from her enchanted her, she knew the risks in opening it.

Something flung itself against the glass on the other side, rebounding off the warding. Then another, its soft flesh making a wet sound as it slid down the clouded glass.

She flinched as a third body hit the warding. "What the hell is going on?"

Davis merely shook his head and crossed his arms as a fourth—fifth, sixth, seventh—*thing* hit the wards. He merely blinked, as if he had seen it all before. "Find a way to strengthen the wards and stop whatever attack is happening beyond. Where do you start?"

Swallowing the lump in her throat, she took a step forward, only to hesitate. "Uh…" She bit her lip, surveying the space; the longer the barrier was physically assaulted, the greater they risked permanent damage. "Identify the attacker?"

Davis shook his head, arms crossed. "You're jumping ahead. Step one, Elizabeth. How can you identify what you cannot see?"

She swore under her breath and squared her shoulders. "Clear the glass. Then identify."

"Correct."

A tingle ran up the length of her arm, starting at her fingertips as she summoned a handful of magic; it spread over her, encasing her like a second skin. Eliza focused on that magic as it swept through her. She envisioned the spell that would reveal what waited behind the mirror.

What waited in Cadira.

Light flared before her eyes, repelling the shadows that dwelled inside the mirror. As the light danced in the reflection, the shadows receded to reveal the Cadiran temple in ruins.

The ancient fire that never extinguished had been pushed to the marble ground, the bowl it resided in snuffing the flame. Standing in the shadows, Eliza could barely make out the form of a person, crouched over a bloody mess of white robes and tangled black hair.

There was a pause in movement as the creatures—demons, Eliza realised with a sickening thought—stopped to watch her and Davis through the now clear glass. They were small, spindly creatures that were enslaved to a master, and had no souls of their own. But they weren't inherently evil. They drew together at the sight of her and Davis, their black, soulless eyes on her, then on each other. One turned its head to a figure in the back. *They're mindless*, she thought, but watching them huddle together with reaching claws, she didn't feel confident in her readings.

"If you look carefully," Davis murmured, pointing to the robes, "you can see their master crouching over the Keeper."

Eliza had noticed it and had tried to look away just as quickly. As if sensing their attention, the Demon Master stood, a hood covering their face. Their fingers twitched, covered in blood.

She swallowed thickly and tapered down on the magic that swelled in response to the threat. A sliver of shadow wavered at the feet of the fallen Keeper. Its spirit clung to the flesh, even though it had been expelled. Death had truly taken the Keeper if she was able to see the spirit finally form.

Slowly, as the spirit came into focus, the Demon Master took a step forward, towards the gateway. In a rush, the demons threw themselves at the mirror. Eliza could almost feel their bodies slam against the ward, slowly but surely disturbing the inner threads of the enchantment.

Davis stepped closer to her, and from him she could feel the crackling of his magic. Hers rose in response, a white light spreading across her fingers.

"This isn't what you had in mind, was it?" she asked. Her grandfather shook his head. As another wave of demons threw themselves into the wards, Eliza could have sworn she heard a *crack* in the foundations. Something inside of her yawned open, and without thinking, she slammed a burst of white energy straight into the middle of the mirror.

Veins of white light splintered across the warding, forming a spider web of interlocking tendrils. Even as she threw her magic into stabilising the wards, she could not stop the next wave of demons from throwing themselves into the glass—could not stop the shuddering explosion of dark, oozing magic that hit the initial crack.

Behind the Demon Master, the dark tendril of shadow came into focus. Confusion and anger crossed the Keeper's features as they gazed down at their fallen body, then at the wards and the demons that attempted to cross.

Only once before had Eliza tried to interact with spirits through magic rather than speech. It hadn't worked quite to her expectations, but she focused on the spirit anyway. Since she could not risk going *across* the border, she *could* lend her magic to someone on the other side.

Sucking in a breath, Eliza focused on her power and sent a wave towards the spirit. Despite knowing how futile it was, Eliza sent a tendril of magic through the barrier. That kind of magic required a different side of her. But she focused, sending the spirit stability in sharp waves. *If he could become solid enough, surely, he would be able to fight back.*

At her side, Davis began chanting; his voice rang loudly in the temple, the words a slew of ancient spells in a dialect Eliza could not understand. But as his voice grew stronger, and the magic around him became greater, Eliza fought the hesitation within her and completely gave herself over to the spirit trapped on the other side of the mirror.

Eliza's gaze was drawn to the Demon Master, to the way he continued to hold control over his minions. His mouth never moved once, but his eyes... if she could draw his attention, she could perhaps tamper with his control.

Pain sliced through her head, but Eliza focused on the spirit who dragged himself through the ruined temple. Demons bit at him, unaware that he was not entirely real flesh, but she could see the hesitation and fear in his face. *Faster*, she thought, grunting at the exertion, *go faster.*

"I can't keep going," she said through gritted teeth. Her heart raced, and black dots danced across the edges of her vision. *More power.* She threw herself into a rhythm of give-and-take, the pulse of magic swaying between her and the spirit.

Davis entwined another spell into his chanting, casting a wave of healing power towards the wards. The strength of his spells sent a shiver down her spine, but it did not stop the agonising thrum inside her skull as she gave her magic to the Keeper.

She watched in fascination as the spirit took hold, almost like a half-assed illusion cast by a Warlock in Cadira. The edges of the Keeper's spirit shimmered, and the light that shot through the ward speared through his body. A dull ring started in her ears as she watched, not aware of anything else, drawn only to what her forbidden magic could do.

But it was enough of a distraction to make the Demon Master blink. His concentration lost, the demons scattered, no longer content on attacking the ward.

The moment wasn't wasted; before Eliza could suck in her next agonising breath, blood spurted from the Demon Master's mouth. The black-clad man crumpled to the ground in a pool of his own blood, limbs twitching before going still.

Eliza dropped her magic, withdrawing from the spirit of the Keeper. She took a shaky step back, away from the now strengthening wards. The demons disintegrated. Back to dust and dirt, the creatures collapsed on themselves, and blew away like ash in the wind.

Davis's chanting came to a sudden halt. Eliza blinked in confusion, collapsing to her knees. In the shadows across from her, she thought she'd seen a figure—a man in armour—but when she blinked it was gone.

Slowly, the wards healed, light knitting together to reform the wall between them and Cadira. As it re-sealed, the shadows that separated them grew darker and denser, until she could no longer see the bodies of the Demon Master and the blood of the Keeper. Until she could see only shadows.

"Eliza?" Hands gripped her arms, and it took her a moment to gather herself enough to climb to her feet. "Are you alright?" her grandfather asked, his voice echoing in her ears.

Brushing the knees of her jeans, she blinked several times at the now secured gateway. "Yeah," she said absentmindedly, nodding shallowly. "Fine. Did you see who did that?"

Davis, oddly quiet, patted her back stiffly. "Who did what?" His eyes darkened from silver to a deep grey. But she caught the recognition in his voice, the *omission of truth*.

She looked back to the wards, now fully restored. "Killed the

Demon Master." It hadn't been the Keeper—Eliza wasn't powerful enough for that. There had been someone else inside the temple. Of that, she was sure.

Her grandfather kept his hand on her shoulder and slowly guided her back through the stone formation, leaving behind the snippet of Cadira and entering the Louisiana bayou once more. *Home*, she thought, squinting up at the pale-yellow sun through the canopy of trees. *This is home*. Not demons and death and masked killers. Home was the smell of wet leaves and the loud jazz music down the road from her house and Bourbon street and tourists.

As she slid into the car, Eliza couldn't help but think over the events of the morning—of the sudden death of the Demon Master and the killer who had disappeared before they could see him. How did her grandfather not catch that?

He did. He saw the person who killed the Demon Master. So why wasn't he telling her?

She spared him an odd look from the corner of her eye. "Why do you think there was an attack today?" she asked finally. His pale lips were pursed, but she saw the shine in his eyes. "Do you think—?"

Davis stopped her with a quick look. "That attack had nothing to do with you."

Why are you keeping secrets? she wanted to ask.

Even as he said it, she couldn't help but doubt his words. "So, you think it *didn't* have anything to do with the king sending for me?" Was it arrogant to think like that? Eliza couldn't help but add up the mysterious occurrences from the last couple of days: the appearance of a Faery Knight and the gold-eyed raven, the ominous letter from the king, and now the attack on the wards by a Demon Master.

Surely, it hadn't all been a coincidence.

Her grandfather said nothing more about it as they left the bayou and headed back towards the city, but she thought about it up until she got home.

Something wasn't right, and she was determined to find out why.

4

AZULA

DEMON MASTERS.

Eliza crossed her legs beneath her as she flicked through the pages of her book. Dim afternoon light filtered through the blinds in their small library, illuminating the thin pages of the old book perched in her lap. White paint flaked from her hands from where she'd been trying to paint one of the walls in the spare bedroom. But rather than helping her keep her mind off the events of the morning, it had only given her ample time to reflect on the attack and her own magic, both of which troubled her deeply. Especially with the arrival of the king's letter and the appearance of the raven and the Fae Knight days before.

The book in her lap held no noteworthy answers to her plethora of questions, but she had doubted it would. Demon Masters were rare in modern Cadira; they were born of a type of Blood Magic that was reserved only to the Blood Witches.

Closing the book, she sat back and huffed a breath. No information. *Why am I not surprised?* Without answers, she was forced to think about the king's message.

And thinking about the king's message would surely send her anxiety over the edge.

Releasing a breath, Eliza cast her eyes towards the darkening world beyond the window. A shadow darted across her vision, inky black wings flapping, the sound echoing inside her head.

The raven appeared at the open door and danced anxiously from foot to foot. Eliza sucked in a breath, her magic rising inside her. The raven cawed, its gold eyes meeting hers, as if telling her to *follow*.

Curiosity won out over worry. Standing, Eliza made it to the doorway as the raven took flight, leaving the floor and guiding her towards the second level, before disappearing.

Frowning, Eliza rushed up the stairs until she could see the bird again. It snapped its beak at her from the doorway of her bedroom, impatient, as if it expected *her* to understand what it wanted.

Eliza shook her head and entered.

"What..." She turned in a slow circle, searching her room for any sign of the raven.

But it was gone.

An eerie shiver danced down her spine as her gaze landed on a black feather resting atop an aged leather book.

Curiosity took a back seat as she hesitated by the doorway. She looked back down the hall for any sign of the missing bird.

She nervously closed her door and flicked the lock behind her. As if that would be enough to stop the powerful magic that surrounded the creature.

Floorboards creaked beneath her feet as she stepped up to the side of her bed. She reached for the feather almost without thinking and blinked in surprise when it turned to ash under her touch.

Weird. Eliza pursed her lips and waved a hand over the ash. It disappeared as magic tingled at the tips of her fingers. Ash clung to her fingers, though, from where she had touched the feather. It echoed with old magic, unfamiliar to her.

Shaking her head, Eliza picked up the book and read the gold lettering that danced across the cover: *The Goddess Azula & A History of Cadira*.

This is a distraction, she thought, *to keep my mind off the king and his summoning.*

A distraction that seemed almost like a blessing in disguise, thanks to the Changed One.

Eliza moved towards her desk and sat, tucking her feet beneath her. The book was heavy in her hands, though looked roughly the size of a common paperback. However, when she finally flipped it open, she realised it wasn't a common history book usually kept in her grandfather's library.

Maybe it's personal, she thought with a twist of her lips. *Maybe I should give it to Grandpa.*

Though the thought ran through her mind, she didn't. Instead, she flipped to the first page and began to read.

~

As the light outside her bedroom window faded—and she was forced to plug in her rusty desk-top lamp—she struggled through the first hundred-or-so pages before stopping at a short entry, handwritten under a poorly sketched image of a woman in a temple:

The Goddess Azula made herself known through peace and power; when the dark ages came to the land of Cadira, all hope and freedom was thought to have been lost. Azula, Princess of the mountain tribes, widow of Eyria, King of the Mountains, rose through the ash of the Jaedera temple and brought justice to the Old King. She fought with a dagger whose hilt was thought to have been carved from the last of the Vaya people, the blade cut from the Irisia rock thousands of years ago...

Eliza skimmed through the passage more, searching for something else, something that might indicate why the raven had chosen this book, but the rest had been crossed out, with the following page torn straight from the binding.

Running her finger over the paper, Eliza wondered what else could have been in there, and why someone would have wanted to destroy it completely.

She shook her head, perplexed. She shuffled an old playlist of jazz music on her phone, the elegant and soulful tone of the saxophone filling her ears. She flipped through the rest of the book, only to come up with a different image—a tapestry of Azula rising from ruins, a dagger in one hand, and a ball of light in the other. Behind her, spirits—Eliza could only guess that's what they were based on the strange, cartoon-like style of the figures—rose towards the only light in the black sky.

But there was no passage, no explanation.

The page beside it had been torn out.

Eliza slammed the book shut and threw it across the room. It landed on her bed with a soft thump.

What the hell is going on?

She ran her hand over her mouth and sat back in her chair. The clock on her desk flashed eight, and darkness had fully descended on the lively city of New Orleans. From her window, she could make out the sparkling city. The city she loved... and would be leaving in five days.

Five days. She wanted to hurl.

Looking back at the book, Eliza gave up, and went to bed.

~

She couldn't get the ringing in her ears to stop, despite the explosions of battle being long behind them. It echoed in her head alongside the screams of all those she'd slaughtered. She couldn't get it out of her head, though she wasn't sure if she wanted to. Perhaps hearing their screams will atone for the wrongs she was forced to commit.

Forced? She laughed at herself, at her naivety. She wasn't forced to do anything, and yet she pushed aside her morality on the eve of war. Could she really blame a spoilt monarch for her decision to fight? She bowed before no crown, and yet she fought for one anyway. She did so to ensure that her love and her sisters would be safe.

But she could not say the same for her soul, for her own life.

Turning to her love, she held out her hand, watching as he took it and squeezed, letting all his frustration and pain flow into her.

"I am glad I got to see you," he murmured, leaning in close to plant a kiss on her forehead. "But I wish you had saved yourself."

She shook her head. "I love you, more than I do myself, more than this kingdom and this world. If your passion is to fight for it with the Brotherhood and the Fae, alongside man, then I shall do the same— by your side." She stood and pulled him away from the campsite where they had been sitting, dragging him towards the tree line. "I wanted, for once, to be there for you, to make sure you were safe. Like you have always done for me."

He kissed her then, hungry and passionately. Her lips parted and he slid his tongue into her mouth. They stayed that way, locked in each other's embrace for several moments before breaking apart, their breaths heavy as they gazed longingly into one another's eyes. Her heart raced, and when she placed her hand over his, she could feel his pulse beat in time with hers.

"I wish we could stay like this," she murmured, before looking up

at him, "because I love you more than I thought I would love anyone."

He gave her a small smile. "Your people won't be happy about this."

"What can they do?" she asked with a grin. "I am to lead them one day. It is, and always will be, my destiny. Loving you will not change any of that."

His dark eyes softened. "No," he replied, smile widening, "no it won't." He pushed her against a tree and his lips found hers again. They stood in each other's embrace for several long moments before the sounds of their fellow soldiers brought them back to the reality that was war.

"How much longer must we wait?" she asked, wrapping her arms around his neck. "How much longer until we can finally be together?"

He kissed her neck, moving his lips up to her earlobe. "I will do anything I have to, if that means getting to be with you." He bit down on the soft spot between her neck and ear, and she moaned at the feeling.

"This is not fair," she murmured, stifling another moan as his hand slid up her side.

He chuckled into the soft skin of her neck. "It doesn't have to be." His hot breath sent shivers down her spine, and she arched her back at the feeling of his skin touching hers.

Shouts sounded behind them, loud and clear despite the fog that seemed to cover the pair. Quickly, they sprung apart, both breathing heavily, both ready for any fight that came their way.

Several soldiers barrelled through the tree line. She stopped one, holding a hand to his chest as his heartbeat raced beneath her fingers.

"What is going on?" she asked, brows furrowed. The mortal man dragged his eyes over her body, over her ceremonial armour and belt full of weapons.

He blanched. "It's looking for you." The mortal pulled himself away from her grip and ran into the trees, followed by the remainder of the human army they had travelled with.

Raising a brow, she pulled her grimoire from the pack tied to her waist, flipping through the neatly scrawled pages, until she came across the spell she needed.

"Stand behind me," she said, as she pulled liquid fire from her belt. She shook the vial three times and whispered a short spell beneath her breath, calling forth the spirits that dwelled within the *forest.*

The first to come to her was that of an old man, hobbled even in death. He limped towards her, and she could see the wounds that had killed him. Half his skull was missing, as was an eye, but that didn't stop him from giving her a calm, sincere smile.

"Do you know what is out there?" she asked, addressing the old man.

He looked down. "Darkness personified," he whispered in his mother tongue. It took her a moment to understand his words, to match them to what she knew.

Changing dialect, she spoke in the native Valondean tongue. "What is the darkness you speak of?"

"It is a monster," the old man said, meeting her stare, "and it is angry with you. You are the one who killed its kin."

Clenching her jaw, she turned to her lover and repeated what the old man had said. She kept her voice low, aware of the other spirits coming to join them. Several were their own soldiers who had been caught in the crossfire.

"If it wants me, then you need to run," she said, resting a hand on his chest. His fingers wrapped around her wrist, encircling the plain silver chain he had given to her—a present from when he claimed that they would be together forever.

She knew he was shaking his head, but she couldn't look him in the eye. "If you die tonight, then I will never forgive myself. Please, go now and take my heart with you," she pleaded. "I will protect you, and I will find you."

He swallowed thickly, voice hoarse as he said, "I will never leave you." She finally looked up into his eyes, so deep and alluring, and planted a long kiss on his full lips.

"Go!" And he did. He stepped away from her, despite his better instincts, and he turned, her bracelet in his hand. He entered the thicket of trees and did not look back.

Guilt made bile rise in her throat; the magic she'd used on him left a bitter taste in her mouth, felt wrong as it died on her fingertips.

Releasing a breath, she turned around and faced her now ruined campsite, exiting the tree line so that she was now out in the open. Several bodies lay dead, scattered in various states; some had been undressing, readying to sleep, while others had settled in for guard duty. She saw the human general laying several feet from her, his spirit standing close.

With a dip of her chin, she raised her arms above her head and sent out a wave of pure magic; it hit the spirits of the fallen soldiers, giving them the strength to take back their bodies.

She did not have to wait long for the darkness; it crawled over an outcrop of rocks on the other side of the campsite, sticky tendrils of shadow wrapping itself over everything in its path. It had no body, no solid form, other than the faint outline of a man controlling the creature of darkness.

"You want me?" she called out, raising her chin. She jerked her hands like a puppet master and animated the bodies around her, bringing them to life. Pointing to the darkness, she sent her small, undead army towards it. "You can have me."

The soldiers raced towards the figure controlling the darkness, throwing themselves into the line of fire. The tendrils of shadow cut through them, but it did not keep them down for long. Each time they stumbled, the undead rose and continued fighting.

She reached for the liquid fire once more. She did not shake the vial, but instead threw it in an arc and smiled as it burned brightly in the centre of the camp, where the bonfire had once burnt.

The fire rose into the night sky until it illuminated everything. The darkness shied away, only to attack with far more vigour than she'd expected. A slimy hand of shadows struck at her fiercely, the blow knocking her to the ground.

Grunting, she commanded the soldiers to attack the figure again, sending her own power towards the spirits that surrounded her. They rose, her undead army, and surged towards the beast, completely untouchable by the darkness. Although the creature attempted to destroy the spirits, they merely re-appeared a moment later.

Something struck her, dark magic doused in something else, something ancient. She stumbled back, confusion rushing through her. Breathing heavily, the witch looked down at herself, at the bloody wound that snaked over her chest.

"You shouldn't be here."

Startled, she looked up and met the eyes of the Fae Knight. The black raven sat perched on his shoulder calmly, looking down at her with its beady gold eyes.

She looked towards the darkness, now gone. Everything was gone.

Except her wound.

Blood continued to bubble from the deadly cut on her chest. "I will die here, won't I?" she asked, shaking. Blood dripped from her lips. One of her lungs had been punctured.

The Knight looked down on her as she collapsed, his helmet now in his hands. "You will. But you will be reborn."

"What about my destiny?" she asked, tears sliding down her face. "What about my love?"

The raven cried out then, as if it were in pain. The Knight grunted. "Your destiny awaits you, as will your love. But it is your time."

"I cannot leave," she whispered. "Save me, so that I can fight this darkness."

The Fae Knight shook his head and looked away. A shimmering, silver tear slid down his face. Fae rarely cried. "I cannot do that."

A shuddering breath left her lips. Suddenly, there were hands cupping hers.

Above her, her sister sat, tears streaming down her face. "You should not have joined this war, Sister."

The witch managed to shake her head. "I had to. It was my duty."

"No," her sister argued, "it was your love that brought you here. And it was love that destroyed you."

"Love did not kill me." She coughed, and more blood dribbled down her lips. Despite all her powers, all her magic, she could not bring herself back to life. It was not her destiny. "That creature did this. Promise me you will find a way to destroy it, Sister. Find a way for it to die, so that when I do come back to this life, I will be able to fight back."

Her sister nodded sadly as the witch's eyes closed, and her heart beat for the last time.

"When will she return?"

The Knight was silent for a moment as the raven cried out again. "I do not know. But you will know when she does. You will feel it in your bones."

When the sister looked up, the Knight and his raven were gone.

"I will find this weapon," she promised, hugging her sister to her. "No matter what. I promise that to you."

~

Fear kept Eliza awake over the following nights; terrifying thoughts wrapped themselves around her every time she closed her eyes. She was caught between curiosity and fear, unable to distinguish either. Her thundering heart and visions of shadow creatures and wars told her to be afraid, but dreams of forgotten lands and a flicker of hope told her to wait before she judged.

It was curiosity and flickering hope that had kept her awake the night before her departure.

As she agonised over what she was supposed to pack into her old, dusty duffle, she thought once more about the dream that now seemed to occur every night. Who were the people—the man and the woman? But there was a flicker of recognition that flared within her when she recounted the dream to herself.

It was just a bad dream. She stared at her pale, trembling fingers before closing her hand into a fist. *A dream and nothing more.* The raven and the Knight had been there, too. That was enough for her to shove her fear aside.

Fear of Cadira. How long would she have to stay? Eliza looked down at her pitiful bag and released a sigh. She had no real memories of Cadira; only flashes of a life her grandfather had once told her about, years ago. Did that count? If she did have any memories, they were overshadowed by her anxiety brought on by the dream.

Dressing slowly, Eliza chose all black; black jeans, a black sweater, even her black docs, almost like she was dressing for any normal day in New Orleans, filled with lessons on magic and afternoons being drilled on both mortal history and the history of Cadira.

Sunrise slowly dawned on the horizon, drawing Eliza's stare to the clock on her desk and the blaring numbers on its surface. *5am.* She had less than an hour left before her grandfather would appear to bundle her up and smuggle her to another world. So, Eliza shoved in whatever clothes she could manage, filling her duffle within moments.

Eliza heard Kay call from downstairs for breakfast. Could she really eat before such a monumental day?

A caw brought her attention to the window, to where the golden-eyed raven sat perched on her windowsill. Eliza sucked in a breath. Standing, hidden by shadows across the street, the Faery Knight waited.

Eliza turned away momentarily and steadied her racing heart.

The raven cawed again, and when Eliza turned back to the

window, the bird flew away. Eliza searched for the Knight, but he was gone too.

She left the comfort of her bedroom. There was an unusual silence that settled over the house as she descended into the courtyard. Waiting at the wrought iron table, Kay poured herself a cup of tea while her grandfather sipped casually from a take-out cup of coffee. Eliza's place across from Kay had been set for her, with an unfilled porcelain cup, her favourite travel mug—filled with black coffee, she hoped—and what looked like a double-choc-chip muffin.

They're buttering me up now. All her favourite things laid out before her, like they were preparing her to never see them again.

Eliza looked down at the muffin. She could smell the bitter aroma of her coffee. Despite not feeling hungry before, she was suddenly certain she could scoff down the food in front of her without hesitation, nerves and fear be damned. *There's no way I'll be getting food like this in Cadira.*

It was that thought that sobered her.

Kay looked her over with a raised brow, face whitening at the duffel bag and satchel, already packed.

"You never really explained if I'd be staying overnight," Eliza said, lips tightening into a frown, "so I packed just in case." When there was no response, Eliza dropped the bags and sat down. She stabbed her fork into the muffin. "What are you going to say to people?"

People like Ambrose, who ran the museum, or Miss Constance next door, who Eliza helped every Thursday with her groceries. What would Eliza's guardians tell her Maths tutor, who already found it strange that Eliza didn't go to regular school?

"We'll figure that out," Davis said quietly, stiffly. Eliza looked up to meet his eye, but he was already looking down at the newspaper spread across his lap. As if finally sensing her stare, her grandfather looked up. He must have seen the nerves—the despair that filled her eyes—because he sighed and closed the paper. "You always have a choice. But I do suggest meeting with King Bastian and hearing what he has to say. It might help you understand."

Eliza sat back, grinding her teeth together. Her nose and eyes stung, like she was going to cry, and it pissed her off. "Understand what? That there are secrets you won't tell me?" She shook her head, exasperated.

Kay and Davis shared a quiet, unrelenting look that made Eliza groan. "I can't do this with you. I just want to get this over with, okay?" She stood, grabbing her bags and throwing them over her shoulders. She raised a brow at her grandfather. "We have to go, don't we?"

Once again, the two adults before her shared a look, and it was then that Eliza spotted the tears that brimmed in Kay's violet eyes. The older woman's thin lips wobbled ever so slightly, and when she breathed in Eliza could see her body shake.

"I'm sorry I never told you about any of this." Davis stood slowly, as if facing off a scared deer. Perhaps that was exactly what Eliza was. Around them, the courtyard brimmed with golden light. *Sunrise.* "I never knew when this would happen." Davis reached for her bag; the bag he had given her when she was so much younger. "I hope you will forgive me."

Eliza stiffened. "For what?" she asked. Her gaze went to Kay, who had tears slipping down her white cheeks.

She would miss Kay. Kay would not be able to follow her into Cadira. Not like her grandfather, not with her exile. Kay would have to stay behind in New Orleans.

Would Eliza see her again? Her eyes shifted back to her grandfather.

She could see how much he wanted to tell her, but she knew he couldn't, knew there would be a price—maybe his position, maybe his life. For five-hundred years, Davis Kindall had been protecting the barrier between this world and Cadira without a fault, and Eliza wasn't sure if she would be the one to break that cycle.

What Eliza knew about herself was incomparable to what she *didn't* know about her grandfather. Did she really expect to learn the whole truth so quickly?

Eliza stifled a sigh and nodded reluctantly. "Fine. I'll wait to hear from His Majesty. It can't be that bad."

Her guardians shared another look.

Oh, I'm screwed.

~

They were running late, but Eliza couldn't bring herself to care. Sitting rigid in the back, nails picking at the worn leather of the car's interior, Eliza gazed down at the floor, unable to bring herself to look out the window and see New Orleans pass her by. She did not want to say good-bye to her home, the only home she could remember, not when she had to have hope that she would see it again.

Despite the melancholy mood, Kay chattered nervously about how much Eliza would love Cadira; "It's different to New Orleans, sure, but it has that same... lively feel to it. That historic feeling you like so much about home? Yeah, Cadira has that. And since you'll be in the south, you should try the wine from the Light Courts! Oh, and they have the best pastries! You'll love them, kid!"

Kay talked until Davis took the uneven dirt road they'd driven down days prior that led up to the old hunting cabin in the bayou. He slowed down as mud and rocks flew up to hit the side of the car. Eliza had always said he should get a truck, but she couldn't imagine her grandfather—always impeccably dressed in sweater vests, pressed slacks and leather shoes—driving a pick-up. *"This car has stories,"* her grandfather would reply whenever she asked about it.

She still didn't know the stories, and now she was too afraid to ask. She didn't want to use up her requests too quickly.

The car pulled to a slow stop outside the temple. Eliza felt tears prick the back of her eyes, and her chest tightened as Kay opened the door for her. *This is it.*

Eliza heard the trunk open and close. Kay had both of Eliza's bags, while Davis quietly donned his traditional white robes, set aside only for the most important of occasions. She could not remember the last time she'd seen her grandfather in his robes, and something within her recoiled from it.

Kay's hand grasped hers tightly as they finally entered the warded, Cadiran temple. Eliza let her fingers tighten around the older woman's, and Davis opened the portal.

"I'll be waiting here for you when you get home," Kay whispered, leaning down to kiss Eliza's forehead. "You were always meant for greater things." A shiver ran down the length of Eliza's spine as Kay pulled away, leaving Eliza feeling cold and empty.

Greater things. What things?

A light flared, and slowly, the mirror began to clear. "We will pass through the barrier," Davis started, stepping up beside Eliza. He took the duffel bag with care, while Eliza hugged her satchel to her chest. "Kay will stay here and make sure it is sealed correctly while the new Keeper does their job on the other end. Keep a hold of me through the whole process though, okay?"

She nodded but could not bring herself to speak. Davis smiled faintly, sadly, before nodding himself. "Good. Let's go."

The glass cleared to reveal an identical room on the other side—the same room she had looked into a week before; the blood had been cleaned from the marble, and there were no demons waiting to throw themselves at the wards. Standing behind the always-burning-flame, a figure dressed in the same robes as Davis waited, their clear blue eyes kind as they watched.

Her grandfather offered her his hand, and Eliza took it hesitantly. Beyond the new Keeper, Eliza could just make out the wavering figures of what looked like soldiers, though they seemed to be hidden by a layer of darkness.

Eliza and Davis stepped up to the glass, and she forgot everything else as they stepped through the portal. Together.

5

CADIRA

Eliza felt hot and cold all over before a strange sensation, one Eliza could only associate with magic, washed over her when she finally made it through the barrier. To her surprise, it reminded her of stepping through a spirit, only icier. Eliza could feel the magic all around her, like a living entity that awoke when she finally entered its realm. Unlike Cadira, New Orleans—and the whole mortal realm—had no natural magic that stemmed from the world itself. Their magic came from whatever seeped through from Cadira, but even that wasn't as much as what Eliza felt. It claimed her, something she never imagined she'd feel. It took only a moment of her being there to sense the depths of her magic rise and strengthen, just like Kay had told her it would.

Opening her eyes, Eliza looked around the marble temple, at the soldiers and the Keeper that waited. She turned back to the barrier, to see if Kay was still on the other side... to see if maybe she could spot New Orleans through the cracks.

But it was already gone, gold mist and shadows taking its place.

"Welcome." Eliza turned back to the Keeper, a young woman with stunning midnight skin, and hair the colour of starlight. When she smiled, she revealed teeth as sharp as razors. "If you would, please follow the King's soldiers. They will take you to the Winter Palace."

The soldiers—Eliza counted ten, though she wondered if there were more hidden around the temple grounds—stood armed to the teeth with heavy-looking swords and daggers strapped to their hips. At least three carried small crossbows the size of their forearms. They all wore armour, metal plates strapped to their chests, arms, legs, and torsos. They did not look like they were welcoming a friend into their land.

Eliza turned to her grandfather—for clarification or to check that he was still with her—but he was already following the party of soldiers, shoulders tense. She suddenly did not feel safe in what was supposed to be her home world.

As she stepped out of the familiarity of the temple, Eliza did not know what to expect.

Trees, so tall they almost reached the sky and leaves made of glass, spread out around her. Burrows and twig huts were built into the branches, like small cities floating in the sky. Some of the trees were bent out of shape, while others moved and danced while no one else watched. Light filtered through the branches, casting the meadow in golden light. Dancing in the beams, Eliza swore she saw sprites and wisps, bathing in the warmth before winter arrived.

She had to remind herself that Cadira and her world were very different. Each season could span anywhere from a few weeks to a year. It was never the same, and there was no scientific explanation as to why. Cadira lived by the laws of magic and magic alone.

A breeze rushed through the glass leaves and they twinkled in response. In the distance, Eliza could make out the sound of rushing water—the border between Cadira and the Fae territories, she remembered faintly.

Something buzzed by her ear—a pixie, shining the colour of rose-gold—while another danced warily in the trees. But in between the magic that seeped through the very pores of this world, Eliza could sense something darker, something that tasted eerily like death.

She turned to her grandfather then, brows furrowed. His eyes danced over the landscape, like it was a place he had not seen in years, before turning to her, nodding sadly. "There is something... *rotten* about the land, isn't there?" he said.

Eliza bit down on her lip; they continued to follow the party of soldiers, Eliza and her grandfather situated in the middle of the circle they had formed. "I mean, it's beautiful, but... yeah. Rotting is a good word for it."

The soldier in front of her stiffened; Eliza could see it in the set of his shoulders beneath the plates of steel. He had taken his helmet off—

several of the others had, too—and he wedged it beneath his arm.

Without realising it, Eliza had speared her magic out into the world, searching, fumbling for the darkness that embedded itself within the magic in the land. Where she should have seen light, she saw only shadows; sensed only fear from the living creatures that relied on that essence.

"There is an absence of light," Davis said, stepping carefully over an exposed root. Around them, green grass glinted like polished emeralds, and in some places, snow melted. Overhead, dark clouds filled the sky, extinguishing the sun's rays. "The people of Cadira are losing their hope, and because of that, they are allowing darkness to take over."

She couldn't help but roll her eyes. "This isn't a movie, Grandpa." She sidestepped what looked like a boot made of wood. When she blinked, it was gone. "It sounds like you're quoting *Harry Potter* or something." She felt his gaze of disapproval slide over her, but she shook her head. "This all happened after the king's wife and daughter were killed, right?"

It took him a moment to respond. Around twenty years ago, a series of attacks befell the King of Cadira, leaving many of his soldiers dead. Eliza knew the story, had heard it a thousand times from her grandfather and Kay. Even wayward ogres and gnomes in the mortal realm recounted the stories to her. Although the king was not harmed, his wife had been killed, along with his eldest—his daughter. And his son, who had only been born two months before, had been taken in the night, never to be seen again.

Eliza knew her grandfather had been a part of one of the search parties who had gone searching for the lost prince, and that he left his position in New Orleans to recover the infant and find the attackers. But, like many, he had found no trace, no evidence of the prince anywhere. It was almost like he had never existed, never left a mark.

"More or less," Davis finally said, releasing a breath. "But it has always been there, a fixture in this world. I honestly cannot remember a time when there *wasn't* darkness here."

They stayed quiet; Eliza's hand now tucked into the crook of her grandfather's arm. They walked at a steady pace with the soldiers, though Eliza's eyes kept catching on the man in front of them with dark brown hair. A silver chain glinted around his neck, though he never made a move to look behind him.

Her grandfather said something to one of the soldiers, who replied in a brisk, curt voice, "Ten minutes." By that point, Eliza had stopped listening.

There were too many thoughts clanging around in her brain, thoughts she could not ignore. Darkness, the king, his lost son. Something insidious stirred within her, like an unquenchable fear. Perhaps she'd be facing her death sooner than she thought.

Between the dense trees, she made out a white wall.

Surprise and wonder took over as Eliza gazed at the Winter Palace. It was made of white marble and designed like it came out of a Victorian period novel; a white stone exterior with too many windows to count, and lush green gardens powdered in snow. Gargoyles surrounded the roof, staring down at her with unseeing black eyes, wings spread like they were ready to take flight. Perhaps they were, since Eliza could not tell if they were real, or just stone. Attached to the grounds, however, spirits wandered unseen amongst the living.

Since their walk from the temple, a fog had settled over the land, casting everything in a muted grey light. The spires became unseeable from their position at the gates, stretching at least four storeys high. Great dark-wood doors stood before them. The palace looked somewhat serene. Whimsical.

Eliza hated it.

When she thought about her audience with the king, she imagined him looking down on her and ordering her execution or locking her away in a tower for the rest of her short, miserable life. She pictured him as malicious and brutal, especially after losing his whole family to this unseen threat.

The wrought iron gates closed behind them as they stepped into the grand gardens of the palace grounds. As their group walked, Eliza made out rows of tents off to the side of the palace, in what looked like the games yard. Soldiers—like their guides—milled about. Fires had been lit at intervals. She could already feel the chill bleeding through her clothes and wished now that she'd packed warmer clothing.

"Why don't they have proper housing?" Eliza asked her grandfather, her voice low enough so the soldiers couldn't hear.

Davis's eyes skimmed over the setting; grey brows furrowed. "In all honesty, I'm not sure. It looks like a small army, doesn't it?"

Eliza pursed her lips but said nothing more. At the foot of the stairs a well-dressed man in what looked like a butler's uniform—black vest over a white dress shirt, an overcoat with pointed tails and pressed black slacks—waited, his hair combed neatly back, and his face impassive. She then noticed his piercing, red eyes and the curl of his lips. He shooed the soldiers away with a look of disinterest, then looked down his nose at Eliza and her grandfather.

"Welcome to His Majesty's Winter Palace." The doorman spread his arms wide. "Please, do follow me inside." Without waiting for a reply, he turned on his heel and walked to the doors. They opened without a sound.

Already, a sense of exhaustion rose within her; the mental strain of the last week casting a haze over the magnificence of the palace. Her mind, too occupied on the meeting with the king and her possible death sentence, didn't quite take in the foyer like she'd wanted to.

Davis, who knew her so well, patted her hand, which was still on his arm, and they followed the bustling man into the palace.

The butler began talking again, his steps growing quicker. Eliza almost snapped at him to slow down. "You will be shown to a set of rooms designed to meet your every need." They approached a set of grand, imperial looking stairs leading up to the second storey. Eliza blanched, but followed, awed by the marble and the elegance of the palace. "In these rooms, you will be expected to bathe, change, and be ready to meet with His Majesty in his private court. You will have two hours to do this. Food will be brought up to you. Appropriate attire will also be provided."

Eliza didn't question the man as they followed him up yet another set of stairs, though she doubted he'd bother to respond. With his hurried pace, she couldn't even look around or take in the strange yet alluring architecture surrounding her. She was too busy trying not to get lost in the maze of halls to pay attention.

They stopped before a set of doors; the doorman rested a white-gloved hand against the gold handle.

She took the time to breathe as he rattled off further instructions. "Your accommodations, Miss Elizabeth. A maid will be waiting for you inside. You have two hours. Keeper Kindall, if you could please follow me."

Fear sparked in her chest, eyes widening at the idea of her grandfather leaving. She'd been in Cadira for all of twenty minutes and already she and her grandfather were splitting up.

Davis touched her cheek lightly. "Don't worry yourself. I'll be down the hall. We'll be apart for a couple of hours." He smiled and stepped away. "You usually hate when I stick around anyway. Don't I embarrass you?"

Eliza narrowed her eyes, crossing her arms over her thundering heart. "Cadira is different."

"You're tired," he reasoned. "Take the time to rest, eat something. Mentally prepare."

Then they were gone, disappearing beyond a bend in the hall. *Mentally prepare.* She snorted. *Mentally prepare for what?*

Silence settled, unnatural and foreign. She shuddered. There wasn't even a spirit to keep her company. But she gave herself the chance to finally look around.

It wasn't hard to guess that Eliza was in the less favourable hall of His Majesty, King Bastian III; it didn't look like it was used often to entertain important guests. There were a couple of threadbare tapestries hanging on the walls around her, and other doors the same red-brown wood as her own. Sconces with gaslights flared every so often, like they were reminding the guests that they were, in fact, there. Unlike the outside of the palace, the inside looked less magical.

She shuddered at the eerie silence. *Totally normal and not weird at all.* With a sigh, she pushed open the door.

The room was much bigger than her one back home; full of light-pink and gold décor, a four-poster bed up against one wall, and large windows that opened onto a balcony overlooking the darkening forest and the soldier encampment below. There was a door to Eliza's right with steam billowing underneath, and she could hear someone humming beyond.

Eliza dropped her duffel bag with a thud, and the humming stopped. Waiting, Eliza watched the door to the bathroom open, and a girl with pretty red hair and striking jade eyes slipped out through the steam. She had to be a couple years older than Eliza, maybe in her early twenties, dressed in a pale-yellow gown with a white apron. *Must be the maid*, she thought, offering the woman a smile.

The girl dropped into a curtsy; Eliza watched, uncomfortable, wringing her hands before her.

"You don't need to bow," Eliza said as the girl rose. A blush swept its way over Eliza's cheeks. She *so* wasn't used to that. "I'm Eliza."

Her smile was frightfully wide, but there were no fangs or needle-point teeth. *Human.* "My name is Clio. And I know who you are," she replied softly, tilting her head. "Follow me, please, so that I might ready you for the king."

Swallowing, Eliza followed her into the steaming bathroom, and noticed the porcelain tub—definitely bigger than the one she had in New Orleans. After a pointed look from Clio, Eliza hesitantly stripped her clothing, cheeks burning in embarrassment.

Her hair was washed, and various oils and soaps were used to make her skin glow. During the quick work, Eliza tried to relax; tried to think about anything other than what was to come. She was going to meet the king. Eliza was dreading it, but at the same time, excitement bubbled in the pit of her stomach.

Eliza lived and breathed New Orleans and the limitless life she'd been living. Being home-schooled, the only authority she'd had to deal with were her guardians. When she worked at the museum, she and her boss were more likely to discuss movies than her lack of ambition. She'd always *assumed* her future had something to do with the wards, but now she wasn't so sure.

When Eliza got out of the tub, Clio wrapped a soft towel around Eliza's shoulders. She was told to dry herself, and without complaint, she did. All the while, Clio prepared the gown.

The dress had long sleeves that slipped off the shoulders and an A-line skirt, all in navy blue with silver-detailing around the neckline and bodice. It slipped over her skin like water... like magic.

Eliza looked herself over with a furrowed brow, twisting to see the back; it dipped, the cut going low, but where she thought she might see skin, she saw silver lace covering her back. *Might as well look nice if this is the day I die*, she thought with a twist of her lips.

An inkling of doubt gathered in her gut. *Would the king really do all this to kill me?* She hoped not.

Clio braided Eliza's hair next, letting it fall down her back before weaving it up into a crown. When she tried to do Eliza's makeup, Eliza had refused, scrunching her face in disgust at the heavy powder and the red lip-paint the maid was about to cake onto Eliza's face. Not even in New Orleans did she wear makeup, save for the occasional swipe of mascara or cute lip-gloss.

A knock sounded at the door, startling Eliza away from the mirror—from looking at the paleness of her skin and the dark circles beneath her eyes.

She was glad that she hadn't downed all the food that had been brought up to her while she'd been bathing, because if she had, she was sure she'd be feeling absolutely sick.

The doors opened after a moment, revealing the butler and her grandfather, who looked just as worried as Eliza. He nodded once to her and offered his hand, to which Eliza accepted, thankful for the support.

"You look beautiful, Elizabeth," Davis said once out of earshot of Eliza's maid and their guide. "You clean up nicely."

Eliza snorted, her heart rate slowing. She sucked in a breath, the corset of the dress no longer so stifling, but it still pinched at her waist and chest. The presence of her grandfather was enough to calm her, to make her *breathe* again.

She tried to crack a smile, but the tightness in her chest stopped her. "You don't look too shabby yourself, Grandpa."

The doorman led them down to the second story, though they did not descend any farther. They took a left towards what Eliza assumed was the king's private court. But they turned away, the doorman leading them down an additional hall, before stopping.

Bile rose in her throat; she should be looking at something besides the door before her, but she couldn't bring herself to look anywhere else. The feeling of being trapped was suddenly all consuming.

"Breathe." Eliza turned to look at her grandfather then, and could see the worry in his grey, ageless eyes. Worried for her? She hoped not. If he was concerned, then something was wrong.

The palace butler swept out a hand as he dipped into an elegant bow; the tails of his suit-jacket brushed the back of his knees, swaying in an almost unfeeling breeze. His other hand deftly turned the gold handle to the king's study. She ignored the off-putting perfection to the way he looked.

Eliza sucked in a breath, urging her heartbeat to slow. Despite her grandfather's steadying presence beside her, she could still feel sweat on her upper lip. That fear of not having answers, of being so close and yet so far from what she sought, left her stomach turning. But she couldn't deny the small seed of curiosity curdling in her heart, a flickering flame in the darkness that dictated her every move.

Davis guided Eliza into the king's office, hand warm and steady on her back. She ignored the racing of her heart as she took in the room—wide, floor to ceiling windows took up an entire wall, and heavy grey drapes pushed aside to reveal the grey, cloud-stricken skies beyond. Heat emitting from a fireplace made her sweat more, but she eyed the portrait hanging above the mantle, at the woman depicted in paint; strong, sharp cheekbones, and glaring sea-green eyes. Her ebony hair was wound like a crown atop her head, detailed with jewels and flowers.

"Beautiful, isn't she?"

Eliza started, turning wide-eyed to the king.

He watched her from the other side of the room, leaning casually against a wall of shelves. His dark eyes took her in, and suddenly, she felt exposed.

He looked younger than she expected, though she truly wasn't sure *what* she had imagined of the king. Bastian's dark hair was neatly combed back, his dark brows set in a frown. His equally black eyes were critical in the way he assessed her.

Swallowing, she looked back to the portrait, taking in the familiar dagger strapped to the woman's thigh. "Is it the Goddess Azula?"

The king barked a laugh as his long fingers stroked at his pointed beard. "No." He walked towards her slowly, and she had the awful feeling that she was being stalked. "A Queen of Cadira, though not by birth. She married into the royal family, but unfortunately bore no heirs."

The king turned his back to her, looking out over the grey sky and forest beyond the window. "I am glad that you made it here, Miss Kindall. Please, do take a seat."

She sat on one of the plush chairs situated by the fire, dress now sticking to her body. She felt the heat rolling off the flames, but it did not stave off the dread she'd felt moments before.

"I suppose you noticed the darkness," he said, back still to her. "How it weaves through the land like a plague."

Eliza shuddered, remembering the twist in her gut when she had stepped out of the temple. She'd sensed it, yes, but to hear it from the king's mouth made her go still.

"It started the day we were attacked, the darkness. Did you know that?" He didn't give her the chance to reply; his voice had taken on a softer tone, like he was lost in a memory. "Perhaps it started before that, but we truly felt it then. The death of the queen and the princess, the kidnapping of my son, Alicsar... it had a ripple effect.

"We thought keeping the search a secret would help the land heal," he said. "We hoped the people would forget, but it made its mark, and for that reason we could never recover. Keepers and Elders alike thought leaving it alone and moving on might help..." The king finally turned to her, shaking his head ruefully. Red-rimmed, his dark eyes and his cheeks looked hollow, skin pale. "Here we are. Twenty years later with a witch who may or may not have the answers."

Eliza swallowed the lump in her throat. She hugged herself tightly, a chill seeping through her gown. Even with a roaring fire, she felt cold. "Why me?"

The king cocked his head. "You tell me, girl. You were attacked by the same men who took my son and killed my family. Eight years *later.*"

She found herself looking towards her grandfather for answers; *he must know the reason*, she thought, furrowing her brows. *If anyone would know, it's him.* But he shook his head, running a hand over white stubble. Disappointment shuddered through her as she turned back to the king.

"I-I don't know, Your Majesty."

Those dark eyes never strayed from Eliza, not even as he sat across from her, folding his large hands over his lap. "I have a feeling you've been chosen for something, something far greater than a small tribe in the wilderness." His eyes narrowed. "If the bastard who stole Alicsar wanted you, then what do you have that he seeks?"

While she'd tried to come to terms with her fear in New Orleans, it came flooding back in that moment. With the king watching her and her grandfather standing only a few feet away, she couldn't stop the racing of her heart.

Oh, Gods, no. What is he talking about? She thought about her magic, her necromancy, bile rising in her throat. *Is he going to kill me? Is that why I was hunted down? Is that why they wanted me?*

Is he going to finish the job?

Eliza's hands shook as she tucked them into her lap. "Why am I here, Majesty?"

He blinked, and looked away, rubbing a hand over his chin. "I've taken your... *image* into consideration, what it could mean if the hunted became the *hunter.*" He stood; she took in the dark pants and polished boots. "Imagine what would happen if a young girl, who had once been hunted by our enemies, found the crown prince of her kingdom?" He turned to her then, a twisted smile on his face. "What would happen should the people once again find their hope in a young witch determined to save her world?"

Heart racing, Eliza felt a wave of dizziness wash over her. I can't... *I can't save Cadira! I'm just a witch from New Orleans. I'm a necromancer. I'll die.*

"What if I don't want to?" she asked meekly, folding in on herself as his eyes darkened.

"Then you run the risk of exile, Eliza Kindall. That world you are so fond of... you will never see it again. You will never see your family again; you will never set foot in this kingdom again."

Her heart stopped in her chest, and without breathing, she looked to her grandfather; he'd gone still beside the wall of bookshelves, his back stiff as a board, his weathered skin as white as snow. But she didn't see an inkling of surprise on his face, nothing to indicate that he hadn't known what she was getting into.

"There is a war threatening to take our kingdom." Her eyes flashed back to the king. He brushed a hand over a mounted map of Cadira, from the desert region of Mesah down to the Court of Light to the south. "We have enemies that we cannot see, bloodshed that cannot be accounted for. There is upheaval in the smallest villages and rebellion in the largest. Entire towns are disappearing and being slaughtered."

"What does this have to do with me?" she asked quietly. The king's eyes snapped to hers, and an unquestionable anger filtered through those dark depths.

Before the king could reply, a hand—warm and familiar—touched her shoulder. "Elizabeth. Show some respect to your king."

Despite the softness of his voice, the scolding of her grandfather's words shuddered through her. Heat flooded her cheeks as she refused to meet the hardened stare of the monarch. To be trusted with a job by the king and then to be treated like a child... She forced herself to suck in a deep breath to calm her racing heart.

It must be a mistake, Eliza thought with conviction but deep down she knew that wasn't true. *It can't be me, I'm* nothing.

Out of all the possible outcomes, she hadn't thought of *this*.

At this rate, she'd rather be shoved into an arranged marriage or claimed by a money-hungry aunt. That was something she could escape—somehow. But this?

To work for the king, to be his personal hunter... the thought left a bitter taste in her mouth.

"I must prevent war at any costs, and to do that—according to my council and advisors—I must consider the people. To uphold an image of complete power means sacrificing control." He took the seat across from her once again, shifting so that he leaned towards her. His voice dropped. "Find my son and stave off a war. Fail, and we all lose."

She shook her head. "I'm just a witch from New Orleans." She barely had any control over her necromancy, not to mention anything in that world. "I grew up there, not here."

The king sat back and spared her a tight smile. "Precisely. I've had my best search for my son, and I've had common people search, too. Each with varying skills, each with an array of powers. None, with abilities like yours."

Eliza swallowed the lump in her throat. The fear she'd been suppressing rose in waves. She clutched the arms of her chair, fingers turning white, seeking a moment to escape.

Icy fingers brushed gently against her neck, and her frantic gaze met her grandfather's. He shook his head in warning.

She looked back to the king, to his calm posture and blank eyes, and whispered, "I don't know what you're talking about." The lie tasted bitter on her tongue, accentuated by her thrumming fear and almost drowned out by the thundering of her heart.

"I know of your powers. That you can hear and see things others cannot."

Eliza turned back to her grandfather, betrayal flashing in her heart. She slid farther into her seat, farther into herself. *How could he do this to me?* She'd seen the words, read them, heard them from Kay's lips: *necromancers were hunted to near extinction.*

Suddenly, she was at the king's mercy, her life now in his hands. She felt her freedom slip from her hands and bundle in his own. If she failed, she'd face death—perhaps her family would, too, for protecting her.

King Bastian continued, as if unaware of Eliza's fear, her thoughts. "Your abilities are almost unheard of in our kingdom."

Yeah, she thought, clenching her fists. *Because rulers like you killed them off.*

"You see, necromancy is *fickle,* but it came to my attention twelve years ago that *you*—a little witch, attacked by Demon Masters, hunted down until all you could do was disappear—had that forbidden kernel of magic." He cocked his head, fascination glinting in his eyes. She couldn't help but narrow her own and glare. "My council and I had to wonder if perhaps you were *vital* in finding my son; what made an unnamed witch so special in the eyes of my son's kidnapper? What could a five-year-old girl do that hundreds before her could not?"

Fear quickly turned to anger. *Unnamed witch.* She'd been a *child,* as much a victim as he. She thought about the lack of memories, the half-truths, the unanswered questions that had plagued her growing up. "*It's nothing you have to worry about,*" her grandfather had said.

But she'd been taken from Cadira, because she'd been a target. She'd escaped, while the king's family couldn't.

She understood his feelings; the resentment that flickered in his eyes whenever he looked at her. She felt the same way whenever she thought about the world she'd been forced to leave behind. Sitting before him was a girl who had escaped a fate his daughter, wife, and son, did not.

"*Where is your sense of adventure,*" Kay had asked her only a week ago. When had Eliza lost that spark of excitement to see what the world had to offer?

"What do you want me to do?" she asked quietly, voice unwavering.

The king smiled. "I want you to use your abilities—discretely—to find my son. Bring him home *alive*, and should you do so, I will give you everything you could ever desire."

Her heart thundered. *Freedom.* Freedom to not check over her shoulder in fear, to not have to worry if what she was doing was *bad*, to finally have a choice, and maybe even the answers to all her pent-up questions.

Doubt cut through her like a double-edged sword, though. What would happen if she *couldn't* bring the prince home alive? Eliza didn't have to ask the question—it flashed in the king's eyes. Fail, and she wouldn't have a life to go back to. Her family would suffer the consequences of her actions, too.

"You will have all the resources one would need for this kind of expedition," the king said. "Horses, gold, clothing, anything you need. I ask that you keep quiet about what I am having you do, because of your abilities. You never know when a spy might be in our midst, and I would like to keep your arrival and departure secret."

She nodded, keeping her mouth shut. She felt the soft touch of her grandfather's hands on her shoulders as he stepped up behind her.

King Bastian continued, "I have already set up a meeting for you with my Captain of the Guard and Keepers like your guardian. They will tell you everything you need to know about that night." Sadness flashed in his hollow eyes, and she watched the façade he'd thrown up stumble ever so slightly. "I will not be present in this meeting, as I have councilmen to entertain. But I'm sure you understand."

Eliza didn't, but she nodded anyway. It wouldn't do her any good, she thought, to piss off the king.

A knock interrupted them, and the palace butler stuck his head in. Those red eyes met hers before looking away. "Captain Jed and Keepers Itzel, Dresden, and Tyr, are waiting in the library for Miss Elizabeth."

The king nodded, and Eliza looked between the two, biting her lip. There were questions she wanted to ask him, though she already knew they wouldn't be given until she'd found the prince.

Curtsying, Eliza left the king in his study, and followed her grandfather and the butler to the next meeting.

6

KEEPERS OF FATE

"Did you know about all this?" Eliza asked. They passed an open window revealing the front gardens; soldiers trained in the game-park below, wet with the misty rain. Their bodies moved deftly, like pieces of a larger machine. "Did you know the king was planning that?"

Davis remained quiet as they followed the bustling palace butler down a series of corridors and onto the first floor. Her grandfather spoke quietly as he said, "I knew, when I took you in, that the king had a plan for you. I did not know what though."

She bit the inside of her cheek. "You know," she said softly, stopping, "it's hard to believe that."

"I know," he replied, taking her hand. His skin was soft, familiar, and he wrapped both his hands around hers before bringing her knuckles to his lips, kissing them softly. "But I have faith in you, Eliza. I always have."

Tears stung the back of her eyes; the butler had stopped to wait for them, his red eyes impatient. They seemed to glow in the dim light of the corridor.

Davis pulled her along, and she let him; there was still a part of her that wanted to fight, to dig in her heels and say no. The same fear that wanted her to stop was what made her keep walking, to enter the small library off to the side of the palace.

While she imagined fairy-tale libraries to be grand, this one was stuffy; bookcases circled the room, dark wood filled to the brim with books. High windows illuminated the room, though the light was dim. More shelves had been erected around the room, and in the centre four tables were set up.

One of the tables was occupied by six people; Eliza identified the Captain of the Guard easily. The captain wore silver armour over his broad frame, inky-black hair streaked with grey, his face clean shaven. Dark eyes roamed over her and then her grandfather. A scar cut through his top lip, lifting it in a way that made him look as if he were constantly snarling.

"Welcome, Miss Kindall," he said, nodding in her direction. He turned his gaze to Davis. "Keeper Davis Kindall."

A robed figure stood and dropped the hood of her ceremonial robes. Tattoos inked their way up the woman's face, stark-black against the pale glow of her ivory skin. Her white hair was bound atop her head in a tight bun that reminded Eliza of a ballerina.

Eliza assumed the woman beside the pale Keeper was the new Keeper of her grandfather's temple, though Eliza couldn't be sure, not when she rarely met others. She smiled warmly at them both but remained seated. The last Keeper was a small man, perhaps shorter than Eliza, but she could feel the power radiating from him. His light hair had been brushed back and fell to his shoulders, curling around his pointed ears.

Two guards sat with them, both with bowed heads as they worked through a series of papers. They wore armour—silver-plated and shining—that stretched over their broad chests and shoulders, though their arms were surprisingly bare, save for the cotton shirt beneath. They were both older than Eliza—perhaps in their late twenties or early thirties.

The first Keeper motioned to two empty seats. Eliza took one silently, while her grandfather quickly clasped hands with those around them before taking his seat beside her.

"We thank you for coming here," the first Keeper said, voice like a melody. She looked to be half-Faerie, like Eliza, though Eliza's own Fae-blood was diluted to the point where there were little to no signs of her heritage. The Keeper looked like she'd just stepped out of the Willican Forest. "We understand the burden that has been placed upon you, Daughter of the Wilderness."

The Fae were known to have strong connections to magic; those with even an ounce of Faerie blood could summon the natural magic of Cadira. Sometimes, there were exceptions; normal humans without an ounce of Fae blood who could wield the magic of Cadira. Most of them trained to become Keepers, like her grandfather.

Then there were the Blood Witches of the Labyrinth Mountains, who descended from the blood of demons and Elves, who did not wield natural magic. They took magic into their veins—into their blood—and they wielded it in a way that could be considered dark, deadly.

But from Eliza's understanding, the Blood Witches were not evil; they were not a blight on Cadira and its light magic. Her grandfather had explained it to her as if the Witches were part of the natural balance to Cadira—without them, the land would fail.

Eliza swallowed. *Daughter of the Wilderness. Unnamed child.* She'd been hunted, and for what? Her necromancy? A skill she'd been born with, one that now haunted her every waking and sleeping moment? Never before had her magic been such a burden as it was now.

"I appreciate you going through this with me," she said, forcing a strength to her voice that she did not feel. *Think of the freedom. Think of Kay and Grandpa.*

"Where would you like to begin?" the second Keeper asked. The smile hadn't slipped from her familiar face, but Eliza could see the stiffness in the gesture. It was forced politeness for Eliza's sake, and nothing more.

"Perhaps names would be a start," Davis said with amusement. He motioned towards the woman with the ballerina bun and tattoos. "Eliza, this is Keeper Tyr, who holds the Capital's wards. Keeper Itzel, my partner. And lastly, Keeper Dresden. He holds the Copenhagen wards."

Eliza's lips formed a small 'o' as she glanced at the man. She wouldn't have thought him much, not with his stocky build and unusually critical eyes, but she had heard Keeper Dresden mentioned several times throughout her childhood.

"The Copenhagen wards are some of the deadliest wards on Earth," Eliza said, eyes wide. There, for a reason she didn't understand, the wards were weak with the darkness that plagued Cadira. If a Demon Master wanted to break through, that's where they would try.

Keeper Dresden nodded. "But on Cadira's side, the wards are heavily fortified in a great castle, hidden by magic. On my side, it's in a basement of an old townhouse I live in."

So different to the wards in New Orleans. Eliza would have thought that, in a couple of years, she'd be studying under Keeper Dresden in the art of defending the wards. He had the most practice, and all who sought to be Keepers trained under him.

Eliza, lost in her thoughts, hadn't realised everyone was watching her with steady, unblinking eyes. Had she said something aloud? Or... She quickly closed her mouth and offered the Keepers around her a smile. "It is nice to meet you all."

Davis, still beside her, slid her a blank notebook and a pen. The look in his eyes when she took it told her enough—*take notes. Ask questions. Do this right.* Eliza gave a shallow nod of her head before turning back to the others.

"Were any of you there, the night Prince Alicsar was kidnapped?" Eliza asked first, pen poised.

Keeper Itzel spoke first. "Unfortunately, no. But I was there when the Warlock Amitel arrived."

"He was the first Warlock to start searching," Keeper Tyr said, pale hand resting on a file. "He's several centuries old, mastered immortality young, and is known to dabble in Blood Magic with permission from the Blood Witches."

Eliza recognised the name, his past. What she knew about him was little—second-hand knowledge—but it painted a rather dark picture of the immortal Warlock. While Keepers were granted with immortality and the Blood Witches drew immortality from their blood, there were some Witches and Warlocks who could ascertain immortality for themselves. It was difficult, and Eliza didn't know the specifics, but the trials usually lasted weeks and could kill any not strong enough to complete the final spell.

"Was he called immediately?" Eliza asked finally. She gazed between the Keepers, but it was the Captain of the Guard who answered.

"It took several days. The entire guard was slaughtered. It was by chance His Majesty was found by suppliers from the town, and some guards who were taking over shifts." He shook his head, eyes tired. "I was not there. But it was a bloodbath."

Something in Eliza's stomach churned.

"As soon as the king was found, more guards and soldiers were called in. King Bastian himself called for Amitel."

Keeper Itzel continued, "Then the Keepers were called."

"Amitel led the search, picking up traces of the young prince and his captors. We followed," Keeper Dresden said. "I, personally, could only spend a couple of days searching—my wards were failing, and I was needed back at my post."

Eliza scribbled several notes. If Amitel, the high and mighty powerful Warlock of Cadira was there first, then she would need to speak with him too. It wasn't enough for her to be receiving information from people who hadn't really *been* there.

The rest of the information came to her slowly, and unfortunately, it wasn't much: the trace first led south, then disappeared. Amitel and others in the search party had gone back to the Spring Manor, where the prince had been taken. When they'd found the trace again, they'd found themselves travelling east into Fae territory before it had disappeared again. They went north, faced off against the formidable desert that covered the northern part of Cadira, with no way to enter or exit. Then, the trace had disappeared, and they'd had to start again.

It was a confusing mess, one Eliza barely managed to wrap her head around.

Like the king had already said—many had searched for the lost prince. Commoners, Keepers, Knights, Warlocks. Keeper Itzel mentioned a convoy had been sent to the Blood Witches in the Labyrinth Mountains, but they had declined to help. Elders and the Fates had been called upon, even dragon riders and their hunters. But every trace was exhausted to the point where nothing would get picked up.

That left Eliza exhausted; she felt it not only in her bones, but in her soul. There were so many missing pieces that it made her head want to explode. The only reason why she hadn't gotten up to pace or leave was her grandfather's presence. It wasn't the fault of the people around her that the traces were screwed up. Eliza was already under the impression that the trail's dead end was on purpose.

When the meeting finally finished, Eliza gathered her notebook and pen and gave her thanks to those who had helped. They each smiled in return before resuming quiet conversation as Davis led Eliza from the library.

The library door opened before they could leave. "Tonight, dinner will be hosted in the dining room by His Majesty. Be ready by seven," the butler said, his red eyes unnaturally bright in the dim light. A moment later, he disappeared without another word, leaving Eliza and Davis to find their own way back to their rooms.

"Do you understand what it is you need to do?" Davis asked as they left.

Eliza shrugged. "It's not like I have much to work with."

"And yet," he said, voice a soft echo as they ascended the stairs, "you have witnesses you can ask." Pausing at the top of the stairs, Davis looked out over the courtyard and the games park, where the soldiers still trained. At some point, the king and what looked to be his council had wandered out to watch.

Her grandfather turned back; his eyes alight. "You can ask the dead."

~

The room had not been empty when Eliza had returned from her meeting with the Keepers and the guard. Clio had been wandering about, cleaning and arranging clothes, packing saddle bags, and checking things off a list that had quickly been pocketed when Eliza had entered.

Sitting at the vanity, Eliza watched Clio's reflection as she pulled pins out of Eliza's hair and brushed out the tangles.

Eliza's mind went back to the king and their meeting. Every thought, theory, and fact filled her head, leaving her with a migraine.

She barely noticed when Clio left, and the door had clicked shut. She flung herself down on the bed, thoughts going back to the meeting.

The king and his assumptions, or rather his knowledge of her power and his promises of freedom, rang loudly in her head. Though, just below the shouts of desire, she heard the name *Amitel*, like a whisper of someone she ought to already know.

The king had revealed very little of her past, but that didn't mean it was completely off limits. Eliza already felt a sense of recognition for the immortal Warlock. Like she should know him already. Maybe, she thought, he'd been there when she'd been found. Amitel had been the first called when Prince Alicsar had disappeared, and so he could have been first called when she was found too.

And then there was what her grandfather had said: "*You can ask the dead.*" It should have been obvious, what with the revelation that the king knew what she was. She had *necromancy* magic, after all. The king had explicitly told her that her power would be useful.

But it didn't stop the hesitancy or the fear. Because while the king didn't seem to care, others might, and they could very well harm her in order to remove her power.

Think about Kay. Think about Grandpa. Think about freedom.

A knock sounded at the door. "Come in!" she shouted, rolling off the bed. Her grandfather appeared, smiling sadly. A knot formed in Eliza's stomach as she took him in. He was wearing his pointed leather shoes and slacks again.

Like he was leaving.

He paused at the door, his hand on the knob. "I'm afraid I must leave you now, dear."

Eliza's heart sank; she fell back onto the bed and sucked in a breath. "I can't do this without you."

"Yes," he replied, moving to sit beside her, "you can. You can and *will* be able to do this."

"Why do you have to go? Why now?" she asked, closing her eyes. *Screw making him proud*, she thought bitterly. Couldn't she just have a bit more time with him? The king hadn't given her a time limit in finding his son.

Eliza climbed off the bed, running her hands through her hair.

Davis sighed and stood, wrapping his arms around her, pulling her close. She breathed in his scent and memorised the familiarity of it. But he pulled away too soon, leaving her alone. "I need to go back to the wards, back to New Orleans to protect both worlds. You know that."

Eliza shrugged, hugging herself. "I thought you'd help me with this."

"You don't need my help, dear. You just need to trust that you can do it." Davis walked to the door, and Eliza sadly watched him go, tears spilling down her cheeks. "Don't fret, Elizabeth. I love you, and I trust that when the time is right, you will find your way back to me... back home."

Eliza didn't get the chance to reply before he left, gently closing the door behind him. "Love you too, Grandpa," she murmured to the empty room, biting down on her lip. She'd seen the pain flash in his eyes, too, before he disappeared down the hall.

She couldn't help it; she buried her face in the pillows. But she could not cry over her grandfather leaving her in a world she no longer knew.

She was alone.

7

KNIGHT OF NOTHING

I need to clear my *head.* Eliza slipped out of her pretty dress and changed into her clothes from home. Though she found comfort in the familiar smell of washing detergent, something felt strange about donning her own clothes. She tried to shrug the feeling away, but it followed her as she left her room and descended the stairs.

Eliza found no trouble when she slipped out the front doors; either no one was watching her, or no one expected her to go far. She wasn't sure what she was doing now. Sucking in a breath, she closed her eyes. Her thoughts wandered back to the king, to the enormous task he had *bestowed* upon her. As she released a breath, Eliza turned towards the old games park, where the soldiers sparred.

Misty rain fell, more annoying than drenching, though it cooled her burning skin. The sky above her was stricken, dark, not like the world she'd imagined.

The soldiers were young—closer to her age, seventeen, and older—pushing themselves not only for the commander present, but for the king and his council that were locked away indoors. She couldn't help but stop and watch, enamoured by the lengths in which they'd go to impress their king, to follow his orders. How far would *she* go? Eliza wondered what she would do in order to attain her freedom and the freedom for those she loved.

Her gaze strayed to the man barking orders. From what she could tell, he was young—older than her, but younger than the men whom she'd been meeting with earlier. He held himself almost arrogantly amongst his men, though he'd taken his shirt off and was sweating with them in the rain. When he turned to block a swipe from an oncoming soldier, she could see his young face focused so intently on what he was doing, that the expression looked familiar to her.

Eliza caught the eye of a soldier, who whistled. *Actually whistled.* She felt somewhat flabbergasted as she stood there, arms crossed over her chest. *People do that here, too?*

She sent a harmless wave of frigid wind snaking towards the soldier in question. She watched, pleased, as the air knocked him on his backside. When he looked back at her with wide eyes, she gave him a vulgar gesture before stalking off in the direction of the gates.

A clear head. She wasn't even mad over the whistle; her frustration was towards the king and her grandfather leaving, not some silly soldiers.

But she hadn't just caught the attention of a few soldiers; the man who had been barking the orders earlier was now watching her with narrowed eyes.

As the front gates opened, she headed straight for them and away from the palace. She was somewhat surprised to see how busy it was; a steady stream of people entered and left the premises, trailing carts, horses, and donkeys with them. She slipped between a couple of servants and joined a rather interesting party of—circus folk? They wore so many different colours it made her eyes hurt.

"Hey!"

Eliza stopped and turned, shoving her hands into the pockets of her jeans. In retrospect, she realised just how poorly she'd handled the situation, but... Eliza plastered a smile across her face and looked up into the unreadable expression of the soldier before her. They stood against the tree line, only feet away from the palace gates.

"Hello to you, too."

He looked down at her, unamused. Eliza noticed—a little sadly—that he was now wearing a shirt, and a sword was strapped to his hips. His dark hair was plastered against his skin, wet with sweat and rain.

The way he moved and watched her reminded Eliza of her dream, of the strange war and the threatening darkness, the man with the piercing eyes who said he'd loved her... Eliza shook her head, expelling the memory. It had just been a bad dream, nothing more. But that didn't stop her from questioning the man before her, questioning the familiarity. The arch of his lips, the whisper of his fingers, it called to something in her blood. It was impossible, the feelings that rushed through her. So, she tried to shoved them aside.

And yet, curiosity rose within her, painstakingly familiar. She couldn't help but wonder why she recognised him, why she'd seen him in the dream.

Unfortunately, Eliza thought it made him look rather... cute. Cuter than some of the boys she'd encountered in New Orleans. His storm-blue-grey eyes were almost swoon worthy, a detail she could imagine she'd have read about in a romance book. He had that heroic look about him, from the broadness of his shoulders down to the broody slant of his brows.

Almost. Eliza checked herself quickly. *Gods,* she'd just said goodbye to her freedom, independence, and family, and now she was checking out a soldier who *probably* had high standards. That, and he was probably going to berate her for her actions in the games park.

She waited for it, but it never came. "I'm sorry for the cadet," he said, jaw ticking. "His actions were inexcusable, and I apologise for how he made you react."

Eliza bit down on her tongue—hard. She couldn't help but wonder why *he* was the one apologising, and not the *cadet.* Hesitantly, she said, "I wasn't expecting an apology. I thought you were going to get shitty about the magic."

He nodded. "I understand that. It won't happen again."

"What?" Her brows rose. There was something about him that made her think twice, like a bad case of déjà vu. Before he could reply, she shook her head.

He probably hadn't meant to, but a smile flickered at his lips. "Commander Brandon Thorne of the king's army."

"Eliza." She stuck out her hand, and albeit slowly, the commander took it and shook. Something in her clicked. "I know you."

Eliza wasn't sure what she saw flash across his face—alarm? It was quick, but she could tell her words affected him; he dropped her hand quickly, like she'd burned him. She tried to play it off, but something deep within her cracked in response. "Uh, you were there, when I came through the gateway. I recognise the chain." She pointed to the silver necklace that appeared over the collar of his shirt.

Thorne visibly deflated, like what she said wasn't what he expected. "How could you tell?" Those stormy blue-grey eyes of his had hardened, darkened, but he was slowly pulling himself together.

She shrugged. "You just seem familiar. And you gave it away."

Commander Thorne seemed to want to object but closed his mouth quickly. Eliza smiled in quiet triumph and turned on her heel.

Though she'd only walked through the forest earlier that morning, it looked somewhat different. *An ever-changing lifeform,* she thought. The burrows in the tall branches looked like they were now part of the trees themselves, and she couldn't make out if there were any sprites or pixies or nymphs climbing amongst the branches. The grass looked grey, almost lifeless. Talk of the darkness flashed in her mind, but she shoved it away. It wasn't her problem, not right now.

A shudder of dread coursed through her. Eliza stopped and turned back to the commander, who had been following her dutifully through the forest. Despite the overcast day, she could see him clearly. "You know following me makes me think you're planning to kill me."

He cocked a brow. "And what makes you think that?"

"Why are you following me?"

The commander straightened, like he was prepared to go on some kind of spiel. It was then Eliza noticed his height. *Tall,* was one way to put it. *Six-two,* she imagined. "My duty is to serve the king, and as you are his guest, I need to make sure you are safe."

"I'm still in view of the guards," she said, exasperated. "I think I'm fine." Her heart fluttered, even if he said he was doing his duty. "But... thanks."

Silence passed between them—Eliza couldn't call it easy, but it wasn't tense, either. She'd just met the man, and although there was a familiarity to him, she tried to brush that away. She had a job to do, even if she doubted that she'd be able to get it done.

If she was going to find the prince, then she wanted to go to the scene of the crime. Eliza had watched shows like *Criminal Minds*, so she knew the drill—even if they were fictional shows. Living in New Orleans and learning about missing persons and murders came with the territory, especially since she could see the dead and understand them.

Eliza began making a mental list of what she needed to do, including going back to where Prince Alicsar had been taken. There was something else that ate at her though—something one of the guards had said about the first warlock to go out searching.

Surely I won't find anything, she thought as she jumped over a moss-covered boulder. But if he was lying... Eliza then decided to find him too, and question him herself.

"Why are you here, Eliza?" Commander Thorne asked suddenly, leaning back against a tree. He crossed his arms over his broad chest, the grey shirt he wore stretching as he did. He watched her with an intensity she couldn't quite escape, like he was seeing her not for the first time—no, they had seen each other before in the temple—but like he was seeing her anew, in a new and changing light.

Crossing her arms over her chest, Eliza decided she needed to start moving again, if only to get the commander to stop *looking* at her like she was a puzzle, or some kind of freak-show entertainer. "I could ask you the same thing," she said over her shoulder.

Eliza could almost *feel* his eyes roll. "You know what I mean." He continued to follow her deeper into the forest. She made sure to stick close to the road that led to the palace, keeping it in the corner of her eye. "Why are you in the Winter Palace?"

She stopped, lips pursed. When she turned, she found the commander a lot closer than before, close enough for her to touch. She stumbled back and swore under her breath. When she found herself caught in his stare, she had to force herself to look away. "You don't know?"

There was a pause, and she sighed. What would be the repercussions of telling him? He was a commander in the king's army, so admitting to him what she was going to do... it wouldn't be a bad thing would it? But she thought back to the king's words of keeping the mission quiet, and her own fears resurfaced.

And yet, she found herself telling him anyway. She almost cursed herself but decided, screw it, the king and his rules be damned. "The king has employed me to find the prince."

His jaw ticked as he looked her over, brows furrowed with worry. "Why you?" he asked, voice low.

"Trust me," she said with a shake of her head, hair bouncing, "I've been asking myself the same question. But I'm still not happy with the answer."

He pursed his lips and looked away, as if he too did not trust that she would be able to find the prince. It was the same look she'd given herself in the mirror.

"No one has found any trace of him," he said slowly. "How are you any different?"

"I don't know."

"Do you even know where to start looking? Do you have any leads, anything that might help you?" He took a measured step towards her, head cocked. He didn't *sound* condescending, at least. But he was analysing her, his stare critical.

Eliza shook her head, relenting. She didn't bother voicing her ideas. "No."

Those piercing eyes of his revealed nothing. "So why you?"

Irritated, Eliza shoved him back with a wave of magic and breathed in deeply. "Because I have powerful magic that'll help me."

That sounded better in my head. She almost cringed but refused to give *him* the satisfaction.

The commander's eyes widened as he shook his head. "That won't be enough. The most powerful Warlock has gone after the prince and has found nothing. How are you going to do any better?"

"Because I have a power that the Warlock didn't." *Keep digging that hole, why don't you?*

Just to break the tension, Eliza started walking again. She had no destination. She just needed to move and stop *him* from asking so many questions.

It would be easier for her to admit it: *she could see ghosts*. But... she spared a quick glance over her shoulder at the hulking man who walked behind her. He brushed his hand through his hair and met her stare. Kay's warning and those fears came back. What would he do if he knew she was a necromancer? Probably kill her then and there... or run.

Eliza quickly looked away as a blush crept up her neck. His gaze continued to reveal nothing, leaving her stomping through the underbrush of the forest.

"What power?" They were coming up to a small glade, the creek already frozen over.

They stopped, and Eliza looked at the canopy of trees—felt the dying sun break through the clouds and wash over her in chilling warmth. The sounds of the forest seemed to cease as they faced each other.

"It's none of your business, actually." Eliza definitely couldn't deny the spike of fear in her heart. She turned back to the frozen creek, to the quiet woods and the muted colours of the forest. Certainly, the darkness her grandfather talked about had seeped into the very life of this place. Even the thought sent a shiver down her spine. The sky darkened as if to reflect that.

When she turned back to the commander, he was watching her with shadowed eyes and lips pulled down in a frown. If she could guess, it looked as if he were caught up in a memory. Maybe he knew this glade or remembered what Cadira was like before the darkness. She wanted to ask but couldn't quite find the words.

Eliza began walking back to the palace when he did not reply, feeling the storm above them grow. The sky opened to release a light sprinkle of rain, which cooled Eliza's hot face, slowly drowning out the thrumming in her head and the confusion that swirled within her.

Even though she couldn't see him, she could still feel the commander a couple of steps behind her. He walked a respectful distance even though he was still close enough to make the hairs on her arms stand on end. In all their time walking through the forest, Eliza hadn't felt unsafe. Part of her knew she should have been more cautious, but she was in *Cadira*, and her magic was stronger than ever.

She never got the sense of *danger* from him, though. Sometimes, if she were faced with a particularly bad customer at the museum, or some weirdo on the streets of New Orleans, she'd get a *feeling*; whether it would be the hairs on the back of her neck standing or a spirit screaming at her.

He smiled when she turned back to check, and the gesture clawed at her chest. She tried to force it down, but the look in his eyes, the way he caught up to her to walk beside her...

Eliza turned away.

Thorne stepped out onto the road, and Eliza walked out behind him. They strode out to the middle, uncaring as the rain intensified, slowly drenching them.

"What do you know about the Warlock who was first sent out to search for the prince?" Eliza asked suddenly, looking up at the commander.

He paused for a moment; eyes narrowed. "He was summoned first because he's the most powerful. Why?"

Thanks for that reiteration, she thought, irritated.

"Because I want to talk to him about what he found that night."

The commander nodded. As they neared the gates, he stopped, arms crossed. "I can set up a meeting with him, if you really think that'll help you find the prince." Eliza swallowed thickly; her mouth suddenly dry. He was offering his help. "I don't know how it will though, since he's revealed everything he knows. And then some."

Eliza smiled, somewhat grateful. The king had never told her that she couldn't get *help*. And the prince had been missing for over twenty years. If anything, *she* was going to need all the help she could get, necromancy abilities aside.

"Trust me. I can get answers; I'll find out what I need to know."

There were no more carts or soldiers heading in and out of the palace gates, though they were still open. The commander let her slip through first and continued to follow her to the slippery marble stairs. Already, the doorman was waiting for her, his lips pulled down in a frown. In his arms he had a towel.

She turned back to the commander, only to find him several steps away. Those stormy eyes of his flashed, and one hand curled into a fist. Beneath his wet shirt, she saw the outline of the silver chain hanging over his heart.

"I'll send word to you when I hear from him," he said, edging towards the encampment. "Get dry."

Eliza watched as he turned around. Some part of her wanted to call out to him—it was the same part of her that screamed déjà vu whenever she looked at him. It was something she couldn't quite escape, and to be frank, it frustrated her and confused her to no end.

"Wait." He paused before turning back to look at her. "Why are you helping me?"

The commander's eyes flickered up and met hers. "Because it's my duty to do so. And..." He shook his head, dark hair sticking to his forehead. "And maybe I want to."

She didn't know what to say; her heart was racing, and that damned blush she tried to fight was now spreading up her cheeks once again. *Damn him*, she thought.

"Miss Elizabeth, please." She turned back in time to see the doorman sigh, to see her servant sidle up behind him. The commander was still behind her, watching. "Out of the rain before you catch your death."

She didn't have a choice; with one last look spared towards Commander Brandon Thorne, Eliza entered the palace with just a little bit of hope.

8

A VISION IN RED

The storm continued late into the evening. It wasn't until after dark that Eliza received a calling card from Commander Thorne. It was only a letter to let her know he'd sent word to Amitel and asked for a meeting, but it was a good start—especially for her. He'd also written that he'd see her at dinner.

When she'd returned to her room earlier—bound in blankets and soaking wet—a bath had been drawn and Clio had set out a pair of comfortable Cadiran clothes for Eliza to wear, telling her that she'd be back at six to help her dress for dinner with the King.

Apparently, it was going to be a rather large feast, including all the visiting councilmen, their wives, their heirs, and all the commanders, officers, and generals present at the Winter Palace. It also now included Eliza, who would be sitting close to the king. As far as she knew, only the Captain of the Guard, the king, the Keepers, herself, and now Thorne, knew about her position, so she knew she'd likely receive unsettling glares and be the source of scandalous rumours by the end of the night... but she couldn't really bring herself to care, especially when she saw what she'd be wearing.

Blood-red and sleek, the dress hugged Eliza's curves, falling to the ground like silk, finishing in a short train. The back of the gown had intricate lace, while its bodice was plain, the same lacy design at the hem.

Clio forced Eliza into a pair of red heels that had her feet aching before the night had even started, while her hair was pinned up with pearls. Eliza refused makeup again and decided against wearing an expensive-looking ruby pendant that the king had given her.

When dinner was called, Eliza was escorted down to the large hall by the king himself. Ornamented in jewels and gold, Eliza looked quite plain beside him, but he complimented her nonetheless, though he did question why she'd refused the ruby necklace.

"It looked really expensive," she'd said after a moment. "The necklace, I mean. It's a lovely gift, but it really didn't look right."

He nodded but did not reply. Eliza bit her lip and kept quiet after that.

Walking in on the arm of the king sent the room into silence. The doorman cleared his throat. "His Majesty, King Bastian and Miss Elizabeth Kindall."

The enormous table was full of people, each with empty plates in front of them, but full wine glasses. There were decorations spread across the centre of the table, leading all the way down; twigs and branches that looked like glass glimmered in the candlelight of the dining room, droplets of crystal hanging from their ends. Bowls filled with emeralds and rubies overflowed in intervals, and there were large, gold vases spread around with purple flowers that danced with the soft music of the orchestra in the corner.

Though there was silence amongst the guests, there was also a clear universal order; every person stood, their backs straight, waiting for the king and Eliza to take their seats at the other end of the table. Based on the direction Eliza and the king had entered from; she was forced to face the preening nobility of his royal court, rather than the assembled military figures they passed.

King Bastian released her arm and strode to the head of the table, while a young servant showed her to her seat, only several spaces down from the king. She waited to sit, like everyone else, until the king took his place.

There was absolutely no hesitancy in the court's whispers when she finally sat.

Towards the other end of the table, Eliza spotted Commander Thorne, who had caught her eye when she'd moved to her seat. She spared him a smile, yet in response he turned away to speak with a woman beside him, ignoring Eliza completely. It stung, but how could she be surprised?

A lady across from Eliza caught her stare. "I am Duchess Yohanna, wife of Duke Josef. Who exactly are you, *Elizabeth Kindall*?"

Eliza swallowed the lump in her throat. "I'm the ward of Keeper Davis Kindall." She looked over to the king, but his attention was elsewhere. "And I'm here as a guest of the king."

The duchess gave her husband the side-eye, making Eliza clench her teeth. The king, however, spoke with the man beside him. The Duchess didn't say anything else to Eliza, content with the information she'd gleaned. She moved on to speak with another woman at her side instead.

Sighing, Eliza picked up her wine glass and took a large sip. No one else bothered to speak to her, and she suddenly felt alone.

Eliza looked across at Commander Thorne but found his attention elsewhere.

The first course was served to the king and then the rest of the table, consisting of a light pumpkin soup. Eliza ate it slowly, savouring the warmth. The room had gone cold suddenly, and even though she knew the fire was being fed and poked behind her, she still shivered. The chill in the air left Eliza feeling rather uncomfortable.

The seat to her left, which had previously been unoccupied, was then taken by a young man. His sandy hair—combed back with enough gel to give him a role on Jersey Shore—glimmered with gold dust. He had narrow shoulders, and the hands of a musician, Eliza thought. Completely different to the commander. His smile was kind as he offered his hand.

"Lord Irvington."

Eliza extended her own and they shook. Heat rose in her cheeks as he searched her face. He was attractive in the same way that she found Disney princes attractive; there was an otherworldly beauty to his sharp jawline and the elegant tilt of his head. He didn't look quite *real* to her, like the colour of his blue eyes was off, or the fact that his hands looked a little too strange to be part of his body.

"Eliza Kindall, ward—"

He cut her off. "Ward of Keeper Kindall and guest of the king." He grinned, showing straight-white teeth. "I've heard. People talk."

She flushed, and quickly took another sip of her wine. She couldn't help but look over to the commander then, only this time, his eyes were on her. She looked away.

"How long have you been in Cadira?" Lord Irvington asked. He leaned in, giving her his full attention. "I'm only asking because I have never seen you before, and I know Keeper Davis works in the mortal realm."

"A day," she said, and smiled honestly. "It is very different."

He quirked a brow. Servants cleared the dishes from the table, replacing the soup with plates of small roasted bird drizzled in a sweet-smelling sauce. There were roasted vegetables pushed to the side with nut flakes sprinkled over the top. A light sheen of golden powder lightly dusted the entire meal.

Eliza thanked her server and blinked as her wine was refilled. She hadn't realised she'd finished off the first glass.

"This land... isn't all that it seems," the young lord said. He didn't touch his food. "There are all kinds of secrets hidden here."

Another memory twisted inside her mind, swirling to the surface. She glimpsed a forest clawing at her before the vision disappeared completely. Confusion swelled within her; she stifled an irritated sigh and bit into a piece of roasted potato. She heard parts of the king's conversation—he spoke to the Duke about some new development concerning a 'missing piece'.

"Do you plan on staying long?" Lord Irvington asked, pulling Eliza from the king's conversation.

She looked back to him, forcing a smile. Small talk wasn't one of her specialties. "I will stay however long the king desires," she said. "I hope to see the land, witness the true magic of Cadira while I am here."

"It is definitely beautiful," he conceded, smile still on his lips. Something was hidden behind it, though; feral, untamed beauty, she thought, heart twanging. *There are all kinds of secrets hidden here.* She was certain she was looking at one.

There was something about the young lord that called to her magic. However, when she sent a spear of magic towards him, she felt nothing; an emptiness that should not have been there.

Turning away, she finished off her meal, and waited for the next course.

~

When the dinner ended, the large party was herded into an adjoining ballroom for music and tea and sparkling wine that made Eliza's head spin. She had tried to think of some excuse to leave, but the king offered his arm once again with expectant eyes, and she was forced to take it with a smile.

Eliza spotted Thorne in the crowd with the same woman from earlier but had lost him when she and King Bastian had been cornered by generals and councilmen alike. But she knew she was being watched by the king, even when she found Commander Thorne.

The commander stood alone by a bay window that revealed the thundering storm outside, a glass of wine in one hand with the other behind his back. Eliza could see herself in the reflection of the window, could see his face and the way he watched her, though he didn't bother to turn around.

Her breath caught in her throat as she watched him for a moment. With his back to her, Eliza imagined the man from her dream walking away from her.

She shook her head. There was a stillness to his posture, a glint in his eyes that almost made her stop in her tracks. His stormy eyes swirled with thoughts Eliza wasn't privy to, and his brows were furrowed in a way that made her think he'd seen something that made him uncomfortable.

Maybe it's me, she thought, hesitating. *Maybe he's waiting on someone else and doesn't want to talk to me.* But she knew how ridiculous she sounded even to herself.

"What did you think of dinner?" he asked, breaking their tense silence. He still didn't turn around to face her—their eyes met in the window, and she held his stare. A foggy memory danced in the back of her mind; a blood-streaked gown, the galloping of horses, a broken crown. She struggled to grasp the memory before it slipped away.

Shrugging, Eliza walked straight up to the window and placed her hand on the pane of glass, just as a bolt of lightning lit up the sky. "It was alright."

Thorne snorted. "Trust me, too many people talk and usually it's bullshit that comes out of their mouths."

"Oh?" She looked up at him. "What kind of *bullshit* are you referring to?"

Commander Thorne met her stare then went back to looking out of the window. Lightning struck again, followed by a crack of thunder. "One woman claimed that you must be the king's new mistress—or bride."

Eliza's eyes widened and she choked back a laugh, covering her mouth with her hand.

Thorne continued. "Another—this time a councilman—tried to

convince everyone that you are an assassin."

Her brows shot up.

"And *another* believes you must be one of King Bastian's bastard children, ready to be legitimised and introduced to court," he finished, finally looking at her.

"And what did you say to all these assumptions?" she asked, biting back a laugh.

He smiled, and it lit up his face. "I told my comrade that my money was on you being an assassin."

Eliza couldn't help but smirk. "God, some people." She shook her head, exasperated.

The two stood in silence for a moment with only the sounds of the orchestra, the loud conversation, and the occasional rumble of thunder to break the stillness. In the background, Eliza could hear the ladies and duchesses talking about her gossiping as to why she had been on the arm of the king, but she decided correcting them would be useless.

Let them talk.

"I have another favour to ask, concerning, well, *everything*," Eliza said, lowering her voice.

Commander Thorne met her stare, eyes shadowed. He stepped closer to her, shielding her from the party. "What exactly do you need?" he asked.

Eliza swallowed thickly, unable to meet his gaze. "I don't know Cadira—the landscape. I don't know the landscape, or to find what I need." She paused, thunder erupting in the sky. She felt the window shake beneath her hand. "I need a guide; someone I can trust. Someone who won't ask too many questions."

Thorne's eyes narrowed and he leaned in, lowering his voice. "Are you asking me?"

"No." She shook her head, but her heart did a silly somersault when she thought too long of the man standing beside her. "Of course not. I guess you're too busy. I just need someone I know I can trust—who you might trust, too, since they'll probably have to get me to Amitel and where the prince was kidnapped." Her cheeks flushed, because some silly part of her *did* want the commander to join her. Stupidly, she knew it wouldn't happen.

Thorne remained quiet for a moment, still extremely close to Eliza. She could feel the heat from his body on her shoulder, noticed his gaze upon her.

Then he shook his head. "I don't trust anyone enough with this," he said, running a hand through his hair, dishevelling it. His eyes reflected the storm outside, swirling with grey and blue and mystery.

Some part of Eliza wondered if his statement wasn't just reserved for the prince. That part of her hoped it meant her, too.

"And?" she asked, heart thundering in her chest as another flash of lightening illuminated the sky.

"And... I'll take you myself."

Eliza blinked, surprising herself at how much she wanted to hear that. Gods, she was turning into a ninny, wasn't she?

"What?" His eyes flashed, and a smirk upturned his lips. Red tinged his own cheeks, but Eliza couldn't tell if it was because of her or the sparkling wine in his hand. "Didn't expect that?"

Eliza shook her head. "No, not really." She cleared her throat and stepped away, searching the crowd for the king. "I'll need to speak to the king with you. I mean, you're a commander in his army. It might be hard to let you go."

"Not if I'm searching for the prince, it won't be."

She searched his face for something more—anything to explain why he would help her. Glory? Duty? Curiosity? Did he believe what the king did? That she had the power to get the prince back? Was he hoping that she would bring up his own status? Eliza internally shook herself at that thought; he didn't seem the type.

"Okay," she said, finally stepping away from him, drifting into the throngs of the elegant and wealthy. "Tomorrow. We talk to him tomorrow. I want to get out of here and start the search."

9

GHOSTS

Eliza was a girl again. *Five, at least. She did not recognise the room she was in, nor the clothes she wore, but she felt wood beneath her bare feet and dirt caked beneath her fingernails. Her hands were small and darkened with a tan. She wore a wool dress and footless stockings that did nothing to keep the cold from seeping into her.*

Is this a memory or a dream? She couldn't tell. It felt real; she could smell smoke in the air, though there was a sweetness, like burnt sugar, that enveloped her. The room she stood in was foreign, though recognition twinged in the back of her mind as she looked over the sparsely furnished area.

A small bed had been pushed against the far wall, a door set into the wood walls across from her. Two windows stood on either side, curtains drawn, giving Eliza no indication of what was beyond.

There was a table beneath the window; it had been vacant only moments before, but now a young woman sat there, face lined with fear. She spoke a language Eliza couldn't understand, not even in her sleep. The words were rushed and murmured, softly spoken. Eliza realised then that there was another girl in the room.

She had to be in her late teens, maybe early twenties. Dark hair cascaded down her back in ringlets that made Eliza envious. Her eyes were bright, but not with fear.

"There is something coming," a voice beside Eliza said, startling her. Turning, Eliza faced a girl not much older than her dream self, perhaps six or seven. She was thin, bony. There was a wildness in her

eyes that Eliza recognised. Her ears, which poked out beneath scruffy white-blonde hair, were pointed.

Eliza looked back as a boom echoed through the room. The woman who had been sitting at the table got to her feet and hurried over to Eliza and the other young girl. Her cheeks were red, eyes wide with fear. She spoke again in that language Eliza didn't understand.

Another boom sounded and the door rattled on its hinges. The woman who had been standing over Eliza ran away, entering a room Eliza had not noticed before. Footsteps alerted Eliza that the other girl, the one with the black hair, had followed, leaving Eliza alone with the little girl as the door rattled again.

She wanted to speak, but found her voice gone. She wanted to ask why the adults had disappeared, why someone was trying to get in. But no words would form on her lips.

The door rattled again, though this time something scraped against the wood. It sounded like nails digging in, tearing at it. Eliza flinched, managing to take a step back before the door burst open.

Darkness unlike anything she'd seen before hurtled towards her. The spear of night dug itself into the wood at her feet before retracting. The creature howled and light flared behind it, but it wasn't enough. The spear hurtled towards Eliza again, in line with her heart. She squeezed her eyes shut, waiting for the pain she knew would come.

But it didn't. A scream of agony pierced the air, echoing through the howling of darkness and the stampede of feet.

Eliza opened her eyes in shock. The girl with the wild eyes and scruffy hair had taken the blow, the darkness bleeding over her small frame. She had probably been six, Eliza realised. Six, and had given her life for Eliza.

She unleashed a blood-curdling scream as the darkness at the door faded in a flash of light, and she awoke.

Unease mixed with fear knotted in Eliza's stomach as she opened her eyes and blinked up at the ceiling. There were no stars glued to the white paint, no strings of fairy-lights winding their way along the corners of her walls. But there was a wide bay window with fluttering curtains that weren't her own, and a comforter so soft she would have called it dreamlike. The room was both familiar and unfamiliar.

Still in Cadira. Part of her had hoped it was just a bad dream, that she would wake up in the comforts of her own bed in New Orleans. But she wasn't in her own bedroom, she was in the Winter Palace. The mission still hung over her head, freedom tied with it.

The dream drifted away from her, her only recollection being the fear that still burned on her tongue. What had she seen, she wondered, to make her heart race like it was?

Eliza squeezed her eyes shut and turned in her bed. Sweat, sticky and now cold, covered her body, forcing her to shift until there was only a thin sheet covering her flushed body.

Sighing, Eliza opened her eyes, and yelped.

Kneeling over her bed was a child—a little girl, maybe ten or so—her red-rimmed eyes staring out the window, her mouth open in a silent scream. When those eyes found Eliza, the little girl hunched over her. Blood covered her mouth, her teeth, though there was a kind of gentleness to her form as she looked Eliza over.

"They're coming," she said, voice soft. Fearful. Eliza swallowed. "They know you're here."

Eliza bit back a scream. "Who? Who does?"

The little girl looked back towards the window, then at the doors to Eliza's room. Beyond them, the floorboards creaked. *Someone's out there.* Perhaps it was just Clio or the doorman, or some wandering noble sneaking back to a lovers room.

Spirits could not hurt the living; Eliza had learned that from an early age. But it didn't stop her from flinching as the little girl crawled closer, making no indents in the ruffled bedsheets. "Demons. Dressed in darkness and shadows. They know you are here. Run."

The little girl disappeared from the bed. Eliza sat up, her breathing heavy, fast.

She remembered what the king had said to her, that creatures like the ones who had taken his son had once come for Eliza, too. Had they already found her? She shook her head in disbelief before clambering out of the bed, sweat clinging to her.

Ruthless creatures of the night, she thought. She threw on a pair of jeans and her hoodie, along with a cloak that Clio had left for her.

She didn't need anyone getting hurt for her; these *demons* had taken out the king's entire guard back then. There was no telling what they would do to a palace full of civilians. What she needed to do was get out of there before anyone could get hurt.

Gathering her meagre belongings—she needed to thank Clio for already preparing the saddlebags and pack—Eliza sucked in a deep breath before cautiously opening the door a crack, but no one was there. She left her room, heart pounding, careful not to wake anyone as she crept through the halls and down the main staircase towards the front doors. Not a living soul walked the halls. *Strange.* There should have been guards.

But if anything were to happen... she wasn't sure what else to do as she opened the door just enough for her to sneak through.

High winds picked up her cloak and her hair as she ran down the slippery steps, careful not to fall. She could barely make out the soldier encampment through the haze of rain, but she held the cloak close to herself as she ran towards the tents. It was still dark, an endless night already in upheaval.

Eliza passed through the gardens soundlessly, hands shoved deep into the pockets of her cloak. The tents came fully into view and the little girl appeared in front of her, untouched by the rain. "Hurry, you don't have much time."

Eliza stopped. "Do you know which tent belongs to Commander Thorne?" Eliza had to yell over the rain, but the ghostly girl heard her well enough to vanish and reappear beside a pitched tent towards the front. She lifted her arm and pointed into the darkness, where Eliza hoped the commander would be.

Without thinking, she ran into the tent and dropped the hood of her cloak. Commander Thorne sat in the middle of his cot, half naked with a sword in one hand and a sharpening stone in the other.

Eliza's cheeks burned as he looked her over with furrowed brows, lips pressed into a frown. When his eyes met hers, Eliza almost stopped breathing.

"Demons," she said, sucking in a breath. "And soldiers. The ones who came after the prince."

Commander Thorne dropped his sword and stood, reaching for his shirt. "How do you know this?" he asked, fastening a belt across his hips, along with a dagger and a raven pommeled sward.

At least he works quickly. Within moments, he was dressed and ready, pulling on his boots. His eyes never left hers. He was waiting, she realised, for an answer. One that she couldn't give. The soldiers were likely after her because she was a necromancer—she wasn't about to give her secret away to someone who might betray her in the end.

Eliza shook her head, biting her lip. "Part of my powers. Just trust me." She cast a wary look behind her, as if the soldiers were already upon them. Her dark hair stuck to her forehead as she looked around.

"We need to alert the king and the rest of the guard and disappear. They're after *me*."

The commander frowned. "It might very well be safer if we just leave."

She shook her head, but before she could argue, shouts echoed through the night.

Eliza tore through the tent with fear pumping in her veins. Fire consumed the other side of the gardens, like someone had tried to create a physical barrier between the darkness and the palace. But it did not stop the creatures that bounded through the trees and flung themselves over the walls, heading straight into the flames and ripping apart anyone who got in their way.

A hand tightened around her upper arm. Eliza looked up to find Thorne looking over the destruction already caused.

This is why the king has an army, she realised with dread. He knew it would happen. That someone would come after her.

Bile rose in her throat. "We can't leave them," she said, as soldiers rushed into the fray. She hadn't realised she'd called for her magic, but it danced at her fingertips, an extension of her that never seemed to end. It drew up from the land itself.

Thorne started pulling her away, back towards the palace. He murmured something beneath his breath, about getting horses and leaving.

The demons and their Masters were there for *her*, not anyone else. How many had died at the hands of these creatures? Not just when the prince had been kidnapped, but when they had come for her as a child? Even now?

Eliza ducked as a demon flew over her head, followed by a flaming arrow that embedded into in its leather hide. The demon howled in angry pain and lashed out at her with bloody claws. Eliza's magic flared, taking the form of fire. Flames danced across her fingers. She threw her hand out towards the demon as it skittered past, and she watched in fascination when it turned to ash.

"Miss Eliza."

She spun to face Clio; her red hair was bound atop her head, and she wore a night gown stained with blood. Her face, white with shock, seemed to pale even further in the glow of the fire around them. In her hands, she held Eliza's duffle bag.

"It's not safe for you out here," Eliza said, rushing to the girl's side.

Her eyes, shadowed and unblinking, met Eliza's. "And it is not safe for you, either."

Eliza bit her lip. Soldiers were now fighting back against the demons, though there did not seem to be any kidnappers in the demonic ranks. Though, it wasn't like Eliza could see anything anyway, and she was too anxious to search for any with her magic.

Where is Thorne? She wondered if he'd already left—maybe he'd realised how screwed up this entire plan was. Her heart thundered, stomach churning. He could already be dead. One of the creatures could have already jumped him and cut him down. She'd seen the commander train, but she didn't know the extent of his abilities.

A spindly, oil-black demon sprung towards her. A fireball left from her fingers; the magic crackled eagerly as it exploded on the demons chest, destroying the creature. It whimpered like a wounded dog as it collapsed to the ground, and Eliza finished it off, her magic turning the demon to dust.

"We need to find the commander," Eliza said, whirling back to face Clio. She gripped her hands in front of her, fingers pale in the light of the fires, bag on the ground. Eliza looked her over, searching for any sign of a wound, but saw nothing. The blood that covered Clio was not her own, though she didn't appear to be hurt. "Did you see Commander Thorne?"

Clio shook her head, lips pursed. Tears tracked down her cheeks, cutting through the soot and blood that covered her skin. She no longer resembled the put-together girl Eliza had first met.

"There," Clio whispered, raising her hand. Eliza followed her line of vision and found Thorne galloping through the destruction, another horse by his side. He sat tall and proud atop the saddle, swinging out with his shining blade at approaching demons. The blade gleamed with black ichor.

Clio shoved her out of the way. Eliza landed on her arm and felt sharp stones and twigs bite into the soft flesh of her wrist. Rolling onto her back, Eliza's eyes widened in horror as a blade pierced through the girl's heart.

Blood bubbled from Clio's lips, her bright green eyes growing dimmer, meeting Eliza's own horrified stare. "Find him," she gasped. The attacker pulled the blade from Clio's chest; the metal slid through blood and flesh and ground against bone. Clio collapsed, blood blossoming along the white of her night gown, bleeding onto the stone path below her.

"No!" But the girl was dead, eyes wide and empty, staring at the grey smoke above their heads. There was no fear marring her soft features; her eyes were empty of everything but courage and hope.

Thorne rode over and cut the attacker down, blade slicing through the man's neck, cleaving his head from his body. Shock drowned out her own repulsion as the head landed not far from her feet. She crawled away, heart shattering. The commander jumped from his horse and called her name, but she couldn't hear him over the blood that pounded in her ears.

Tears stung the back of Eliza's eyes as Thorne grabbed hold of her arm. "We need to go," he murmured. "There is nothing else you can do."

She looked up, finding his stare, but her vision blurred. *There is nothing else you can do.* But there was, she thought. She could fight back. She could use her magic, help everyone.

"Eliza." His hand tightened, and then he was lifting her off the ground, pulling her to her feet. Eliza thrashed in his grip, but he was stronger, pulling her away from Clio's body, from the destruction she had brought.

If the king hadn't sent for her, the attack would never have happened. The attack was because of *her;* she had no naïve thoughts on whether that was true, not with the evidence piling up. There was an *army* sitting at the king's feet. He knew what might happen.

But it was still her fault.

Through the screeching and clashing of swords, Eliza heard a raven caw, too loud to be possible over the cacophony of sound. Searching, Eliza spotted the gold eyes of the raven perched on a branch, its feathers like ink against the dancing flames. Eliza's heart skipped a beat as she stared at it. And standing beneath the branch, Eliza caught sight of the ghost-girl.

The spirit beckoned Eliza with pale, luminescent arms, motioning towards a break in the wall where the gate should have been. Beyond, Eliza only saw darkness. The girl disappeared, wide eyes filled with terror, before reappearing in front of Eliza.

"You must go, Elizabeth Kindall, before they get you. I'll show you the way."

Before Eliza could respond, the girl disappeared again, reappearing beneath the branch from before, though the raven had already vanished. Her small hand beckoned to them.

Numb, Eliza allowed the commander to help her onto the back of her dapple-grey mare. The horse nickered and swung its head, dancing warily from side to side as Thorne mounted his own steed. He'd taken hold of Eliza's reins—she didn't care, not when she could see Clio's broken body from the corner of her eye.

"We can't just leave her here," Eliza said, voice cracking. Thorne was already shaking his head in disagreement, forcing Eliza's mare into a trot.

His eyes, though, were sad when they met hers. "I know, but we cannot stay."

"They're after *me*," she whispered.

They barely managed to get through the throngs of the attack; Thorne fought off demons and shadow soldiers that pursued their horses, while Eliza managed to use her magic during moments of consciousness when she broke out of her state of shock. The king's soldiers swarmed Eliza and Thorne, and fought off the bony, leather-hided demons, their swords clashing and sliding through the thin bodies.

Ahead of her, Thorne hissed. Blood seeped from a wound on his cheek as a demon scuttled up the side of Thorne's horse. The commander cut the creature down quickly, only to be preyed on by more demons that scuttled over to them from the direction of the king's army.

Something cracked inside of Eliza. The sight of Thorne's blood against his golden skin sent a shock through her.

No one else needs to get hurt because of me. No one else needs to die.

Almost like a switch had been flipped, Eliza summoned the power that dwelled deep in her body. Lightning spread across her fingers, and like arrows, shot from her hands and into the bodies of the scattering demons.

Eliza spurred her mare ahead, pulling Thorne along with her. She couldn't remember ever riding before, but the motions came naturally, something she didn't question in that moment.

The demons parted as flames leapt from her out-stretched hands, screeching back into the darkness that surrounded the palace. They ran for a thicket of brush leaking dark magic, leaping into a chasm in the earth that swallowed them whole.

Eliza's magic burned in her veins. She had felt the difference and growth of her magic after stepping through the wards, but she hadn't had the time to truly delve into the well of her magic. Now it threatened to overflow without the control she should be able to maintain.

If she couldn't control her magic, then she would become a greater threat than the demons and their masters.

"Eliza." Thorne stopped her by curling his fingers around her wrist. Her pulse quickened beneath his touch. "Where are you going?"

She pointed to the dark underbrush. The ghost-girl's transparent form wavered by a hidden trail. The trees moved around the girl, parting for them, creating a path through the brush.

Thorne did not release Eliza's hand. "Are you sure?"

"The forest wants us to go that way," she said. She'd wanted to mention the ghost-girl but couldn't bring herself to bite through the fear. Necromancy was still illegal, still hated. She didn't know the commander well enough to reveal that side of her; the side she knew she should be ashamed of but couldn't justify hiding.

Eliza met the unyielding stare of the commander. Was he trying to untangle the web of lies she'd spun to protect herself? Or was there something else hidden in his gaze?

Eliza's hands shook until he finally bowed his head in understanding. A flicker of recognition darkened his eyes, and when he released her hand, she went cold at the loss of his touch.

Somewhere behind them, a horn sounded. "Retreat," Thorne muttered, spurring his horse into action. The commander took the path first, sword angled in front of him.

As Eliza lifted her hand to summon light, the commander shook his head. "Light could mean attracting attention."

Eliza dropped her hand and spurred her horse. The mare snorted and walked on, treading carefully behind the commander. "We can't see though."

"Like you said," he murmured, eyeing the evolving path, "the forest will guide us."

10

RAVENS IN FLIGHT

Eliza gripped her wrist, which had been sprained from Clio pushing her. She dug her nails into the soft flesh until all she felt was pain. Her thoughts were still stuck on the attack; she hadn't seen the ghost-girl since finding the path and dreaded seeing her transparent form once again.

It was different from seeing Miranda, her ghostly friend from New Orleans. Different to when Eliza traipsed the cemetery in the dark with the spirit by her side. Even with Davis or Kay, Eliza could let herself go with the two-hundred-year-old spirit, but with Thorne...

Eliza swallowed and averted her eyes from his tense back. They'd managed to escape the demons and their Masters. As Eliza and Thorne had ridden through the forest, the path had opened before them, closing quickly after they'd ridden through. And not for the first time, Eliza had been left speechless by the beauty of Cadira; the moss-covered tree trunks alight with glowing mushrooms, trapping darting pixies in their light. Overhead, shimmering spiderwebs created a net, carrying small, elf-like creatures to and from different trees. Several times, those creatures—with long, pointed ears and white hair, black eyes and no clothing—dropped into Eliza's waiting hands, leaving her berries, stones, or crystals as they went.

The beauty she witnessed was almost enough for her to forget the creeping darkness. She didn't see it in this part of the forest; it hadn't spread so deep, but it was still weaving its way through the land.

Thorne had been right; the forest had guided them back towards a road. Dawn slowly approached, breaking through the bank of clouds that constantly threatened rain.

"We'll take a couple of hours before leaving for Harrenhal," Thorne said, leading his steed off the main road. Branching off the side was a beaten path, perhaps forgotten over time.

It sent a wave of nostalgia through Eliza as she followed the commander, careful to avoid the reaching limbs. Twigs snapped as they made their way through the green undergrowth. It reminded her of *home*, of the New Orleans bayou and the hidden beauty of the city. If she concentrated on that, she might be able to allow herself some kind of peace, but anger quickly shot through her, followed by guilt-ridden wretchedness.

Nothing compared to the remorse that rushed through her over the attack on the Winter Palace; on the death that she had wrought. The king had thought they would be safe hiding with an army of soldiers camping within the palace grounds, but he had been wrong. Whoever or whatever wanted Eliza didn't seem to care or fear the forces of King Bastian. They had come regardless.

Eliza blocked out the memories of the Winter Palace as bile rose in her throat. *Clio died for me, she died so I could get out... oh, Gods, what have I done?*

Eliza had already vomited three times since leaving the smouldering remains of the once whimsical palace gardens. She couldn't escape the guilt and fear that was building inside her. Not even the murky rain could cool her as heat—fed by her fear and apprehension—seemed to take hold of her body, leaving her trembling.

The Demon Masters had been after *her*. *The king* told *me they wanted me*. And she'd been there, ripe for the picking. It made her sick.

And Clio... Eliza clenched her fist, biting back the sting of tears.

They arrived in a small clearing, overgrown with moss-covered tree trunks and emerald grass that looked like gems even in the grey dimness of the day. Autumn leaves of brown and gold did not touch the clearing, almost like...

"A pixie circle." Eliza dismounted and stepped into the plush grass, surprised to find it dry and crisp unlike the rest of the forest. She saw the crystallised mushrooms circling the clearing then, creating a ring of protection around the space. "How did you...?"

Thorne dismounted and led his horse farther in to a trickling stream cutting through the other side of the glade. "I have a knack for finding the little creatures. You help one, plenty will help you in return."

She eyed him warily, the reins of her mare clutched tightly in her hands. "I've only ever read about these things in books. My guardian used to tell me stories about the creatures who roam these lands." Eliza took a hesitant step in, heart racing as she thought about the fabled creatures that danced there when the moon was full, or when the sun had set. She couldn't help but wonder if the immortal Fae ever walked through this land.

The commander motioned for the reins, and with trembling fingers she handed them over. Their skin brushed, and she quickly pulled away, clearing her throat. "When did you save a pixie?" she asked.

Eliza took a seat on an overturned tree, buried half beneath the ground. She stretched her legs out before her, wriggling her toes in her boots. The commander watched her from the creek, eyes hooded with weariness.

"You know, we should probably get to know each other," she said, though she did it only for her own benefit. A part of her didn't care if she knew him, not with the white noise that filled her ears or the shock of the night's events that had her trembling. Every time she closed her eyes, she'd see Clio's lifeless body decorated with blood that had yet to dry.

He rolled his eyes, dropping the reins of the horses. She cocked a questioning brow. "They won't run, if that's what you're worried about."

She shrugged. "Fine. Story. Now." She needed the distraction, to keep herself from retching.

"I was a cadet in the royal army. Some idiots from the capital, who had barely been exposed to the magic that roams the lands, caught a pixie. Tried to shake the thing to death. I caught them with her, got the poor creature out of their grasps and reported them to the on-duty commander."

Eliza rolled her eyes. "Oh, how heroic, you snitch."

Thorne shot her a withering glance, but a smile twitched at his lips, nonetheless. "You're the one who asked."

Silence passed between them; Eliza's stomach churned as her thoughts strayed back to the attack, to the pluming fire and the ash raining from the sky. The beady eyes of the demons flashed in her mind. The blood rushed from her face and she slumped forward, resting her head in her hands. "What do we do now?" she asked.

"We go to Harrenhal," he said, cutting her a glance. His eyes softened as he took a seat beside her. "We see Amitel, and then I take you to the Spring Manor."

She swallowed. "What if they attack again?"

"Then we'll be ready."

The sky turned pink, washing away the hazy grey of the hours before. "I've been here all of, what, a day?" She looked over to the commander, noticed his eyes on his clenched fists. "What happened?"

The commander released a breath. "It wasn't always like this."

"Really? Does it have anything to do with the attack on the king?"

He shook his head, running a hand through his dark, tousled hair. "It... changed everything. Cadira turned into something I don't even recognise anymore." She waited for him to continue; fingers cold as she balled her fists. "You know the other kingdoms call us the *Shadowland* now?"

"I thought..." It had always been a *nickname* of sorts, the name *Shadowland*, as it had always harboured the most magic and was the only direct route into Eliza's world. She'd heard it once or twice from the mouths of other exiles like Kay but she had never thought they meant it literally... until now.

"I know." He looked to her then, eyes searching hers. "Everyone can feel it—the darkness. Even those without magic can sense it running through the land. *I* can feel it sometimes, can even see it seeping through the forests."

"The king thinks I can stop it," she said, voice barely above a whisper. "He thinks if I find the prince, he can spin the whole thing into some fantastic story and drive the darkness away. He thinks *I* can bring hope back to the land."

Thorne touched her hand, wrapping his fingers around her arm. Her heart rate accelerated as his thumb rubbed circles around the inside of her wrist. Her mind flashed to the dream. "I think the king has a point."

Does he? Because I certainly don't think so. Eliza pulled away, standing. Her legs ached, but she had to move, had to stop thinking. "People shouldn't rely on me."

"What?"

"They shouldn't rely on me!" she said, spinning to face him.

"Look. I'm just a girl from New Orleans. I was pretty much kicked out of Cadira when I was five and now, I know it has something to do with the king's *twisted* idea that I have something to do with his missing son. I'm just a witch with a little extra magic, that's all."

She sucked in a cooling breath as the commander watched her, shoulders hunched. He stood and slowly approached her. Something in his gait reminded her of a man who had all the answers—someone who could reveal truths not even she would understand.

Eliza knew almost nothing about the commander, other than he was in the king's army, and that he'd saved a pixie once. But she couldn't deny how her body responded to him, how her blood seemed to answer a call she didn't hear.

Kay, with the stories of the Courts, would have said Eliza and Brandon Thorne had known each other in another life. That was Kay's forte, her magical ability. Eliza had always nagged Kay about her power, but it remained a mystery to Eliza. But the Courts had their own stories, own beliefs.

Thorne touched a hand to her cheek, forcing her gaze to his. Heat flared in her cheeks. "You were targeted for a reason, both times. Whether it has something to do with the prince or that little extra magic you have. But that is not *your fault*. The attacks were not instigated by you. It's not something you can control."

She wrapped her arms around her midsection, releasing a shuddering breath. "Clio is dead because of me."

"She saved your life," he said. "Giving up now would only throw her sacrifice in her face." He brushed his knuckles across her cheek, wiping away a tear that had escaped.

He tucked a strand of hair behind her ear, grinning as his fingers brushed what should have been the curve of her ear. "Your ears have changed."

Her breath, previously stuck in her throat, escaped with a laugh. "My ears?"

"They're pointed."

Eliza's brows furrowed as she reached for them; she hadn't even felt the change, not physically or magically. It must have happened overnight, during the time between the dinner party and before the attack. But her ears were now pointed, barely hidden behind her dark hair, a clear marking of the heritage she didn't understand.

Heat flushed her cheeks as Thorne grinned at her. "Seems the Fae in you is marking its territory."

"You make it sound like my bloodline is a dog!" she said indignantly. But she couldn't keep a smile from spreading across her face. A weight lifted from her chest in the process, too. *He didn't run away from the ears.*

The marking of Fae-heritage was always something of debate in Cadira. While there were many with slightly pointed ears, or magic stemming back to Fae ancestry, some towns and even regions were less enthused about the strange-natured and immortal beings that once lived across Cadira. Some shrugged, but others—those with a bad history with the beings—were more likely to refuse even looking at people like Eliza. It both disgusted and emboldened her to show off the heritage she had once wanted to hide.

Shaking her head, Eliza let her hair fall over her ears, cheeks flushed. Thorne still stood close enough for her to feel his warmth. Her heart raced. She'd felt it before, and she could feel it now, that sense of knowing him though they'd never met until the day before. It pressed down on her.

Eliza stepped away from the commander, gasping for breath, head spinning.

"Is everything okay, Eliza?" he asked, coming to stand beside her. This time, though, he did not touch her.

She nodded. "Yeah, everything's fine."

"Are you sure?"

Meeting his stare, she tried to smile reassuringly, though it felt forced and wobbly on her lips. She wished she had Kay with her; Kay, who would know why Eliza was feeling this way towards the commander, who could diffuse the situation and make Eliza *think*.

She nodded and walked over to the horses. She pulled her saddle bag from her mare's back, stroking her neck as she did. Eliza rifled through the contents, finding her notebook and spell book.

The white leather-bound spell book had been a gift from Kay, enchanted to always have blank pages, though it looked no bigger than a three-hundred page book. Within it, Eliza held all her thoughts and spells, enchantments and charms. What she had learnt from her guardians, she'd written in the book.

With a sigh—and her head lowered so she didn't have to look at the commander—Eliza made her way back to the fallen tree.

She took a seat and flipped open her spell book, turning the pages slowly. If she couldn't dwell on how her presence at the Winter Palace had caused an attack, then she'd do her best to try and stop it from happening again.

Kay told me a story about enchanted tunnels that spread beneath Cadira. She said there were points of entry across the land. Apparently, there's one at King Bastian's Spring Manor, protected by a giant maze. How cool is that? I wish I could see it...

Eliza stiffened. Vaguely, she remembered something her guardian had told her. Kay, who had once belonged to the scholars of the Courts, had learnt of a Cadiran story, long since forgotten by the people. Once, when Eliza had first arrived in New Orleans and had suffered mild insomnia, Kay had told her all kinds of stories she'd collected from her time in the Courts. And Eliza had written them down—actually, she'd scribbled them down in half English, half chicken-scratch, which only she could understand.

Sitting cross-legged now, leaning back against the fallen tree, Eliza flicked through her spell book, searching for any other mention of the tunnels. It hadn't been something she had thought to ask about.

"Hey, commander..." she started, but trailed off. In the sunlight that filtered through the glade, the commander was haloed in glowing, yellow light. He'd stripped down to a white undershirt that hung to his mid-thigh, his weapons belt in the grass and boots off, left to dry in the sun.

The image dredged up a memory; a boy who looked an awful lot like Thorne, pulling himself out of a clear-blue lake, golden skin pink with heat from the sun. His smile was big, and it had reached his eyes, making him seem younger, innocent. There was a happiness in his gaze that Eliza wasn't sure she'd seen before.

The memory disappeared as the commander looked over, brows raised. He'd tucked his shirt back into his pants and tied his weapons belt around his hips once more.

Eliza cleared her throat and hoped her cheeks had stopped flaming. "What do you know about tunnels running beneath Cadira?"

"What? Like the ones used beneath the palace for the royal family?" he asked. Thorne picked up his boots and dropped down in front of her.

"No," she said, looking back down at her spell book. "Like a system of caverns running all around Cadira, with hidden entrances." She shook her head and closed the book. "Never mind, it was dumb to ask."

"I've never heard of them. But that doesn't mean they're not real." Eliza watched from the corner of her eye as he shoved his boots back on and stood, offering his hand. His skin was calloused and warm. "We need to leave for Harrenhal now if we want to make it before nightfall."

~

Dusk had settled on the horizon when the pair finally found Harrenhal. The roads went from packed earth to cobblestone, while the trees slowly thinned to reveal manors and townhouses, storefronts and inns. Carriages carrying the wealthier populace passed them, along with other lone riders or donkeys pulling carts. A strange mix, Eliza determined as they rode towards the closest inn, but not uncommon for a town working close to the Winter Palace.

Eliza decided to trust the commander, if only because she doubted that she would have gained an audience with the esteemed Warlock on her own.

"Excuse me," an older woman said, stopping Eliza by a worn vegetable cart. "Did you come from the palace?"

Before Eliza could reply, another woman stepped in, a baby bundled in her arms. "We all saw the smoke. Few survived, apparently."

The woman with the baby continued, "I just hope my husband returns. He's one of the palace guards."

It's all my fault. He's probably dead because of me. Bile rose in her throat, but she swallowed it down, forcing herself to answer even though her head was spinning. "I'm sorry—I'm so sorry."

Eliza didn't wait for an answer as she rode off in Thorne's direction, who waited patiently outside the inn. The exterior was simple; wooden beams and grey-stone blocks, cloudy windows and a slightly crooked door. Windows were barred with iron rods, the sign above the door shaking silently in the breeze.

She sucked in a shaky breath. "They asked me about the palace. And I couldn't—" Her breath left her in a half-sob, her stomach clenching. She wrapped her arms around herself, unable to look at the commander or anything else.

Slowly, Eliza forced herself to peer at him. "There was nothing you could have done," he said. "We've already gone over this."

"Seriously?" She shook her head, breath hitching. Eliza dismounted on shaky legs, ignoring the bark of pain in her thighs. "I could have done *something*."

"Or," he said pointedly, fluidly stalking over to her, "you could have gotten yourself killed. Or taken." He looked between her and the inn before rubbing at his eyes.

"Wait here while I take care of the horses," he said, dropping his bags at her feet, doing the same with her own. He took the two horses down a short alley, where she noticed a trough and a hitching post set up in what looked like a small stable.

Eliza picked up her bags and threw them over her shoulders; she waited with her arms crossed and hands trembling.

You could have gotten yourself killed. Taken. At least she could have helped. Instead, she'd ran, and she hated herself for it. Not to mention, her stomach was twisted into knots over her impending meeting with Amitel. She couldn't help but hide her current idea about the tunnels.

The Keepers hadn't mentioned any hidden tunnels—perhaps they, too, had forgotten the old stories. Kay had belonged to the Courts, a pocket of land in the south that ran on creativity. If the king hadn't sought their help, and they hadn't offered their knowledge about Cadira's history, then Eliza couldn't help but wonder if these tunnels were only that—a story. Telling Thorne had been a shot in the dark, but he hadn't known anything either.

A bird cawed overhead, and Eliza stiffened, head snapping up to meet the beady gold eyes of the raven. "Shoo!" The raven merely stared at her, cocking its head. "Go!"

The raven shifted impatiently, cawing as it bobbed its head.

Turning around, Eliza spotted something she hadn't noticed when she had ridden into Harrenhal—an obsidian statue depicting a raven in flight, and in its talons, a dagger, much like the one Eliza had seen paired with the legendary Goddess.

Eliza snapped her head back to the raven, but it was gone.

Rubbing her eyes, she didn't hear Thorne as he approached, and almost jumped when he touched a hand to her shoulder. She blinked slowly, then lowered her head, shaking it. "Sorry," she said, rubbing her eyes. "It has been a long day."

The commander looked down at her with furrowed brows, lips twisted up in an almost-smile. Warmth spread through her at the look, and the near-comfortable way in which they stood together.

Of course, it dissipated just as quickly, and she was reminded of why they were there—why they *weren't* at the Winter Palace.

Eliza turned back to the statue, if only to break the silence that seemed to wedge itself between then. "What does this symbolise?" she asked, pointing towards the statue, biting down on her lip.

Thorne turned to the statue, brows still furrowed, but recognition flashed in his storm-blue eyes. "This is where they believe the Goddess Azula was last seen."

She crossed her arms tightly over her chest to stave off a chill that shuddered through her. "Why the raven though?" Eliza asked. She'd been taught from a young age that coincidences should always be taken into consideration, especially when magic was involved and *especially* in Cadira. It couldn't have been a coincidence that she and Thorne had ended up in Harrenhal, and that it was a *raven* that had pointed out the statue.

Thorne shrugged, though she could see his shoulders tense. "I don't know," he said, stepping back with a taut roll of his muscles. "There are a lot of legends that surround the Goddess and her being. Harrenhal is one of many towns and areas that is believed to be where she was last seen. Some think that her final form was that of a black raven."

Frowning, Eliza stared at the raven. *Coincidence.* It couldn't be anything more.

Eliza shook her head. She had one goal, and that was to find the prince, win her freedom, and get the hell out of here. She tried to push the raven out of her mind completely. But it was hard; something nagged at her, nipping at the corner of her thoughts, like a memory long since buried.

The look on the commander's face stopped her from asking any more questions, and Eliza quietened quickly. It didn't stop her from wondering, though, about what he might be hiding. What he might know.

11

AMITEL

Eliza had expected the summons to come immediately, yet they waited two days before they heard anything from the mysterious Warlock. In that time, Eliza had wallowed in self-loathing after the attack. During that time, survivors had flooded the town, and out of the two hundred or so that had been staying within the palace walls, there were so many more that needed to be accounted for.

But the clear and concise message awaiting them hadn't left Eliza feeling any better. Anxiety chewed at her as she read the words aloud. *"Watermill. One hour. I speak with her alone."*

"Absolutely not," Thorne said, shaking his head. He dropped his sword onto the bed, crossing his arms.

She squared her shoulders. "I'm sick of feeling useless. You won't let me go down and help people *because of my safety*." She dropped into a chair. Guilt felt like a rock sinking in her stomach. She wouldn't let herself forget that the attack had been because of *her*. "This is my mission and my responsibility."

"He wants to be with you... alone." Thorne shook his head, running a hand through his hair, over and over, before running it over his face.

"How is that bad?" she asked, furrowing her brows. Thorne didn't reply. It was a good start, Eliza thought. She would have access to whatever Amitel knew. He could have information the Keepers didn't have. Eliza could only hope he had more for her—more than what everyone else was giving up.

Thorne made a sound in the back of his throat but did not reply.

He didn't argue either as they left the inn. The sun rose high in the sky and glared down at her despite the crisp wind that scattered leaves over the cobblestones. The shutters of windows waved to her. Where there were people—both injured and healthy—there were spirits; some young, others old. Soldiers, crones, small children with the pox. Eliza saw them all and tried to hide her stare.

The smoke from the Winter Palace had finally cleared; the king had escaped with his council, some said around Eliza, but many hadn't been as lucky.

"Thank the Gods the king survived," an older woman said, her voice ringing out in Eliza's ears.

White flags of mourning had been hung from many windows and Eliza tried to swallow down the bile that rose in her throat.

Thorne looked at Eliza from beneath the hood of his cloak as they entered the shadows of the forest. "Amitel doesn't usually ask to be alone with someone he doesn't know," he said

She narrowed her eyes. "Is it really a bad thing? I won't hurt him; he probably won't hurt me. I don't see why you're so worried." She pointed her finger at his chest. They were already far enough into the winding forests of Cadira, that she had no problem with speaking her mind. "You're talking as if you two have met before. Why are you so sure?"

"Because," he stated, teeth gritted, "he is the most powerful Warlock in Cadira. *Everyone* knows him. He will hurt you if you ask the wrong questions."

Eliza bit her lip. "I don't care," she said. "I still want to talk to him. I need to. Obviously, he knows something." She stepped carefully over a root. "If it didn't matter, then you wouldn't be here. But it does. So, you will wait for me. If you have a problem with that, take it up with him."

Without a second thought, Eliza marched through the forest gilded with red, yellow, and green leaves. Their destination was in sight, and she darted towards the old, crumbling building where the Warlock awaited.

She heard Thorne sigh, followed by the crunch of his footsteps as he jogged to catch up with her. When she turned her head to look at him, she noticed the stoniness of his face, how his brows furrowed.

Eliza snorted at Amitel's choice in meeting place; the old

watermill looked to be over fifty years old, and hadn't been occupied in the last twenty years, Thorne had told her. There was no water running in the stream, and the dry creek bed revealed odd-coloured stones and what looked to be skeletal remains.

Grimly, she turned back to the commander, arms crossed. "You aren't my protector," she stated. He met her stare with a deep frown. "And you aren't my grandfather. You are my guide. You're here to help. But don't think you can just *decide* what I can and cannot do concerning this mission."

Through gritted teeth, he said, "I didn't. I was merely warning you."

Eliza shrugged. "Either way, I'll make my own decisions about how I conduct this search. Don't stand in my way about this. I have a feeling."

"A feeling?" He barked a scornful laugh and finally met Eliza's gaze. "Is this *feeling* going to end up killing us?"

Eliza ignored how he said 'us'. She forced it from her mind and refused to let it hurt her—hurt the feelings she was slowly developing for the commander so hell bent on helping her. *We've known each other for a couple of days, and by the Gods, I want to throttle him half the time.*

"Look," she said, stopping him. "You don't have to believe me, but believe this: my freedom—my life—is in the hands of the king, so I have to do as he asks. That means finding the prince by any means possible. I have my magic, so don't underestimate me."

A breath of silence passed between them. The leaves rustled on a soft, quiet breeze, and there was little activity from the forest folk who dwelled within the canopy. Even the old mill seemed quiet. Forsaken.

"Fine," he finally said, and Eliza released a shuddering breath.

She forced down a shiver and strode to the rotting door before knocking. It opened on silent hinges, but there was no one there, no other indication for her to enter besides a shift in the air, indicating magic.

Eliza walked in, Thorne one step behind her. His grunt made her look back. She shook her head. *Typical.* He slammed a hand against the force of ancient, binding magic blocked him from following her. A look of desperation crossed his dark eyes.

"Blood Magic," Eliza breathed in awe—and fear—as she turned back to face him on the other side. "It's keeping you out and won't let me leave." She slammed her hand against the shimmering boundary to prove it. "Now I don't have much of a choice."

Blood Witches, the only beings able to harness Blood Magic, were dangerous, and their spells—out in the open—were rare. Any who tried to practice the forbidden art were cursed by the Witches themselves. Eliza couldn't begin to imagine why Amitel would be going to such lengths. To protect himself perhaps?

Thorne watched her from the other side of the barrier, his hands raised as if to reach for her. "This could be a trap." She could tell he was blaming himself for letting her enter first, but he couldn't have known about this kind of magic. Not many did. He certainly would not have known about Amitel having the ability to use it.

Desperation flashed in his eyes, and the smell of smoke filled her senses. *Stupid dream*. But she shook her head. She knew that at some point she'd have to do the work on her own.

She swallowed thickly, stomach churning. Squaring her shoulders, Eliza looked back into the dusty darkness of the mill. "I'll be fine," she said. "Just wait here." Before he could reply, Eliza walked into the mill.

Crumbling in most places, the mill looked as if it could collapse at any moment. Dust rose as she stepped around pockets of decayed wood. She stopped when she felt the familiar tingle of another spell, a ring of magic masked by shadows.

"I'm not stupid," she stated, turning in a full circle, "I can tell that you're here. Might as well show yourself."

Eliza heard him laugh before she saw him. Covered in a large, oversized cloak, Amitel stood over six feet, his head lowered so that he wouldn't hit a low-lying beam. By his voice, Eliza could tell he was young—younger than she expected. He had definitely mastered immortality young.

"Oh, I didn't think you were stupid," he purred, finally revealing his face. Young, unblemished and smooth, his face hid years of torment and secrets, but she only wanted the memories of the prince.

"Gullible maybe?" she asked, gesturing to the door. "Or uneducated?"

The Warlock only grinned. "Neither."

Eliza clamped her mouth shut, following his every move with her eyes; he watched her like a beast stalking its prey, circling her, his hands still at his sides, though Eliza could sense the tingling of magic between his fingers. Golden hair fell over his forehead, and his eyes—

molten gold, flecked with red, and darker than the ravens—watched her unblinkingly.

"I'm only here to talk," Eliza said, standing still outside the ring of magic. He merely cocked his head. "I just need answers, then Commander Thorne and I will be on our way."

Amitel smiled, revealing dimples, his golden eyes brightening. "Is that so?" But there was a darkness in his stare, ancient and foreboding, despite his youthful appearance. It sent a chill down her spine, made her own magic rise in response.

"I'm here on behalf of the king."

The Warlock paused, lips turned down in a frown. "Is that so?" he repeated, though he didn't sound as if he were mocking her.

He drew closer so they were almost touching and Eliza sucked in a breath, steeling herself. "I'm here to help find the prince, and you have information—whether you realise it or not—that I need." She paused to gauge his reaction, but his face was impassive, a single brow raised. "Don't play games with me, Amitel. I don't have the patience."

His smile reappeared, though this time smaller, calculated. It did not reach his eyes. "And how do you know the prince is still alive?"

"Know?" Eliza asked, spreading her hands. "Don't you think he is, since you were the first to start searching, and the last? Don't you still have a shred of hope?"

The Warlock stopped prowling and shoved his hands into his pockets. Casual, like they were talking about the weather. "My hope began disappearing," he said, narrowing his eyes, "the day the shadows and darkness began seeping into this realm. My hope disappeared when our land was given the name 'Shadowland', and the name Cadira was nearly forgotten."

Eliza swallowed, thinking back to the conversation she'd had with Thorne in the pixie circle. "Help me make it stop. Help me fix it."

There was a pause; Eliza wondered if the Warlock would instead kill her rather than help. But quietly, he said, "How will you do that?"

She closed her eyes for a moment and sucked in a breath, releasing it slowly. How could she explain herself to him, to a Warlock hundreds of years older than her, with twice the amount of power? How could she assume that she could do more than him, who had mastered Blood Magic without dying, had been the first to search for the prince and found nothing? How could Eliza believe she was any better?

"Hope," she said, meeting his stare. "It's not much, and I don't have much of it myself, but the king believes that by using me, hope will come back to the land. I have a different motivation and different skill set. I have knowledge from another realm that will help me. I have Commander Thorne to guide me, and I hope, I will have you there to help me too."

Heart pounding in her chest, Eliza stepped towards Amitel and held out her hand. "Help me save this realm, so we can bring hope back to the people."

Her breath caught in her throat as Amitel reached out his hand and grasped hers. A tingle shot through her palm, and her magic seemed to sing in recognition to his. "We have a deal, little witch," he said, smirking. "I help you, and you help me."

Eliza smiled, and her heart did a little somersault in her chest. "Let's get to work. I need to know everything about that night."

The Warlock took a seat, elbows resting on his knees. "I was there first. The guards were all dead, the queen was lifeless outside her bed chambers. I found the king rocking back and forth with the princess in his arms."

A chill danced down Eliza's spine. "And the prince?"

"No sign of him." Amitel didn't look at her, the shadow of memory dancing in his golden eyes. "I could barely catch a trace on the assassins. It was hard," Amitel said, leaning back in his chair. "But there was just a small trace, enough for me to bind it in a location spell."

Eliza nodded, eyes focused on him. "And then?"

His lips tilted upwards, as if he enjoyed the attention. Eliza tried not to roll her eyes. "Well, I cast the spell, and I began looking. It was a goose chase; I searched the forest, sent out copies of myself to look farther. Sometimes, the trace would disappear, and I'd have to start again. I had to go through the labyrinth several times, to no avail—I only found more and more bodies, the death count growing."

Eliza made note of what she could, about the forest and lands surrounding the manor. But Amitel never once mentioned the underground maze, and Eliza decided to leave it out.

It's a dumb question anyway, she thought. *He'll just laugh about it.*

The immortal Warlock continued; brows furrowed. "We traced the assassins all the way down to the southern border, and that's where we lost them. Of course, we lost them in the North and West too."

Something didn't quite sit well with her as she mulled over the information she had been given. Was there a chance the assassins worked for a southern or western kingdom? That the prince was a prisoner of war, rather than this just being a calculated attack? From what Eliza knew, Cadira had no prominent enemies; there were feuds, and the occasional mishap, but there was a lasting peace between the surrounding kingdoms, ever since the Great War fought between man and beast. And the Courts of Light, sitting at the southern border of Cadira, were a peaceful nation.

But Eliza didn't voice those thoughts to the Warlock, either. He studied her with those golden eyes, as if waiting for her to say something—anything—about the information provided. She thought about the possibility of the tunnels, of how *that* might affect a location spell; underground, hidden, and most likely spelled to be undetectable, Eliza made a mental note of checking a location spell, too.

Thank you, Criminal Minds, for your help.

"Thank you for giving me this information," Eliza stated, rising from her seat. He followed, offering her his hand.

"If you need anything else," he said, that same, arrogant smirk appearing on his face, "send me a summons."

Nodding, Eliza took his hand and shook it.

"Wait," she said, heart fumbling in her chest. Hand still clasped in hers, Amitel quirked brow. "Do you know anything about my heritage?"

The other brow shot up in surprise. "An interesting question. You don't know anything about yourself?"

Eliza shook her head. "I left this world when I was five; I have no early memories of my life here. I only know that I was hunted down by the same force that stole the prince."

The Warlock eyed her warily, all surprise gone. "I'll look into it for you," he said, the uncertainty disappearing only to be replaced by what Eliza would have called a 'smarmy smirk' had it been on anyone else's face than his. "For a price, of course."

She felt the magic around them dissipate, the boundary that trapped Eliza within the mill retracting, allowing her to leave—and Thorne to enter. She heard him stir beyond the door, heard it open; she turned around to see the commander, but when she looked back to Amitel, the Warlock was gone.

"Are you alright?" Thorne asked, rushing into the empty, murky mill.

She nodded mutely. *Why did he have to disappear?* She would have thought he'd be somewhat happy to see Thorne, but as soon as the boundary let up, he was gone.

"Eliza?"

There had to be something she was missing. She'd assumed the boundary was because Amitel himself used Blood Magic, but he hadn't seemed to notice the boundary itself until it was gone, unless he'd never noticed it...

She shook her head. Was there another player setting up their side of the game? She knew it was never going to be easy, but...

If there was someone else out there, then Eliza wasn't sure what she was going to do.

12

SPRING MANORS

They left Harrenhal as soon as their meeting with Amitel ended. Eliza hadn't been able to take the proximity of being so close to the Winter Palace—to the massacre and death that filled the air.

She couldn't shake the darkness, either. It moved through the veins that kept Cadira alive. It spread its fingers like endless vines; wherever she looked, it was there, suffocating the natural magic that filled the land.

But she couldn't help but wonder if the darkness followed her. *Maybe necromancy really is evil.*

A shudder worked its way down her spine. Stiffness ate at her bones and muscles; since leaving Harrenhal, they only rested a couple of hours at a time. When they did, Thorne would disappear to hunt, returning to Eliza with fish or rabbit, easy kills that would fill them until they made it to the abandoned spring home of the king.

Eliza knew they were close when she noticed how the king's road became overgrown; where there were once cart marks in the road, weeds now spread into the forest on either side of them. Fences made of carved wood, now broken and half consumed by forestry and vines, lined the road. It had taken them three days, but they were finally getting close.

Eliza stopped her mare. She sucked in a breath and closed her eyes, reaching out her magic. She sensed the trace of the assassins, of Amitel and her grandfather and every other magical being that had been at the manor. She grasped at the strings of their magic, and let it pull her towards the manor. Her magic explored the dead landscape, but it found no living being. "We're alone," she said.

They continued at a slow walk towards the manor; Thorne had a look of dread and grief, obscuring the handsomeness of his storm-blue eyes. When he met Eliza's stare, he frowned, lips pursing. Eliza shared his sense of dread, though hers was mixed with apprehension and... excitement. Dread, because she feared she might find nothing, might have wasted so many days without any leads and apprehension because she knew she was close. The sense of excitement came from hoping she might find more than anyone expected.

The manor came into view, and Eliza felt her heart stop in her chest; hundreds of spirits milled around the decrepit estate, disappearing in and out of the ruins, sometimes stopping to stare at another spirit before moving on. Eliza noticed how they didn't cut through the maze, but rather how they manoeuvred it the same way the living did.

"There was so much death here," Eliza noted aloud, halting her mare again.

Ahead, Thorne stopped and looked back to her. "After the assassins killed almost every guard here, and the king completely abandoned it..." He nodded towards the ruined building, that once would have been as grand as the Winter Palace. "There was a fire that killed whoever was inside the manor."

Eliza shuddered. "That's... horrible. But the maze stayed intact?"

"Yes." Thorne looked over to the still green hedges, at the white flowers that bloomed on the outside. "An old magic, one that came before the king, protects it from being destroyed."

They guided their horses up to the maze entrance, stopping to dismount. Eliza wound her reins around her sore hands, careful to keep them from shaking too much. Only briefly did Thorne spare her a glance, face blank. A terrible sense of undeniable fear shuddered through her. *Maybe we shouldn't be here*, she thought, stiffening.

Although long and tedious, the maze wasn't hard to navigate—at least, not for Thorne. He guided her through the thick hedges without fail, his movements quick and thorough, leaving no chance for Eliza to question him on their direction. It was almost like he'd made the trip before, she mused. When they made it to a large, white-marble fountain, she stopped to look up at the figure spouting water.

"Who are they?" Eliza asked, facing the statue. It depicted two people: a man with pointed ears, wearing armour with thorns etched into the breastplate, and a woman holding a dagger to her chest.

Eliza went cold, a shiver dancing down her spine. She knew who they were.

"That is the Goddess Azula and her lover." Thorne started to turn away, but Eliza stopped him.

"I thought she was married to a mortal king," she said, staring at the Fae man, who resembled the Knight who had been following her in New Orleans. She could not fault the coincidence, or the resemblance of the two.

Thorne shrugged. "There are different variations. In this depiction, she's a Goddess. She picked a Fae as her lover because he, like her, is immortal, and they can be together forever."

"Romantic," Eliza muttered, pulling on the reins of her horse. "Why is it here?"

The commander was hesitant in his reply, his eyes flashing to hers. "Some say this is where they gave up their first-born child nearly two-thousand years ago."

Eliza's brows rose, and she couldn't help but blink; in all the books, all the stories she'd heard, she never knew that the Goddess had a child. Never knew that there could be a possibility, and from the way Thorne had said it, there was more to the story than just that.

"I've never heard anything about this." She clenched her jaw and eyed the pair. "I've never heard of this lover, never heard of any of her children. Hell, I barely know anything about this Goddess, and here she is, everywhere I look!"

It took a moment for the commander to respond, but when he did, his eyes were narrowed, like he wasn't quite seeing her properly. "There are different stories based on different areas. Don't worry about it too much." He made a move to leave, but Eliza hesitated.

Something about the space screamed *power*; whether it was the white-marble fountain that continued to spout water like it was still connected to a source, or the fact that, despite the considerable death that surrounded them, none of it breached the sanctuary of the maze.

"Thorne." The commander turned back to her; eyes now wary. "Let's try here, first."

"Why?"

She bit her lip. "This place is *teeming* with magic. The power here, at the maze's centre... I can use it to connect with the maze and maybe find something." His brows furrowed, and she sighed, handing off her reins. With a flick of her hair, she pulled it back into a bun. "The maze itself is like... a living thing; it might very well be hiding the entrance to the tunnels."

"Why are you so determined to find these tunnels?" he asked. *Why aren't you?* She wanted to argue but didn't.

Instead, she sucked in a deep breath and sat amongst the emerald-green grass of the maze, crossing her legs, lifting her chin so that she could peer up into the faces of the Fae male and the legendary Goddess who looked down upon her with marble-white eyes.

Connect to the maze. Eliza searched for the maze's unique, ancient magic, grasping for tendrils that reached for her before snapping away. Furrowing her brow, Eliza tried again, reaching further into the forgotten magic, and held on to the tiniest flare of power she could find.

Tethering herself to the maze's magic was easy, but getting it to accept her magic, to accept her as an equal and not a threat, became hard; although the maze was stagnant, never changing and protected, it was a living entity, full of secrets and lies, crevices and alcoves that hid things it didn't want found. Tethered to its magic, to its essence, Eliza could feel the maze move and reshape, changing one corridor into a dead end while opening another wall into a hall.

Protection and safety. It *allowed* her and Thorne to find its centre, to understand; whether she liked it or not, Eliza knew then that the maze had been born, not of any magic she knew, but of a magic created and honed by the Goddess herself.

That was why the Goddess Azula stood at its centre like a beacon.

It wasn't until she understood its changing nature that it opened to her.

'*Ask,*' it seemed to whisper, accepting her into its magic hesitantly. '*Ask and you shall receive.*'

'*Did you help the assassins escape? Did you provide them with safe passage by use of underground tunnels?*' Eliza asked. She felt the magic of the maze pulling from her, could feel it reeling back, as if the questions were too personal, too hard for it to answer. '*Please. You are the only being that can help.*'

'*No witch has referred to me as a being. I am a thing. Not living.*'

'*I don't believe that.*' Eliza had seen it for herself, had seen and felt it move and reshape and reform. It had willingly guided her and Thorne through its brambles and thorns without any issue, like it had *wanted* them at the manor.

'*Please,*' she pleaded, '*please help me, so that I can try and help you.*'

The maze did not respond. Instead, Eliza felt the ground beneath her tremble, heard the crack and crumble of marble and stone. Somewhere in the distance, Thorne shouted, but it was drowned out by the clanging of swords and the furious images that sprang into Eliza's mind.

~

The darkness was as thick as blood. It rolled over the forest like a wave of ink, smothering the stars. Nothing was spared as shadow soldiers crept through that thick blackness with their blades drawn, and evil magic protecting them.

Thunder struck blindly without the illumination of lightning, for the light of that, too, was choked out by the bleeding darkness. Natural magic shied away from the forbidden enchantments spilling over the estate.

The maze wept before it fell asleep.

In that darkness, even the faces of the fountain shifted to dread. Even the Goddess feared what would happen next.

They moved like shadows, the soldiers, bleeding through the darkness in droves. Guards who were blinded by the rain were caught unaware; blood soaked through the cobblestone and the grass, into the stones and over the marble staircase like a waterfall. Even the rain turned to blood.

The walls were scaled, the windows broken into. Any who met the shadow soldiers faced death. Their screams were drowned out by the rain, by the thunder that had nowhere to strike.

In the bedchambers, the queen awoke first. Dread twisted within her like a warning from the Goddess. She did not wake her husband, peacefully asleep after the stress of the day's work.

She went to her son, her beautiful sleeping son. He usually did not sleep through the night.

The queen did not notice how the darkness stifled all the light, and she did not hear the wails of her servants and guards as they were slaughtered. She heard nothing, saw nothing, but her beautiful son.

The shadow soldiers found the infant asleep in his crib, ripe for the taking.

In the doorway, a young girl screamed. She screamed so others could escape. She screamed for her father, she screamed for the Goddess who could not save them.

They slit her throat and let her tumble to the ground. Her blood soaked their shoes, but they did not glance twice at her young face.

The youthful queen found them, found her daughter and her wide unseeing eyes. She said a prayer and with anger thrumming in her veins, she used what little magic she had to protect her son.

But she was not fast enough.

Soldiers slit her throat next, leaving her beside the crib.

One stowed the young prince in their cloaks, hiding him away from the enchanted weather. But he awoke and wailed. There were doors leading to a balcony in the nursery. A shadow flung them open and let the rain and wind fill the room. The reek of sulphur almost washed away the stench of death.

As the soldiers climbed out of the nursery, the king stumbled in. He wore no shoes, his bare feet quickly soaked with the blood of his young daughter.

He did not weep. He only stared.

The assassins took to the darkness, the infant wailing still.

The king could not save his wife or his daughter, not even his son, as darkness consumed his land and his heart.

The guards were dead, the servants slaughtered. The blood that drenched the assassins was quickly washed away by the rain.

With dark magic in their veins, the soldiers walked through the now sleeping maze. The old magic that had created it bowed to the dark magic they wielded. Darkness overcame light.

Death overcame hope.

The infant stopped wailing.

The Goddess who stood within the depths of the fountain wept tears of blood as the soldiers stepped into her water. With the magic they wielded, the soldiers became shadows, became night themselves, and disappeared beneath the water.

~

The visions died, the sound of the thundering rain nothing more than an echo in her ears. Night turned to day before her eyes, and if she squinted, she could almost see understanding in the white-marble eyes of the Goddess towering over her.

'Thank you for showing me this,' Eliza said at last, and pulled herself out of the ancient spell. She felt the magic glide over her like the caress of a mother, thankful and sad all at once.

Brushing herself off, Eliza stood on wobbly knees. "The shadow soldiers put the maze to sleep. Its magic is old—older than anything I've ever encountered, but it's *alive*. It led us straight here."

Thorne turned to her, the reins in his hands slackening. "And?" he asked, wary.

Eliza breathed in deeply. "And it showed me. It showed me how the soldiers got in, how they stole the prince."

Thorne crossed his arms. "So, did it show you anything about this underground maze or tunnels?"

"Yes!" Eliza replied, smiling again. She pointed at the fountain. "That's the way in. That is how the soldiers got out with the prince."

Those storm-like eyes darkened, face twisting into dread. There was apprehension in his glare as he strode over to the marble fountain. Warily, he ran his fingers over the high rim before looking back at her. "How?"

"You step in and go down."

Confusion clouded Thorne's features for a moment before his eyes cleared. Almost like something had clicked, there seemed to be a new resolve about him that made Eliza giddy. "Alright. Get your things—whatever you might need down there. Rations, water, your spells, weapons. Get mine too. I'll take the horses and hide them..."

With a simple nod, Eliza grabbed her bag and rifled through it, double-checking she had enough water and food to last them at least a week. She made sure her spell book was strapped to her side.

She just hoped that whatever they found down there would lead them in the right direction.

"Do you know anything about what's down there?" Thorne asked as they stared into the water. Eliza wondered if he was searching for a physical doorway amongst the gently lapping waves.

She shook her head. "The maze didn't show me anything about what might be underground."

"And how did you know about any of this again?" She caught the hint of caution in his voice and glared at him with a deepening frown.

Without a response, she stepped onto the rim of the fountain's base. Thorne followed, and held out his hand. Heart racing, Eliza took it, holding on tight and interlacing her fingers with his. A deep burn made its way up the base of her neck, and she tried not to look at him. "One of my guardians told me about the maze... a story about it anyway."

Thorne grunted in response. "Ready?"

Am I? Eliza nodded, unable to respond.

Together, they stepped into the water. Eliza held her breath, feeling the water rise to her shins, then to her chest, and finally her neck. Magic danced over her skin like a phantom wind, crisp and refreshing, ancient and consuming. Despite the shallowness of the fountain, the water continued to rise, until finally it fully covered her, submerging her in darkness.

Eliza didn't release her breath nor Thorne's hand until she felt the magic of the fountain slipping away, until she could feel solid ground beneath her feet. As the water ebbed—and she was somehow not drenched—she finally opened her eyes.

Beside her, Thorne coughed. "What the..."

Releasing his hand, Eliza spun in a full circle, brows raised as she took in the entirety of the underground civilisation that surrounded them.

"You said tunnels," Thorne said, spinning around as well.

Eliza shook her head. "I thought... I thought they were. Kay said... Holy shit."

Like another realm in its own, the seemingly abandoned underground city looked untouched by the world above it. Directly in front of Eliza was another towering statue of Azula and her legendary dagger, this time accompanied by a raven on her shoulder, and her lover standing behind her other shoulder. At the foot of the statue were skeletons, cloth and skin still hanging to their bones, all surrounding Azula, stretching skeletal arms towards her.

Behind the statue lay a towering city complex; there were no windows in the frames—whether there had been originally, Eliza wasn't sure. The buildings were made of white stone that had discoloured over the course of time.

Bodies of all shapes and sizes littered the ground, perhaps hundreds—*thousands*—of years old, each in a state of complete decay.

Were they worshippers? Eliza took in the out-stretched hands and upturned skulls.

She noticed there were other statues, too; of Azula, her dagger, the raven, and the Fae Knight, spread throughout the underground city. Everywhere she looked, there were more statues and bodies. A city so grand it couldn't have been real.

At her side, Thorne said a short prayer. "This can't be right," he whispered.

"Do you think this is where the shadow soldiers have been this whole time?" Eliza asked, turning to the commander. She reached her hand out and summoned a ball of light, throwing it into the air to illuminate the rest of the city.

Thorne shook his head. "No. If they were, we'd probably already be dead." He turned around again, though this time he no longer looked amazed at the city. This time, he turned slowly with a critical eye, searching the area for entrances and exits, tunnels that may have given the assassins a way out.

"So far we only know of one way in and one way out," Thorne said, looking up at the portal. "But there are bound to be others. I can see three tunnels that branch out of this main cavern, which might mean three more portals."

"Or three more cities." Eliza frowned and shook her head, still perplexed by their finding. "Have you heard of any cities dedicated to Azula kept underground?"

Thorne shook his head. "No. I didn't think she ever had any large-scale monuments either. The Goddess had temples and small statues and fountains, and the occasional tapestry. But nothing this big."

Eliza looked around again, heart racing. "Why?" she asked, staring at the large statue, at the Goddess and her Fae lover, and the raven. "Why all this? Was there a secret cult following for her?" Her thoughts wandered back to the books, to the missing pages. It hadn't been a coincidence, she realised, but that still didn't answer the question of *why*.

"Possibly." Thorne shrugged, pulling his sword from his sheath. He stared down at the hilt—at the raven carved into the pommel. "Don't most Gods?"

Eliza stayed quiet, biting her lip. Ever since she'd seen that stupid raven and the Fae Knight in New Orleans, she kept finding references to Azula and making connections to the dead Goddess that couldn't be possible. Everywhere she went, Azula was there. So, what did the Goddess have to do with anything? What was so important about her?

She stopped and cocked her head.

Holding her breath, Eliza listened for a moment, willing her heart to slow, to silence for a split-second to give her the chance to listen. In the distance, Eliza made out the sounds of beating wings.

Spinning around, Eliza spotted the gold irises of the raven, perched on a root that stuck out of one of the cavernous walls. It flapped its wings again and flew down an adjacent corridor.

"Shit." Eliza ran after the Gods' forsaken raven. She dodged skeletons and jumped over fallen columns, sprinting into the darkness of the tunnel where she could still hear the raven flying.

"Eliza!" She didn't have the breath to reply, and instead threw her hands up to illuminate the tunnel, expelling the darkness that circled her.

Eliza came to a stop, her breaths rapid and her heart racing. Her legs ached, and she fell to her knees, confused and downright annoyed.

The raven was already gone.

Thorne came to a stop beside her and knelt, placing his hand on her shoulder. "What the hell was that?" he asked, forcing her to look at him.

"I think," she said, pointing down the tunnel. "They went down here."

"A feeling?" Thorne questioned, incredulous.

Eliza shook her head. "I think the Goddess is showing me the way."

Thorne looked down the tunnel, at the darkness Eliza's light could not penetrate. He then looked down and frowned at the footprints leading into the darkness.

"Those aren't yours?" He pointed to the tracks in the dirt.

Eliza sucked in a breath. "No." She shook her head. "The feet are too big. And look, there are multiple pairs."

"These can't be that old," he murmured, touching them. "At least, not old enough to match any of the bodies back there. These have to be new."

"So... that might be from the shadow soldiers. This could lead us to wherever the prince might be." Excitement flooded through Eliza, filling her with a sudden giddiness. *This is it! We might actually be able to find him!*

Beside her, Thorne replied. "Maybe. He might not be there anymore."

"Way to kill the mood," Eliza said, frowning. "Either way, we have a better lead than *anyone* has ever had. I can actually get a better trace on him from here."

Thorne shook his head and stood, taking a step back. "We should alert the king. Contact his trackers."

"No!" Eliza stood and turned on him, shaking her head. "This is supposed to be my mission. The one entrusted to *me*. If he wanted his trackers doing the job, he would have asked for them."

Eliza saw the war within Thorne. Like many, he'd been taught to take orders from the king and let him handle the tough decisions, especially concerning the fate of the kingdom. But here he was, entrusting this responsibility to a seventeen-year-old girl from another realm that the king had brought in to save his son.

But then she saw it; the indecision disappeared, like a light switch had been flicked. He trusted her.

But why?

"Fine," he said, low enough that she had to step closer to hear him. "But if that's the case, then everything stays between us. We can't get *anyone* else involved."

Eliza nodded her agreement. "I think someone on the inside, close to the king, knows about the soldiers and the kidnapping, and all of *this*. I don't think we can trust anyone."

Thorne smiled ruefully. "It may be true. We may not be able to trust anyone. Hell, I don't even know why you chose to trust me." The wariness in his smile almost stopped her; why *had* she trusted him?

She felt her cheeks heat and redden and was suddenly thankful for the darkness. "Because you could have been like everyone else, you could have dismissed me the first chance you saw me. But you didn't." She cleared her throat and ran a hand through her hair. "And if you were against me, you wouldn't have let me come here, or let me speak to Amitel. And I would know, too, if I couldn't trust you."

"Your feeling?" he asked, smirking.

"More or less," she replied, shrugging. If she couldn't trust him, she doubted the ghost of the little girl would have let Eliza leave with Thorne, and she doubted him saving her life meant anything other than him being on her side.

Thorne stepped away from her and began walking back to the main cavern where their belongings were still at the portal. He gestured for her to follow. "If we're fast, we can restock and come back here to follow that tunnel. We're going to need more provisions though. We don't know how far the tunnel goes."

"You don't think we have enough?" Eliza asked. She knew she had at least two full water skins, along with the one strapped to her hips. She also had dried meat wrapped in her bag, stale bread, and whatever fruits and nuts she could find. Eliza knew it wasn't enough, but the itch to search and keep going made it hard for her to step away from the tunnel's entrance.

Carefully, she looked between the commander and the tunnel, and that shred of hope that readily ignited in her. For the first time since starting this mission, she felt like she had a chance.

But she trusted Thorne and followed him back to the tunnel's entrance with a smile on her face.

Hope, she thought. *I must have hope.*

13

TUNNEL OF TRUTH

"We should head straight into the tunnel and see where it leads us," Thorne said, wrapping a rope around his torso. He handed the other end to Eliza, who begrudgingly tied it around herself, for the purpose of not losing each other in the darkness. "We'll walk until we get tired and stop for a couple of hours. We won't have any concept of night or day down here."

Finishing the knot, Eliza shrugged. "Maybe it's a good thing—at least we'll find the end in no time."

It had been easy enough to stow their horses with an old couple—though Eliza had the sneaking suspicion they might sell the horses, but she hadn't said anything aloud—and while they'd managed to find a trading store with rope and dried and cured meats, Eliza couldn't quite stamp out the feeling that something bad would happen.

The town had been desolate; barely a living soul there. By chance, drifters and a few farmers had been around and they'd been able to buy any supplies they needed, but it hadn't been much.

Thorne shook his head and didn't reply, though a smile tugged at his lips. Instead, he checked his weapons again, then his packs, before gesturing for Eliza to turn around so that he could make sure she was secure with her own bags and limited weapons.

"When we return," Thorne said, meeting her stare from the corner of his eye, "I will teach you how to use a sword."

She rolled her eyes. "I know enough to get by."

"You cannot always rely on magic," he said. "It won't always be there."

Instead of responding, Eliza looked away.

The pair walked slowly towards the far tunnel, taking their time to step over the remains of those who had once inhabited the large city. Eliza kept her gaze directed at the tunnel and the enormous arches with grand carvings so that she wouldn't see the bodies of the children huddled together. Their remains reminded her too much of the Winter Palace.

"I wonder what happened down here," she said finally, gazing up to the ceiling. Bile rose in her throat.

Thorne shook his head, at a loss for answers. "I've never heard of underground cities—never heard a mention to any that were built for Azula. There could be a number of reasons why." There was a stiffness to his voice, one Eliza barely noted. What was he hiding?

"Do you think the king ever knew?" she asked as they passed through the arch, entering the cavernous tunnel. Darkness spread around them, thick and tangible. Eliza could taste the staleness of the air on her tongue, could feel the shadows wrap around her, stifling.

Thorne barely spared her a look over his shoulder. "I can't say." He stopped when the darkness did not give way. Eliza raised her hand and a ball of light appeared. She threw it up towards the ceiling, lighting the way. "But I don't think so. He would have sent trackers down here otherwise, just in case."

Eliza didn't respond, too busy glaring at the depth of the tunnel. She wondered how an entire civilisation had managed to survive underground without being noticed—or missed. Why were there bodies everywhere? And how, she wondered, did Kay know about it at all?

~

The warmth that surrounded Eliza pulled her into its loving embrace. There was a familiarity to the feeling she couldn't escape. But she knew the warmth couldn't last.

Eliza peeled her eyes open and yawned. The haze of sleep slowly disappeared, slipping away from her as she finally came to consciousness. But not all the darkness was gone. It still clung to the edges of her vision, a reminder of where she was.

However, the pain in her butt and back was enough of a reminder of her less-than-comfortable sleep. She couldn't help but ask herself *how* she'd managed to even fall asleep.

The tunnel was dark, save for their dim torch, which had rolled to the end of their feet. It flickered occasionally but remained steady.

But the warmth never left here.

Something heavy slowly shifted from her shoulders. "You're awake?"

Eliza frowned and straightened. Now, the warmth was gone. *Oh Lord.* The warmth had originated from the commander. His arm had been wrapped around her shoulder, her cheek against his shoulder.

Heat rose in her cheeks as mortification settled upon her. She'd fallen asleep on the commander.

Eliza grimaced as she sat up. "I'm sorry."

"For what?" Thorne asked, frowning. "For sleeping?"

"For sleeping on *you*." She shook her head as a smile twitched across his lips. "It won't happen again, I promise."

Thorne chuckled and stood, stretching his long limbs. His shirt rose, untucked from his pants, revealing a line of bronze skin marred by pale scars. What had happened to him to earn those scars? Even as he lowered his arms and hid them from her view, she could still see them, branded across her vision.

"What?" he asked, frowning at her.

Eliza shook her head. "Nothing, sorry."

"We should keep moving." Thorne reached for a pack but didn't shoulder it. Instead, he pulled out a water skin and drank. "Walk for a couple of hours, then rest."

Nodding, Eliza said nothing as he sat across from her and rifled through her pack. She watched mutely as he produced their rations and set the bread and cured meat between them.

It reminded her of a picnic, like the ones she, her grandfather, and Kay had gone on when she was a child. Eliza sometimes took her elderly neighbour, Miss Constance, to the park for a picnic. *Used to,* Eliza thought bitterly.

A lump formed in her throat as she picked up a slice of bread. "Why are you helping me?"

Thorne's eyes flickered from hers to the shared bread between them. If the question took him by surprise, he didn't show it. "It's a long story," he said. His hands tightened into fists.

"We have time." Eliza cocked her head. "Something, anything.

Give me an actual reason as to why you're helping me."

"Can't you just trust that I'm here to help?" he asked quietly.

She eyed him for a moment, then shook her head. "I need to know, especially now."

"Why?"

For a moment, the tunnel grew cold, frigid under the weight of what he wasn't telling her. Something deep within her told her not to push, and yet she couldn't stop herself. She didn't understand why he wanted to help her, not really. She wondered if it had anything to do with power, with wanting to prove himself to the king, but one look at the commander told her that wasn't the case.

Perhaps he saw those questions warring in her eyes because he finally sighed. "I once knew someone who was taken by the same soldiers who attacked you and kidnapped Prince Alicsar." He cast his gaze downwards, where his fingers touched a silver chain.

A flash of familiarity struck Eliza as she stared at the chain. *Her dream...* she'd seen the same one in her dream. She'd seen it again when she'd first met the commander, but it hadn't struck her as odd until now.

"She died protecting the people she loved," Thorne murmured, eyes glassy. "I refuse to let her sacrifice be in vain."

Eliza swallowed thickly. "That's why you decided to join me. To avenge her."

His eyes flickered to hers. "Among other things."

She didn't know how to respond, and instead sat back against the stone. The weight of her mission settled on her shoulders as she watched the commander from the corner of her eye. She'd thought it would be a simple explanation, but there was nothing simple about him.

~

They walked for hours before stopping at a decline in the tunnel.

"We can stop here, rest for a bit. Eat," Thorne said.

Eliza nodded her agreement and pulled off her pack, which was giving her serious back pains. She dropped it to the ground, which had gone from sandy dirt to hard rock after a while, meaning they'd lost all the footprints from the soldiers.

But the prints had been enough for Eliza to catch a trace—old, but still useful—and they used that to find their way, even though the tunnel hadn't branched... yet.

Groaning, Eliza fell to the ground and rested her head against the stone. Her cheeks were hot and sweat dripped from her brow. Thorne grumbled but sat beside her, the rope still holding them together.

"I'm dying," she said, wiping her brow. "It's so hot down here. *How* is it so hot down here?" She fanned herself, wishing she had access to her clothing back in New Orleans. It was still autumn, winter slowly taking over Cadira. Not summer in hell.

Thorne shrugged off his cloak and rolled up the sleeves of his shirt, stretching his arms over his head. Eliza noticed sweat coating his face as well.

"We must be going deeper underground," he muttered, closing his eyes. He pulled out his water skin and took a long swig of it before wiping his mouth. "Have you still got the trace?"

She felt for the strange tug of magic, the remnants of what had once been the assassins over twenty years ago. It shone like liquid silver in her mind, ever dimming but ever present. She let her magic slide over it and follow it farther into the darkness of the tunnel.

Slowly, she nodded, taking a swig of her own water. "Yeah. It's weak, but it's enough. I don't sense any forks in the tunnel." She furrowed her brow and closed her eyes. In fact, she didn't sense *anything*. Just darkness and a deep abiding fear that something was going to happen.

"Good. We don't need any surprises."

She grunted in agreement and rubbed her eyes, growing more worried than she thought she should be. If she didn't sense *anything,* was there a chance that there was no portal and it was just an endless tunnel, its only way out being the direction they had come through? She shook her head. It made no sense, and she knew the shadow soldiers wouldn't have gone down that road, only to turn back. No, there *had* to be a way out.

If she doubted herself, she knew she'd lose the trace, lose any courage or pride she had. Eliza hadn't sensed the portal back at the manor, so there was a chance that they'd just happen upon it without really knowing it was there. At least, Eliza hoped that would be the case.

Opening her eyes, Eliza sucked in a deep breath and released it slowly, concentrating on the hope she harboured that it wouldn't all be for nothing.

Beside her, Thorne tensed; she could feel the coiling of his muscles as his arm slid over her chest, keeping her back. "Do you hear that?" he asked quietly, head cocked.

For a moment, she heard nothing, but then... scuttling, like claws on stone. Eliza leaned forward and searched the darkness at either end of the tunnel... but saw nothing. She couldn't even sense another presence, whether it be dangerous or not, and there were no spirits in the tunnels to guide the way.

"What do you think it is?" she whispered, leaning in closer to Thorne. His arm tightened around her.

He shook his head, and through the dimness of the light, she could see his jaw clench. "It could be anything."

Eliza's heart sped up, thundering in her chest. The hairs on the back of her neck rose, and she dropped the orb of light that had been guiding them, submerging them in thick darkness.

They continued listening, noting how the scuttling grew louder—and closer.

When it was directly over them, Eliza summoned the light source and yelped. Beside her, Thorne growled.

Above them, a demon screeched; either at the suddenness of the light, or at seeing them, she wasn't sure. It wasn't like the creatures that attacked the temple or the Winter Palace; this one was larger—and hungry. Eliza only caught a flash of its teeth before Thorne aimed a dagger at its skull.

The demon fell with a wet thump, dead upon impact.

The commander uncoiled himself, though he did not remove his arm from around her. He held her back as he inspected the body, his other hand rubbing tiredly at his chin.

"The hell is that?" Eliza asked. It was human in size, skin pulled taught over thick, long bones. Its skull resembled that of a goat, but with teeth like a sharks. The demons palid skin was marred by burns and swollen cuts, like it had been tortured before descending into the tunnels.

"It's an Igiulon demon, very rare and very dangerous. I didn't think they dwelled this deep underground."

"Do they travel in packs?" Eliza asked. She watched as the body turned to ash, stomach roiling.

Thorne shook his head. "No. Usually alone. They're also supposed to be incredibly smart. But this one... this one wasn't right."

"Are you sure it was an Igiulon then?"

He was quiet for a moment, running his hand through his hair. Eliza watched as he gnawed on his bottom lip, dark hair falling over his forehead. In the dim light, his skin took on a bronze colour, making him look otherworldly as his eyes darted over every piece of evidence.

Snap out of it! Eliza shook herself and averted her eyes, pursing her lips. *He doesn't think about you like that, so you don't think about him.* When had she started noticing the little things? They had been together all of a week, searching for the prince. They had nothing in common other than that. *Crushing on the commander will do me no good. If I find the prince, then I'll be gone the next day, back to New Orleans.*

Eliza cleared her throat. "So? Was it an Igiulon?" Their eyes met, and he quickly looked away.

"Yes," he replied. "I'm positive. I've seen them before. They're intelligent, humanoid, but this one... this one looked as if..."

"Like it had been brought back from the dead?" Eliza quipped, crossing her arms.

Thorne shook his head and smirked. "No, more like it had been starved into insanity."

Eliza cringed and swallowed thickly, taking a step back. "You're right. But if they're so smart, how do you think it got trapped down here?"

Shrugging, Thorne picked up his pack, and she did the same. "I'm not sure. But did you see which direction it came from?"

Wide-eyed, Eliza looked down the tunnel, where the trace still pulsed from where the demon had sprung from. "It could have come through a portal without realising it."

Thorne nodded his agreement. "It might also mean that we aren't the only ones to come down here. Those demons are like you and me, they need to eat regularly, which means it's been down here for at least a couple of weeks, and it definitely didn't come down here on its own. From the sounds of it, someone with magic needs to open those portals."

"How can you tell?" Eliza asked softly.

"Too thin," Thorne replied. "Usually they're much larger, muscled. That's why it's advised you be careful if you face one."

Eliza's heart sank. "So that could mean that someone else made those footprints in the city."

"There is only one way to find out." He tugged on his end of the rope, forcing Eliza to follow him. "We need to find the end of this tunnel and get out of here."

~

A dead end. Eliza stared at the looming wall before them, studying the intricately carved images etched into the stone; Azula wielding her dagger, the Faery Knight at her side. The raven in flight, its beak open as if laughing at them. She could almost imagine its gold eyes glimmering at her.

"Can you sense the portal?" Thorne asked, touching the wall. "Can you get us out?"

They'd travelled what had to be four days below ground before finding the dead end and what had to be a portal. But when Eliza reached her magic out towards the ancient doorway, she felt... nothing.

Shaking her head, Eliza narrowed her eyes and concentrated her magic back to the portal—back to the exit. Her magic reared its head in response, searching. "Nothing," she said, incredulous. Dread settled over her. "It's closed."

Brows furrowed, Thorne turned to her. "And you can't open it?"

Eliza looked up towards the ceiling. "It's not that easy." She focused again, pushing against the magic that had closed the portal. "Someone with really powerful magic forced this closed, and my magic isn't enough to open it."

"Impossible." He cursed foully under his breath. He punched the wall in frustration, swearing again and again, irritation and anger evident on his face.

Eliza's heart sunk, and her stomach turned. "I can't open it."

The silence that surrounded them was deafening. She wished Thorne would shout again, or curse, but he didn't. He merely stood in front of her, completely still, and stared down at her with a look of utter calmness that freaked her out.

"Thorne?" she whispered, stepping back. He shook his head and closed his eyes.

"Let's turn around and go back."

But she didn't move. "Which direction did we walk? South?"

"I don't think so," he said, voice rough. "I think... I think we walked north."

Frowning, Eliza shook her head. "In the opposite direction to what Amitel and everyone else believed."

Something caught her eye; Eliza knelt down and ran her hand over the stone. Her fingers came back dusted red. The dirt they had walked through in the city had been brown.

"It would make sense," Thorne mused, "because the Mesah desert is in the north, and no one who enters the desert makes it out—not usually. It would be the smartest place to hide royalty, especially if you become untraceable." There was a note of awe in his voice.

She asked, "Why did no one look there before?" *It made sense.*

"They did," he said carefully, "but the traces led south. The king wanted to focus his assets on the evidence. And the desert meant the prince couldn't survive."

She met his stare and showed him her fingers. "The shadow soldiers could have easily had a boat and travelled north. This is sand. Red sand."

Eliza closed her eyes and spoke quietly under her breath until a cold, hard object appeared in her hands. The small vial was only as long as her pinky, but big enough for her to take a sample of the sand. She stared at it for a moment, thoughts a flurry of questions. But she slipped it into her bag.

Thorne released a breath and touched his fingers to hers. "Like in Mesah."

Eliza stood, wiping her hands on her pants, and began walking again, back down the tunnel towards the ancient, sweeping city.

I know where you are, she thought, a smile twitching on her lips, *and I'm going to find you.*

14

KEEPERS OF KNOWLEDGE

Along with the ache in her legs and the hunger pangs deep in her belly, Eliza felt empty. *A week.* They'd wasted a week travelling through the tunnel. The feeling of failure wrapped itself around her gut.

She and Thorne had barely said a word to one another as they made their way back to the city and to the portal. Eliza, too wrapped up in her own thoughts—the lore and stories she knew of Mesah— couldn't fill the silence with useless chatter. Especially after the revelations made earlier.

Had they truly found something, or had they been led on a wild goose chase like Amitel and the trackers had been almost twenty years ago?

Eliza couldn't help but think about Thorne and the woman he had loved. She'd been killed, but for whatever reason, he was here. He was helping her.

Everywhere they went, there was a distraction; some kind of trap or test. Did the soldiers and whatever higher entity ruled them know that they were getting close? Or could it all be pre-planned traps that would eventually amount to nothing because the prince was already dead?

The questions ran through Eliza's head over and over again until she couldn't think about anything else. She knew the prince had to be her main priority, but she couldn't stop dwelling on the man she was tied to. There was something pulling her to him, something inside her awakening at his presence.

The portal's magic washed over them, like it had when they'd first gone underground. It brought them to the surface, where darkness reigned freely, and rain poured from the skies above.

Eliza swore quietly and stared up at the sky. Her luck. Perhaps Cadira was more in tune with her than she realised.

The murkiness of the sky with the added rain that fell like sheets made it hard for her to see. Was the manor up ahead? Or the road? Her hair, plastered to her skin, became a curtain she could barely see through.

Thorne untangled the rope, giving her a strong tug before leaping out of the fountain. Through the darkness and rain, Eliza could just see the glow of his eyes.

"Really?" he asked, holding out his hand. "You enjoy being soaked?" A chill passed through her and she shuddered, wrapping her arms around herself tightly.

With the ache in her legs and the pains in her stomach, and her wet clothes now clinging to her chilled skin, Eliza climbed out of the fountain, docs soggy and pants already chafing. She took his hand hesitantly and tried to ignore the racing of her heart as his warmth shot through her.

Thorne made his way through the darkened maze, hand still wrapped in hers. As the manor came into view, she had to squint to see the outline of it properly—and to try and disentangle the spirits that rose up in response to their arrival. She could see them in her peripheral vision, noticed them watching her. The commander tugged on her hand and they ascended a crumbling staircase, then with a gentle push, he guided her into a small, dry place under a low hanging beam, lowering his head to fit underneath with her.

His hair dripped onto her face as she looked up at him. They were standing closely together—closer than they had been over the last several days.

Wiping her face, Eliza scowled, trying to ignore the racing of her heart. "Take a step back, Thorne."

He merely grinned, but he took a small step back. Eliza, for reasons beyond her, wished he hadn't... that he'd stayed close.

Shaking her head, she ran a hand over her wet hair, smoothing it down. "What now?" she asked, meeting his stare. The sound of rain echoed in her ears. "Are we going to wait out the rain?"

Shrugging, Thorne looked her over before his eyes flickered out towards the maze. "I suppose we will, since we're stuck walking until we can get the horses."

Eliza frowned. "Horses would come in mighty handy right about now. What took us four days on foot will take only two or three by horse, right?"

Thorne nodded. "Something like that. We also need more provisions, and a proper place to sleep."

Eliza turned her face away from Thorne and tried to forget what had happened in the tunnels between them. *Between them.* There *wasn't* anything between them, though, and she knew she had to remember that.

"Of course," she said, scrubbing a hand over her heated cheeks. "We don't have much in the way of money, though."

Thorne shook his head. "There's a military base a couple of hours away—a day at the worst. If we get stuck..." Eliza groaned, shutting her eyes and leaning against the wall beside her. "Much of the nobility will be in the capital with the king, so we can't count on them for aid, especially after what happened at the Winter Palace."

"Of course," Eliza replied. Her heart dropped at the memory; the smoke, the blood, Clio jumping in to save Eliza... "And how far away is the capital?"

"A couple of days *out* of our way, towards the east."

Eliza decided not to answer, and instead watched as the rain hit the gravel and ruins around her, how it washed over the maze and the fountain. She could only guess that it had just turned midnight, especially since there was no sign of the rising sun on the horizon.

"Doesn't the capital have a port?" she asked finally.

He nodded, narrowing his eyes. "It does. A day's ride from the city."

"Does the port have a direct trade route north?"

"It does," he replied, smiling. "And I thought you said you knew nothing about the land. Looks like you don't need me after all."

"Ha, very funny." She rolled her eyes. "Now the problem is getting the horses."

"I might be able to help with that."

Eliza spun around as the commander unsheathed his sword, raising it to meet their sudden visitor.

A man with long white hair and ebony skin stood behind them

amongst the rubble of the manor, dressed completely in black. Dark eyes met hers, and when he smiled, it was like a sense of déjà vu settled over Eliza, like she knew him—and he her. It didn't feel like the same sense she'd had when meeting Thorne; no, this was different, and for the most part, it unsettled her.

"Who are you?" she asked softly, unable to raise her voice over the rain.

The older man laughed softly, like how Eliza's grandfather did when she asked silly questions. His dark eyes flashed; there was little humour to be found in them. "I am Henry Ivo, a Keeper from the east."

Eliza watched Thorne from the corner of her eye, saw the recognition on his face.

"Shouldn't you be at your Temple?" Eliza asked, uncrossing her arms. "A Keeper was killed recently, so you should be protecting the wards."

"I agree," he replied, mildly amused. "But I am no longer the Keeper I was—my place has been taken by another, and I now do the bidding of the Gods."

It explained why ancient markings tattooed his skin, just noticeable under the cuffs of his coat and above the collar of his grey shirt. But Eliza didn't understand why he was there with them, standing in the pouring rain. Had the Gods asked him to find them? Or was he there of his own volition?

"Why are you here?" Her heart pounded in her chest. There was already one pesky God involved with her business; she didn't need the others getting involved as well.

She knew just how powerful a Keeper could be; her own grandfather had been offered many times to give up his position to join the Elders, the portal Keepers who had joined with the Gods. But Davis had always refused and wouldn't give her a reason why. But he did tell her how powerful those Elders were.

Henry Ivo only smiled. "I am here to help, Miss Kindall, as a favour to Davis."

"You know my grandfather?" Homesickness rushed through her. In that moment, she realised just how much she missed New Orleans; she missed the faded stars at night, and the smells of the French Quarter, and all the memories that clung to the old city.

"Yes, I knew him very well." The older man gestured to the inner ruins of the manor. "Would you two like to follow me? You are both very wet, and there is better cover farther in. I have much to tell you, as I have been waiting here for some time."

Behind her, Thorne grabbed her hand, but he didn't pull her back; instead, he held on to it. She'd seen the recognition in the commander's eyes, and he didn't seem too concerned with the Elder, which calmed her racing heart.

The Elder summoned an orb of light, illuminating the wreckage of the manor. Within the ruins, Eliza could make out the remains of those who had been trapped in the flames, of those who could not escape. Henry Ivo led them farther into the darkness, until he came to a stop at an old set of stairs that led down into what could only be a cellar.

"It is safe down here," he said, sending the light into the cellar. "Just watch your step."

Eliza followed the old man down the stone stairs. Thorne, still grasping Eliza's hand, went last, a small dagger now grasped in his free hand, poised and ready to strike.

"So, you two found the ruins of Azula's temple and her great city," Henry mused, turning back to them on the last step. "Was it as magnificent as the scrolls describe?"

"How did you know?" Eliza asked, releasing Thorne's hand. "Neither of us knew anything until we ended up down there."

Henry smiled and gestured to some old chairs and a table, where a pot of steaming water waited, along with a jar of what could only be tea. It reminded her of home. "Please, take a seat, and I will explain to you what I know."

Eliza sat first, suddenly grateful for the chair and the warmth that came from the pot of tea. It took a moment before Thorne followed, taking the seat directly beside Eliza and inching closer to her.

Henry poured three cups of steaming tea before continuing. "When one becomes an Elder, they are entrusted with scrolls older than registered time. In those scrolls there are legends and truth, especially about Azula and her offspring, and the temples, cities, and sacred lands that were dedicated to her. One of those sacred spaces was an underground city completely dedicated to the Goddess, with her children ruling over it."

Children. Thorne had mentioned one child. Now Eliza understood why Azula and her Faery lover had chosen this place to give that child up.

"How come Amitel didn't try the portal? Or any of the other

Keepers?" she asked.

Henry's silver brows shot up in surprise. "Because no one asked the maze."

Thorne leaned forward; lips pulled down in a frown. "And you didn't think to tell the king that the maze might have been used as an escape route?"

The old Keeper sighed. "We Elders do not fall into Cadiran politics. Even if I had wanted to help, I couldn't have. This is beyond me, beyond the other Elders. We do not get involved."

"Until now?" Eliza sat back, crossing her arms.

"You must understand," Henry said, pausing to sip his tea. "The Elders take their work seriously. The fact that I am here at all is more than the Elder Council is willing to offer concerning this mission. We only give aid in true crises. The matter of a stolen prince is, well I'm sorry to put it this way, beneath us. The king has another heir."

"Why wasn't this other heir ever an option?" Eliza asked. Thorne shifted uncomfortably. "What?"

The commander spared the Elder a glance before shaking his head. "It's complicated. King Bastian's last heir is... not here, with us."

Eliza furrowed her brow. "That makes no sense."

"That is the way of the world," Henry replied. "It is not what is important."

Eliza released a breath and scrubbed at her eyes. "What now? What will the Elders do with us?"

"Oh, nothing." Henry placed his cup down on the table with a shake of his head. "Until this issue is resolved with whoever is controlling these demons—the leader—nothing. You've violated no laws."

Eliza cocked a brow, heart hammering. "So, there is someone calling the shots."

"We've believed that was the case for some time, but there has never been any proof," Thorne said, leaning forward in his seat to wrap his hands around his cup. "No sightings, no proclamations. This *dictator* seems to be letting his minions do all of the work while he sits back and barks orders."

She wanted to ask why he'd never told her, but she held her tongue. Something about Henry stopped her from speaking up. Thorne was already keeping things from her. She didn't need him to close off completely.

"Exactly," Henry agreed, taking another sip. "And if that is the case, then we must believe that whomever this is knows what we know and more."

Eliza fidgeted with a loose string on her tunic, mouth suddenly dry. *A leader.* Of course, there was someone barking orders, but she just hadn't added them to the ever-expanding equation. "So, there's a chance that this is an Elder gone rogue," Eliza speculated. "An Elder who enjoyed power and wanted more of it maybe?"

Grim faced, the old Keeper nodded. "Yes, it is a likely possibility. Our compound has had no intrusions, and it is unlikely they found the city by chance. We have determined that someone in our ranks is responsible."

"I did," Eliza stated. "I was told about the possibility, and I asked the maze."

"And that," Henry replied, smiling, "is where you two are different. The maze gave you that information because it believed you could help. But whoever found it and used those passages to smuggle the prince out of this manor did not seek its help, nor did the maze give it willingly."

"They put the maze to sleep. Because of that, they could gain access," Eliza said.

"Indeed." Henry took another sip of his tea, then set it to the side. "I am here to help you, Elizabeth Kindall, not only because it is my duty as an Elder, but it is my duty as a former Keeper under the king's rule."

For a moment, Eliza stayed silent, as Thorne did beside her. She stared down at her tea, searching it for answers she knew she'd never receive. Could she trust this man with the information she thought she had? Could she risk anyone else for their cause, have their deaths on her hands?

Uncertainty flooded Eliza, as did a disturbing chill that had not been left by the rain. As if sensing her unease, Thorne rested his hand on her thigh beneath the table, forcing her gaze to his. In the storms of his eyes, she could see every emotion she felt mirrored; the unease and uncertainty, the fear that if they placed their trust in another it would be betrayed. Eliza wanted to see the logic in whether it would be smart to trust the Elder, but she couldn't be sure, not anymore. She reached out with her magic, feeling for his own, but felt only the unfamiliarity of it.

Clearing her throat, Eliza turned back to the Elder. Nothing in his eyes gave away his intentions. And yet, Eliza still felt unsure about him.

Standing from her seat, she held out her hand. "Thank you for your time, your knowledge, and your tea, but we will have to respectfully decline your offer of aid, as Commander Thorne and I have our leads. And you must be extremely busy as it is. I would hate to take you away from your work for the kingdom."

Before he could say anything to sway her judgement, Eliza left the cellar with Thorne by her side, and she did not look back.

15

THE DARK MASTER

When they left Henry Ivo in the skeleton of the Spring Manor, it had stopped raining. Eliza and Thorne had gone straight to the neighbouring town, only to find it deserted. Tumbleweeds had been rolling through the streets—*like an old Western,* Eliza thought—but there had been no proof that anyone had stepped foot in the town for almost twenty years.

By chance, they'd found their horses in the stables of the old farm couple they had stumbled upon; fed, brushed down, safe. Like they'd been gone for a couple of hours, and not a week. It had only taken them a moment to load their bags in the eerie silence and then they were gone, determined not to leave another mark on the town.

"What do you think?" Eliza asked, guiding her horse around the commander, grimacing. Eliza hadn't been able to shake the feeling that something had changed between them after going down into the tunnels, and even voicing her fears now sent an unexpected shiver down her spine. "Do you think it's possible that something else is out there? Watching us?"

"This is Cadira," he said finally, slowing the pace of his nickering horse. "Eyes are everywhere; I'd be surprised if we weren't."

Eliza noticed his gaze go to the forest, fenced off by a ravine of crystal blue water. The barrier between them and the creatures that dwelled within the Fae Territory.

Someone in her bloodline had come from there. Almost

subconsciously, she reached up and touched the points of her ears. *Yeah, because* that's *normal.* Some part of her didn't want to care about that, but... Eliza looked over to the legendary Willican forest and stared into the emerald depths of the trees, gazing upon the strange ruby and sapphire coloured flowers that blossomed amongst the branches.

The forest that protected the Faery realm remained untouched by the greedy hands of the mortal kings and queens that ruled Cadira. The only way in—and out—was a direct invitation from the Faery King himself, and Eliza understood how rare that would be. Even if she wanted to locate her bloodline, she had a hard time believing that would happen.

Maybe Bastian knows. The thought popped into her head before she could brush it aside, before she could extinguish that small flare of hope that arose with the thought.

She tried not to let the thought get to her; what would happen if she *did* learn more about her past? Were her parents alive? Dead? Did she have family in Cadira and the Fae territory?

Continuing to watch the forest, Eliza almost didn't notice a dark figure standing just behind the tree line, surrounded by an army of woodland creatures. Deer with antlers that held nests with beautiful green birds, and bears with fur as brown as bark and horns shaped like twigs. Squirrels, bluebirds and other animals emerged from the trees too, all enchanted by the strange magic that dwelled within the territory.

The Fae Knight stood silently among them, the raven perched on his shoulder. One hand rested atop a sword's hilt, while the other clutched something else, something white. *Paper.* Although he wore his helmet, Eliza could see the brightness of his eyes as they followed her down the king's road. The raven, too, watched their slow parade.

Furrowing her brow, Eliza waited until they were only a speck amongst the tree line before turning back to the path ahead. Though, she knew it wouldn't keep her from wondering.

Why are they here? Eliza spared her companion a glance. She hadn't consulted Thorne about their followers; she couldn't bring herself to mention it to him. It was the strange magic that stopped her from approaching them—her fear of Cadira that turned her blood to ice whenever the ancient creatures appeared. Her curiosity and need for answers screamed for her to ask why they followed her, but despite that, she didn't. Deep down, she knew she couldn't. Not yet.

Eliza turned back but there was no one there.

~

"We're coming up to the troll bridge." Thorne stopped and turned, shoulders tense. His jaw ticked as he spoke. "Stay close to me, no matter what. And don't say a word."

Ahead, the tree line faded, and a river cut between their path. The rushing water could be heard from where they waited at the bottom of an incline, their horses becoming increasingly agitated as they waited, as if sensing the danger ahead.

"Have you got the gold?" Thorne asked suddenly without facing Eliza. "We'll need to pay our way across."

Eyes narrowed, Eliza scrunched her nose and pulled out a rather light coin pouch. "The king actually lets the trolls toll the bridge?" she asked, handing over the purse.

A light breeze ruffled the commander's dark hair, pushing it across his brow. "They've been here longer than the kings of Cadira and are expected to be here longer than the Shadowland." He carefully dismounted and wrapped the reins tightly around his hand, indicating for Eliza to do the same. She did, waiting for him to continue. "The king has no jurisdiction over the creatures that have inhabited this land for thousands of years. It's a part of the treaty. So, when we come across their *territory*, we abide by their rules."

Swallowing a sigh, Eliza followed his lead.

Gravel loosened under her feet as they trekked up the incline towards the bridge's opening. Tall, gnarled and oddly angled trees lined the path. The raging river, which branched off the ravine that protected the Willican Forest, disappeared into the trees, winding toward the open ocean.

They stopped, waiting for a small family to pay their way across.

Trolls of different shapes emerged from the green-grey foliage; they were not like the trolls from modern mythology, Eliza realised as she gaped at them. They were like Nordic Trolls, with thick noses and stone-like skin. They had long, curled hair of different colours; some were grey-haired, while others were fair, brunette, or red-haired.

They looked almost peaceful, but they were not the isolated creatures she'd read about in Norse folklore. No, these were Cadiran trolls, and they could be deadly if provoked.

Eliza watched with bated breath as Thorne paid for them to cross. The trolls surrounding them stopped as Eliza stepped onto the bridge behind the commander, steering her horse beside her. She tried not to openly stare at the creatures that watched her with beady-black eyes.

When Thorne mounted his horse again, she followed, feeling the air around her change as she did.

It happened faster than Eliza could catch; the slow march across the stone bridge quickly turned into a hastened escape, with Eliza stuck at the end of their party. Beneath her, the mare reared at the appearance of a troll rushing them. She tumbled off its back, hitting the ground and rolling, her shoulder smashing into the hard stone as screams arose to drown out the river.

Trolls spilled onto the bridge quickly and effortlessly, their bulging bodies encircling her. It was the stench that hit her first—rotting carcass and mould—then their voices, gruff and low in timbre. Through the haze of confusion that swelled in her already muddled brain, she could just make them out through the curtain of hair that covered her face.

"The master will reward us for her capture," one said, sticky fingers reaching towards her.

Eliza threw up a protection shield around herself and stumbled to unsheathe a sword Thorne had given her after leaving the tunnels. Yet, the troll's words stopped her. *Their master.* What had it meant by that? She looked up into the three eyes of the misshapen monster and searched for confirmation, even if she didn't know what he was talking about.

Had the infamous leader of the demons and shadow soldiers bribed the trolls to stand against Cadira? Eliza finally removed her sword from its sheath and brandished it before the trolls.

The one with the three eyes spoke up again, a twisted smile marring its rotund face. "You think your steel will hurt us?" He chortled, protruding stomach jiggling as he laughed. "You cannot penetrate *this hide!*" The rest of his brethren laughed as well, leaving Eliza rather... perplexed.

She slowly got to her feet, pushing her hair back from her face. The protection spell began to dim. Behind the circle of trolls, Thorne had managed to clear the bridge of its previous occupants and threw himself between them and the danger. He had his sword raised in his right hand, while a dagger was poised in his left, but there was a calmness to his stance that gave Eliza chills.

Turning back to the trolls, she took in each of them. There had to be at least five in total surrounding her, while she had no doubt that there were more lurking below the bridge. It was just a question of how many. Three more faced off against Thorne, keeping him from approaching her, while two more cornered off the other side of the bridge.

As the shield around her disappeared, Eliza struck; magic rushed through her, dancing through her veins. She felt it burn the tips of her fingers and she sent a wave of light out in an arc around her. Trolls fell—not dead but stunned—while others stumbled off the side of the bridge. Somewhere behind her, there were more screams.

Their clubs and axes clanged against steel as Thorne and the remaining trolls sprang into action. She wanted to check behind her, but the trolls she had knocked down were slowly getting to their feet— and they were *pissed.*

"I would kill ya," one troll snarled, spit dripping from his swollen lips, "but the master wants you *alive.*"

The troll struck out with one meaty hand, aiming to grab Eliza by the hair. She ducked with the intention of rolling away, but instead backed herself into the awaiting paws of another troll. He gripped Eliza's arms and pulled her into his body, the smell of rotten fish and stale water assaulting her nostrils.

"You're mine, pretty thing," the one holding her said, squeezing tighter. Eliza yelped in pain as the troll forced her to drop her sword.

Without thinking, Eliza started burning. It was a simple defence mechanism she'd figured out when she was young. When in a bad situation, she'd set herself on fire. She'd done it all of three times in New Orleans before she knew she could control it.

It was enough for the troll holding her to drop his hands and howl in pain.

A wave of dizziness washed over her before she picked herself off the ground, forcing herself not to sway. Thorne fought his way to her, having cut down two trolls. The one Eliza had gotten rid of was still screaming over his burnt hands, and those who surrounded her now watched in wary fascination.

She didn't give them a chance to attack as she picked up her sword and ran. Eliza threw all her energy into leaving the bridge and making it onto solid, sturdy ground. Where, she hoped, the trolls wouldn't follow.

Unfortunately, Eliza wasn't fast enough.

A hand closed around her ankle, sending her to the ground once more. Eliza reached out a hand to stop the fall, and instead landed heavily on her wrist, yelping in pain. Gravel embedded itself into her palm, but as the pain washed through her, her hand grew numb.

She flipped over and reached out her good hand, intending to throw another blast of magic towards her assailant.

But the troll dragged her backwards, away from the safety of the forest beyond. Her clothes caught on the stone and tore, but the troll—who had his back to her, a wooden club in his other hand—paid her no attention. It even hummed a jaunty tune.

From where she was being dragged, Eliza couldn't see much of the fighting, but she had to assume that Thorne was making headway with the other trolls. She could hear grunting and cries of pain over the pounding of her own blood, but she couldn't be sure who they belonged to. Had they taken Thorne down? Were they now terrorising the people?

She threw her hand up as heat warmed her, racing from her core and up her arm. The fire formed in the ball of her hand until it was the size of a softball, and she threw it at the troll. The force knocked him into the ravine, the echo of water splashing forcing her to turn to the next assailant.

Eliza scrambled to her feet, wincing as pain sliced through her. She surveyed the area, spotting two trolls left standing, deciding on whether they should continue fighting Thorne, or if they should just go straight for Eliza. The civilians that had managed to cross were now nowhere in sight.

They could very well be dead, as far as Eliza knew, but she hoped Thorne had helped them escape.

"He knows you're coming." Eliza spun to face a withered troll who grappled to pull himself over the edge of the bridge. "The Dark Master. He's always watching. He's always there."

Eliza's heart stopped in her chest and a coldness seeped into her bones. Icy fingers seemed to grasp her from behind and encircle her neck, and she choked back her response, because there was *nothing* she could say to that.

Before she could form any kind of answer, the troll smiled and slipped down beneath the bridge. Those remaining followed suit, leaving Thorne and Eliza alone with the sinking sun, and her sinking gut.

The Dark Master. Somewhere, in the back of her mind, a memory tugged at her. But she caught sight of the commander, who sunk to his knees at the foot of the bridge.

The breath rushed from her lungs. "Thorne!" Eliza ran towards him and threw her arms around his neck, breathing in his familiar scent—of freshly cut grass and the calm before a storm. His face crumbled as he wrapped his arms around her.

They sat there, folded upon one another, breathing. "I thought I'd lost you for a moment there," she said, unable to speak any louder than a whisper. The trolls and their words echoed in her head. "That wasn't a coincidence."

Thorne shook his head, dark hair falling in his face. Several cuts marred his skin. His lips parted, and it was then that she was aware how close they were to one another.

Before he could reply, Eliza pulled away, and cleared her throat.

Something in his eyes darkened, and his smile was strained when he finally replied, "You can't get rid of me that easily. We still have a mission to complete."

16

DRAGONS OF GOLD

The admission of the trolls echoed in her head. *The Dark Master.* The name tickled something in the back of her mind, like she'd heard the words before, in passing, or spoken in a different context. It sounded like a nickname passed on to Voldemort in *Harry Potter*, but—*no*. It was the way it had been spoken that grated against her memories.

They stopped as soon as Thorne declared they were a safe distance from the bridge and away from any trolls that might be lurking in the nearby forest. Eliza's heart hadn't stopped hammering.

The sky above them opened and a misty rain covered Eliza's clammy skin. She lifted her face and let it cool her. But it didn't quite calm her; it only made her more aware of her surroundings. There was someone searching for her, someone powerful enough to command the loyalty of the ancient trolls.

"What happened?" the commander finally asked. His voice wasn't harsh but rather, tired, worn from the fight.

Swallowing, Eliza shook her head. "I don't know." The words wouldn't form in her head, at least not in a way that would make sense. Eliza ran her tongue over her bottom lip. "They—the trolls—they wanted me, wanted to hand me over to their 'Dark Master'."

Thorne stayed quiet for a moment, unable to meet her stare. "We were lucky," he said, voice low. "What are you thinking about the Dark Master?"

"Nothing." She released an irritable sigh and hung her head. The cool rain brushed over her neck. "I wish I had something, but I don't. One of the trolls, though... they said something that caught my attention."

He gave her an expectant look, brows raised in question.

"They said the Dark Master is always watching. That he knows I'm coming."

She was afraid, terrified, of what this Dark Master could mean to her and the mission, to her life and the lives of her guardians. That fear ate at her insides, chipping away at the wall she'd placed around herself after their failed attempt at following the tunnels. Finding the prince was enough of a challenge, but with the Dark Master and the presence of the Blood Witches at Eliza's back...

She sucked in a choking breath. *Freedom. For me, for Grandpa, for Kay.* Eliza needed to protect her family. The Dark Master, for all she knew, was nothing more than a scare tactic.

But that small kernel of hope she so desperately tried to cling to was slowly being chipped away.

A chilled wind swept over the desolate road, picking up her hair, which had come loose from the braid she'd had it in. Thorne's hair ruffled only slightly, despite its ever-growing length. The thick, low-lying clouds hanging over them only threatened more rain.

"We should find somewhere to set up camp," Thorne finally said, his voice a whisper. Above them, a crack of lightning illuminated the sky.

Eliza grimaced when the thunder followed. "I suppose we'll make it a two-day ride to the capital?"

~

It was during the second day that she noticed a change in scenery; although the area around her was a maze of jutting mountains and rolling hills towards the ocean, there were expensive mansions dotting the landscape, each one just as beautiful as the last. The shadows of darkness infected that façade of beauty though, touching it in simple ways; rotting vines and blackened trees, abandoned buildings and dull faces peeking out from beneath hoods.

Driveways paved with loose pebbles broke off from the main road they travelled on, leading up to the occasional estate. Most of the homes had an old, eastern European feel to them, decorated with iron balconies and vines climbing up beige exteriors. From the road, Eliza could even make out fountains sprouting water, similar to the design outside of the king's old Spring Manor, though no goddesses were in sight.

Or ravens.

In the breaks of forestry and hills, there were wineries, which gave Eliza the image of Italy. How so many different parts of her world seemed to work their way into this kingdom, she wasn't sure.

Between the manors and winding streets lined with towering trees, the darkness rotted tree trunks where pixies and nymphs seemingly abandoned, grotesque buildings now skeletons of their former beauty. A dark reminder of what was happening in Cadira.

Every so often, Eliza sent out tendrils of her magic, feeling for the shadow that wormed its way through the land. Where there had been brightness, there was now darkness, and where there was once hope, there was now death.

She couldn't ignore it, either; tethered to the darkness, spirits dwelled in larger quantities than she ever would have imagined. They walked along the veins of blacknesss; phantoms locked in endless turmoil.

As they passed over a ridge, Eliza finally saw the entirety of the Cadiran capital.

Directly in the centre of the bustling metropolis stood the marvellous palace. Spires and turrets reached for the grey sky, and a wall stood between the castle and the common people. Statues and gargoyles decorated the eaves, while bridges branched between towers.

The palace glittered like quartz in the dying rays of the sun; from where they stood on the ridge, Eliza could plainly see the beautiful reflection of the palace shimmering in the clear water of the giant lake it was built by.

Around the perimeter of the curtain wall were multiple churches, temples, and what could only be the entrance to the Royal Catacombs below the palace. Eliza had seen the entrance sketched in her grandfather's books; two Gods, their names lost to her, hands clasped outside of the stone doors. Even from a distance, Eliza could make out the temple and the descent into darkness.

Surrounding the palace, Eliza could distinguish the social hierarchy that took over the rest of the bustling capital. The mansion-sized houses surrounding the palace were clearly marked as the upper class, with clean streets and gas lamps lining the cobblestone paths. Small parks dotted the area, along with blocks of townhouses, and what looked to be a huge shopping district.

There was a clear change in the working class quarters, as it rimmed the outermost city, leading into a darkened spot by the lake's edge that Eliza identified as the slums. Darkness did not spread as freely throughout the city; where she had expected to see lines of it feeding off misfortune, she could only see the streams of light, of... *hope*.

Her stomach dropped. In the distance stood the *Labyrinth Mountains*, home to the Blood Witch tribes. Protected like the Fae Territories, the mountains remained untouched by the worlds monarchs. There, the darkness did not spread; even it feared the wrath of the Blood Witches and their terrifying matriarch.

"We should go straight to the castle," Thorne said. Eliza peeled her eyes away from the mountains shrouded in low-lying clouds and looked to him. "Hopefully, the king will give you a room for the night."

Eliza frowned. "Just me? What about you?"

Thorne shrugged, wariness filling his eyes. "I have some business to go about while I'm here. I also have an apartment in the city. It'll be easier for me if I'm out of the palace." He smiled as if sensing her uncertainty. "Don't worry though, I'll still be with you throughout the day. You won't lose me."

Something didn't sit well in Eliza's gut about her having to stay within the palace while Thorne wandered the streets of the capital. What if something happened to him? She knew she wouldn't be able to live with herself if he was hurt. Especially after Clio and the attack on the Winter Palace.

He replied to her questioning look with a shake of his head. "I grew up in this city. I know it like the back of my hand. I will be fine, and you will be safe in the palace, with or without me."

Eliza narrowed her eyes. "Alright," she said, huffing. "But the minute you suspect that something is wrong, or if the Dark Master is around with his creatures, then you better be back at the palace. And we need to be out of here. The longer we're in one place..." she trailed off, unable to finish the sentence.

The longer we're in one place, the easier it'll be for the Dark Master to find us and attack. She hated to think it, but it was true.

Hopefully, he wouldn't touch the capital.

Thorne pursed his lips but gave a tight nod. "Let's get you to the palace first and go from there, okay?"

~

As the sky darkened, Eliza and Thorne quickened their pace through the bustling, maze-like streets. They didn't stop to marvel at the storefronts or relish the freshly cooked Cadiran delicacies from the street vendors. Eliza didn't even get the chance to take in the sights, as Thorne made it clear that they had to make it to the palace before nightfall. So, they rushed towards the sun-bathed palace, leaving the city in their wake.

The process of entering proved to be far easier than she thought it would. The anxiety of being turned away ate at her insides. She wondered if maybe the king would even let her stay, after what had happened at the Winter Palace; would he blame her for the attack and wish her gone?

Sucking in a breath, Eliza lifted her chin when the guards called her forward. "Name?" one asked, tall and heavily built, like Thorne.

"Elizabeth Kindall. I am here to seek an audience with the king, who should be waiting for me." The words tumbled from her with a kind of strength she didn't know she had. She almost smiled at the wariness that passed over the guard's eyes.

Instead of turning her away, the guard before her called a runner over—a lithe girl with red braids—who took the message and ran towards the palace, hopefully to the king.

The palace was not what she'd expected, but it was everything she had dreamed it would be. Spires of glass and white stone lifted the sky, the stained-glass creating rainbows despite the dreary weather. Every part of the palace's exterior made it look like a gothic cathedral and a whimsical fairy-tale palace had a child.

It took all of twenty minutes before a young man arrived, an easy smile on his handsome face. "The king will see Miss Elizabeth Kindall."

Eliza released a grateful sigh and ushered her horse forward, which was quickly taken away by another guard, who skilfully removed her gathered belongings and handed it over to an awaiting servant. Eliza watched with an open mouth as that servant rushed off in the direction of the palace, leaving Eliza with Thorne and the young man.

Turning to the commander, Eliza pursed her lips. "You might as well join me for the interrogation, Commander."

Despite the less than enthusiastic look in his face, Thorne forced a small smile onto his lips, and nodded.

A look passed between the on-duty guards, but they said nothing as Thorne handed the reins of his horse to another stable boy, stressing the importance that his belongings should be left with the steed, completely untouched.

Eliza and Thorne followed the young man past the wall of the palace and into the expansive courtyard. Hedges of bright green lined the cobblestone path they walked. Eliza spotted a well-dressed woman with a parasol in one hand, dressed in swaths of gold and sapphire and onyx that swallowed her whole, and a menagerie of servants trailing behind her. It reminded Eliza grimly of her dirty clothes and unwashed body.

When they were close to the entrance, Eliza stopped, brows furrowing. Halting the commander, she pointed at a gold mound to her left. "What is *that?*"

Thorne barked a laugh, while the young man stared at her, dumbfounded. "That's the Cadiran Protector!"

"What's the 'Cadiran Protector'?" she asked, frowning.

"A myth," Thorne said, just as the man replied with, "A dragon!"

Eliza took in the young man's lean physique and the sandy ashen hair that brushed his bronze neck. He was handsome in a classical way, different to Thorne, she thought. The young man's eyes were a startling emerald in colour, a much different shade to Eliza's. He wasn't as broad as Thorne either, though beneath the grey-knit sweater there was a toughness to him that reminded Eliza of her companion.

Eliza's brows shot up as she turned back to the commander. Thorne, exasperated, shook his head. The man's grin was wide and excited, and his green eyes only brightened at Eliza's obvious lack of knowledge.

"A mythical dragon?" Eliza crossed her arms over her chest, fidgeting. "I thought Cadira didn't have anything to do with dragons?" She directed her question to Thorne, but it was the man who replied, smile broadening still.

"During the Great War," the man said, "Cadira was desperate for allies. Which included getting help from the Dragon Riders of Laziroth."

Eliza couldn't help but smile in return, if only because she found his excitement infectious. The young man grabbed her hand, his fingers warm as they circled around her wrist. He dragged her towards the monolithic creature, bringing her around to its side so they could see the creature's full size.

The size of a blue whale, the dragon took up a large portion of the palace's front garden. Its sleeping figure was mostly obscured by towering hedges and a smattering of crystal-leaved trees.

The entire creature was gold, Eliza realised, almost like the body of the dragon had literally been dripped in a pool of liquid gold. She could make out clearly the veins in the beast's wings, and the slit of its eyelids. Every scale was refined and detailed, the claws looking like they could still rip a body apart.

Swallowing thickly, Eliza unconsciously reached out a hand.

Don't.

Eliza snatched her hand back. "This is really cool," she said, heart racing. "Which king commissioned it?"

"It wasn't made," the man said, still excited and completely unaware of the way Eliza's breathing had become unsteady. "A thousand years ago, this dragon actually protected Cadira from the forces of Valonde."

She directed a questioning gaze to Thorne, and he explained, "Valonde no longer exists. It disappeared beneath the ocean a thousand years ago when the Lazirothian Dragons and Cadiran Warlocks sentenced it to destruction. The war they waged was... it was terrible, the ancient texts say."

"Wow." Something inside her mind squeezed at a memory, a memory of endless oceans and the screams of people.

Remember.

Eliza shook her head. *Remember what?* She knew little of Valonde, of the war and what happened.

Thorne shrugged, his eyes on her. Something in his features darkened. "It isn't something that is taken lightly. The war killed hundreds-of-thousands, and it still hurts many to speak about it. An entire civilisation vanished. It's not something we commemorate normally."

"So, why memorialise the dragon?" Eliza asked. "Why not do something else?"

The young man replied, "Because if it weren't for this dragon, we wouldn't have won. She was the king's personal advisor and friend and

THE LOST PRINCE OF CADIRA

risked everything to bring Valonde down. She fell, right here, just like this." The man looked at the creature with admiration. "The king had a Blood Witch come down from the mountains and turn her to gold."

Eliza's blood ran cold. *A Blood Witch?* She hadn't realised that her hands had started shaking.

"My mother told me stories about it." The young man sighed wistfully. "I don't remember much. In Mesah they don't tell these stories often."

The young man's eyes were on the dragon, but his fists were clenched. What he'd said stuck with Eliza, even as Thorne placed a hand on her arm and said, "We should go see the king."

Eliza almost jumped out of her skin, yet her gaze stayed on the young man. She couldn't help but be intrigued over him. His eyes had darkened as he looked between the commander and her. But he shook his head and began leading them to the palace entrance.

Around them, guards began changing shifts, while servants bustled around the palace with work to do. Night now seemed to send a wave of silence over the palace and the capital.

Yet, even as they walked through the white-stone doors and into the front landing, Eliza couldn't stop thinking about the golden dragon, or the reappearance of the Blood Witches in Cadiran history.

The raven hadn't made an appearance since the troll bridge, and it half surprised her; mentions of the Goddess and the Blood Witches seemed to be following her on this journey of hers, but she couldn't quite connect the dots.

~

The king looked at Eliza and the commander with heavy lidded eyes, though she didn't dare try and seek out her companion as she slipped into an awkward bow. Bastian wore a robe; she hadn't even considered that he might have been otherwise occupied when they'd arrived, but she was grateful that he'd chosen to meet with her straight away rather than putting off the meeting for the following day.

"The last I saw you, Eliza, you were escaping into the night like a phantom," he said, voice tired. His dark eyes roamed over her, though not in a way that made her uncomfortable. His eyes never lingered where they shouldn't, and his gaze found hers almost immediately after. "I had thought perhaps that you had run away. Then you were spotted at the spring manor."

Eliza swallowed the lump that had formed in her throat. King Bastian motioned for them to enter the room; it looked like a parlour, or a tearoom, though Eliza didn't know the difference. She called it the tearoom, since a round woman with greying red hair settled a silver tray on a small table between her and the king. A teapot steamed, smelling of mint.

Armchairs faced a fireplace, while a deep burgundy rug, worn with age, covered the white stone floor. Windows behind Eliza looked out over gardens, though not the dragon. A fire roared in the hearth, warming the room enough to make Eliza sweat.

She shifted uncomfortably, unsure of how to answer, and cast a wary glance to the commander. The king knew she could see spirits, but Thorne didn't, and the longer she kept it from him, the harder it became for her.

"The day of the attack, I spoke with Commander Thorne and asked for his help in locating the Warlock, Amitel," she said, mouth suddenly dry. "The commander offered to help me. When the attack happened, I thought they were coming for me, because of the mission, and the commander got me out."

The king watched her carefully. "Many died that day."

Tears of shame and guilt burned behind her eyes. "I know. I wanted to stay and fight but—"

"I forced her to leave, Majesty," Thorne said, bowing his head. "I believed it would be safer if she got out under the cover of the attack."

King Bastian nodded, though he didn't look like he was paying attention to the details. "Have you found anything?"

"I met with Amitel. He gave me all the information he had, and then we went to the Spring Manor." Eliza cupped her hands around a cup of mint tea, though she felt no urge to take a sip. She took comfort from the warmth. "There was an underground city, and a tunnel which we believe was used to carry your son out. But I cannot tell you where. I don't want to put you or anyone else in anymore danger."

"Danger." The king scoffed, rolling his eyes.

Eliza set her cup down. "Please, Your Majesty, you're just going to have to trust me when I tell you it's best you don't know." She sucked in a breath and closed her eyes. *Time to tell him the worst part.* "I think the attack on the Winter Palace was orchestrated by the same person who stole the prince and sought me out twelve years ago. And I think they're hunting me now. Their leader might be going by the name 'Dark Master'. There was an attack at the troll bridge, where the *trolls* came after me."

The king watched her with dark eyes. "They could be unrelated," he said, but sighed in defeat. "But you do have a point. The attack on the palace was only the beginning. I thought perhaps taking you there and meeting with the army might ward off any chance of attack, but I was wrong."

She swallowed. "I'm sorry. I don't want to be here any longer than necessary, but I do need to ask something of you."

"And what might that be?"

This time, Thorne answered, leaning forward on his elbows. "Maps. We ran into Elder Ivo at the Spring Manor and found out that the Elders have access to resources that we might need to find the prince. We need you to ask for these resources."

"The Elders will not help," the king said, dismissive.

Eliza blanched. "Please. We need those maps."

She wasn't sure what it was that clicked inside the king's mind, but she saw the resolution before he uttered a word. "Alright. I cannot make any promises, but I will send word. I do not know if they will answer this request." He closed his eyes, weariness settling over his strong features. "What is it that you need?"

17

UNFOLDING MYSTERIES

Pale, white light filtered through the cracks between the gold drapes, bathing Eliza's room in a magical glow that could only be achieved by mid-morning sunlight. A tired groan escaped her lips as she rolled over in her bed, smothering her face in her pillows. For the first time since arriving in Cadira, she had managed to sleep without jerking awake from nightmares or being roused by Thorne. There were no slithering snakes or pesky pixies forcing her from blissful darkness.

All was peaceful, and she lay in the warmth provided by the heavy duck-feather duvet, unbothered by Thorne's snoring or the whining of their horses.

But nothing was simple, she knew, because she still had a mission to complete, and a prince to find, and a past to uncover.

That last thought, she understood, would unfortunately have to wait.

Eliza rolled over again and climbed out of the bed. She stretched her arms over her head, hearing the joints in her back and shoulders crack. Oh, how she enjoyed sleeping in a comfortable bed. Nothing compared to it.

But it didn't stop her stomach from churning. Thorne had left as soon as they'd been released by King Bastian. The commander had walked her to her room but had left as quickly as he could. He hadn't even left her an address for his apartment in the city.

Outside her window, birds sang. Eliza dragged her feet to the balcony and threw the doors open, wincing as the frigid air hit her. "Winter," she said, crossing her arms over her chest as goose bumps rose along her arms. "Right. Cold."

As she turned, Eliza caught sight of sandy-blonde hair and the broad, tall frame of the handsome young man from the day before. He hurried across the courtyard, an easy, wide smile on his face. He looked to be wearing palace clothing, though she wasn't sure.

She couldn't turn away, and as if sensing her, the young man looked up to her balcony.

Heat flooded Eliza's cheeks as she waved awkwardly in his direction before disappearing back into her room. She slapped a hand to her forehead and shook her head. *Good work. You made yourself look like an idiot.*

Eliza bathed and dressed quickly, all the while wondering if Thorne would find her. But as she brushed her wet, tangled hair, and pulled on her boots, she wondered if she should *bother* waiting around. Surely there was something she could do *without* him.

A knock at the door brought her out of her thoughts. She hurriedly tied the laces of her boots and stumbled to the door, flinging it open to reveal a green-clad messenger. They—beneath a large cap and caterpillar eyebrows, Eliza wasn't sure if it was a man or a woman—handed a note to Eliza and disappeared down the hall.

Her shoulder's slumped, disappointment flooding her. She bit her lip as she read the note:

Eliza,
I will be following a lead today. It would be safer if you
remained at the palace. The city is crawling with demons.
Thorne

She huffed. Crumpling the note into a ball, she threw it into the corner of the room before leaning back against the wall. *What am I supposed to do?* She couldn't just sit still; her blood thrummed with the need to do *something* to help. Knowing Thorne was out there looking for answers, leaving her to sit back in the palace, made her stomach twist. All she knew was that she couldn't stay in her room all day.

With that resolve, she left her rooms in search of answers.

Servants rushed through the halls, though none made eye contact with Eliza as she slipped down to the main floor of the palace. From there, she had no idea what to do; the gardens were easy to access but every time the doors to the palace opened a wave of frigid air swept through the foyer. The giant chandelier above Eliza's head rattled every time, like a warning. It gave her enough time to step out of the blast zone.

Several guards dressed in silver plated armour with shoulder capes and polished spears passed Eliza without sparing her a glance. Somewhere wedged in the tight formation, she heard giggling, and saw the plume of a feather sprouting from the centre.

Nobility. Eliza rolled her eyes and headed in the opposite direction of the procession. Pointed arch windows lined one wall down the hall, looking out over a small courtyard hidden by stone walls and vines. There were prettily dressed ladies in gowns of emerald-green with skirts that looked like tents, heavy cloaks, and white gloves. From the window, Eliza could see their breaths.

She sighed and put her back to the wall, feeling the chill of winter seeping through the stone.

Where is your sense of adventure? She could almost hear Kay's voice inside her head. She could almost imagine her guardian standing beside her with a wicked grin, leading Eliza farther into the palace.

Her stomach churned with the image; shaking her head, Eliza pushed off the wall and continued walking, eyeing the arched corridor with wonder. Light from the fixtures in the walls cast the ceiling in shadows, giving the creatures that dwelled in the darkness—several floating pixies, who peered down at Eliza with wide, unblinking black eyes—malicious features and dark expressions.

Only once did a servant pass Eliza, but the farther she went, the quieter it became, until Eliza was standing alone before a bolted door. Cobwebs that shimmered like diamonds glittered in the corners, and when Eliza tried the handle, dust covered her hand.

The door opened on creaking hinges to reveal a round room. Dusty red drapes lined the walls in all directions, and a black grand piano stood on the other side of the room. The floor was a giant mosaic of what Eliza could only assume was the Fae Territory; a giant forest, the tips of the pine trees reaching the piano. The twin moons of Cadira, one full and one crescent, could be seen hidden beneath the piano.

Hidden in the dusty trees, Eliza made out the sharp faces of the Fae.

"What are you doing in here?"

Eliza jumped and spun around. The man standing behind her had silver-threaded brown hair that reached his shoulders, and hazel eyes shadowed with age. Lines marred his square face, and his lips were pressed into a thin, unyielding line.

He wore a navy-blue jerkin tucked into black breeches and knee-high boots. All his buttons glimmered gold even in the limited light. There was a flush to his pale cheeks, almost hidden behind a beard.

"Well?" he asked impatiently, tapping his foot.

Eliza looked around, searching for guards who were ready to kick her out on her butt. Yet none came. "I... Sorry, I got lost."

He lifted a brow before sighing. "Miss Kindall, you should not be wandering around the palace alone. His Majesty has requested that you be watched."

"Watched?" she asked, heart thundering. "What does he think is going to happen? And who are you?"

The man bowed his head briefly, though the look in his eyes told her that he wasn't impressed with her. "I am Advisor Inko. The king is worried that danger might come to you."

"I should be safe at the palace, though."

Advisor Inko nodded. "We also thought you would be safe at the Winter Palace, but you weren't. This palace is large, Miss Kindall, and while we take great measures to ensure the safety of everyone within these walls, there are still ways one can get in, especially if they are after something."

A shiver danced down Eliza's spine. *There are still ways one can get in.* Rather than risk any more embarrassment—being berated by a man she didn't know and who clearly knew of *her* was bad enough— Eliza nodded solemnly and stepped out of the dust-covered room, moving around the advisor as he closed the door behind her.

"What's the room for?" Eliza asked. She twiddled her fingers as the advisor peered down at her with furrowed brows.

"It used to be a smaller ballroom, but it hasn't been used in over twenty years." He started walking, Eliza hurrying to catch up. "The king would prefer that you *didn't* poke around the palace."

Of course, he would. Eliza tried not to snort as the advisor guided her back to the palace entrance. What else was she supposed to do?

~

Eliza proceeded to get lost another four times—two more ballrooms, and two court gatherings, and each time she was conveniently saved by the king's advisor, who in the end strictly decided Eliza *shouldn't* roam the palace on her own. Or at all.

Someone doesn't like babysitting duty, she thought, crossing her arms. She watched the advisor leave her in what she *hoped* was the hallway where her room was. He hadn't specified *where* she was, though she doubted he'd give her any more clarification than *stay put*.

Eliza sighed and looked down either end of the hall. There were no servants dancing around her, no guards peering down at her through the slits in their helmets. The advisor's footsteps had long since faded, now but a distant memory.

What am I going to do now?

"Lost?"

For the second time that day, Eliza almost jumped out of her skin. She whirled around to face a grinning spirit; half hidden by the wall. His face was youthful, round, but the glimmer in his eyes told Eliza he was older than he looked.

"Actually, you look bored," he said, cocking his head in a bird-like manner. Russet hair fell over his face as he looked her over. "I could show you something fun."

Eliza cocked a brow. "Aren't you surprised that I can see you?"

"You wouldn't be the first. Doubt you'll be the last," he said with a shrug. "So, you in?"

Her heart pounded, and her uncertainty wavered; the advisor had told her to stay put, to stop looking around. But he had told her to stop wandering around on her *own*. If she had a spirit to guide her through the palace...

"Alright," she said with a sigh. "What do I have to lose? Think you can get me to the library?"

The young boy snorted. "Of course. Is *that* where you were trying to go before?" He disappeared behind the wall, voice but a whisper as he continued, "You have a *terrible* sense of direction."

The wall the spirit had disappeared behind groaned, a section splitting off from the rest of the hall. It disappeared into darkness, setting Eliza's nerves on edge.

"Are you going to be helpful?" she asked, sparing the young spirit an irritated glance. She stepped into the darkness and looked around, jumping as the door closed. "Or are you going to spin me in circles?"

"I'm going to help," he said. There was a spark of light, and the thin corridor they had entered lit up with candles hidden behind dusty glass sconces. A cheeky grin spread across his dead face. "This way."

Eliza followed the spirit despite the uncertainty that swirled in her gut. As they walked, Eliza noticed indentations in the walls where doors would be, and occasionally they stumbled across rickety stairs that reached for the upper or lower levels.

Maybe I should have just asked the advisor for help.

Dust rose with every step Eliza took. "What is this?"

"An old servants' passage."

She coughed and waved her hand in front of her face. "They don't use this one anymore?"

The boy looked back at her. "Nope. Couple of servants died in here. Guards too. You'll see soon. Closed this one up."

Eliza shuddered and wrapped her arms around herself. "Then why have you brought me in here? Is it even safe?"

Oh, Gods, what have I gotten myself into?

She could almost imagine the horror movie scene she was walking into: darkness, rattling chains and creaking floorboards, the bitter, metallic smell of dried blood, and then—

The young boy stopped and turned to her. There were no indents in the walls where the doors should have been. *Where the hell am I?*

"You've gotten me lost, haven't you?" she asked.

He shrugged. His body grew transparent. "Have fun getting out."

"No!" Eliza lunged like she could hold on to him, like she could drag him into the dark with her. But the boy vanished, leaving her alone in the dusty passage with only the lights of the flickering candles to keep her company.

I'm going to have to walk all the way back and find a door, aren't I? She just hoped a little bit of magic would get her out of her sticky situation.

So, she started walking, keeping her footsteps light, remembering the deaths that the spirit had listed. Part of her wanted to brush it off, but with the amount of dust that coated the passage... She could at least be sure no one used the passage anymore.

"Why did I do this?" she wondered aloud. "I could have said no. I could have walked away or found my room. But *no*. I just had to—"

She broke off with a screech as a panel in the wall beside her opened. A hand grasped hers and pulled her out into the bright hall of the palace.

Eliza spun to face the handsome young man from the day before; his sandy hair swept over his brow as he looked down at her, an amused quirk to his full lips. Laughter danced in his eyes as he looked her over; it was then that Eliza realised the state of her clothes and hair, which were both dusty and ridden with cobwebs.

"That didn't sound like fun," he mused, releasing her arm. With both hands free, she watched silently as he toyed with a candelabra, which pushed the wall back into place. "Although I'm not sure *how* you managed to stumble across something like this."

I stupidly followed a ghost in there. Then he left me. Little shit. She didn't say that. Instead, Eliza shrugged, cheeks warm. "I got dropped off by the king's advisor. He told me to stay put, and..."

"And instead you decided to play with the walls?" His eyes were pretty as they danced between her and the now sealed door. Eliza could almost imagine it hadn't been there to start with. "Something could have happened. It isn't safe."

She couldn't help but roll her eyes. "Yeah, I know, I got the memo from Advisor Inko. *Don't wander around the palace alone.*" She sighed. "Look. I just need to get to the library."

"All you had to do was ask."

The young man lifted his hand in an 'after you' kind of gesture. Eliza began walking, her stride slow. There was something about him that drew her in. The better part of her was telling her to not follow, to do as the advisor instructed and go back to her room. But the curious side wanted to know more—about the palace, the world, and maybe about *him*.

But something deep within her forced her to keep walking with the young man. "I'm Eliza, by the way," she said, offering him a smile.

His own smile widened. "Dorin."

Her grin widened to match his. Looking away, Eliza tried not to think too hard on her current situation, especially with Thorne always in the back of her mind, reminding her of all the complications in her life.

She was good at not getting tangled in the webs of boys and broken hearts. When she looked at Dorin, she could tell that's exactly where this charming man would leave her. There was no point in befriending him. In the end, it would prove more trouble than good. It could get him killed.

As it was, the maps would arrive in a matter of days. She and Thorne would be gone, off to Mesah, and she'd likely never see Dorin again.

They stopped at a set of doors; Dorin bowed at the waist, smile still playing at his lips. High above them, the windows let in golden light that reached Dorin's sandy hair. In this light, it looked almost golden, like the halo of an angel.

Eliza cleared her throat, reaching for the library door. "Thanks for your help," she said.

"That's alright." He turned to leave but stopped. "Honestly? This is going to sound strange, but I'm kind of glad I got to see you again, even if I was saving you from a servants' passage."

A smile cracked Eliza's face, and she laughed. "My hero."

Those wide green eyes, framed by dark lashes, brightened. "Always, Milady." He took a step back, then another. "Until we meet again."

Eliza hadn't the heart to point out that might not happen; if the maps arrived tomorrow, then she'd be gone, and she wasn't sure if she'd ever return.

18

LIBRARIES & STORMS

Eliza gazed longingly at a pile of palace records. If she were going to discover anything about herself, then surely, it'd be in there. She'd managed to find records from the year she'd arrived in New Orleans, though she wasn't even sure if the dates would correlate. How long after the attack had she spent in Cadira? Had she gone directly to New Orleans with Davis? Or had she been at the palace?

If only I could remember.

Biting her lip, she dragged the records to her. *I'll look into the prince*, she promised herself, though who was she kidding?

The first several pages were nothing more than stock intake, servant names—Eliza dog-eared that page, just in case—but paused at what looked like a new addition. The page had been shoved in and pasted down, the ink bleeding as if the writer had been rushed.

Eliza skimmed the contents warily:

Bastian had two legitimate children: Princess Emmylia, second of her name, Heir to the throne of Cadira, and Prince Alicsar, third of his name.

However, King Bastian also has one known bastard child. It is rumoured that he sold the child to Witches in order to hide it from the court and his wife. The child was never spoken of again. Some believe that the child never existed, and that its mother—who has remained anonymous for many years—has never been found.

Eliza's brows rose in surprise, though she wasn't sure why. Monarchs *always* had bastard children. *Well,* she amended, *maybe not always. But most of the time.* Eliza couldn't help but wonder what might happen if the king were presented with his bastard child. With a second option.

She shook her head, disgusted in herself. *They're people, not objects.*

There was nothing else about the supposed bastard, leaving Eliza with more questions than answers. There was nothing about herself, either.

Her disappointment flared; sighing, Eliza reached for a geographical tome about Mesah and slid the thin, red leather-bound book towards her. The face was worn soft, the corners bent with age.

Mesah, for the most part of a millennium, has been overrun with ancient magic unfamiliar to even the Blood Witches of the Labyrinth Mountains.

Eliza rubbed at her eyes. *Yeah,* she thought, *no shit.* Sighing, Eliza looked back to the page with bleary eyes, thoughts drifting back to Thorne and his whereabouts, and then to Dorin, who seemed to be at the edge of her mind. She couldn't escape it.

And again, she read.

~

Rain thundered outside her room; the downpour hadn't stopped since early this morning, flooding the streets and games park of the palace, leaving most confined to shelter. Thorne had sent word to her, again, telling her he'd be somewhere in the city until the evening, and it left her stomach churning.

Eliza hadn't seen him since arriving at the palace the day before.

She hadn't bothered leaving her room, anyway, too wrapped up in palace records and books she'd borrowed from the library. Her fingers skimmed the weathered pages, careful as she flipped through the pages of a dusty tome. Every new passage had her heart accelerating as if she expected to find an entry about her past. But disappointment flared every time she found nothing.

Why am I not surprised? I mean, it's not like the king is going to keep a detailed record of my life laying around. Still, it left her feeling more disappointed than she had been over the tunnels. Something as simple as finding the names of her birth parents shouldn't be as hard as it was proving to be.

Groaning, Eliza flopped back on the bed and scrubbed tiredly at her eyes. It was already nearing midday, she was hungry and a heavy feeling of foreboding had settled on her chest and wouldn't lift. It had been like that since she'd entered the city and hadn't lifted since.

With Thorne *out* doing whatever it was he was doing, Eliza wondered what her next course of action should be. She was still waiting on the maps of old Cadira, ones that might reveal to her the locations of the portals and the tunnels. It was a long shot, given that Henry Ivo had already told her that those kinds of records were kept under lock-and-key.

But why hadn't the Elders shared that knowledge earlier? Probably because they didn't care. What's one prince in the grand scheme of things?

With a shake of her head, Eliza slipped from her bed and pulled a heavy coat over her shoulders. Her spell book fit into a satchel, resting beside a book of Cadiran history that Eliza had pulled from the library. If Thorne wasn't there to help her, then perhaps she could find something to help herself.

At least now she knew how to get from her room to the library without trapping herself in the walls or walking in on court meetings.

Eliza dodged servants with tea-trays, their faces blank and eyes cautious. They all wore simple clothing: white aprons over beige or black dresses, slacks and simple tunics and vests. Every so often, Eliza thought she saw Clio, with her fiery red hair and enthralling green eyes, but the familiar face was lost amongst those of the living.

Clio was dead—spirit bound to the Winter Palace—or gone. Eliza would not round a corner and face Clio again.

The thought brought up bile in Eliza's throat.

"Eliza!" She paused at the landing of the stairs and waited as Dorin—bright eyed and grinning, cheeks pink with the cold—caught up with her. He was dressed casually, black breeches and a deep-green sweater sprinkled with rain. His boots were wet. "Hi."

Eliza's heart fluttered, though she tried to stop herself from showing anything more than pleasantness. "Hey."

"Haven't gotten lost again, I see." He looked her over with a smirk.

"Shame. Looks like my services have been rendered useless."

Eliza couldn't help but smile. *What is it about him?* she wondered. *This is just a shallow appreciation of a pretty boy*, she decided, *nothing else. What do I even know about him?*

She forced herself to start walking again, to make her way down the stairs. Guards peered up at her through the slits in their helmets but didn't make to step towards her or speak.

Dorin followed close behind, the sweet smell of rain and wet grass following his movements. At the foot of the stairs, Eliza paused and looked up at him.

"Look, Dorin, I know you mean well..."

"Oh no," he said, cocking his head. "You're going to tell me to go away, aren't you?"

Eliza's cheeks blazed, shame mingling with guilt. "I'm sorry."

"Don't be." Dorin smiled sadly. "I get it. You have better things to do. And not to mention your... friend."

"Friend?" she asked, brows rising. Eliza's cheeks blazed a fierce red now. She crossed her arms over her chest tightly and gave him an embarrassed laugh. "The commander? He's my friend and nothing more."

Now Dorin's cheeks blazed. "I'm sorry. I didn't know..."

"It's alright." Eliza shook her head and laughed again, earning a timid smile from Dorin. "We work together. That's why we're here."

Eliza started walking again, needing to move. Dorin trailed her.

She stopped. *Attraction.* She was attracted to him. But there wasn't some deep pull in her like there was with Thorne. It was simpler, just a basic attraction, that she might just blame on being lonely.

Dorin stepped in front of her. "Come with me," he said, holding out a hand. "I want to show you something."

Eliza bit her lip as she looked between him and the bleak weather outside the window. There wasn't much she could do, not without Thorne. Where was the harm?

Kay would have jumped at the opportunity, at the adventure. Kay wouldn't have let anything hold her back. That's what Eliza admired about her guardian; a woman who defied her court, who did what she believed was right, and who took her punishment without an ounce of fear.

That's who Eliza wanted to be in that moment, staring at Dorin's outstretched hand.

Without another moment's hesitation, she wrapped her fingers around his, and let herself go.

~

"Where are you taking me?" she asked, unable to help the hint of curiosity that entered her voice. She looked up at the handsome young man, raised a questioning brow, before tugging hopelessly on the hand that was still gripped in his.

He laughed softly. "It's a secret."

"Oh no." She shook her head, smiling. "No, no, no. Nope."

"What?" he asked, turning to her. "Are you afraid?"

Eliza rolled her eyes. "Of what? Being alone with a stranger who plans on taking me to a secret location? Who won't *tell* me where we're going? Who could possibly be a murderer in disguise? Of course not."

He laughed and pulled her towards him. "Come on. Don't you trust me?"

She raised a sceptical brow in response, and his laughter filled the darkness once again. "Seriously though," she said, pulling him to a stop so she could look around the corridor. It was unfurnished save for a row of faded tapestries that could barely be deciphered. There was nothing exciting about the space. "Where are you taking me?"

Eliza's thoughts wandered back to her brooding partner, who she hadn't heard anything else from since his note about remaining in the city. Her stomach churned. A whole day had passed since she'd seen him, and in that time, she hadn't been able to prevent the mess of thoughts that had arisen in his absence.

Is something wrong? He'd tell her if there was, wouldn't he? She hoped so, though nagging doubt had wedged itself within her.

Why hasn't he come back? She bit her lip. *Why isn't he here?*

Part of Eliza knew there was a chance that Thorne wasn't just using his time in the city to find clues as to the prince's whereabouts; he had a life outside of the mission and her, one that seemed to escape even her notice. She'd missed the strange, immortalising magic that guarded him and instead had followed her gut in trusting him.

What did she really know about him?

"Is everything okay?"

Eliza looked up startled, forcing a smile onto her face. "Yeah, of course."

Dorin raised a brow. "Are you sure?"

"Yeah," she said. "Anyway, where are you taking me again?"

They resumed walking; Dorin looked over his shoulder with a crooked smile, eyes bright and hopeful.

Hopeful. Eliza's heart squeezed.

Dorin stopped at a towering door and looked it over, eyes narrowed. "I should tell you now," he started warily, "that we aren't actually *allowed* in here. However, I have a key, so..."

Without another word, Dorin slipped a key from his pocket and inserted it into the lock. Eliza watched with bated breath as the old lock clicked over, echoing in the quiet corridor.

The high, glass dome roof allowed for murky light to filter into the abandoned greenhouse. Light clung to the leaves of crystallised trees, bouncing off the petals of glass roses. Vines, black and murky green, slithered over the stone paths and climbed up the walls, encircling iron fixtures.

"Wow," Eliza breathed, pulling her hand from Dorin's to spin in a circle. The soft patter of rain against the glass filled the space. "This place... what happened?"

A soft smile played at his lips as he took the space in. "From what I know, this was the queen's pride and joy. When she died, the king had it closed off. Someone built a new greenhouse on the other side of the palace." Dorin paused and looked around, eyes glistening. "No one has been here since."

"Sad." Eliza shook her head.

Dorin shrugged. "Shame, really. Don't you think the queen would have wanted this place to stay alive? For her?"

"The king is still hurting," Eliza said, surprising herself. "Twenty years and he still holds on to hope."

"Hope." Eliza looked over to Dorin, who had seated himself on the rim of a stone basin. "Seems a bit late for that, don't you think?"

"I don't know." She should have said no—that there was always going to be hope. That was why she was in Cadira, wasn't it? *To bring hope back to the people.*

Eliza watched as Dorin picked something up and dusted it off before shoving it in his pocket. She raised a questioning brow.

"What?" he laughed, coming to stand before her. For a moment, their breaths mingled.

Eliza's heart quickened. *Is he going to kiss me?* Did she want him to? She wasn't sure. But she hesitated a moment too long, and Thorne came to mind. Reliable Thorne, who she would be leaving with.

"I'm sorry," she whispered, taking a step back. "I should go."

"Wait, Eliza."

But she didn't; Eliza hurried out of the greenhouse and didn't look back.

19

WARLOCKS & HEDGES

The icy air filled Eliza's lungs as she stepped out of the barracks, legs shaking and arms aching. She couldn't help but send a scathing glare in the direction of the commander, who had woken her at the crack of dawn to *train*, after two days of silence.

Eliza hadn't realised Thorne would push her so hard; the lap around the grounds served as a double warm-up, as it took them at least half an hour to complete at a fast jog. Then in the barracks, they had spent an hour working on her swordsmanship, then a half hour on integrating her magic into a fight, and then another hour on close combat with a dagger, because she couldn't handle a sword.

During the hours spent in the barracks and training fields, however, there was no mention of what he'd been doing in the city.

What a thorn in my side.

She was still waiting on the maps, and going on two days now, she couldn't help but start feeling impatient. All she'd managed to do was research and try to keep herself from seeking out Dorin.

Leaning against the doorway, Eliza sucked in a breath. Thorne was still inside, packing their weapons and discussing 'important' things with the in-house guards, but Eliza had to get out of there. Although well ventilated and open, the training space had started to feel claustrophobic after the first hour, and it had become hard for Eliza to breathe.

The hairs on the back of her neck prickled and a weight settled on her shoulders. She had the sudden sensation of being watched. Eliza closed her eyes, ready to reach out with her magic, but hesitated.

An image of a shrouded figure, donning shadows as a mask, rose from the depths of her thoughts. A hulking man, smoke and darkness emitting from his shadow-cloak. Demons from the deepest pits of hell surrounded him. Soldiers of death formed his army behind him.

He is always watching. A shudder ran down her spine. *So am I.*

When she blinked, the image was gone, only a figment of her imagination.

The barracks, situated towards the west wing of the palace, took up just enough space for the three hundred guards working the grounds, and housed their own kitchens, training facilities, board, and private stables. Thorne hadn't given her a chance to check out the layout of the manor-styled building, but she had an idea of what it was like, especially when he mentioned that all of the housing was located on the lower floors and underground. Connected to the lower level were tunnels that fed in and out of the palace, along with tunnels straight out of the city in case of an attack.

Tunnels. Like she hadn't had enough of them. During the days spent in the capital, Eliza had been more or less confined to the palace, and while she had *tried* to look around, she'd gotten lost one too many times.

Sighing, Eliza looked up to the blazing sun; it gave off little heat now that winter was in full swing. They'd already heard reports that the south was being ravaged by snowstorms—"*lucky for them,*" Thorne had muttered—but that same weather barely touched the kingdom's capital.

Cold air swept through the branches of the leafless trees. Gardens surrounded the barracks, leading all the way up to the palace proper. The scattered trees—weeping-willows and giant oaks—looked strange, tangled with the crystalline shrubs and glass rosebushes that made up the gardens. Eliza couldn't help but think the juxtaposition of foliage looked like it was out of a movie set.

A caw sounded from the tree in front of Eliza, startling her from her thoughts. Looking up, she narrowed her eyes at the gold-eyed raven dancing along the tree branch, sleek black feathers reflecting the sunlight. As far as she could see, the Knight was nowhere in sight, but that didn't mean he wasn't watching, waiting.

"Why the hell do you keep following me?" she whispered. Shaking her head, Eliza tried her best to turn away from the bird, when a figure across the gardens caught her eye.

Tall and narrowly built, Henry Ivo was easy to spot. Since meeting him at the remnants of the Spring Manor, Eliza had had a feeling she'd inevitably meet the Elder again. A wariness had filled her after their initial meeting, though she couldn't quite place where it had come from. Maybe it was because her grandfather had never mentioned him, or the fact that she still had that strange sense of recognition whenever she saw him. Something about it just didn't sit right with her.

Eliza stepped back into the safety of the doorway, entering the shadows, hoping the old Keeper wouldn't catch her eye. He stopped not far from her and looked into the trees. Following his stare, she glanced warily at the branch where the raven had once stood.

Ivo shook his head and began walking again, disappearing down a hedged pathway that led back to the castle.

Releasing a breath, Eliza turned back to the barracks and contemplated what she should do next. There was so much she had to still do, and yet she didn't have much to go on.

Eliza shook her head and scrubbed a hand over her face, stifling a groan. Without any word from the king, Eliza could only go back to research or wandering the halls of the palace until someone found her.

"What's wrong?" Thorne asked, eyes glazed with worry. He touched her upper arm lightly, fingers warm despite the chilled air.

Guilt seized her, but she forced a smile. "Nothing," she said, voice thick, "everything's fine."

His eyes darkened. "I was going to go into the city again, see if I can find us any more information. Since we're stuck here until the king gives us those maps." His brows furrowed as he looked down at her, though he hadn't dropped his hand. "But I can stay if you want. Help you here."

Eliza's mouth had gone dry, but she found herself shaking her head. "No, it's alright. I can stay here, research. You go out and look into whatever you have."

"Are you sure?"

She nodded, smile stiff. "Yes."

A look of disappointment flashed in his eyes.

I have to talk to him. She opened her mouth, ready to do so, but hesitated. Magic brushed against hers, light as fingertips. She recognised it—the trace familiar to Eliza's own magic. She reached out, heart racing, but it danced away before it could be touched. *What the hell?*

"Eliza?"

She searched the gardens, looking for... *someone*. Guards, servants, and nobility milled about the gardens, though none radiated familiar magic.

"Go into the city," she said distractedly. "I'll see you later."

Eliza took off, leaving Thorne standing at the barracks. He called after her, but she ignored him.

She dashed through the garden, heading in the direction of the palace. Several preening nobles looked in Eliza's direction as she passed but paid her no more attention than that.

The magic brushed against Eliza again, almost like a purr, sending shivers down her spine. She paused by a grouping of hedges and looked around.

An arm wrapped around Eliza's waist while a hand covered her mouth. Pulled back into a hedge, Eliza felt the leaves and branches scratch at her clothes. The hedge closed around herself and the assailant, locking them within the confines of the hedge.

Just as quickly as before, the hands were gone. With as much space as she was given, Eliza spun around to face Amitel.

"What the hell was that?" she asked, brushing away small twigs that had gotten caught in her clothes.

The Warlock shrugged. "I needed to get you alone."

"There are better ways than giving me a heart attack," she remarked, crossing her arms. "I could have attacked you."

A smile worked its way onto his lips, making his face appear younger. His eyes softened; golden hair slightly ruffled. "I'm over a thousand years old," he purred, eyeing her. "You couldn't hurt me, even if you tried."

Eliza blew out a hot breath, averting her eyes. "Okay." She drummed her fingers on her arm. "Why did you drag me into a *bush*?"

"It's a hedge," he said with a grin. "And to give you a warning." The smile disappeared from his face, and his eyes darkened. "Be careful with the Dark Master."

Eliza narrowed her eyes and stilled. "What do you know about the Dark Master?" Had he known about the master when they first met? She wondered, heart skipping a beat.

Amitel merely shook his head, golden eyes piercing hers. "Enough to warn you to be careful."

"I already know that." Her jaw clenched and she could feel her cheeks heating. "But how can I be careful when I don't know what is really going on?"

The Warlock was silent for a moment before replying. "I can't tell you much."

"If you tell me, you'll have to kill me?"

Amitel was not impressed. "It could kill someone else if I tell you."

Eliza's heart dropped into her stomach. She knew straight away that she should take the warning seriously, even if something inside her—the childish side that didn't want to believe any of this could be possible—couldn't quite comprehend that this was now her life. The fear she had been trying to supress for so long reared its head.

She gave a silent indication for Amitel to continue.

"I heard about the attack on the troll bridge. Your every move is being watched and monitored. This city could be attacked next. You *need* to learn how to protect yourself and hide your tracks."

Amitel released a sigh, and Eliza realised then that he looked nervous, like he, too, was being watched, *monitored*. "I can name only one kind of magic that could potentially keep you and Commander Thorne safe." He paused, eyes flickering over her face. "Blood Magic."

Eliza froze. *Blood Magic?* She should laugh at the absurdity of it, but the seriousness of the request chilled her.

Amitel continued, "I know it's dangerous—"

"Then don't ask!" she snapped. Her fingers trembled.

"Eliza, listen." His voice grew soft as he placed both his hands on her shoulders. "Blood Magic is about blood. You don't know it yet, but you have a strong connection to your blood. Use it."

"Why are you telling me this?" she asked, shuddering. Her voice would not go any louder than a whisper. "Why now? What's changed?"

Amitel's lips thinned. He shook his head again. "The game is always changing. I've just decided that I want to be on the winning side. Being stuck in the middle doesn't do me much good anymore."

Eyes narrowed, Eliza stepped back and bumped into the hedge behind her. "That's it?"

The Warlock shrugged. "That's all you need to know; all you should care about knowing." Something flashed in his immortal eyes. Fear? Or shame? "By telling you this, I've put both of us in danger. But the Blood Witches are the *only* beings that can outsmart and finish off the Dark Master."

"Then why don't they?" Eliza asked, suddenly angry. Red flashed across her vision. "Why don't these all-powerful Witches stand up and actually *do something about this!?*" She shook her head in frustration, clenching her fists. "Oh, right, because they can't do *anything*. They'll leave it all to the little guys, or only step in when it suits them!"

With a flick of her wrist, Eliza forced the hedge to reopen. "Next time," she started, chest heaving with emotion, "give me information I can *use*, rather than useless stories that don't help." She didn't turn around.

Eliza went to take a step but froze with his next words. "The spell I used to trap you in this hedge was born of Blood Magic. You merely flicked your wrist and undid my spell without even realising it." Fear swelled in her stomach. "Heed my words, Elizabeth Kindall, because they *will* help you on your mission, whether you think so or not. Beware the sands. They lie."

When Eliza turned around to question the Warlock further, he was gone, leaving only a pile of red sand in his wake.

20

THE BROTHERHOOD

Standing on the balcony of her room, Eliza watched the darkened sky with a frown. She'd tried to avoid the room as much as possible, but with Amitel's warning in the back of her mind and Thorne not giving her the whole truth, it was hard for her to settle down.

Instead, she eyed the golden dragon down in the courtyard of the palace, elbows resting against the balcony-railing. She drummed her fingers against the gold detailing, frowning at the figure that cut across the gardens. He was headed towards the closed palace gates.

Where is he going? The figure paused by a fountain, stopped by a set of guards. Thorne had told her he was going straight back into the city, but instead he'd stuck around at the palace.

Eliza sighed. *What am I going to do?* There was no way she was going to be able to sit still, not with what she'd learnt.

It took only a moment for her to let her curiosity get the better of her. She left her room without considering the consequences. Manoeuvring through the palace, she quickly ducked outside, entering the crisp night with only thoughts of catching Thorne before he left the palace grounds. Sticking to the shadows, she watched him shoulder his pack, horse nowhere in sight.

She crept out from her hiding place, inching behind a bush. Although she had no doubt that he could make any distance easily on foot, she hoped the lack of horse meant he was staying close to the palace. At least then, she decided, she'd be able to retrace her footsteps back to the entrance. And hopefully, she wouldn't get caught.

Sticking to the shadows, Eliza followed several paces behind the commander. There was an ease to his gait that she'd never noticed before.

Thorne turned a corner, passing under a gaslight. From where she waited, Eliza could make out his features; jaw clenched, Thorne looked like an avenging God with his thick brows furrowed and eyes focused on the path ahead. Despite the darkness around him, she could see his fists clench.

What is he doing? She considered turning around and heading back towards the palace. He didn't seem to be doing anything important, and part of her was disappointed. She shook that away, and guilt nestled within her instead. *What am I doing? This is Thorne!* Eliza took a step back, ready to return to the palace, but stopped.

Damned curiosity, she thought. She'd pushed aside her questions about Thorne and his past relationships, but now she was throwing it all away.

When he disappeared behind the next corner, Eliza crept forward, keeping her eyes peeled for both Thorne and anyone who might disrupt her sleuthing. If there was one thing she knew she was good at, it was sneaking around. Growing up in New Orleans, surrounded by the numerous cemeteries and nosy spirits, Eliza knew how to use stealth to her advantage. At a young age, it had become a rather useful talent, and there was no reason for that talent to go to waste, especially in Cadira.

The commander stopped at the end of the narrow alley, almost completely shrouded in shadow. At the other end, Eliza could make out what had to be a canal, branching off the main lake that took up most of the capital. Moonlight reflected off its surface, sending refracted light off the small, white-capped waves.

Eliza rushed across the street and into a shallow alcove, pressing herself into the sticky bricks at her back. From where she stood, she had a relatively good view of Thorne and anyone who might enter the alley.

She felt a small bubble of magic swell within her as she willed the shadows to her and hid herself completely from sight.

"It's been a while, kid." The voice, low and gruff, echoed through the alley, forcing Eliza to duck back into her hiding place, despite the magic that shielded her. A shiver danced up the length of her spine, and goose bumps rose along her arms.

I know that voice. She didn't know from where, but she

recognised it, like she was watching an animated movie with a well-known actor voicing a character, but one she couldn't place. *But how?* Was he someone from her past?

And why was the commander meeting with a stranger in a back alley?

Thorne grunted. "Not long enough," he replied. Eliza heard footsteps against the damp cobblestone, then the whine of a sword being pulled from a sheath. "Look, I wouldn't have contacted you if this wasn't urgent."

The man who had spoken before replied with a malice that made Eliza shudder. "You gave up the right to call on us when you left the Brotherhood."

The Brotherhood? Eliza peered out from her hiding spot; there were three of them, all tall, standing at least six foot, roughly the same height as Thorne. They each wore a hooded cloak that covered their faces. She couldn't make out their features, and she wasn't sure she wanted to. They looked dangerous enough, and the middle man—the one who had spoken—had drawn his sword.

Magic danced at her fingertips just in case any took a step towards the commander.

Is this what he had been doing? Eliza's gut twisted.

"I know." Thorne sounded hesitant, uneasy. Wariness rolled off him like a stench; like he didn't want to be there any more than the men around him. "But I need your help."

The same man barked a humourless, taunting laugh. "Our help?" he spat incredulously. "You want our help? Boy, after what you did—"

"I know what I did." Defensively, Thorne took a step back, and he lowered his voice. Eliza strained to hear what he had to say. "But I wouldn't be asking if this wasn't a life or death situation."

Another man spoke up, his voice kinder. Eliza strained to see him from the shadows. "Does this have anything to do with the girl you've been travelling with? The one who is supposed to find the prince?"

The blood in Eliza's veins ran cold as Thorne nodded stiffly. *How do they know about me? The mission?* The king had been firm in keeping it a secret—she was still surprised he'd even allowed Thorne to continue working with her.

But to be out in the open the way the commander was... Panic seized her, quick as lightning, and she searched with her magic for anyone who might be listening. She used her natural connection to the land to feel for life, but only found a strange, ancient force coming from Thorne and the three men.

What are they?

The kind of magic that radiated from them made her stomach twist. It reminded her of...

Several drunkards stumbled past the mouth of the alley, loud and obnoxious as they sang some gaudy tune about a woman in a flouncy dress. Eliza flinched, and wrapped the shadows around herself more tightly.

At the end of the alley, the four men fell silent, and Eliza could have almost imagined that they'd disappeared.

Finally, there was a sigh—she couldn't tell from who—and she stuck her head out from the alcove to watch them. "She cannot receive help from us," the kinder man said. Eliza noticed Thorne's shoulders drop at the words. "The power of the Ecix is her only hope."

Confusion swirled in Eliza's gut as Thorne's head shot up at the term. *What the hell is an 'Ecix'?* The blood in her veins ran cold, then boiling hot. She knew the word, just like she knew the men and other little things. Déjà vu just wasn't cutting it for her anymore. *What the hell is going on?*

She flinched again as Thorne stepped away from the three men, shaking his head. "No," he said, thrusting a hand through his tousled hair. "No."

What did he know?

The middle, scarier man nodded his head. "Yes." There was a pause that sent Eliza's stomach lurching. "I know you have a past with the Ecix. But the Ecix is the only one who will be able to guide your girl to where she needs to go. The Blood Witches foretold it."

Again, with the Blood Witches? Eliza pursed her lips. What did the Witches have to do with anything? They had a strange way of showing their heads when she least expected it, Eliza realised. Wherever she looked, there they were, eerily watching her. Just like the 'Dark Master'. *What did the Blood Witches have to do with any of this?* She wondered.

She was starting to learn there was no such thing as coincidences.

The kinder man picked up where the gruff one left off. "Because of our oath and your isolation, we cannot interfere."

So many questions swirled around Eliza's head. They muddled themselves in her mind until her blood sang in her ears.

Eliza had to admit there was a lot that she didn't know about

Thorne; she didn't know anything about his background, his past, or his family. Hell, she wasn't even entirely sure about his *age*.

"So, you cannot give me *any* information about what I seek? Nothing about the Dark Master?" Thorne asked quietly, almost like he was afraid to ask the question.

The kinder man shook his head. "We can tell you nothing else. Our oath forbids it."

Disappointment shuddered through Eliza; she hadn't realised that she, too, had been hoping they might say more. Even though she wondered about their motives and who they were, she wanted any— and every—piece of information she could get.

The breath rushed out of Thorne as he ran his hand through his hair again. "Alright."

But he didn't sound particularly disappointed, not like how she imagined he would be.

Confusion swirled in her gut as the commander turned his head, almost like he'd spotted her in the alcove.

The middle man clicked his tongue. "Anything else you want, boy?"

Thorne shook his head. "No. You've done enough."

~

It was the spirit of an old man in a white bed-robe that told Eliza it was safe for her to leave the shadows. She wasn't too sure how long she ended up staying in the alcove, replaying everything that had been said about her and this 'Ecix', but her knees cracked when she finally fell out of the shadows and into the dim streetlight.

How was she connected to the Ecix? And how did this all tie into the Dark Master and the Blood Witches? There was just too much she didn't know about this world. Hell, she didn't know that much about *herself*, it seemed.

Eliza released the shadows that had kept her hidden from Thorne's retreating form. She'd noticed that he had turned right, rather than left, heading in the opposite direction of the palace.

She had no desire to follow him that time.

Stepping out of the alley, Eliza turned left. The palace loomed ahead of her, spires and turrets now dark claws that reached for the heavens. They had an eerily menacing look about them as she headed towards the palace. The looming hedges behind the curtain wall didn't help the dark imaginings that swirled inside her mind.

A cold chill wrapped itself around Eliza, forcing her to stop in the middle of the street. Icy tendrils of doubt and darkness enveloped her now shivering body. The hairs on the back of her neck stood on end. Above her, the gas lamp flickered. In the back of her mind, she heard the word: *run.*

Taking off in a sprint, Eliza headed straight for the castle, bypassing the guards on duty. They called out to her, but none made a move to follow her.

In her haste, Eliza had completely missed the boy who had been standing across the street smiling.

She hadn't noticed the way his fingers had curled around a delicate blade, or his eyes: green, like summer grass, which hid the monster within.

21

SECRETS OF THE WITCH

Dark crescents lined Eliza's green eyes. Though she'd finally dragged herself from the comfort of her bed and down to the palace library, she still wished to be asleep, dreaming away all her unanswered questions.

She had to forget what had been revealed by Thorne and his acquaintances, but she found it hard to push the Ecix from her mind.

The sand. Eliza closed her eyes and heaved a breath. Two vials, cold with the winter air, filled with sand that could lead her straight to Prince Alicsar. She knew she needed to see Thorne, tell him about Amitel's sudden appearance and the message, but she stopped herself.

Eliza sucked in a breath and released it slowly.

She started towards a wall decorated with maps, hesitating when her eyes landed on the scarcely explored landscape known as the Mesah Desert. The only travelled areas of the desert were the outskirts and an old slave prison located close to the villages, tucked into a remote mountain range that once had been accessible by a river, Eliza noted. Every other part of the map was uncharted.

Beneath the map lay a large glass door cabinet filled with maps—none of which, Eliza mused as she picked through them, would lead her through the desert. If they did, she would imagine that the prince would have already been found. What she needed was an ancient map, and those were kept under lock and key.

Eliza pulled one of the maps from the case and started for a table. "Priority one. Make sure we aren't sent on a wild goose chase."

For the most part, the library remained quiet. Scholars kept to themselves, their robes a whisper as they walked the long rows of books. As she sat, she unravelled the map and used discarded books to flatten the edges.

She pulled the vials from her bag and set them down on the map. They rested atop the markings of the Labyrinth Mountains, home to the Blood Witches. Eliza pushed them from her mind as well. She didn't need to go over what Amitel had revealed in the garden. She didn't want to.

Swallowing thickly, Eliza pulled the stoppers off the vials and tipped the sand directly onto the map.

Closing her eyes, Eliza rested her hand an inch above the map, the tracking spell clear in her mind. The intricacies of the spell played out in her head; the draw from the magic of Cadira as she willed the sand to move, to wind its way back to where it came from. A warmth spread over her palm where it hovered over the sand.

The warmth disappeared a moment later. She released a slow breath before opening her eyes.

During the spell, the sand had moved, shifting so it covered the desert.

"Yes," she whispered, eyes widening. "*Yes.*"

They weren't on the wrong track. The sand Amitel had left her, and the sand from the tunnel, came from the desert.

Was the prince actually there?

The urge to tell Thorne rushed through her, but she still wasn't entirely sure about him, not after his meeting with the Brotherhood.

"Next priority," she muttered, standing, "figure out what the hell is going on with Thorne."

Eliza waved a hand and the sand returned to the vials. She tucked them back into her bag, before returning the map to the case. She started for a random wall of books next, hoping to find *something*. She couldn't tell if there was some kind of order to the library that she wasn't seeing. But then again, what she was searching for might not have been common knowledge, especially to the resident scholars.

Not if the Blood Witches were involved.

She sighed and shook her head. There may have been a scholar who could help, but she was too afraid to ask.

She didn't even know what the Brotherhood *meant*.

"Maybe I shouldn't even bother," she muttered, shaking her head. "Maybe I should just... let it go."

"Let what go?"

Eliza jumped and spun. "*You.*"

The spirit who had deliberately gotten her lost grinned. "Hello again."

"Go away," she hissed, starting for a different section of the library.

The boy reappeared. "But it looks like you need something."

"Not from you."

He pouted. "But I swear I can help!"

Eliza shook her head. "No, you can't."

"Tell me what you're looking for."

She stopped and looked him over warily. "Alright." She sighed, rubbing at her eyes. "I'm looking for anything relating to the Brotherhood."

The boy's eyes went wide. "Why?"

"Does it matter?" she asked.

"It's just..." The boy began floating through the stacks. Should she follow?

She followed.

"The Brotherhood are *legendary*," he said, stopping by the far wall. He pointed to a book, which Eliza cautiously picked up. "My brother went to join them."

Carefully, she flipped the book open, and to her surprise, found direct references to the Brotherhood. She looked up and met the boy's stare. "What happened to him?"

The boy shrugged. "Not sure. Never saw him again. Then again, I did *die* a month later."

"I'm sorry."

"What for?" He grinned. "Now I get to live *forever.*"

He disappeared before she could reply, and she huffed. "I don't think that's how it works," she muttered, "but okay then."

Book in hand, something inside of her changed. Perhaps it was the weight of what she was searching for, or perhaps something else entirely, but Eliza almost recognised the book in her hand.

Like she'd seen it before. Read it.

She shook her head. *Impossible.*

The main section of the library had a space dedicated to reading, so Eliza headed towards one of the many empty desks and sat herself down, the tome in front of her. The brown cloth of the cover had a layer of dust sticking to the leather, and when she finally opened to the introduction, Eliza spied crossed out passages, and it looked as if someone had gone through and torn out pages.

But she read anyway, her curiosity getting the better of her.

The Brotherhood are a league of warrior knights sworn to protect and obey the wishes and orders of the Blood Witches. They have existed for over seven hundred years. They were organised by the head knight, Aerelm Vyncis, who served under High Witch Valazena, and saw the resurgence of the Valondeans.

She stopped. She'd had an inkling that the Brotherhood had somehow been connected to the Blood Witches, but she hadn't realised *how.*

It is said they were created in response to a threat to the Blood Witches, though historians believe it was to combat the need for Blood Witches to converse personally with ruling Monarchs.

Brothers are chosen by a pool of young men presented to the Blood Witches. Only five from each group remain to take the Brotherhood's oath. There is nothing said about what happens to the others.

Men who join the Brotherhood do not leave. They take oaths that are kept until death. Once chosen, they are gifted with immortality and blessed by the Witches in other ways, most of which are unknown to us.

In recent years, they, like the Witches, have kept their distance from the neighbouring kingdoms. During the attack on the Cadiran King, King Bastian—

The passage ended there.

Eliza sat back and ran a hand through her hair. Her heart had dropped into the pit of her stomach.

Had Thorne's connection to the Brotherhood been the reason why he'd been so intent on joining her for the mission? Eliza tried to shake the thought from her mind, but... it seemed like too much of a coincidence to her.

She hoped it wasn't, but...

If she wanted to know more, be *sure*, then she'd need to brush up on her knowledge of Blood Witches.

Casting a glance over the library, Eliza headed towards a section dedicated to the magic of Cadira. Scholars dressed in grey robes filled the isles of this section, some pulling manuscripts and scrolls from the hard-wood shelves, while others packed them away. There was one section though, that caught Eliza's attention: Blood Magic.

That part of the library was cordoned off. Glass surrounded the books and scrolls in that area, while two guards stood idly by, hands clasped in front of them, their weapons just in reach.

Eliza stopped a young scholar. "Why are those books under lock and key?"

The scholar hesitated before answering. "Since the prince's disappearance, the king has had all books regarding *that* kind of magic stored away for safe keeping."

"Why not just destroy the books?" This time, Eliza met the stare of the scholar, who shook her head.

"It is not that simple," she said, frowning. "They are ancient tomes that have been interlaced with their own unique kind of magic. They simply cannot be destroyed."

Pulling away from Eliza, the scholar girl bowed her head. "Sorry, I cannot be of more use. Only the Masters know the truth behind those books." She hurried away without another word, leaving Eliza standing alone.

Gods, the restricted section of Hogwarts would have been easier to infiltrate, she thought bitterly, pursing her lips. None of the scholars made any attempt at even looking *into* the case, almost like casting your eyes on the forbidden magic was grounds for treason.

Something within her recoiled from the case. But something *else* wanted her to go in and take what she wanted. Magic warmed the tips of her fingers. *One simple spell...*

"If you want to read what is within, then all you need to do is ask."

Eliza, startled, turned to face a green-skinned, blue-horned woman. A long burgundy cloak covered her tall body, matching the colour of her piercing eyes. Hands clasped in front of her, the woman eyed Eliza.

Something twisted in Eliza's stomach. Since arriving in Cadira, Eliza hadn't seen any of the Faery beings. Like herself, they were the offspring of the Fae and mortals, though rather than having the pointed ears of the Fae, they were touched in other ways.

It still startled Eliza to see them look so human yet so different. Though rare, Eliza couldn't help but be amazed by the beauty of the scholar.

"Do you want to know what is inside the case?" the woman asked, a smile forming on her face. "Or do you just want to stand there?"

"I, uh..." Eliza trailed off, unsure how to answer. It seemed almost too easy, being able to just get what she wanted.

The horned woman cocked her head. "I can see the uncertainty. It wars within you."

Eliza bit her lip. "It's just... why are you letting *me* into that case?"

"I am under strict instructions from the king to give you whatever information you might need for your mission. If it means allowing you access into the forbidden shelves, then so be it."

Furrowing her brows, Eliza nodded half-heartedly. "Alright. Well, I need access to all the books on Blood Magic, if that's alright."

The woman bowed her head, pulled a key from her cloak, and walked towards the glass case. The guards who stood by watched Eliza closely, and watched the woman too, with an air of distrust. But the guards let them through without a word, giving Eliza enough space to gather old books into her arms, and carry them towards a nearby table.

"If you need any help, then please let me know."

Alone, Eliza set to work.

~

Hours slipped by without any thought. Eliza sat at her table, transfixed by the Blood Witches' magic. Ancient spells and curses marked the pages in a language she could barely understand. Not only spells filled the pages... at least three of the books she'd read had folklore and history about the Witches, though it was scarce. Despite being a very well-known and powerful coven, with tribes dispersed throughout the mountains, there was not much written about them. Most of their customs and history—even their exact whereabouts—were unknown.

The High Witch of the Blood Witch tribes has protected the secrets of the Labyrinth Mountains for centuries. There have only ever been three High Witches recorded since the discovery of these Witches. It is unknown if there were more, or for how long these Witches have lived in Cadira.

Some scholars theorise that the Blood Witches belong to the Brithien Elves, a species of Fae now rumoured to be extinct. The Brithien Elves, who are said to be the children of Thrinarv, King of the Gods, were enslaved in the old prison of Mesah before they disappeared. There are few left alive to know what the Brithien Elves looked like, or the kind of magic they wielded.

I am uncertain as to the reason behind the scholars' theories about the Blood Witches. There is no evidence—written or otherwise—that we have access to in order to make these assumptions. There is even a scholar who believes the Blood Witches descend and worship the Goddess Azula, though there is no evidence.

Other scholars claim that Blood Witches are Changed Ones (a Changed One is a being able to shift into their animal familiar). This magic has, for a long time, been inaccessible to regular magic users. Those who claim to attempt this magic—or curse others with this ability—have said that their magic has been cut off, or they have developed terrible migraines which have stopped them from further attempt...

Eliza stopped reading and sat back, drumming her fingers on the table. The lantern on her table flickered as the library descended into hushed whispers and quiet footsteps. Alone in her little corner, Eliza could almost imagine that she'd stumbled across these documents in a forgotten room.

She pushed the book away. Mentions of Mesah and the Changed Ones made her stomach roil. She'd suspected that the raven was a Changed One, but the idea that the Blood Witches were too, and that they linked to the Goddess Azula somehow...

Eliza rifled through another text about their history.

The Blood Witches created the Brotherhood, a sector of immortal Knights sworn to these Witches, in order to potentially combat an unseen threat against them. This threat, which has targeted leaders of the coven, cropped up after the Great War, when—

A sharp pain sliced through Eliza's skull, behind her eyes. She drew in a breath as she dropped the book, stopping her from reading on. Icy fingers wrapped around her throat, and her heart beat frantically in her chest. Fear gripped her stomach, leaving her gasping for breath.

"Miss Elizabeth?" The cold and fear quickly receded, and Eliza sucked in a deep breath.

"Miss Elizabeth, this is for you." A green hand reached out and placed a folded note onto the book in front her. On the front, scrawled in a neat and legible hand, was her name.

With frozen fingers, Eliza opened the letter and read through its contents quickly.

Miss Elizabeth,
I apologise for the lateness of this letter, but I must see you at once.
I will be awaiting your arrival in the catacombs.
King Bastian

Fear gripped Eliza's chest once more, but not like before. Instead, she pushed it down and nodded to the scholar. "Thank you," she said, swallowing the lump in her throat, "I don't think I'll need these books anymore."

The woman bowed her head. "Of course."

Eliza thanked her, and without another word, followed the guards to the royal catacombs.

22

SECRETS OF THE DEAD

The catacombs were as desolate and creepy as Eliza imagined they would be. They stretched onwards into darkness, occasionally broken by flickering candlelight. Down there, the darkness was heavy and overwhelming, stifling. Eliza fumbled to find a torch, almost too afraid to call upon her magic after the episode in the library. She didn't quite trust herself with that.

Her stiff fingers curled around the staff of the torch as she approached the darkness with a straight back. She knew the king was down there somewhere, waiting for her, but now she wished he'd asked to meet back at the palace, despite her growing curiosity at what was down there. It seemed, no matter where she was—New Orleans or Cadira—she was always drawn to graves.

Eliza gave a quick shake of her head and quickened her pace, forcing her breath to come out evenly. She was sure that if she didn't quash her anxiety, she'd most likely run. Her chest tightened the farther she walked. Something about being underground with the dead monarchs of Cadira didn't sit well with her. Almost like she didn't deserve to be down there.

Thankfully, due to some old magic, there were no spirits haunting the underground graveyard. That gave Eliza a chance to release a breath of relief.

Ahead, there was a sharp corner, and beyond that she heard a voice. Deep and commanding, she didn't have to guess that it belonged to King Bastian.

Rounding the corner, Eliza noticed how the king stood alone, without guards and without any weapons. His dark hair had been slicked back, outlining the sharp structure of his face. He wore a plain red cloak over his broad shoulders, and a pair of black gloves. Standing tall and strong against the flickering torchlight, he looked like a wraith guarding the dead.

"I have been putting off having a statue created for my son. I keep thinking about how he will come home eventually and take my place as king."

Eliza swallowed the lump in her throat, unsure of how to respond. Was there even a chance that the prince was still alive?

"I have no other heirs," the king continued, voice soft. "I do not know what I will do if you do not find him." His gaze remained on the two statues he stood before, and it was then Eliza realised who she was looking at.

The queen, with a small smile on her narrow face, looked almost serene standing beside her daughter. Eliza tried not to think back to the vision the maze showed her, of their gruesome deaths. The blood, the gaping wounds. It almost made her sick.

How would the king memorialise his son? Would the statue be of an infant? Or would they wait until the king was dead, when they could carve Bastian's statue holding his infant son?

Guilt and uncertainty drummed inside of Eliza's stomach. She couldn't help but second-guess her abilities. She knew he was relying on her necromancy, but would that really be enough? Especially against enemies like the Dark Master and the Blood Witches.

Bile rose in Eliza's throat, panic seizing her, but she asked anyway. "I thought you had another heir?" She recalled the whispers she'd heard from her grandfather and Kay years ago, and the forgotten records she'd found in the library. "Would they not be able to rule after you pass?"

"I do," he said quietly, as if he weren't surprised that she'd asked. Eliza suppressed a shudder. "But it is not that simple."

"Isn't it?" she asked honestly.

A small, amused smile tipped his bearded lips. "There are some secrets, Elizabeth Kindall, that not even you can uncover. I know I have placed a tremendous amount of pressure onto your young shoulders, but I see no other choice."

"Have you been to see the Fates?" she asked, wringing her hands, hoping for some kind of assurance. Eliza thought of the far-off island where the sisters resided. Kay had told her stories of the Fates, though it was usually kings and queens of great empires who sought out their destinies.

The king's head dipped. "Indeed. They, too, have placed their beliefs in you."

Eliza's stomach rolled. "I don't understand why you have so much faith in me." She could no longer look at him, or the statue of his dead wife and daughter. Instead, she averted her gaze, taking in the bust of a hundred-year-old queen, perhaps forgotten by time, only to be memorialised there. Eliza shuddered.

"Because," he said, fully turning to her, reaching a hand out to the statue of his dead wife and daughter, "faith and hope is all I have left in this world. Without it, I'm afraid I would have lost my will to keep fighting long ago. And I would have given in to those who wish to assume power."

The king continued, "I cannot let just anyone take my throne. It should be my blood. Since what happened, I have been cursed with the inability to bear more children, and I do not trust any *bastard* child that I have."

"But you trust me?" she asked, lips thinning. Her heart raced faster in her chest. "I'm a stranger to you. Why?"

King Bastian's eyes were knowing as he gazed upon her. "I know that you will find my son, Elizabeth Kindall."

"How are you so sure that he's even alive?"

At that, the king smiled. "Like I said, I have faith. But I also believe that if he were dead, the Dark Master wouldn't be trying so hard to keep you away."

Her heart dropped into the pit of her stomach, and she watched as the king turned back to his wife, caressing her cheek lovingly.

But Eliza could no longer breathe; not in the catacombs, not with the stench of death and smoke filling her senses.

"Are you alright, Elizabeth?"

She looked up into the worried eyes of the king. Her blood pounded in her ears, and when she tried to speak, her mouth went suddenly dry.

Her heart thundered in her chest as the weight of the king's expectations finally settled over her.

Eliza took off in a stumbling sprint towards the catacombs

entrance, instead finding herself in a completely different section of the old, underground graveyard. Eliza breathed heavily as she took in the grey-block walls that surrounded her, and the yellowed marble of the royal statues that resided in the blocked-off tombs.

Queens with bowed heads, and kings with no heads surrounded her. Ancient and unforgiving, this part of the catacombs sent a chill down her spine.

Her eyes darted over the old statues, and the plaques that gave details of the monarchs.

Queen Kilandra, King Consort Gerome

Their heir resided in the next section.

The light of her torch flickered off the faces, and Eliza stopped at the reflection of herself etched in gold.

King Kamdon.
Ruler during the Valonde Wars, Rode the great Dragon
Zevanya.

Eliza looked upon the face of the young king. Beside him, there was no wife. The next ruler was his brother.

Immortalised, Zevanya and King Kamden led Cadira and
Laziroth into victory against Valonde. Featured, the Blood Witch
responsible for the immortalisation of Zevanya.

Eliza took a step back, and then another. Her blood went cold. She would have missed the bust had she not been reading, would not have thought to look at it.

But there, off to the side, behind the great King Kamdon, was *her.*

23

MASKS & MAGIC

You are hereby invited to King Bastian's Masquerade Ball. Within this package you will find appropriate attire for the ball. You will be expected after sundown.

Eliza shifted to show Thorne the note and watched as his eyes roamed over the words before picking up the box and sliding it open. "It's nice."

She cocked a brow. "*It's nice?* Thorne, do we really have time for a *ball?*"

"Do you have those maps yet?"

She huffed. "No."

"Then I don't think we have much of a choice. The king is planning something with this ball."

Eliza looked between him and the dress, brows raised. Sweat had dried along Eliza's brow after their long workout that morning; running through the gardens had done wonders in clearing her mind of the anxiety she was feeling about waiting. And had made her conveniently forget the catacombs as she'd been too focused on remembering how to breathe. Already, she feared that they'd been in the capital for too long, and the lack of attacks only made her stomach churn.

What is the Dark Master waiting for? She knew she shouldn't be thinking like that; she should be rejoicing in the lack of deaths in her name. But Eliza couldn't ignore the pit in her stomach, the ever-growing chasm of fear that seemed to expand the longer she waited.

Quietly, Eliza asked, "Do we even need the maps? Maybe it would be best if we just... left."

Thorne met her stare evenly, without judgement. She'd told him about Amitel and the sand, about the cryptic message, and she'd been prepared to talk about the Brotherhood, but had faltered when she'd spotted the box lying on her bed. Part of her had expected something to jump out of it and attack. But nothing had happened, except for a whole lot of tulle to escape the tight confines.

"We can use this ball to our advantage," he said, eyeing the gown. "We need those maps, Eliza. I don't think we should take the risk of leaving without them."

She sighed. "We've lost so much time already. And we know he's there." Eliza itched to leave, to finish the mission. It wasn't just her or her guardians' freedom on the line anymore; the lives of innocents were caught in the crossfire, dying because the king wouldn't compromise, wouldn't find another way.

"How much longer can we wait, Thorne? The Dark Master doesn't care if we have maps or not, he doesn't care about the tunnels. He cares..."

"Eliza." She stopped and sucked in a breath. Thorne rested his hands on her shoulders. His touch sent shivers down her spine. "I know I haven't been here for you the last couple of days, that I've been in the city and haven't told you much."

She swallowed. *Is he going to tell me about the Brotherhood?*

"But trust me when I tell you that *we have time*. We have to wait."

Eliza nodded sharply and eyed the dress again. She deflated slightly. "I guess I can't change your mind?"

"I honestly thought you might enjoy the break." When she looked back at him, he was grinning. "The king throws the most elaborate balls."

"Sure." She huffed, thinking back to all the dances she *didn't* go to in New Orleans. Thanks to being home-schooled, she hadn't had the chance to experience those kinds of mundane things. When she was fourteen, she had been invited by a boy from her neighbourhood, but she'd refused—chickened out, really. Kay had gotten Eliza a dress and everything. But Eliza had been an outsider in that regard.

What's one ball? she thought, biting her lip. *What's one more night?* Surely, she thought, the Elders would deliver maps the following day. What's one more night of faux freedom when her doom might be upon her in a matter of weeks?

Sighing, Eliza finally nodded. "Alright." *It might be my last one anyway.*

~

The gown wasn't as heavy as Eliza had thought it would be. The black chiffon fell around her legs, covering the extensive bruises and scrapes that spread across her body. The bodice itself was tied tightly around her chest, giving her cleavage an unnecessary boost, shaping her figure into something feminine. A thick black ribbon tied around her waist and knotted at her back, adding a flair of innocence to the look.

A young woman stood behind Eliza with black roses sticking from her mouth, skilfully winding them through Eliza's hair into an elaborate array of curls that fell down her back. Eliza watched in the mirror as the black roses were artfully pinned to her hair into a crown that wound around her head.

Eliza reached a hand up and touched her hair lightly. *Pretty*, she thought, lips parting. *I actually look* pretty. The mask she'd been given fit over her face easily. It was made from the same shimmering black material as her dress.

The young woman bowed her head and left the room. Eliza watched her, unsure of what to do. She'd wanted to thank the woman, but thoughts of Clio, of the winter palace and the fancy dinner, stopped her.

The night grew cold and dark, stars now scattering the clear winter sky, surrounding the moon that lit the city. From her room, Eliza could clearly hear the beginnings of an orchestra as they began testing their instruments, fighting a war against the howling wind that blew off the lake.

She stood from her vanity and grabbed a black cloak; the thin material fell to her feet in a pool of silk, but it gave her the protection she would need against the chilly corridors. Even with only her balcony doors wedged open, she felt the bite of the night seeping into her room, sending goose bumps along her bare flesh. The rest of the palace would surely be warmer, but she didn't want to take that chance.

"This is one night," she said to herself, wrapping the cloak around her hunched shoulders. "I just have to deal with one night of pampering and stares and *Gods* I need to stop *whining*." Shaking her head, she stepped into a pair of black boots and tied them at her ankles.

A brisk knock sounded at her door. *Thorne.* Eliza glanced at the time. He was early.

Sucking in a breath, she rolled her shoulders back, checked her lipstick, and walked to the door.

Brandon Thorne stood tall in a tailored uniform; a black suit rimmed in emerald green and gold; the buttons of his coat polished to reveal pure silver. The coat reminded Eliza of a British general's uniform from the eighteenth century. Several medallions lined his right-breast pocket, some gold and others silver. *Merits of war.*

Overall, he looked... *handsome.* Her lips parted as she looked him over, from the slight tousle of his dark hair, to the storms of his eyes, and the line of his lips. The plain mask he wore highlighted the sharp lines of his features and made his eyes look darker.

"Is something wrong?" Thorne asked, voice low. Pink brushed the bronze of his skin, high on his cheekbones.

Eliza looked up from his lips, cheeks heating, and gave him a smile. "Of course not."

Thorne offered his elbow and Eliza took it with trembling fingers. "You look..." Thorne shook his head, colour rising in his cheeks.

Eliza was forced to remember what he told her in the tunnels, about his past love. *It can never be anything more*, she thought. Not with his secrets about the Brotherhood, about his past.

The corridor seemed uncharacteristically quiet despite the gradually building tempo of the orchestra in the ballroom, the music echoing hauntingly throughout the hall. Eliza had expected all kinds of people to be rushing around the corridors, preparing for the unexpected ball, and yet, she and Thorne were the only ones in sight.

There was an unnatural chill in the air too, but Eliza tried to ignore it, despite the churning in her stomach.

"Are you still sure this is a good idea?" she asked, voicing her doubts.

Thorne looked down at her, a wisp of dark hair falling into his eyes. She yearned to reach up and brush it aside, but her hands wouldn't move. "Yes. I know for a fact that someone important is going to be here tonight. We may need their help... if they offer it."

Eliza swallowed thickly. She wanted to ask if it had anything to do with this 'Ecix' he was hiding from her, but the words wouldn't form on her dry lips. Guilt stopped her from asking.

Eliza returned her gaze to the empty hall.

They descended the opulent staircase that led to the entrance of the palace but turned left towards the music. It floated steadily through the halls, gradually growing louder the longer they walked. Masks and feathers hung from the ceiling, while servants dressed in elaborate costumes lined the walls. They wore masks that covered their faces; some wore the faces of Fae—gold-skinned with silver eyes—while others wore the faces of horned monsters. Each carried a different drink though, and Eliza plucked one from a Faery-faced server. Thorne took one from a monster.

She sipped at the sweet beverage hesitantly. It tasted like a cocktail she'd tried in New Orleans, though she could feel magic on her tongue this time. She lowered the drink.

"The king doesn't joke around when it comes to parties," she murmured. Now, the hall was littered with guests who drank continuously from the glasses that lined the walls. Although she doubted they'd repeat anything she'd say—because she doubted they'd remember this night—she couldn't help but eye the few that did not have drinks in their hands. "Even the servants are dressed up. Gives the dinner a murder mystery vibe."

Thorne cocked his head so that he was closer to her. "This is all a façade. Remember that." His body tensed as they finally entered the ballroom.

Streamers of black, gold, and burgundy lined the walls and ceilings, while feathers and dripping candles of the same colour-scheme floated mid-air. Hundreds of people danced to the jaunty music of the orchestra, while others conversed beside a buffet table against one of the far walls. There were tables and chairs scattered about, too, but Eliza couldn't spot many using them. They were either too entranced with the music or the company of others.

From where she stood, Eliza could clearly see the king, sitting upon his gilded throne. He wore a more extravagant version of Thorne's uniform. He had twice the number of medallions, and they stood out above all else. The emerald lining of his suit was more prominent, the expensive material exquisite to look at, and silver lined his cuffs and collar.

Sitting upon his dark hair was his golden crown, detailed in emeralds that glimmered. Diamonds glistened like teardrops, while rubies shined like freshly spilt blood, shaped like interwoven vines and flowers to hold the beautiful jewels. On his face, he wore a silver mask.

Eliza touched her black mask. Their masks matched, except in colour.

"It looks fine," Thorne said, breaking through her thoughts as he touched his own mask. Silver, like the king's. Anyone with military status wore something similar.

Nodding, she pulled her cloak from her shoulders and handed it to a passing servant, who took it with a bow of their head. When she turned back to Thorne, she noticed—with some surprise—that his eyes travelled up the length of her body. Eliza watched as they roamed her figure until his eyes met hers once again.

"Is something wrong?" she asked, repeating his own words.

Before he could reply, silence cut through the room like a knife. The orchestra died mid-song, and the guests all turned to face King Bastian's dais at once.

Eliza did the same, heart pounding in her chest.

King Bastian stood before the crowd with his arms raised, resting his eyes on Eliza.

But it wasn't the king's stare that caught Eliza's attention; it was Henry Ivo's.

The older man stood to the left of the king, hands clasped behind his back and a look of placidness smoothed over his lined face. His silver brows furrowed, but she could see the ghost of a smile tipping his thin lips. A look of concentration flashed in his dark eyes.

"He would appear *nicer* if he smiled," a voice whispered in her ear.

Eliza pursed her lips in order to hide her smile, but she couldn't help it. "Grandpa, what are you doing here?" she asked, voice low. The king started his speech, but she gave up listening.

Her grandfather slipped his hand into hers. "I wanted to check up on you." He gave it a squeeze before releasing it. "But it seems to me like you are in good hands. Henry is one of my oldest friends and contacted me straight away when he ran into you. He said you looked fine. But I wanted to see for myself."

Tears sprung to her eyes. Turning her head slightly, Eliza caught a glimpse of her grandfather's face, and she committed it to memory, like she always did. Like she would always do. His silver hair was combed back, thick and slightly curled with the cold air. The robes he wore were ceremonial; the ones he'd worn the last time she'd seen him.

Not seeing him while being in Cadira... her heart grew heavy in her chest. She blinked, and he wavered slightly, the outlines of his body shimmering like that of an illusion. When she blinked again, however, it was gone, and her grandfather smiled at her broadly.

Perhaps the wine is getting to me, she thought with an inward shake of her head.

Davis indicated to the old Keeper. "Henry is one of the best Warlocks I know, and the most trustworthy. If you need anything, go to him."

Before she could reply, Davis Kindall disappeared into the crowd.

24

SECRETS HIDDEN IN THE DARK

Despite the room being packed, Eliza attempted to make her way across the dancefloor, heart still pounding. Over and over again, she replayed the moment with her grandfather; his voice, soft in her ear, and his hand holding hers. She wanted so badly to hug him, to go back to her life in New Orleans, but the heavy burden the Cadiran king had placed upon her shoulders weighed her down.

The king sat idly on his throne; his chin propped lazily on his hand. *Bored already?* she wanted to ask.

Straightening her spine, Eliza approached the king, but was stopped when a hand lightly touched her back, beckoning her away from King Bastian and his posse of Dukes and Lords.

"Elizabeth, might we have a word?" The voice didn't give her a chance to deny. Before she could react, Henry Ivo swept her back onto the ballroom floor in a single, flourishing movement, and tricked her into dancing in time with the orchestra and the rest of the pressing bodies.

"Elder Ivo," she said, blinking in surprise. "What can I do for you?"

The older man smiled pleasantly. "I saw old Davis with you on the balcony. He looked well."

Pain burned in his eyes then, like the mention of her grandfather hurt him.

She smiled. "He was just checking up on me, thanks to you

contacting him."

"I'm sorry," he replied, frowning, "if I got in your way by any chance."

"No!" Startled, they missed a beat, and hurried to regain their tempo, along with the other dancers beside them. "I just... I just didn't expect to see him so soon, is all. Thank you for that, I guess."

The old Keeper gave her a nod. "That is no problem, my dear."

They remained quiet for several beats and continued to dance steadily across the floor. Henry spun her, and she dipped underneath his arm, her dress flying out around her.

"I did not pull you away just to dance and reminisce," Henry said, voice low. His face darkened for a moment. "I have those maps you requested. That is also why I am here. However, you will need to have a meeting with King Bastian before they can be handed over to you." He looked around warily for a moment before spinning her. "You must also be careful when dealing with the Blood Witches."

Fear uncoiled in her stomach as a chill danced over her skin.

The old Keeper continued. "I am afraid they may be working with the Dark Master. I do not understand how he would be able to control such an army otherwise."

"What army?" she bit out. But she knew. The demons, the Demon Masters, and the Shadow Soldiers. Was there a chance that Blood Magic was giving him the ability to control his creatures?

Henry cast a look around the crowd. "You can trust only a few, Elizabeth Kindall. And for those you do, it must be with your *life*. I cannot stress this enough."

Breath catching in her throat, Eliza directed her stare to Thorne, who stood imposingly at the sidelines, his eyes on her. At his side stood a woman dressed in gold, her mask in one hand and a letter in the other. She stood with her back to the dancefloor, facing the commander, but from what Eliza could see, he wasn't quite paying attention to the dark-haired girl before him.

Henry spun them away from the commander and back into the middle of the dancefloor. "Do you trust that man with your life?"

Eliza hesitated for a moment but she didn't get the chance to reply. Henry Ivo was gone, leaving only a gold feather in his wake.

~

Head spinning, Eliza managed to stumble towards a refreshments table and collect herself enough to grab a glass of champagne. The dry, bubbly liquid filled her mouth, and she swallowed with some difficulty.

"What did Ivo want?" Thorne asked, coming to stand beside her.

Eliza shrugged. "He was giving me a warning concerning the Dark Master." She fiddled with the glass in her hands. She put it back down on the table, half empty, and instead ran her hands over her dress to smooth out the skirt.

When she looked up, Thorne had moved closer; his body half shielded her own, and he carefully put a hand on her waist. His lips, so close, moved to brush her cheek, breath caressing her face.

Warmth shot through her, and gasped softly. "What?"

"We're being watched."

"And you think whatever this is will help?" Eliza's heart hammered in her chest. Electricity fired through her veins. Was it the alcohol, or his nearness, that was making her dizzy? She hesitantly lifted her hand to rest on his shoulder.

He uttered a low chuckle in her ear. "Everyone is too drunk to recognise you. But there are a few..." he trailed off. Of course, there were. The king had eyes and ears everywhere.

Pursing her lips, Eliza subconsciously leaned into Thorne's body, relishing in the heat he radiated. Suddenly, she was just *tired*. Tired of the ball, tired of her dress, tired of her entire mission. She just wanted to go *home*.

"What now?"

Thorne didn't respond. Instead, he pulled Eliza towards the dancefloor and wrapped his arms around her body, pulling her close.

She could smell his aftershave and the woodsy scent of being out in the gardens and in the barracks. She could feel the crispness of his uniform beneath her calloused fingers, felt his strength beneath the jacket.

With Thorne, Eliza was safe; the minute they began dancing, her doubts and worries seemed to slip away from her. A sense of security washed over her. And the way they danced... they met the tempo step by step, enraptured by the songs' quickening beat. But they managed to stay together without fault.

Despite the safety she felt while in the arms of Thorne, she couldn't quite remove Henry Ivo, or his warning, from her mind. Those doubts and worries that had slipped away came tumbling back into the forefront of her thoughts, and they pounded her with questions that she didn't have time to answer.

"Ivo thinks the Blood Witches are working with the Dark Master." They missed a beat. Thorne's eyes widened. "That the Dark Master is using Blood Magic to control his armies. Thorne... it isn't a long shot. It would explain their refusal of helping the king find his son. What if *they* were the ones who instigated the kidnapping?"

Thorne shook his head, lips pursed. "They wouldn't. They have too much to lose."

"How do you know that?" she asked, heart thundering in her chest once more. But she remembered the Brotherhood and their connection to the Witches. Eliza's mouth went dry.

"Because," he said, enunciating each syllable pointedly, "they *do* have a stake in whether or not the prince is found."

Eliza shook her head incredulously. "Now you're just being vague. What stake? How do I know I can trust them?"

"You can trust *me*," he said.

It was those four words that almost stopped her on the dancefloor. But the music hit its crescendo, and the orchestra paused for effect. Thorne held Eliza close then, eyes pleading with her as the music reached its finale. As Thorne spun her, the world around her slowed.

Who could she trust? Thorne was the obvious choice; so far, he had done all he could to protect and help her on her mission. Together, they had fought side by side, but they'd fought each other, too. Eliza couldn't deny how she felt for the commander, her friend. They had their secrets, but beyond that, they were a team.

But then there was her grandfather, who had implored that she trust in Henry Ivo. Could she trust a man who she didn't know? Davis hadn't once mentioned Henry to her. She'd never heard the name, not until she met him at the Spring Manor. That was what scared her.

Mind spinning, she hadn't even noticed the song end, or the fact that she now faced Thorne, not touching. They bowed to one another, and before she could escape the throng of dancers, she was thrown into another dance as the orchestra started again, though this time, Thorne was not her partner.

"Dorin!" she gasped as he swung her into the next dance. His green eyes were bright behind the black of his mask, hair combed back and sprinkled with gold. His full lips pinched up in a smile as he took her in.

"You look beautiful," he said earnestly, spinning her in a waltz.

The music was calm, not like the hypnotic clash she'd danced with Henry to, or the simple passionate waltz she'd shared with Thorne. There was something magical about Dorin as he moved her across the dancefloor, the skirt of her gown sweeping the floor with every dip and spin.

"Thanks." She looked him over, taking in the black suit jacket over black slacks, the blood-red vest over his white dress-shirt. "You don't look too bad yourself."

"I hope so. This suit cost a small fortune. The king *really* likes to throw last minute parties, don't you think?" Though he smiled, Eliza couldn't help but detect a bitterness beneath his words.

I wonder why.

Then she realised: he was a servant of the court. He wasn't supposed to be out *dancing* with the guests, least of all *her*.

Eliza's heart fluttered, and she scolded herself.

Heat rushed Eliza's cheeks as they danced. "I'm glad you're here."

Dorin lifted her off her feet in a spin, his hands warm where they rested against her waist. She felt the heat of him through the thick layers of chiffon and satin. His eyes bore through the mask, through *her*, like he could see directly into her soul.

As he placed Eliza back on her feet, Dorin pulled her close, breath fanning her exposed neck. "Look, Eliza, there's something I need to tell you," Dorin said quietly as the music slowed. His eyes roamed the dancefloor before finding hers again. "I'm not exactly who I say I am."

The blood rushed from her face. "What do you mean?" she asked.

"Amitel sent me."

She wasn't sure how to feel at that revelation.

A darkness flared in his eyes, sending shivers of distrust down her spine. There was something about the way his gaze went to the dark windows that made her stomach churn.

"I need to go," he said, voice low.

Eliza's stomach somersaulted. She tried to pick Thorne from the crowd but couldn't find her mysterious companion amongst the dancers. He'd disappeared, leaving her with Dorin.

Dorin didn't give her the chance to respond. Instead, he released her and started for the gardens, his stiff posture only adding to her sudden uncertainty.

What if something happens? she thought. She searched the ballroom for Thorne again. She'd almost lost sight of Dorin, only to find him slipping through the glass doors and into the gardens like a shadow.

Oh, screw it. She had her magic, and she could fight back. There were guards everywhere, too, and she knew—hoped—Thorne would find her if anything happened.

But she couldn't let Dorin get away. It made no sense for him to drop a bombshell like that only to disappear immediately after.

Eliza slipped unseen through the throng of dancers and followed Dorin outside. Magic sung in her veins, a reminder of what she was capable of.

Hitching her skirt, she stepped carefully down the wide staircase that led into the maze of crystal trees and sweet-smelling roses. The darkness had almost swallowed him whole, but she spotted his figure cutting through the gardens.

Eliza noticed the top of Dorin's head, golden in the light of the lanterns, moving towards high hedges. She started towards him, fingers tightening as she gripped the skirts of her dress. Gravel crunched beneath the heels of her boots, too loud in her ears. The music sounded like a far-off whisper as she approached a bench hidden amongst foliage, out of sight from the guards and dancers.

Secret.

She shuddered.

The hairs on Eliza's arms stood on end. Dark, strange magic touched the back of her neck in warning. Eliza reached for her magic as a wave of dark energy knocked her to the ground.

Struggling to her feet, another wave slammed into her. It spread over her skin like she'd fallen into a pit of spiders. She gasped, falling back, head slamming into the bench. Something stood over her, made of shadows and darkness.

She blinked as blackness crawled at the edge of her vision. As the dark magic rose again against her, she thought she heard the familiar *caw* of the raven somewhere in the distance.

She couldn't fight back as the darkness took her.

~

"Are you alright?" The voice wavered in Eliza's ears. She could barely hear it over the pounding of her own heart. Her eyelids flickered, and between her lashes, she thought she could see Thorne. "She's waking up!"

Groaning, Eliza sent out feelers of magic and sensed three other presences with her, though none of them had an inch of the malicious power she had felt earlier.

Memories came springing back to her of her grandfather, Henry Ivo, the Blood Witches, and Thorne. And finally, Dorin, who she had followed into the gardens.

There was a lingering uncertainty within her when she thought about the pretty palace boy, but she couldn't understand why. There was a layer of haziness surrounding her memories of him, of the night.

Mouth dry, Eliza tried to speak, but there was no sound leaving her lips.

"Celia." *Thorne,* she thought. That was his deep tenor, unmistakable, even with her spinning head. "Gather whatever supplies you think we need and head to the port. It isn't safe here anymore. We'll meet you there."

Darkness blurred her vision, and a weightlessness washed over her as Thorne held her in his arms.

From the corner of her eye, she spotted the gold gown of the dark-eyed girl she'd seen with him earlier. Something deep inside Eliza cracked as she met the girl's eyes.

"Don't worry," Thorne said quietly, breath fanning over her face. "I'll protect you."

25

MAPS OF BLOOD

Eyes closed, she smiled as the rays of the high sun warmed the skin of her chest. The chills of winter broke temporarily to the warmth of spring, blooms of the Goddess breaking through the harsh, frozen soil.

She opened her eyes and turned to where her sister sat amongst the flowers, her dark head bowed.

"Why aren't you enjoying the sun?"

Her sister looked up, a frown tipping her bow-shaped lips. "Because we came out here to work, remember?"

Isolde heaved a sigh, lying back on the ground. "You came out to work. I came out to enjoy the sun I so missed the past couple of months." Closing her eyes again, she breathed in the scents of grass and wildflowers. "When I come of age, I will make sure we never have to deal with another winter again."

Several feet away, her sister sighed. "Then I suppose we'll be forced to endure several more horrendous winters, won't we."

Rolling her eyes, Isolde turned her head so she could take in her sister's hunched form. The flowers she picked were lavender, but they smelt sweet like powdered sugar, and tasted bitter like citrus when ground into tea. They were a hybrid creation, grown only by the shores of Lake Mab, blessed by her waters.

Isolde made a disgusted face as memories of their mother force-feeding them the petals as children resurfaced. "You want something *sweet? Fine," she'd said. "Have one of these."*

They never tried to steal from the bakery again.

"What?" her sister asked, frowning darkly. "What are you looking at?"

Isolde grinned. "I'm just remembering those precious moments we spent being so afraid of those flowers. Now you drink it like you'll never see it again."

Her sister snorted loudly and rose from the patch of Mab flowers. Her smile was faint, but it was there as she moved towards another patch. "It grew on me."

Isolde rose from the grass. Her gaze fell on the lapping water of the lake, its blue depths endless, harbouring some of the most dangerous beasts Cadira had ever seen. Would never see again.

"Iss," her sister said, drawing Isolde's attention to the edge of the lake. "What do you think is going to happen to us?"

Frowning, Isolde wandered over to the edge of the water and stared down into the murky depths. A flash of silver caught her eye, but it disappeared into the darkness of the lake; into the sweet embrace of Mab, who looked over that part of the valley. What would Mab do, Isolde wondered, if the kings of Cadira angered her like they had centuries before? Would she unleash her dark children on the earth?

"I think," Isolde said, "in the end it will not matter what happens to us. What matters is the ending."

"I will do anything to make sure this ends differently," her sister whispered, voice thick with tears.

Isolde bowed her head. "I know."

Darkness fell over the valley, coating the legendary lake in shadow. In the distance, the caw of a raven sounded. It turned her blood to ice, sending shivers down her spine.

She turned in a slow circle, brows drawn. Wariness washed over her.

To the end, she thought, closing her eyes. Beside her, her sister took her hand. The end.

Eliza woke with a pounding headache. Her vision blurred as she tried to blink her eyes open, but she found them pasted shut with sleep. Her memory of the night before was hazy at best, but she remembered the ball, the cold air and the music that whispered like a ghost in the back of her mind.

"How are you feeling?"

She startled and turned her head towards the voice. She recognised it—albeit slowly—as Thorne. She felt her hand tucked into his, felt the warmth of his skin seeping into her cold body. Slowly, she peeled her eyes open and took him in.

Dark circles lined his eyes, the storms of his irises shadowed with worry. His tousled hair looked messier than it usually did; for some reason, Eliza felt the urge to run her fingers through it like she used to.

I've never done that before, she thought with a jolt. *Maybe I'm still out of it.*

With her spare hand, she touched her forehead gingerly, wincing at the sudden pain. It felt like her whole forehead was bruised and sore to the touch.

"I feel," she said slowly, voice hoarse, "like my whole head has been smashed in."

Thorne nodded, as if he understood. "It was powerful magic that knocked you out. Do you remember anything?"

"I went out," she started, fumbling through her memories, "to see Dorin."

The commander straightened in his seat, a stoniness settling over his features. "Who's Dorin?"

Oh, right, she thought, wishing she could hit herself. *He's the boy I've been hanging out with while you've been gone. You know, the one we met when we first arrived? Yeah, him.*

She didn't say that; instead, Eliza reached for the pitcher of water beside her bed, but the commander beat her to it. Pouring her a glass, he handed it to her without meeting her stare.

Eliza swallowed it selfishly, guzzling until the cup was empty. "He works in the palace, and knows Amitel," she finally said, setting the cup on the nightstand.

Thorne sat back, arms crossing over his chest. Eliza had the sense that he wasn't pleased with her revelation, and that he wasn't entirely certain he believed Dorin knew the Warlock. But she had no reason not to believe him, she decided. She wasn't sure why, but it sent a pang of guilt through her. That deep, unfamiliar need to protect Thorne rose within her.

"Dorin was sent to the palace by Amitel. I met with him a couple of times while you were in the city, and he only mentioned Amitel last night," she continued.

"I'm not entirely sure if I believe that, though," Thorne said. "Why were you in the garden last night?"

Eliza hesitated and searched her memory, but she remembered only dancing with Dorin last. She hadn't *had* a reason to go into the garden, had she?

Eliza struggled to sit up, groaning as her head thrummed. *How hard was I hit?*

Thorne leaned forward, resting his elbows against his knees. "I don't like this, Eliza," he murmured.

She shook her head. "Dorin is fine. If there was something wrong with him, then I would know, right?"

Something deep inside told her otherwise, but she shook the feeling aside.

"Anyway," Eliza said, climbing out of bed. "We need to see the king. And we need to leave, now."

~

"Majesty," she said, eyeing the king's office. The room was all dark mahogany and velvet; old tomes lined the walls and a heavy desk sat in the centre of the room. A fire crackled in the hearth, illuminating the room and casting dancing shadows across the walls.

The king rose from his desk, face impassive. Dark eyes found hers, and she held his stare unflinchingly.

"I take it you have decided to leave," King Bastian said, moving to stand before the desk. "I am sorry for what happened last night."

Eliza bobbed her chin, careful to keep her stare respectful. "It's alright. I feel fine today."

The king regarded her for a moment with cool eyes. "Elder Ivo and I received those maps you were searching for, Miss Kindall. I must say they are an interesting find."

Her heart thundered in her chest, relief washing through her. She held her breath as an old, worn map was handed to her. Yellowed with age, the corners were darkened and torn from use.

With steady hands, Eliza unrolled it and held her breath; marked with a raven in flight were the different entrances to the underground cities. One at the Spring Manor, one on the outskirts of Mesah. There were others scattered across the map—three, though there could have been more if the ink wasn't so faded—but the one she needed...

Eliza lightly ran her finger over the spot. "Thank you, Majesty. I appreciate you getting these."

When she looked up, she found the king staring at her with an openness that left her feeling uncomfortable. Hope. Unburdened and unrestrained. "I'm sure you do," he said, crossing his arms, shutting the hope away. "Is there anything else you require for your journey?"

Eliza bit her lip, looking down at the map again. "There is one thing, actually, that might help me."

"And what might that be?"

She looked up and met his stare. "Your blood."

~

Eliza stepped back as Thorne checked the saddles of the horses. The two dark, chestnut mares nickered as he rubbed their silky necks. A softness entered his gaze as he worked through the motions of checking their supplies, though Eliza could tell his mind was elsewhere.

She couldn't stop thinking about the attack at the masquerade. Where there should have been a trace of magic, there was nothing. But she'd *felt* the slam of darkness, the formidable magic that had swept her off her feet. It had been enough to knock her out entirely, but not kill her.

Why? What was the Dark Master playing at? Why *didn't* he kill her?

"What are you thinking about, Eliza?"

Those thoughts were pushed to the back of her mind as she took the commander in. He still looked tired, eyes deeply shadowed, and his usually bronze skin was pale.

She gave a stiff shake of her head and sighed. "I just can't believe we're finally leaving and that we might know where the prince is." Handing her satchel over to be packed into her saddle bag, Eliza paced the courtyard. "Do you think we have a chance of getting him back?"

Mid-morning light brightened the dreary day, though Eliza was happy that it wasn't raining on them. *Yet.* But a bank of clouds hesitated on the horizon, and even with the mostly clear sky, there were few who braved the cold air and icy wind.

"I think it's a possibility," Thorne said. "I think that attack on you was a last resort to stop you from getting any closer. The Dark Master might be afraid of you finding Prince Alicsar."

The wind swept Eliza's hair off her shoulders. It reached below her shoulder-blades now, dried out from the cold air. Irritated, she pulled it back. "I just don't get it. Why now? What's so special about it? And don't get me started on the idea of keeping the prince alive. None of this makes any sense, Thorne."

The commander sighed, stepping away from the horses as the captain of the guard approached, his inky hair swept aside by the wind.

Thorne touched her arm before pulling away. "I know. Let us find him first. Asking these questions now won't help."

"There are three weeks' worth of rations and enough gold to help you on your journey," the captain said, voice gruff. The scar that cut through his upper lip made him look like he was forever sneering, though Eliza doubted he minded. It made him look scarier.

Eliza smiled as his gaze found hers. "Thank you, Captain Jed."

He nodded; dark eyes hard. "Bring him back, girl."

The captain walked off stiffly without another word, armour clinking with every step. When he disappeared behind the hedges, Eliza released a breath.

"Sure. Because it's *that easy*," she muttered, stomach churning.

Thorne stepped up to her side. "Eliza, we'll find him."

Their eyes met, and her worries washed away with the sincerity of his gaze. Just like the king, Thorne believed in her. Had *hope* that she'd find the prince.

Eliza pulled her gaze from his and walked over to her horse. The mare nudged her stomach, as if understanding her doubt.

How is one girl supposed to defeat a bad guy, save the prince, and bring hope to an entire land?

Without meaning to, Eliza snorted, realising she'd just found herself in the middle of the *Young Adult* section of the bookstore. *Katniss Everdeen who?*

"Hello you two. Thank the Goddess I caught you before you left."

Eliza jumped and spun around. "Amitel? What are you doing here?"

The Warlock grinned. Dressed in all black, he truly looked like a dark God with his golden hair and red-gold eyes. He stood tall and straight, somehow bright against the grey skies. "Good to see you're doing well, Eliza."

She stiffened, remembering the hedges and his words. *The sands lie.* "I'm fine now. But I doubt you're here because of what happened last night," she said, curling her hands into fists.

He rolled his eyes, smile disappearing. "That is *part* of the reason why I'm here, actually."

Behind him, a boy leading a horse appeared. Sandy hair caught the wan light of the sun. Eliza checked her surprise, merely raising a brow as he approached in dark riding leathers.

Her voice, however, came out as a whisper. "Dorin."

Amitel spared Dorin a quick, unamused glance. "Yes. You've already met my *friend*." The Warlock didn't sound too *friendly*, she noticed. "He's been an informant for me here in the palace for a while, and I asked him to watch out for you while you were here. He informed me of what happened at the ball last night and, well, since I was already in the capital, I thought I might offer my help."

The commander stepped up. His stiff shoulders did not relax an inch. "And what help might that be, Amitel?"

"Good question, Commander." Amitel pointed to Dorin, who had finally caught up. "You'll likely be in need of a guide to get you to Mesah."

Dorin didn't meet her stare, and instead looked between her and Thorne. "I grew up there. I know the roads from Port Beewold like the back of my hand, and I know most of the cities there."

Finally, his eyes met hers.

"It would be helpful," Amitel drawled, stepping into Eliza's line of sight. She didn't miss the way Dorin watched Amitel with distrust.

What is that about?

Thorne cleared his throat. "Celia is arranging safe travel for us now."

Eliza's attention snapped to him. "Too many people..."

She knew that name though. Somewhere in the back of her mind, she recognised the name. *From her dreams.* The memory of gold, of worried eyes and something else warmed a deep part of her.

Eliza shook her head, feeling sick. After the attack, she wasn't sure if she even wanted *Thorne* with her, not with the chance that he could be targeted by the Dark Master just for helping her. But taking Dorin and now *Celia*... Eliza wasn't sure if she was comfortable with the amount of lives being put at risk.

"We'll have to make do," Thorne said with a sigh. "Celia is a powerful witch, and we'll need the extra protection. Neither of us know the desert well enough, and we would have needed a guide as soon as we got there, Eliza."

She shook her head. "I don't want to put anyone else in danger."

"I'm helping because I want to, Eliza," Dorin said quietly, surprising her. "I'm putting *myself* in danger. And like the commander said, you need the added protection. Let me do that for you."

Amitel looked her over with shadowed eyes. "After last night, the Dark Master—if it even *is* the Dark Master who has the prince—is getting bolder. It's clear he's after *you*, Eliza, and for that reason, having others help protect you on your mission will perhaps save *your* life and the life of your prince."

"Let me help you, Eliza." Dorin stepped around Amitel, his horse joining hers.

"I need to go. Dorin has his horse prepared, and he has a way to contact me if needed." It looked as if the Warlock wanted to say more, but he held his tongue, instead nodding in the commander's direction.

Eliza stepped up and touched his arm, throat tightening. "Thank you, Amitel."

He winked and swept down in a bow. "All in a day's work. Now, I *really* should be off. Say hello to Celia for me, it's been a while since I saw her last."

The Warlock nodded to Dorin before clasping hands with Thorne. *How long have they really known each other?* she wondered. If she was right and Thorne was immortal, what did that mean when they finished the mission?

She tried not to think about that.

As Amitel turned to Dorin, Eliza pulled Thorne aside. "How well do you know Celia?" she asked. She kept Dorin and Amitel in the corner of her eye.

Thorne frowned. "For a long time. Why?"

"You've never mentioned her before. And I think it's weird how you've invited her to join the mission, like we're just going for a stroll in the gardens."

"Eliza..." he sighed and shook his head. "Do you remember when I told you about the girl I once loved?" Mutely, Eliza nodded. "Celia is her sister."

Blood running cold, Eliza said nothing as Thorne stepped away. She heard him bid Amitel farewell, but her mind was reeling.

Someone touched her hand, and she startled, blinking up at Amitel. "What?"

The Warlock grinned. "Be careful out there," he said, before stepping back.

Amitel met her stare one last time before turning away from their party. Eliza gazed at his retreating form, and not for the first time that day, felt a little lighter, like there was hope after all.

26

DREAMS OF DEATH

When the coast came into sight a day later, Eliza, Dorin, and Thorne led their horses into a copse of trees and tied them to a branch before heading back to the road to scope out the port city.

Fishing boats dotted the water, while massive transport and trading ships filled the horizon. Farther along, Thorne pointed out the navy harbour and the hundreds of vessels that filled its small port. Most of which were being tended to.

But the city itself was cramped and overpopulated; squat buildings bled into one another, while the docks were full of people and vendors. The city centre seemed to be the hub of activity. The city bled outwards, spreading across the coast and into the hills beyond until there were only scattered hamlets and farms.

That wasn't what worried her, though.

As her magic danced across the hills of the coast, Eliza sensed the essence of demons, barely hidden by the city. Demons weren't inherently bad, but they were easily manipulated. It required powerful and dark magic to control the hoards, though.

"They're patrolling," she said, opening her eyes and turning to Thorne and Dorin. "Demons. A hundred *at least*. The Dark Master knows we're here."

Thorne cursed under his breath and disappeared back into the trees. Eliza waited, casting a glance over the open lands again. A chill ran down her spine. *Something isn't right here.*

Dorin followed Thorne into the trees, neither speaking, leaving Eliza to run messages. She understood Thorne's lack of trust.

She frowned and made sure she was alone before walking farther onto the road until she was amongst the trees across from their newly-chosen campsite. The trees were thicker here, growing closer together. Moss-ridden rocks scattered the ground, and Eliza carefully stepped over them, heading towards the centre of the grove.

White flowers sprouted from the emerald green grass. A light breeze brushed over Eliza, picking at the hair clinging to her forehead, rustling the leaves above her.

A shiver danced down the length of her spine, the temperature chilling significantly. She crossed her arms over her chest and spun in a slow circle, brows furrowing.

There's nothing here.

Not a spirit, or a sprite, or a demon. Nothing. The grove was quiet, almost unwelcoming.

She heard her name called from the road. Eliza carefully picked her way back towards the horses.

"I'm here!" She cleared the trees into the open sunlight and shielded her eyes.

Thorne and Dorin were not alone on the road; beside them stood the girl from the ball. Her dark hair was braided back from her face, blue eyes bright with untouched emotion. She wore indistinguishable riding leathers, but there was something about the way her brows furrowed that reminded Eliza of the girl from her dreams.

Somehow, Eliza had forgotten the mysterious woman would be joining them at the port. *Looks like she found us though.*

"We thought you'd been taken." Dorin sighed, rubbing a hand over his face. A ring Eliza had never seen before glinted on his hand. She couldn't quite make out the sigil, but it looked almost like a dragon in flight.

Eliza cocked her head and smiled. "Sorry guys, but you can't get rid of me that easily."

Thorne narrowed his eyes, ready to reply, but Celia stepped forwards and offered her hand.

"I am sorry we did not get to properly meet the other night," she said, a thick accent stilting her words. "I'm Celia."

Eliza looked over her again and tried to identify the origin, but nothing came to mind. Yet... Eliza recognised the accent, as if she'd heard it before in passing, but she couldn't place where. Celia had pointed ears, too, a mark of her own Fae heritage.

Eliza took the woman's hand and shook it. There had to be maybe be a four-year age difference between them, though they stood at similar heights with nearly identical builds.

"Yeah," Eliza replied, tucking her hand into her pocket, "sorry I got knocked out."

Celia smiled. "I do not believe that was your fault."

Thorne cleared his throat, forcing everyone's attention to him. Eliza rolled her eyes.

"Niceties aside, unfortunately we need a way into the port and onto one of those ships. It'll take too long to get around the mountains, and we don't have that kind of time. Celia, you've managed to get us passage?" Celia nodded, and Eliza's brows shot up. "Good. That means we don't have time to waste getting around those patrols. We still have maybe four hours of sunlight. So, let's make the most of it."

~

The streets were packed with vendors: fish mongers shouted their prices and flailed their possessions, while trinket stall owners stalked out in the open and cornered unsuspecting shoppers, coercing them into buying things they didn't need. Some stalls had travel supplies, and it was towards those that Thorne directed their small party, careful to keep away from the unassuming shadows that drenched the port. In those shadows were demons hunting *them*.

"We have anything and everything you might need in making a journey! Are you searching for treasure? Wealth? A lady? Well, you are in luck good sir! I have the map for you! Enchanted by the legendary Blood Witches, this map will lead you wherever you desire!" The market vendor shoved the map into Thorne's hands. "Trust me when I tell you it works! Found me wife with that thing! We have ten bastards because've it!"

Thorne dropped the map and ducked away from the vendor, who shouted after him. "Nothing of value there," he said, voice low. Celia and Eliza stuck to his sides so they could hear him clearly over the raucous shouting of the market. "We have everything we need."

"We don't have a map, though," Celia hissed. She looked back at the vendor, who had moved on to some other man. "Here... they are an expensive commodity."

"I have a map of the old cities," Eliza said, directing the attention to herself. "A couple of newer ones, as well. But I haven't looked at them since the capital."

Beside her, Dorin released a breath. "Are those the ones Henry Ivo gave you?"

"Yes," Eliza replied. "Thank the Gods he finally got them to us before we left."

Celia shook her head, a smile plastered across her face. "How am I not surprised?"

"What?" Eliza asked, frowning.

Thorne took both their hands, dragging them along the boardwalk and away from the exciting market. He pulled them towards a section of buildings where ships were being repaired. Dorin followed at a slower pace, caught up in the excitement, his eyes wide as they took everything in.

"Okay. We have maps. We have supplies. And we have our tickets out of here." Thorne looked around them, searching the shadows. "From what I could tell, the demons didn't catch our scent."

"I masked it," both Eliza and Celia said in unison.

Eliza groaned and Celia laughed.

"Good," Thorne said. "We cannot stay here. We have two hours of daylight left and if we are caught in the city after dark, then we are completely exposed. We just need to know our route in and out. Which ship are we on?"

Celia explained the fishing boat she had procured, noting how inconspicuous it was and how the captain had promised them safe passage to Beewold, where he had already been heading.

Eliza drowned the two of them out; Thorne would tell her again when they got back to the horses, and then again in the morning and twice more after that. She didn't bother listening to what they said. Dorin seemed to be animated in the discussion though, as he spoke about the route from Beewold to Mesah.

Behind them, the market bustle carried on like there weren't malicious demons stalking their every move. Eliza could make out the calls for fish and strange pocket watches and smell the rotting meat.

Shaking her head, Eliza turned back to Thorne, Dorin, and Celia, but stopped. At the mouth of an alley, a spirit beckoned her. She could have sworn it was the little girl from the Winter Palace.

"Thorne," she said, pulling his attention from Celia. "We need to go down there, right now." She pointed to the alley.

"What?" He looked between her and the darkness, brows furrowed. "Why, Eliza?"

She looked at him pleadingly. "Trust me. We need to go there *now*."

Without waiting for him or Celia, Eliza dashed across the street towards the alley, Dorin not far behind. The little girl stood at the mouth once more, two other children at the other end. The girl disappeared when Eliza approached, reappearing in a sunken alcove.

Eliza went in behind her, pulling Dorin, Thorne and Celia along with her.

"What are we doing in here?" Celia asked, frowning. She stuck her head out, bright blue eyes searching the alley, but Eliza pulled her back in and placed a finger to her lips.

They waited in silence for ten minutes before they heard footsteps. A cloaked figure appeared at the mouth of the alley, darkness swimming and rippling around them. The figure used it to mask its appearance, but Eliza could tell straight away that there was something... *demonic* about the way it appeared.

"We have tracked the girl to this *port*," the hooded figure spat, kneeling before another, more sinister creature. Eliza couldn't see it clearly, but shivers racked her body when it spoke.

"Good." The word slithered over her.

Thorne cocked his head, eyes narrowed, and Eliza placed her hand over his. He knew they were talking about *her*. Who else would they be tracking?

"The girl is not alone," the hooded demon said, shaking its head. "She is in the company of others."

The other figure came into view. It was not an actual figure, though, but an outline made of smoke.

"Do not harm the girl," it said, moving around the demon with ease. Eliza shot up a wall of shadows, and she felt Celia do the same, making sure to keep themselves hidden. "Her... *friends* on the other hand. Keep them around just long enough so that I can kill them."

Eliza's blood ran cold, and her heart stopped.

The hooded demon bobbed its head in response.

"Have you sensed her magic?" its master asked.

It bobbed its head again. "Everywhere. The girl is everywhere."

Eliza could almost feel the shadow man *smile*. "Good. Her magic is almost at its peak. Soon, I will have the power of the Ecix. Go, gather your demons. Make sure to keep an eye on them."

The shadow man disappeared with a wave of his hand, leaving the demon to twist the shadows around himself until he, too, was gone.

They waited twenty more minutes before exiting the alcove and dissipating their shields. Once in the open, Eliza sucked in a breath, tasting the salty air of the port on her tongue. But she didn't care. She just needed to *breathe.*

"We need to go." Dorin had his hand on Eliza's back. Thorne held on tightly to Celia's hand. Was there a chance that Eliza was completely wrong? That perhaps they weren't talking about *her*, but rather, Celia? Eliza knew nothing about her, especially whether she was the *Ecix* or not. And the Brotherhood back in the capital had mentioned Thorne's past with the Ecix.

Eliza nodded, meeting Dorin's worried gaze. "Let's go back to the horses. We don't have much time left before it gets too dark."

Thorne nodded, eyes a storm of tightly wound emotions, and they all entered the market once again.

Eliza almost missed the raven, perched on the shoulder of the Knight. It almost gave her the reassurance she needed.

Almost.

~

Darkness enveloped the world; it covered the land in smoke and dust, in writhing shadows that reached for her no matter how fast she ran. It crept out of crevices and slithered over ruins, all in the hopes of consuming the light that warded it off.

Eliza ran, but she wasn't sure why. There was something behind her, chasing her. Something inevitable.

She ran, nonetheless.

Fear spiked in her heart, pumping her blood faster, harder, forcing her to run from the darkness that stalked her. In her wake, she heard whispers.

Dread shuddered through her.

Run faster. *She did.*

You will die. *She believed that.*

You will be the death of everything. *That scared her most.*

Her breathing accelerated until there was no breath left.

Oblivion. It felt like an abyss and she was falling, down, down, into nothingness. She was unaware of the things around her, unaware of what happened outside of her oblivion-like dream.

For a long time, she ran. Time was an illusion; non-existent, something of the mind but not in being. It was useless as she ran, tirelessly and continuously. There was no need to stop—Eliza couldn't feel anything other than the breathlessness in her chest. She just needed to run.

She tripped, foot catching on the edge of something hard. Eliza tumbled to the ground, landing on a heap of recently dug-up earth, the substance cool and soft under her numb fingers. She didn't dig at it. Eliza wasn't curious as to what lay beneath her, but rather, what she had tripped on.

Turning her head, Eliza squinted. The dark object jutted out from the ground, rectangular in shape, covered in moss and blood-red roses, the only colour in the Gods-awful dream. It stood out bright and crimson against the darkness of the protruding object she had tripped on. It looked like freshly spilt blood.

With a shaky hand, Eliza pushed the moss and vines away, brushing away dirt and hard clumps of soil, outlining words with the tips of her fingers.

A grave and a tombstone.

Eliza managed to brush away everything, leaving the tombstone bare, engraved with a flourish of words that, for some reason, didn't surprise her.

Elizabeth Kindall, born unknown
Death unknown, born of Fae Blood and Witch Blood, mixed
Necromancer

She swallowed thickly. The words tumbled through her head over and over again until one thing stood out.

Run.

Eliza got up and started running again before the darkness could finally catch her.

Awaking with a start, Eliza sucked in a cooling breath, relishing in the cold air that filled her lungs and eased the racing of her heart. Her heated cheeks slowly cooled, and the panic she had felt in her dream slowly drifted away.

It was a dream. Nothing else.

222

Then why did it feel like more?

For weeks, Eliza had the sense that she wasn't remembering something important. For weeks, she had been having all kinds of dreams, but she always awoke remembering nothing. It pained her knowing it had something to do with the past she didn't have access to.

The dream stuck with her tonight; the creeping darkness, her own grave. Although she felt nothing in the dream, she certainly felt it *now*. Panic, pain, and *fear*.

Eliza struggled out of her sleeping wrap and paused at the sound of voices. Although low, she could make out what they were saying.

"This isn't safe," Celia started, voice wavering. "I do not think we should continue with this mission."

Eliza could only imagine Thorne shaking his head. "We don't have much of a choice. Not now. There is too much at stake."

"I am not ready to risk anyone's lives."

"We follow Eliza's lead," Thorne snapped, quickly lowering his voice as he continued, "if she goes ahead with this, then we need to be there for her. Her life is on the line. The life of her family. Everything she's ever known."

"She will only get herself killed. Just like Isolde."

The two were silent for a moment. Thorne must have responded because Celia snapped, "She was my sister, Brandon. I loved her before you did. Remember that."

Eliza sat back and wrapped her blanket tightly around herself, the chill of the night finally sinking into her bones. *Isolde*. Thorne's ex, the girl he had loved. He'd said she was dead, but never how.

She will only get herself killed. What had happened to Isolde? And how was she connected to Eliza?

Thorne and Celia's voices faded. They'd stopped talking. Maybe they'd heard Eliza. She didn't care. Between the two of them, they were keeping more secrets than the Dark Master himself. Who were they *really*? Since she'd met him, Eliza had always known there was something different about Commander Brandon Thorne. But the secret meetings, his unforthcoming stories about his past, and his connections with Amitel and Celia...

And Celia... Eliza knew absolutely *nothing* about this woman, but that didn't stop her from feeling like she *knew* her somehow. Knew *both of them*, without really knowing them at all. Eliza couldn't explain the feeling, but her mind had tugged at some image, some memory that didn't quite belong in her own head. Like it was someone else's memory, and they had merely shoved it into Eliza's mind for safekeeping.

Eliza rubbed at her eyes and laid back down. *When am I going to get answers?*

27

GHOST STORIES

"Aye, the stories are true!" the old sailor cackled, tipping his head back. Watered-down ale dripped from his cracked lips and he wiped it away with a weathered hand, smudging it across his silver beard. But he didn't care; the pause for effect strengthened the ghost story he was about to delve into.

I hate boats. I hate fish. And I hate ghost stories. Never. Again, Eliza thought miserably.

"We've been stuck here *two days*," Eliza muttered, sitting back against rotting wood. She was almost tempted to try the ale that had been shoved into her hands, but she refrained. One look from Dorin gave her enough information about the stinking beverage that sloshed in her hands. "We should already be at Beewold."

Celia nodded; arms crossed over her chest. "What is taking so long?"

"A storm is coming from the north," a fisherman interrupted, ale dripping from his chin. Eliza winced. "It be holding us 'ere until we can make dry land. And there is no wind for us to sail."

"I can make wind," Eliza replied, rolling her eyes. Dorin spared a smile in her direction.

The storyteller rapped his knuckles against the hard wood of one of the tables, gathering the attention of the crew once again. He stroked his wiry beard with one hand, while the other clutched a bottle of rum. His eyes searched the cabin, meeting the gaze of every present crew member, along with Thorne's, Celia's, Dorin's, and Eliza's. His gaze lingered on her for a moment longer than anyone else, and it sent a shiver down her spine.

In Cadira, there were no boundaries. Back in New Orleans, magic had its limits—and its prices—and many of those who knew how to harness it from Cadira were either powerful and banished or were sworn to protect both worlds. Because of that lack of boundary, anything in Cadira was possible. That was what made the stories more dangerous.

Eliza banished the thoughts from her mind. Any other day of the week, she realised, ghost stories wouldn't scare her. But something about being in Cadira made her stomach twist at the possibilities.

The sailors quietened; their drunken voices now slurred as they listened to the storyteller. "Aye, we be travelling down the Gyles Channel in a day, and most sailors know the legends that follow that stretch o'water." Whispers erupted.

He ignored the crew, slamming his wooden mug down onto the table several times to direct their attention back to him. Their whispers died, and soon they could only hear the rattle of their cargo, the rumble of thunder, the crash of the waves against their hull.

"Yes, there are many legends of the channel, but I'll tell ya' there are more than meets the eye. The locals that live above the cliff have their own version of what happens in the depths of the ocean. They have their own tales about the Wailing Woman who inhabits the caves dug into the cliff face." Silence followed his words, thick and filled with awaiting tension. The silence stretched until Eliza could only hear the *thud, thud* of her heart.

"Not long before her untimely death, a lone bride went to the cliff. She was dressed in nothing but her undergarments after being stood up on her weddin' day. And there, she sang a haunting tune, her voice carrying on the northerly winds. It distracted the sailors below and they crashed into the rocks, their ships sinking. And there she stood, an omen of death.

"As she came to notice their deaths, she seemed to glow with glee. She was no longer in pain, watching others come upon it. But it still wasn't enough to mend her broken heart or warm her lonely soul.

"In the midst of the destruction, her groom came upon her, and took her in his arms. He whispered sweet nothings in her ear while she continued to sing her haunting tune. But before he could continue his devilish works, she changed her song, luring him to his death. She soon followed, still singing, heard by all the townsfolk." Silence.

Something thudded above their heads, and Eliza jumped. She almost chided herself with her foolishness. *That was just a story. Hell, they have the same ones back in America! All around the world they do! This was just one of them.* But from the looks of everyone else, they seemed to believe it—even Thorne and Dorin. *The difference between here and America is the fact that here, the stories and legends are often true.*

"Of course, some think she was actually a siren, or a demon, or a Goddess in disguise." As the crew clapped, Eliza's eyes drooped, and the thought of her uncomfortable hammock had her yearning for her own bed back in New Orleans. Or even the campsite at their last port.

Rising from her seat, Eliza nodded at her host and gathered her cloak. She walked onto the deck and let out a deep sigh, ignoring the rotting fish smell, enjoying the fresh breeze that came of the ocean. Both moons were out, one full while the other waned. They were bright, illuminating the night sky and the dark ocean. Stars twinkled against the wisps of clouds covering the darkness like a curtain. On the horizon, Eliza could faintly see the Tower of Oranth, a deserted outpost on an equally deserted island. And farther, the kingdom of Laziroth.

"What's wrong?"

Eliza turned to Thorne, who stood beside her, his features shrouded in shadows. His deep eyes were cast out to sea, never staying on the same point. He pursed his lips, knuckles white where they held on to the edge. Feet firmly planted, he seemed as strong as a tree, reliable, dependant, trustworthy. The way he stood almost felt like an opening for Eliza to spill her dark secrets, to tell him about her strange dreams and admit her necromancy.

But she remembered the secrets he'd held onto. They hadn't spoken about it since the port, but Eliza wanted to know more about the Ecix. Part of her feared asking because of the response she might get.

Deep down, she had a feeling he already knew about her necromancy and didn't care. And yet she couldn't bring herself to say anything. Her fear was irrational, but she knew if she said something now it might push him away.

Eliza mimicked Thorne and pushed against the railing. "Nothing, just tired. Exhausted, really."

Thorne nodded absentmindedly. He didn't say anything for a

while, content to just stand there and watch the waves and the reflection of the moons over the dark water. Every once in a while, the fin of a siren could be seen, diving through the currents, their chilling laughs spreading through the night.

Then everything was silent, the only constant being Thorne's warmth as it seeped into Eliza's arms. They stood there, staring out into the endless ocean, neither talking nor making any move to leave. Peaceful, even.

Eliza shivered. From the corner of her eye, she met the gold eyes of the raven. Shock speared through her as the bird took flight, heading in the direction of the Gyles Chanel.

She wanted to smile, but she couldn't ignore the unease that welled in her stomach.

~

She stood over the cliff, white dress shredded and bloody. Her hair billowed in the wind, wet with blood. Everything that had happened before that moment was a blur, foggy. There was a fleeting memory, but she was unable to grasp it before it fell away.

She shook her head, matted hair clinging to the sides of her face. Her nails dug into the palms of her hands as she clenched them, feeling the stubs of her nails bite into soft skin.

A thick layer of clouds covered the sky, blanketing the stars and moons. The ocean below her crashed heavily against the cliffside, the waves the only sound penetrating the uncommon silence.

"Ecix..." a voice whispered. She spun around, moving away from the cliff. She knew that name but couldn't remember where. "Ecix... I will come for you..."

"No!" she screamed into the darkness, heart pounding in her chest. Behind her, there was more blood. It trailed like a path to her own destruction.

"Ecix..."

The voice seemed to come from all directions, saying the name over and over again. Sometimes from above, other times from amongst the waves, but the voice was always there, always taunting. It called out again.

"Eliza!"

Sputtering awake, Eliza stumbled from her hammock. She could still *feel* her dream around her, feel it pulling at her consciousness. But she fought it back and willed her heartbeat to steady in her chest.

"Are you alright?" Celia asked, gently resting her hand on Eliza's shoulder.

Eliza nodded warily. "I think so. It was just... a bad dream."

The other woman's brows furrowed. "Are you sure? Sometimes, dreams can be interpreted as warnings."

"It was just a dream, don't worry." Eliza didn't want to think of her nightmare as anything more, especially not when it was beginning to fade away, any trace of it being locked away into the recesses of her mind. "Are we any closer to the port?" she asked, running a hand through her tangled hair.

Celia nodded. "Brandon went and spoke with the Captain once the sails gathered wind. We will be in Port Beewold by midday tomorrow."

28

PORT OF DARKNESS

Port Beewold was *not* impressive, nor was it big. A section of taverns and inns surrounded the docks, along with a small market in the centre. Surrounding that were stores and some housing, though there was nothing flashy about any of it.

Squinting against the sun, Eliza rolled her sleeves up, suddenly aware of the hot wind that rolled in from the north where Mesah lay.

In the northern sectors of Cadira, the days were short and hot—the sun pale and harsh even through winter—while the nights were long and frigid. It usually made one wish that they had the sun as a blanket. Dorin had informed them there was no in between, sadly, in the valley of the dead.

"Some say the slave encampments brought on the droughts and the endless nights and the scorching days," Dorin said as he handed Eliza one of her bags while shouldering the other with a smile. "Others say the King of the Gods, Thrinarv, God of War and Wisdom, punished the lands for the enslavement of his children—the Brithien people, the Elves."

Eliza swallowed. The elves were also said to be ancestors of the Blood Witches.

"And the lesser of the few," Thorne continued, forcing Eliza, Dorin, and Celia away from the boat, "believe there is something else in Mesah that keeps it that way, something far more powerful, far more destructive, than one would ever know."

They descended onto the dock and into the middle of a less-than-busy marketplace.

"Those who think this are either thought to be crazy, radical, or meddling in the darkest arts, foreshadowing some horrible fate that will be the end of Cadira. It's these people that have been hanged for their outrageous statements," Dorin finished. "But no one has ever known the truth."

A shiver ran down Eliza's spine. *I will,* she promised. *I'll find out the truth.*

~

Eliza watched from her perch at the window as Celia disappeared into a crowd of fishermen and dockworkers. They had a day before they would journey to the dry plains of northern Cadira, towards the Mesah desert and its main city, Dorin's home.

She closed her eyes for a moment before turning back to her companions. Dorin studied a map silently at a table pushed against the far wall, his back hunched over the paper. His sandy hair flopped over his forehead as he searched the page, for what, Eliza wasn't sure.

Thorne, however, seemed content on sharpening and polishing his sword. The raven-headed pommel stared at her from the bed.

Both men had secrets, were hiding what they knew about her, or about the mission, and Eliza was tired of it. She normally wouldn't care, but the secrets were piling up, becoming overwhelming. She just needed to find out *why* they were hiding things from *her.*

Finally, Eliza gathered her courage and stood. "Look, I get that you both have your own crap to deal with," she said, heart racing, "but you're both keeping things from me." Her eyes flickered to Thorne, who looked up from his sword. "You're keeping information from me that might actually *help me*, and I need to know why."

Gathering her cloak, Eliza strode to the door and flung it open. "If either of you want to talk, I'll be downstairs in the tavern."

Eliza didn't wait for either of them to respond before slamming the door behind her.

With most men out working the docks, or preparing to sail south through the channel, not many filled the inn's pub. Those who did looked perpetually drunk. Anyone else either worked there or needed reprieve from the harsh sun.

Eliza sunk onto a bench in the farthest corner away from the windows or doors, where she could sit in peace. It seemed more like sulking if she thought about it long enough. Which she certainly did *not* want to do.

What she wanted was for Thorne or Dorin to talk to her. She knew Thorne found it hard to express his feelings, especially with all that he had lost, but after the Brotherhood, she wasn't sure what she believed anymore.

"You want anything?" one of the barmaids asked. Her dark painted lips twisted in a frown, thin brows rising.

Eliza bit her lip before nodding. "Just a wine." Like she'd drink it, though. She couldn't help but feel bad for just... sitting there and not doing anything.

The barmaid shrugged and left, disappearing behind the bar before returning with a wooden chalice, filled with a dark red liquid. The bitter smell hit Eliza full force as she stared down into the cup. The smell was strong enough she could already taste it.

As footsteps approached, Eliza expected to look up and see the barmaid and her unimpressed glare again, but to her surprise, Dorin stood beside the table. He didn't smile as she met his stare. Instead, his eyes glistened with guilt.

He sighed. "I'm sorry, Eliza." Hesitantly, he pulled out the seat across from her and sat. "I honestly didn't realise how much this would affect you."

"I don't understand why you kept it a secret," she said. "Why not tell me you knew Amitel? And I know there's more you're keeping from me."

"I know." Dorin sucked in a breath. "I met Amitel a couple of years ago in Mesah. I was a kid, and my mother needed the money. So, I followed him around, did what he told me to." He trailed off and stared down at his clasped hands.

Eliza didn't say a word and waited.

"Amitel saved my life," Dorin whispered. "He saved my mother's life. When he came to me and asked me to be his eyes and ears inside the palace, and to look out for you, I couldn't say no." Dorin looked up from his hands, and their eyes met. "I didn't say anything right away because it wasn't my place. I didn't want to go against Amitel. But when I started to learn more about you, I realised I *had* to say something, because..."

Her chest tightened as Dorin's eyes bored into hers. "I like you,

Eliza. A lot. And I don't want to ruin whatever is between us by keeping secrets from you. I promise I don't know any more than you do. You have my word."

Eliza swallowed thickly. All she could do was nod.

Could she believe what he was telling her? The sincerity shined in his eyes, and although she didn't want to believe him—not fully, at least—she couldn't help but trust that what he said was true.

Finally, she sighed. "Thank you for being honest with me."

Dorin stood and held out his hand, a half-smile tipping his lips. "I'll make it up to you," he said. "I promise."

Something churned inside Eliza's stomach, but she took his hand, warm and soft and familiar. The light of his eyes brightened, which sent Eliza's heart racing. "Alright," she replied. "You better."

His smile turned into a grin. "When I make a promise, I mean it."

"I'm sure." Eliza stood from the table and left two silver pieces for the wine, which still sat untouched. She really had to remember she wasn't great with wine. When she was fourteen, she'd stolen a bottle from Kay and had passed it around with a couple of kids who lived near her, thinking it would help her make friends.

It hadn't. Instead she'd wasted her first kiss and had been left with a major hangover. She'd learnt her lesson.

Eliza stared down at her hand, still clasped in Dorin's, and flushed. It took her a moment to pull her hand from his.

The sun dipped lower towards the horizon, but the day wasn't over yet. Daylight—and the heat that clung to it—stayed longer. It touched Port Beewold and left the seaside villagers working long into the warm night. Eliza saw the exhaustion on the faces of the men and women who continued to slave away at the docks.

"I'm going to go find us some food for travel," Dorin said, making a face. "I should help Celia."

Eliza nodded, sparing the wooden stairs a glance. If she went up there, she'd be left alone with Thorne. Maybe Dorin was giving them a chance to talk.

"Okay," she said, smiling. "I'll see you soon."

Sucking in a breath, Eliza braved the stairs. *It's going to be fine*, she thought. But she couldn't know that, not with Thorne. Since they'd met, he'd been secretive, and for the most part, she'd brushed it off. She had no right to know all his secrets, but the longer they were together, the more she'd realised how much he knew and wasn't telling her.

The Brotherhood, the Ecix, his connection to Celia... there was so much he had yet to reveal, and it weighed heavily on her shoulders.

Eliza hesitated before the door to their room, hand hovering above the doorknob. She closed her eyes. *It won't be that bad*, she thought.

Releasing a heavy breath, Eliza entered the room.

Thorne looked up from the bed, his stormy eyes wide. "Eliza," he said, voice somewhat breathy.

She swallowed thickly. "We need to talk."

"Eliza—"

"Wait." She closed the door behind her, closing them in. "Let me just say something."

Hesitantly, she made her way to the other bed in their dingy room and sat. "I know you don't have to tell me everything," she said, meeting his heated stare. "I know there are things you probably don't think you can tell me. But there are things you are keeping from me; things that could have made this mission so much easier. I just want to know *why*."

Thorne stayed quiet for a moment. No emotions showed on his face. Eliza couldn't help but wonder if he was going to respond.

But he sighed and shook his head. "I wish I could tell you everything," he murmured. "I really do. But there are things I cannot reveal."

"*Things you cannot reveal?*" she asked, scoffing. "Bullshit, Thorne. Can't, or won't?"

His eyes hardened. "Enough."

"Seriously? What about the Ecix? Or the Brotherhood? Or maybe the *real* reason why you're even helping me? It has something to do with Celia and your past, I know it does. And who is Isolde?"

Thorne's jaw ticked as he rose. "I said enough."

Eliza shook her head, disappointment shuddering through her. "Fine," she said through gritted teeth. "Fine." She didn't spare Thorne a glance as she turned her back on him and dropped into the seat by the window. Closing her eyes, Eliza fought back tears, and waited for Celia and Dorin to return.

~

Blood dripped from a cut on her hand, pooling until it mixed with the dirt beneath her bare feet. It dripped onto her dress, staining the white cloth red. But she let it fall.

Around her, there was nothing but blood.

Pools of it surrounded her until all she could see was a crimson ocean. It fell from the sky like a horrendous rain, but none of it touched her. No, she was only wet with her own. It left a bitter, rusty taste on the tip of her tongue, filling her nostrils.

"This is what you will become," a voice whispered in her ear. She spun, finding only emptiness. "You will destroy everything."

She spun again. Tears pooled in her eyes as she waited for something to jump out at her, as she waited for some sign that she was not alone.

But nothing came.

Eliza stepped away from her little island, stepping into the crimson river before her. She walked through it, noting how it only came up to her ankles. The hem of her dress turned red, veins of crimson seeping up the cloth.

"Hello?" she called out before stopping. She twisted again and realised that her little island was nowhere to be seen. The maroon liquid sloshed as she stepped towards it and stopped again. "Is anybody here?"

More blood rained around her. She released a shaky breath as she gazed at her bare arms. Still, though, it did not touch her.

Fear swelled in her heart and pounded through her veins. At her sides, her fingers twitched. She could hear her own blood thrumming in her ears, drowning out the soft patter of red rain around her.

Something sounded above her, and she looked up, stifling a gasp with her hand. The tears that had pooled in her eyes now finally fell as she beheld the source of the blood rain.

Thousands of people hanging from the sky, dead.

Thousands of people looked down at her, dead.

Thousands of people, dripping blood, dead.

Eliza screamed, and screamed, and screamed, until her voice went hoarse. She screamed until her throat burned, but kept screaming anyway, because she knew she couldn't escape the horror above her.

"This is what you will do," the voice whispered in her ear. "You will be destruction, and plight. You will bring famine and death and war. You will be the greatest weapon Cadira has ever seen, and you will pay for it."

Ominous chanting sounded in her ears and she fought back a wave of nausea. Above her, something—someone—shifted amongst the hanging corpses. It dropped heavily into the river, shrouded in darkness and shadow. It was the voice, she realised, but it was not the source of the chanting that steadily grew louder in her ears until it was a constant buzz.

"You did this," the dark figure said, voice barely audible over the continuous chanting. "I will make you pay for what you have done."

It appeared before her within a blink of an eye, just an arm's length away. It struck out with the force of a freight-train and sent her into the air, landing in the blood.

More of her own blood seeped through her dress, now at her chest. Eliza touched a shaking hand to the wound and pulled back quickly, crying out in pain.

"You will suffer, just as they have." The figure came at her again but froze. It growled, low and hungry. "The power of the Ecix will once and for all die."

It struck again, and the world fell away.

She was dead.

Eliza cried out as the dream finally disappeared, reeling from the pain that shattered her chest. The whisper of the shadow weapon burned against her flesh. She could almost feel the blood dripping onto her chest, feel the life draining from her as it stood over her.

"Eliza?" Celia hovered over her, hand covering her mouth. Thorne and Dorin were at her side a moment later, eyes wide. "Oh my..." she trailed off, reaching for Eliza.

Although pain and weariness still coursed through her, Eliza was lucid enough to understand something wasn't right as Celia pulled back the blanket that covered her.

Celia whitened as she stared down at Eliza's chest. "Brandon, I need a medical kit. Eliza, I want you to lay very still, please."

Blinking rapidly, Eliza ignored Celia as she touched a hand to her chest. When she pulled away, *real* pain shot through her, and she whimpered.

In the lamp light, Eliza could just make out the blood that stained her fingers before passing out.

~

"And you do not remember *anything* about the dream?" Celia asked again, dragging her eyes over Eliza's body. She paused at the steadily healing wound on Eliza's chest. Blood and puss seeped through the gaping cut, but so far, there had been no change to Eliza's health.

Eliza shook her head tiredly. "No, I don't," she lied, pushing back the memory of the hanging bodies and the blood river. "I just remember pain and waking up with *this*." She gestured to the cut. In her dream, it had killed her, though her real, physical wound was only a quarter of an inch deep at least. But it stretched over her chest, going from beneath her right breast, over her ribs, until it ended at her heart.

The lie had tasted bitter on her tongue, like the blood had in her dream. But if she'd admitted what the dream had been about, then it would have been too real for her. The lie was better, safer.

Celia ran a hand through her tousled hair. Since Eliza had passed out, she hadn't seen Thorne or Dorin, and whenever she asked where they were, Celia brushed off her questions. Instead, she'd dragged a chair over to sit beside Eliza's bed, a plethora of clean bandages at the ready.

"We should already be on the road," Eliza said. "If this is happening *now*, then we must be getting close!"

"No," Celia said with a frantic shake of her head. Fear blossomed in her clear-blue eyes. "You need to rest, Eliza. Whatever it was that attacked you was a warning. Something was sending you a message."

The door to their small room opened; Dorin entered first, sandy hair in disarray. He dropped a bag of what looked like fruit onto the spare bed, weary eyes finding Eliza's almost immediately.

Thorne was slower to enter, his body rigid. Eliza could see the tension in his shoulders and neck from her position on the bed. When had he last slept? And what had they been doing?

Eliza looked between them questioningly, a frown creasing her brow.

"What happened out there?" Celia asked, knotting her fingers in her lap.

Dorin took a seat on Eliza's bed and ran his fingers through his hair. "There are certainly some interesting rumours spreading through the port. Many are trying to travel south."

Eliza straightened, wincing. "South? Why?"

Thorne dragged a chair to the end of the bed and sat, meeting her gaze warily. Dark circles lined his eyes. "A couple of pirates who docked here told us an army for hire walked into the desert and just... disappeared. Only one survived to tell the captain."

Dorin dragged his eyes from Thorne to Eliza. "The man then killed himself shortly after giving his report."

Celia sucked in a breath, resting her hand over Eliza's. "That's horrible."

"But how is that even possible?" Eliza finished, shifting anxiously in the bed. "I've heard of protective magic that could perhaps cause an *illusion* like that, but I don't know about making an entire army disappear."

Dorin shook his head. "Mesah, I think, exists outside the normal parameters of magic. It is ancient. Whatever happened..."

"Well, it's a good thing we won't be going *through* the desert," Eliza said. "We'll be going *under*."

Thorne met her stare evenly, no trace of fear in his eyes. "We leave at nightfall," he said finally, breaking her stare. "As soon as Eliza can move, we leave. If people are fleeing, then we need to use the coverage to go north."

Eliza spared Dorin a glance. "Will that help?"

"Of course," he said with a smile. Eliza's heart fluttered. "Demons could be on the hunt for us now that we're getting close. We should use whatever distraction is at our disposal."

"Good." Thorne stood, the chair scraping against the hardwood floor. "We have three hours. Will you be okay to move by then, Eliza?"

She nodded, feeling Celia's grip on her hand tighten. If she had her way, Eliza was sure Celia would try and keep them there longer. But Eliza itched to move, to reach the desert... and find the prince.

29

STARGAZING

Pain sliced through Eliza's chest as she awoke from another fitful sleep. Her head ached with the reminder of her nightmares; shadow creatures wielding weapons made of darkness, a war so ancient people whispered its name, and a girl whose destiny it was to die, over and over again.

Eliza touched a hand to her chest lightly. The bandages that wrapped over her chest and shoulder were damp with sweat, the poultice Celia had smeared across the wound sour under the Mesah sun. The pain didn't recede though, even as she pulled the white cloth away to see the scar that marred the top of her breast and sliced down to her sternum, stopping at the top of her torso. Magic had healed it enough over the last couple of days.

"If you keep touching it," Celia said, rising from her bedroll, "it won't heal."

"You sound like one of my guardians," Eliza muttered, but she let the bandage go. She searched the campsite for Thorne, but he was nowhere in sight. "Where—?"

Celia sighed. "Checking the perimeter."

Eliza nodded, quiet. Since she'd confronted him, Thorne had grown more distant. She wasn't entirely sure if it had something to do with her confronting him, or something else, but Eliza couldn't deny that they'd grown apart since the attack on her at the palace.

"Let us go for a walk," Celia said, reaching for Eliza's hand.

Despite the exhaustion clinging to the edges of Eliza's mind, she nodded, and climbed to her feet. She winced at the ache in her chest but pushed it from her head. *I just need to do something to help*, she thought. Since the dream, everyone had been hesitant around her, wary. Celia's behaviour mirrored a doting grandmother who watched over a sick child.

Eliza was, for the most part, sick of it.

Celia hefted one of their bags over her shoulder. Dorin didn't look up from the fire as they passed. His head was in a book, sandy hair falling over his forehead.

Hesitantly, Eliza touched his shoulder. "We'll be back soon."

Dorin blinked and met her stare. For a moment, a dark look passed through his eyes. But it passed, and a smile spread across his lips. "I'll let the commander know when he returns."

Eliza nodded, and said nothing else as Celia guided her through the trees that surrounded their campsite. Since they'd arrived the day before, Eliza hadn't braved leaving the camp to explore the forest. It would be the last forest they'd likely see for a while. Mesah and the surrounding villages were bordered by sand, the closest jungle miles from their destination.

"What's the plan?" Eliza asked, stepping warily over a boulder. "Because I doubt we're just going for a casual walk through the forest."

Celia smiled over her shoulder. "Brandon told me there was a small clearing filled with flowers. I hope to find you something to help you sleep."

The clearing appeared ahead. Light filtered through the trees to create a whimsical scene of tranquillity and quiet, like it had been stolen right out of a fairy-tale.

"I am glad you came," Celia said, smile soft as she knelt by the base of an old, weathered tree. Red darkened her cheeks as she met Eliza's stare. "I thought you would not be up to it."

Eliza shrugged, sparing Celia a smile as she wandered over to another tree in the clearing. Growing in a small patch of sunlight, surrounded by tall green grass, white-petaled chamomile grew in small patches. A ladybug so dark Eliza almost couldn't see its black spots climbed over one of the flowers before buzzing off to land on a collection of wildflowers at the edge of the clearing.

"Collecting herbs is quick, easy," Eliza said quietly. The last time she'd done something like this, she'd been with Kay. Their herb garden back home had been large enough with a variety of different plants, both from the mortal world and Cadira. Sundays had been their day of collection, gathering the plants and preparing them for being dried and sampled. "Anyways, two sets of hands are better than one."

Something about the clearing nagged at Eliza, before a memory sprung to mind: a lake and two girls, wildflowers and talks of the end. Eliza shook her head. It had been a dream, and yet... she couldn't shake it from her mind. Because... Celia looked an awful lot like the girl from the dream.

Impossible. Eliza had seen Celia twice at the ball, and that had been why she'd dreamt of Celia. There was no other reason.

The smile on Celia's face faltered for a moment before she sighed. "Is there something wrong, Eliza?"

"No," Eliza said, shaking her head. She sighed, bringing her knees to her chest, sitting in the tall grass. She rested her chin on her knees, eyes averted. "I just... I feel like I'm missing something. Like everyone knows something that I don't." She eyed the swaying grass. "There's a whole part of my past that I don't know about. And there is so much that I don't feel like I can tell you or Thorne or Dorin. And I think that means they can't talk to me, either."

Celia dropped to the grass beside Eliza and rested her hand on Eliza's shoulder. Her voice was soft as she spoke. "It's okay. You can talk to me if you need to. I will not pass judgement or criticise, for my own life is not entirely complete and open either."

Eliza swallowed and considered the other girl carefully. "I have necromancy," she whispered, a weight lifting from her as she said the words. "I know it's forbidden and everything, but the king thought that maybe... maybe my necromancy might actually help. I don't know. But it's helped so far." She sucked in a breath, unable to look at the other girl. "I'm afraid to say anything to Dorin or Thorne. I don't... I don't want them to judge me for it or fear me. I'm afraid they'll run away, because for so long necromancy has been feared, and I don't want them to see me differently."

Celia touched Eliza's cheek; hands soft despite the callouses that lined her palms. Eliza forced her eyes to Celia's and swam in the warmth of the other girl's gaze. "I know you fear your magic. But you must not."

"Witches have been *hunted* for necromancy."

A soft smile tipped at Celia's lips. "I know. But there are places—"

Eliza scoffed, fear rising in her chest. "Like the Labyrinth

Mountains?" Eliza already knew what the Blood Witches thought of necromancy. While the magic was feared throughout the realm, that fear had never reached the tribes living within the mountains. They thrived on darkness and unnatural magic, and worshipped necromancy because of it.

"I never feared my magic before meeting the king. I *knew* it was dark—that's common sense. It's dark voodoo in New Orleans." Eliza sucked in a breath. "But it wasn't until getting the letter from the king that I truly started to fear what I could do, what it could mean for me and everyone I love."

"You do not wish to have this power, do you?"

Eliza shook her head in response.

"Oh, dear girl," Celia whispered. Her arms wrapped around Eliza's shaking shoulders; Eliza wasn't even sure when she'd started shaking. Her cheeks were wet, and she wondered if she'd been crying for long.

Eliza collapsed into Celia's arms, the weight of her secrets finally shattering in her hands.

Celia cleared her throat carefully. "You know, I once lost a sister who possessed a magic similar to yours. For that she was killed by a creature made of shadows. I vowed to find a way to destroy it." Eliza stiffened, her breath catching in her throat as Celia turned to her fully. "I will make a vow to you now to protect you. This magic does not have to be a terrible burden. It can be good, too."

Eliza nodded, but that did not stop the fear that rose from her words.

Killed by a creature made of shadows.

Eliza couldn't help but wonder if it was the same one that haunted her dreams.

~

Celia and Eliza returned with their flowers and herbs tucked away in leather pouches. Eliza wasn't entirely sure how to help in turning the camomile flowers into tea, so she handed that duty over to Celia. Kay had always been the one to work with the herbs and flowers after they'd been picked. Eliza had never been properly taught.

She sighed heavily and dropped onto her bedroll. All she wanted to do was sleep, but fear of the nightmares kept her awake.

"Are you okay?" Dorin asked, moving to sit across from her. He cocked his head, their eyes meeting.

Eliza nodded slowly. "Just tired."

"You should try and sleep."

"No," she said, shaking her head. "I don't think I can. Not without..."

"The nightmares." Dorin nodded. "It is getting dark. We'll have to keep moving come sunrise."

She hadn't even realised that it had gotten so late. The walk through the forest and harvesting the flowers had taken most of the day. Eliza had spent a good amount of their time crying amongst the tall grass. But she never thought she'd spent all that time away from their camp.

Dorin stood and offered his hand, a smile playing across his lips. "Do you remember when I said I'd make it up to you? For all the secrets?"

Eliza looked down at Dorin's outstretched hand and frowned. "Yes..."

"Well," he said, "I know just how to do it."

She raised a brow. "You do?"

"Of course." Before she could respond, he took her hand and pulled her to her feet. "You need to get out of your head."

He pulled her away from their makeshift campsite. Celia, with her back to them, waved them off. Eliza had no idea where the commander was. She hadn't seen him all day and wasn't sure if she particularly cared.

But I do care. She shoved those thoughts and feelings aside. Dorin was right—she needed to clear her head. She'd been a mess of emotions all day, so what she needed was some time to herself.

Dorin guided her away from the camp, down an incline towards a small field that overlooked the road. The road itself was hidden by dead bushes, concealing the spot from anyone who rode past.

A blanket had been laid out on the dry grass, just wide enough to fit two people. "What's this?" Eliza asked, surveying the space.

"I told you I'd make it up to you," Dorin replied, motioning towards the blanket. He took a seat first and patted the space beside him. "So, I thought you might enjoy star-gazing."

She couldn't help but laugh as she sat. *Stargazing.* What an odd choice, she thought, looking Dorin over. But she couldn't deny the peace that settled over her as she took in the darkening sky.

"This is... nice," she said finally. They'd spent so long sleeping under the cover of trees or in abandoned buildings that Eliza hadn't had the chance to really see the night sky.

Closing her eyes, Eliza took in the silence of the night. Cicadas played their song in the long grass near their campsite, and the crackling fire was carried in the soft breeze. She could almost imagine they weren't on a life-threatening mission to find the lost prince.

"I like this," Eliza said, smiling over at the boy beside her. "Thank you."

Dorin, already grinning, met her stare without flinching. His cheeks were flushed pink, the colour rising high on his cheekbones. There was an easiness to him, to the way he smiled at her that made her heart race.

There were no expectations for her to do the impossible. Thorne expected her to excel at fighting, or using her magic, and the king expected her to find the prince. With Dorin, however, those expectations disappeared.

Somewhere in the distance, Celia and Thorne were probably sleeping by the campfire, hidden in the small copse of trees that protected them. Wards that Eliza had put together with Celia's help were holding strong, protecting their group from prying eyes.

"The stars are different out here, I find," Dorin said, linking their fingers. "Maybe it's our position, but the stars are brighter, clearer." He grinned. "And I still needed to apologise for the way I've been acting. It wasn't fair on you."

Eliza took in the night sky, and gasped. It reminded her of seeing the sky in the country, without the smog and pollution of the city. Bright, twinkling stars broke out around them, vivid in a way that made Eliza think that if she reached out a hand now, she could touch them.

She spied constellations she had pinned to her ceiling in New Orleans: the Queen of Hicantha, pointing towards the west, her crown of Treiss pointing north; the wings of Algeran, the dragon who rode the winds of Cadira before the riders of Laziroth tamed them; and the Goddess Azula. All looked over her, all surrounding the twin moons of Cadira.

"This is beautiful," Eliza said honestly. "I've never really looked at the Cadiran sky."

"I don't blame you," he said. "You've been preoccupied with this mission."

Eliza sighed. "We're getting so close now. I just…"

Dorin rose on his elbows and looked down at her, filling her vision. Eliza held her breath in anticipation. "You look beautiful in the moonlight," he murmured, fingers stroking her hair. Dorin knelt over her, face close enough that their noses barely brushed. His breath fanned over her lips; he smelt like dew and mint and the night.

His eyes flickered from hers to her lips. She read the intention in his stare. Her heart thundered in her ears. It wasn't like she hadn't been kissed before. She'd been fourteen when that had happened, a boy she'd nicknamed Toad having taken that experience, but sitting under the stars with Dorin, it felt different.

But with Dorin hovering over her, and her heart ready to leap out of her chest, she wondered what it would be like to kiss a boy she liked, one who looked at her like she was everything in the world.

Like how Dorin looked at her, eyes glazed over, lips slightly parted.

"Are you going to kiss me or what?" she asked, sucking in a breath as a smile spread across his face.

He didn't respond. Instead, he bent his head and lightly brushed his lips over hers, sending sparks of desire through her. Eliza hesitated before melting into his touch. Dorin slipped a hand over her lower back and pressed his chest into hers, deepening the kiss as he swiped his tongue over her bottom lip.

The kiss wasn't chaste or giggle-worthy like with Toad. There was nothing chaste about how his hand skimmed her side to cup her thigh.

Dorin broke away first and sucked in a breath, eyes bright and half-lidded. Eliza bit down on her lip as she looked up at him.

"I'm afraid if we continue, I won't know when to stop," he whispered, lifting himself off her.

Eliza felt the loss of his body and slowly sat up. Her eyes flickered to Celia and Thorne's sleeping figures.

"We should go back," Eliza said. Dorin held out his hand, helping her to her feet, and for the rest of the night, she kept her hand clasped in his.

That night, she did not dream.

~

It took three days for Eliza to feel whole again, to pretend that her dreams hadn't taken more than a small part of her soul. But the dreams—nightmares, really—were always at the forefront of her mind, replaying behind her eyelids. Hanging bodies and oceans of blood; men wrapped in shadows and lost destinies. Eliza couldn't escape it, but she wrote everything down per Celia's request.

Sweat rolled down Eliza's neck and beneath the collar of her thin camisole. The sun had a bite, but Eliza's olive skin tanned more than burned. Celia and Dorin, both with naturally pale skin, had tried to cover up as much as possible, but both had burnt noses and ears, shoulders and forearms. Thorne, like Eliza, only went a deep bronze.

The protective shield they'd put up to defend their camp did nothing to fend off the sun or its heat. The cotton pants Eliza wore were damp with sweat. The closer they got to the desert, the more the heat grew and the closer they came to tracking down and securing the prince.

Eliza blew out a frustrated sigh. "Still nothing," she called out, opening her eyes and taking her hands off the map. "I can't get a read on his energy."

"Maybe he's being hidden," Dorin replied, biting into stale bread. "If the Dark Master is hiding him, then there is a chance magic has been used to keep him off the maps."

Eliza huffed and sat back against her bedroll, wiping sweat off her face. "I still don't understand why this is *my* job. Locating spells are *not* my forte. I'm better with defensive magic."

"Well," Celia said, dropping down beside her, "if you happen to know any defensive magic that might help us track the prince, then by all means, use it. Otherwise, keep trying."

Eliza blew out another frustrated breath before closing her eyes once again, focusing on the map.

"Do you really think it'll work?" Dorin asked no one in particular, his mouth full.

"Hush," Celia chided in response. "Let her concentrate."

"I can't concentrate if you two keep talking." Irritation shuddered through her as she pressed her lips into a thin line, but she suppressed a smile.

Eliza sucked in a breath and released it slowly as she focused her energy on the map in front of her, and the several drops of blood she'd managed to take from the king back in the capital during their last meeting. Although he hadn't been keen on the idea, Eliza had gotten it anyway, and had stored it in Thorne's bag for safe keeping.

The vial of blood sat in the corner of the map, while a drop had been mixed with dirt she'd taken from the side of the road and blessed. She wasn't fortunate enough to have a fully stocked arsenal of potions and witch-y relics that might help her. But since they were getting closer, Eliza had hoped the locating spell might work. That, and it was Blood Magic. Amitel had told her it would help, and she hoped it wouldn't fail her now.

She felt the dirt shift on the map. Pushing more magic into the spell, she could almost *feel* the dirt moving, though when she opened her eyes, it had stopped at the edge of the page.

"It was working," Dorin said, moving closer. "I swear I saw it move."

Eliza groaned and cleared the dirt from the map, carefully stowing it back in her satchel. Beside her, Celia looked up from the pages of Eliza's journal.

"You will get it." Celia looked back down to the pages, flicking through them.

"I don't think so," Eliza said, standing. She stretched and cracked her back, feeling some of the tension leave her body. "I'm going to go find Thorne. I need to look at something other than that map."

Celia waved a hand without looking up, and Dorin merely smiled, sitting back against his own bedroll.

Eliza couldn't stop heat from rising in her cheeks as she met Dorin's smile with one of her own. She thought back to the kiss, to the night under the stars.

More than once during their nights on the road, she'd awoken beside Dorin to find her hand clasped in his. It usually left her cheeks flushed but sleep usually pulled her under before she could make much of the situation.

Eliza rose and looked around the camp. Their party had chosen to rest on high ground, with a small riverbed below them. From their vantage point, they could see the road and several homesteads, two of which were unoccupied. With the land slowly growing drier, it was becoming harder to find fresh supplies and even harder to find safety during the night.

Thorne had chosen to take first watch, slowly circling their campsite. They'd managed to find a copse of trees, though they didn't offer much shade. But the horses were able to rest against them.

The commander stood with his back to Eliza, shoulders tense and rigid. Since her last episode, they hadn't spoken much to one another. Eliza had wanted to talk to Thorne about it all, but he'd shut himself off from her. She supposed she was no better, but she ached for the friend who had been there for her after the Winter Palace attack and the troll bridge and the masquerade ball. She wanted *Thorne*, but he had locked himself away. Had she done this? She mentally shook herself. *Surely not*, she thought, but the coil in her gut told her otherwise.

"It didn't work," Eliza said in greeting, sidling up beside him. "Something keeps stopping me before I can get any further than the edge of the page."

"Is it someone else's magic?" he asked. "Or something that you are doing yourself?"

Eliza frowned and narrowed her eyes. "If you're suggesting that I'm sabotaging the mission, then you can go shove it. I'm trying to find him, trust me, but the Dark Master is a hell of a lot more powerful than I am."

"That attitude will get you nowhere." Thorne turned to her. Before he could say another word, Dorin's shout echoed through the glade.

Eliza and Thorne looked at each other before rushing back to the campsite.

A vision flashed before her eyes; of a man wielding shadows like a sword, of dead men rising and fighting. She shook the thoughts from her head. *Not now.* Nausea and light-headedness washed over her.

They found Celia on the ground, blood dripping from her nose. Dorin sat beside her with her head in his lap. He looked up as they approached, and he shook his head.

"I don't know what happened," he said, looking back down at her. "One minute, she was standing there, and her nose was bleeding. The next... she'd fainted and hit her head."

Thorne leaned over and felt for her pulse, which roused her.

"What happened?" she asked groggily, blinking. She reached a hand up and wiped away the blood, frowning down at her hand.

Thorne released a breath, pulling her up. "You'll be fine. You probably haven't had any water."

Celia nodded distractedly, her eyes widening a moment later. Before Eliza could ask what was wrong, the other girl was on her feet and pulling Thorne towards the road, and away from Eliza and Dorin.

"What was that about?" Dorin asked, moving to stand beside her.

Roughly the same height as Thorne, he stood over her, even though Eliza herself was rather tall. It had something to do with her Fae heritage, apparently, but most guys her age hated how she rivalled them in height.

Eliza shook her head, and hushed him, before reaching up and circling her ear three times to enhance her hearing.

"What's wrong?" Thorne asked, once Celia was sure they were far enough away.

Eliza heard her sigh. "The council is not happy with me. They were sending me a warning."

"Why?" he asked.

"I am too far away, and that was not part of the deal."

"Then you should go back, for your own safety. I can protect Eliza."

Eliza could hear the worry in Celia's voice when she said, "I know you can. But I have my own reasons for being here. And I want to help."

"The council won't like that," Thorne said. Worry darkened his voice.

"I do not care as to what they like or dislike. I made my sister a promise, and I made Eliza one too. I will stand by her until the end, or until she tells me otherwise."

"She'll tell you to go," Thorne said. "She'll choose your safety over her protection. You know that, right?"

"Then I will not tell her about the warnings."

Beside Eliza, Dorin nudged her arm. "What are they talking about?" he whispered, closer to her than she'd realised. His breath fanned her neck and she shivered.

Eliza shook her head and bit her lip. "I'm not entirely sure, but it didn't sound good."

Thorne and Celia broke apart and looked up to the camp; Eliza met Thorne's stare, noticed the flare of anger in his eyes. Celia took her time in climbing back up to the campsite, Throne reaching them first, eyeing Eliza sceptically, before saying, "I'll be going back to look-out duty." He stalked back to his previous position, leaving them.

Releasing a frustrated breath, Eliza turned to Celia. Sweat poured from her body, dampening her clothes. Rushing to her side, both Dorin and Eliza helped her back to her bedroll.

"Are you sure you're okay?" Eliza asked, sitting down beside her. "If there's anything I can do…" she trailed off, hoping Celia would open up. But the other girl shook her head.

"I just need to rest."

Eliza moved back to her bedroll, sitting down, careful of her satchel and what was inside. Her spell book and journal were both tucked inside, along with her maps and the sand, none of which could answer any questions she had about Celia.

30

FALL OF THE PROTECTOR

It took three days of constant travel to reach the desert.

The outlying towns were worn ragged by the incessant sandstorms and the lack of rain. From those almost abandoned towns, it took them an additional two days of travel east, where Dorin's home awaited them, along with the tunnels that would get them under the desert.

In those long days—and longer nights—Eliza found herself slipping from Thorne and Celia as they closed themselves off. After Celia's episode, there had been no confidential talks between them again, no time spent together.

Eliza and Dorin hadn't revisited the intensity of their kiss, though it wasn't like she didn't want to. If her nightmares gave her a break, she replayed the feel of his lips against hers, the heat of his hands as they slipped beneath her thin shirt and roamed the skin of her stomach—

Eliza's cheeks heated at the memory, and she spared her riding partner a wary glance.

A crooked smile danced across his pink lips, awe settling on his face as he gazed over the landscape.

There were no more trees dotting the horizon, but instead hills and mountains made of sand. Where the Mesah Desert began was obvious; a wall of sand blocked any view of the remaining desert. The constant storm that brewed beyond the border between them and Mesah made it a tough border to cross. Those who tried, like the army for hire, usually ended up lost and dead. Others, if they were lucky like

Dorin, managed to escape before they got too far.

"We'll find him," Dorin said. "You just have to have faith."

"I do. I really do have hope. But it's hard when they... they don't talk to me." She gestured at Celia and Thorne, who rode ahead. Occasionally, they would check if she and Dorin were still behind them, before going back to their heated conversations.

Dorin sighed loudly. "They do."

"Sure. Is that why they give me the stink eye, or when they ignore me? I can't tell."

He laughed loudly, causing Thorne to look back. Eliza couldn't help her smile; partly due to Dorin's infectious, hearty laugh, and partly because Throne's frown deepened when she did.

"Either way, it shouldn't matter," he continued, eyes crinkling. "So long as you believe in yourself. Maybe that's your problem. You're so focused on what those two think of you, that you no longer think of yourself at all."

Eliza pursed her lips. He wasn't wrong. She did weigh everything she did with what Thorne and Celia thought. It was a strange feeling—even the thought process behind wondering if those two approved of her choices tasted strange on her tongue, but the familiarity of it startled her more than anything. They were her friends, but something deep inside her clutched desperately at Thorne and Celia, and it felt their loss more than Eliza could understand.

Thorne pulled back from Celia and trotted back to Eliza and Dorin, his frown gone. "We should be a couple hours' ride from Mesah and the city. But we need to rest soon. Celia isn't doing too well."

Eliza looked towards her, where she sat hunched over her horse, shivering despite the climbing heat. "Maybe you two should stay back while Dorin and I go ahead," Eliza offered. She couldn't imagine going ahead without him, but something at the back of her mind told her she should. "Catch up when you can. At least then I'll be able to do some research in town."

Thorne was already shaking his head, though, before she could even finish. "We stick together, that was the plan, remember?"

"Plans change," she said, harsher than she intended, but it hit its mark. He flinched. "Look, Celia obviously needs help. Even a blind man could see that. You two can stay back so she can rest for a couple of hours. I won't go any further than the city."

His eyes searched hers, roaming over her face. She needed to go on, with or without him. she was getting close, so close that she could almost taste victory on the tip of her tongue.

Her mind told her to leave them behind, but her heart... it ached at the prospect of leaving Thorne—even Celia—behind. And yet...

Eliza eyed Celia and her shaking form, then turned back to Thorne.

He must have found what he was looking for, because he sighed and rubbed a hand over his face. "Alright. Let me see what she has to say first though."

Leading his horse back up to Celia, Eliza could see their lips moving as he told her the new plan, and straight away she could see the fight between them. It wasn't audible—Eliza couldn't hear a thing due to Celia's hoarse voice and Thorne's murmur—but she could tell Celia didn't agree.

"You're doing the right thing," Dorin said from beside her. "She needs to stop, and you need to keep going. I'll go with you as far as you let me, Eliza."

Meeting his stare, Eliza nodded her thanks.

Thorne started back, Celia at a slower pace. "We will head back into the last town, rest at an inn," Thorne said, stopping his horse. Eliza and Dorin stopped as well, their own horses nickering. "You two will get to the city by nightfall, and we'll be there by midnight at the latest."

Eliza nodded. "Be safe."

"I do not want to let you go," Celia said, voice raw and soft. Dark circles rimmed her eyes, and since leaving Beewold she'd dropped weight like it was nothing. "Please, just wait."

Shaking her head, Eliza said, "I need to keep going. We're running out of time. I'm sorry."

Eliza met Thorne's stare and let it linger before nudging her horse onwards without looking back.

~

As darkness fell, Eliza was able to get a full scope of the desert and the surrounding lands. Through the constant sandstorm at the border, Eliza could just make out the silhouettes of Mesah's mountain range, where the slave camp sat in the mountain's shadow. Through the haze, she swore she saw turrets looming into the sky, but when she blinked, they were gone.

"It plays with your mind, the desert," Dorin said, staring out into the sandy hills. "Sometimes I think I see a person wandering through the sand, but when I look again, they're gone."

Eliza nodded. "It's strange how it works. I just... I don't understand."

"Warlocks, I swear." Dorin threw a hand up in exasperation. "No one believes me though."

"I wonder why," she muttered, though she smiled at him. "You sound like a madman."

Dorin grinned and pointed to a large building in the centre of the city. It stood four storeys' high, twice the size of any other building in the bustling city. There had to be hundreds of people running about, finishing their day before night fully fell.

With the setting sun, Eliza could just make out the city, could see the great wall that separated them from the destructive desert. "It's beautiful," she murmured, cupping her hands over her eyes. "Where does your mother live?"

"Right... there," he said, pointing to the largest building. "Or, well, right beside it. Closer to the wall. That's the marketplace. Every storey has a different use. The first floor is food and drink. The next, cloth and clothing. The third is weapons and other tact gear. And the last storey... I don't know what goes up there. Trinkets, I think."

Eliza smiled, her eyes roaming over the large city again before landing on a fountain. She couldn't quite make out what the statue depicted, but she was almost sure it was of Azula.

"Can we go to the fountain, first?" Eliza asked, amusement disappearing. "I just want to check something."

Without waiting for a reply, Eliza led her horse down the rocky path towards the city, praying that she'd make it before the sun completely set. She had a lantern, but it was already stiflingly hot—she didn't want to add to her discomfort. Winter definitely didn't reach Mesah.

The entrance to Mesah City wasn't guarded, though she doubted that any sane monarch would want to overthrow the government there. There were, however, several vendors spread out around the entrance, shouting about the treasure they had found in the desert, or promising camels fit for whatever one needed.

"The horses will barely survive here," Eliza said, dismounting. Dorin followed, patting his mares hide. "They'll probably die in this heat."

"My mother has a stable. They'll be fine there." He led her into the city, waving to several vendors who called him by name.

"How long have you lived here?" she asked, following him farther in. Shops were beginning to close for the night, vendors packing up their wares, and mothers chased children about the streets in an attempt to settle them down for dinner.

Dorin shrugged. "My whole life. My adoptive mother found me in my father's arms out here on the streets. He was dead. I don't remember much of what my life was like before she found me. I owe everything to her."

Eliza's eyes softened, and she could feel a smile growing on her lips. There was a strength to his innocence, she thought, but a pain in his eyes. She never realised how guarded he was before. It sent a shiver down Eliza's spine.

"What about you? What is your mother like?"

The smile disappeared from her face. "I don't know my mother. I was raised by my grandfather and his friend, Kay. I guess she's always been like a mother to me, but she was never really the maternal type."

"Do you know anything about your parents? Either of them?"

She sighed. "My grandfather never went into detail about either of them. I don't even know anything about my life before I was five. I don't know their names, or what happened to them." She met his stare, and he gave her a reassuring smile.

"Look," he said, pointing towards the stone fountain. "We're here."

Much like the fountain that stood in the gardens of the Spring Manor, Mesah's portal to the underground cities and tunnels stood fully intact. Much larger than its copy further south, it stood several feet higher and much wider; water spilled easily from the outstretched hand of the Goddess Azula as she reached towards those below her, offering a way to survive the endless days and stifling heat.

Eliza reached up a hand, but recoiled, holding it to her chest. A chill ran up her spine as she looked over the fountain.

"Is it the right one?" Dorin asked, voice hollow. She turned back to him, brows furrowed, but his face gave nothing away.

Eliza released a breath slowly as she sent out her magic, feeling for the portal's opening, for the tunnels that may lay beneath.

Something seemed to connect with her as a flash of light burned behind her eyes. "This is it," she breathed. Relief washed over her.

"This is the one."

When she met Dorin's stare, she thought she'd seen a flicker of anger waver in his eyes, in the way he set his lips. But when she blinked, it was gone, and in its place was a broad smile.

"Good," he said, nodding enthusiastically. Eliza forced a smile. "I suppose we'll be waiting for Thorne to arrive then."

She pursed her lips and looked back towards the fountain, to the opening. Did she really want to wait? She couldn't answer that question.

I'll prepare myself. Get supplies. Pull out whatever magic I might need in the meantime. Until then, I'll wait for him. If he isn't ready, then I'll go by myself.

Eliza offered Dorin a tight smile. "We'll see. But for now, let's go see your mother. She's probably missed you."

His wide smile faltered slightly. "Yes, probably."

~

Sleep eluded Eliza as she tried tirelessly to replenish her magic. The moment they had stepped foot into Dorin's adoptive mother's home, she had felt a sense of welcome, of acceptance. It radiated off the weathered woman who had greeted them, who had kissed their cheeks. And it had been brought through in the hearty meal she'd cooked her son and his friend.

But when midnight struck, and Thorne and Celia were nowhere to be seen, Eliza couldn't take the damning silence any longer, or Dorin's protective position by her bed, though he'd fallen asleep an hour before her.

Pushing aside the covers, she slipped out of the bed and into her waiting boots, tying them quickly and quietly as she watched Dorin for any signs of movement. But he didn't stir, not even when her satchel rattled as she pulled out her map and spell book. A dagger of Thorne's slipped into a sheath at her side.

Eliza bent down and planted a soft kiss to Dorin's forehead, letting her lips linger a moment longer than necessary. But he still didn't stir. Had she wanted to wake him?

Eliza had noticed how the floorboards had creaked earlier and tried her hardest to step around the loose wood. She'd barely succeeded, though, and flinched when the door whined on its hinges.

When he didn't stir, she sighed, and escaped into the night.

31

SHADOWS BEWARE

No one walked the streets of Mesah during the night. The only souls occupying the darkness were those forced into the crevices of the alleys for protection, drunkards stumbling home from the pub, or the literal spirits that wandered aimlessly down the streets. Eliza worked her magic to conceal herself from the living, decidedly afraid of what they might do if they saw her alone at midnight.

She didn't want to think of that, but the thought had crossed her mind countless times.

Eliza licked her parched lips, aware of how her heart accelerated the closer she got to the fountain. The way the water droplets hit the pool below was like music to her ears, compelling her to get closer and drink what it offered.

Shaking her head, Eliza stopped several feet away from the fountain, and waited for whatever spirit had been chosen as protector over the ancient doorway. She quietly called out for it, offered her aid in whatever it might need.

But there was no response.

"I know someone guards this gate," she said louder, carefully taking a step closer.

In the water droplets, she thought she heard a voice. '*Ask.*'

Eliza released a breath. "Was this portal used in taking the young Cadiran prince through the desert?"

There was a moment of silence, almost like it wouldn't answer.

'It was.' Eliza's heart thundered in her chest. Tears pooled in her eyes. Had she done it? Had she found the prince?

The voice continued, 'But he is no longer here.'

Eliza's heart stopped, then started thundering again. "Here? What do you mean 'here'?" Her breathing grew rapid, like she was running out of time. Was she too late?

'He has been back and forth through these tunnels with his master, and he has not returned.'

"He's free?" Eliza took a step back, reeling. "What master?" Blood turned to ice in her veins at the mention of the 'master'.

The voice did not reply. Instead a wind pushed her towards the portal, towards its opening.

But dread settled deep within her, and some part of her already knew what master. She didn't want to admit it, though; didn't want to dwell on those thoughts. The guardian had already given her enough; he had been here.

With one last look towards the empty street, Eliza stepped into the fountain's water and went down.

~

The city under the Spring Manor had mostly been intact, with few changes since it was abandoned.

But the city under Mesah was destroyed.

Almost like a storm had swept through the only tunnel in sight, sand covered most of the ancient city. Spires and turrets had crumbled to the ground, leaving debris scattered throughout the cavern. The once enormous statue of the Goddess had been split in half, the raven gone, buried beneath the rubble and sand.

Eliza cast her eyes skywards, towards the portal, and marked where she had landed. Darkness mostly consumed the cavern, though streams of light originating in alcoves with illuminating crystals penetrated shadows. It gave her enough light to notice that there was only the one tunnel, and that it was directly in front of her, leading into the heart of the desert.

She rubbed a hand over her face and stepped towards it, careful to remain silent as she did. If the spirit who guarded the portal was right, then there was a chance that the prince—and the Dark Master— would be using the tunnels, including their shadow army.

A scattering of rocks made her stop, one foot outstretched. It sounded far off, somewhere inside the tunnel itself.

Probably a demon, she thought, releasing a slow breath. *I can handle them.*

Could she handle an entire army though? She pursed her lips and stepped back under the portal's opening. If anything, she would need an extra set of hands, someone who could watch her back, whether it be Dorin... or Thorne. But she needed to find the prince.

"I'm ready," she whispered, looking up to the portal. Her voice echoed unnaturally in the cavern. "Take me back up."

The transition between the cavern and the fountain was painless; Eliza landed in the fountain above ground, her feet wet and her skin once again sticky with sweat. The night was illuminated by the stars above her, and the scattered oil-lamps that gave light to the empty streets.

Eliza stepped out of the fountain and cursed. She frowned. The bottom of her satchel was wet too.

"Just my luck," she muttered, taking another step from the fountain.

She sensed the attacker before they struck. Raising a hand, she threw a ball of light at the first soldier and ducked to avoid a blow from another. Focused on those two, she missed the third. He grabbed her around her midsection, forcing her arms to her side. He was large enough to pick her up and managed to cart her back into the fountain.

Fear and panic struck her in an instant, and she screamed.

But it was too late. Her screams went unanswered. They were going back into the tunnel.

Eliza fought back the wave of panicked tears and stopped fighting, forcing herself to breathe. The soldier that held her was twice her size. He carried her without an issue; her feet didn't touch the ground, but his head was still above hers. If she slammed her head back, she'd only hit his chest. So, she had to think of a way to break free.

Magic.

Closing her eyes, Eliza concentrated on the earthly magic that flowed through Cadira. She focused on her connection to those veins of pure magic... but found the connection lacking.

Gone.

Eliza's eyes snapped open and her panic seized her once again, tearing through her chest as her attackers dragged her towards the tunnel.

She could have torched herself, become a living flame to get herself out of the situation, but the connection to the land—to the elements and to her natural magic—wasn't there.

Blood Magic. The words were whispered in her ear like a saving grace, but still she hesitated. Despite what Amitel had told her, she couldn't get Henry Ivo's warning out of her head.

But did she really have much of a choice? She couldn't summon her defensive magic, and she knew little of Blood Magic, other than spells she'd stumbled across in passing.

Illusions, the voice whispered again. Sweat dripped down Eliza's back, the attacker's arms tight around her. They were entering the tunnel now, sealing her fate.

This is it. This is my only chance.

Eliza closed her eyes again and breathed in. Illusions, she remembered, required concentration. Her breathing evened out. Eliza bit down on her lip until she tasted blood and let it dribble down her chin, forgetting the pain entirely.

And she felt it like a chord snapping into place, the thrum of power that belonged to her blood. No longer did she have to rely on her connection to the land. No longer was she subject to *natural magic*. Blood Magic was raw and unfathomable and *powerful*.

Eliza kept the illusion simple to start with.

First, she imagined water, dropping from the ceiling. It echoed louder the farther they went, until it was almost deafening.

The attackers did not react.

She added another side to it, then. Sloshing water, almost like a river. It surrounded them, drowning out their footsteps.

Clearing her head, she pictured the demons clear in her mind: the talons as long as her middle finger, arched enough that if they hooked their claws into flesh it would tear like cloth. Next, she pictured their eyes, black like tar and just as slimy, paired with teeth sharp enough break bones.

She imagined the spindly demons running back towards them, their screams filling the ears of every soldier that surrounded her.

Then she imagined water filling the tunnel. It dipped towards them, as high as the ceiling. There was no other escape but to turn back. She made sure to add the spray of water, let it hit their faces and her own.

Her blood thrummed in her veins, and her magic poured through her.

The soldier holding Eliza dropped her, took hold of her forearm, and dragged her back towards the main cavern, while the others swore quietly under their breaths. Their footsteps thundered in her ears, because she couldn't hear what they could, or see what they did.

She grinned.

Their party broke through the tunnel and back into the main cavern, their footsteps faltering.

The water should have reached them by now.

They turned to her, and she struck.

Eliza hit the shadow soldier holding her in the throat, remembering the early morning training Thorne had forced upon her. The man stumbled back, tumbling to the ground in shock.

Eliza unsheathed her dagger and brandished it before her.

After weeks of training, Eliza knew she wouldn't beat them with only her weapons. She wasn't strong enough physically, and they likely had *years* of training. But she persisted, swinging her blade in arcs, hitting theirs. She brought back her illusions to aid her; the water disappeared, and now there were creatures manifesting in its place. They fed on blood, and tasted fear. They had horns and three eyes and ten arms. These were creatures of nightmare, twice the size of the soldiers.

Eliza pushed half her magic into the five creatures she'd created, willing them to do her bidding. They were real enough; they struck at the assassins and small demons with ease, sending them into the rubble and sand. One creature had three of its limbs cut from its body, but she manifested six to replace it.

Sweat poured from her body as she was left to face one shadow soldier. He stalked her, eyes black and unnerving. He did not fight with weapons, but instead with his hands.

Eliza was no good at hand to hand combat. Thorne had told her as much. It had been one of her problems while training, and though she tried hard to do better, it hadn't been enough.

"If you think I'm dropping this, you're fooling yourself," she breathed, holding up her dagger.

The soldier said, "I don't need you to." He dipped and swung his leg out, aiming for her feet, but she jumped back.

"I'm from New Orleans," she laughed, shaking her head. "I know how to fight dirty."

Choosing offensive, Eliza swung her blade, aiming for his chest.

Eliza felt her illusions slipping from her, though. She was no longer bleeding. Wide eyed, she cut herself on the leg, wincing as the blade cut through skin. Blood bubbled from the gash, but she didn't stop.

Silence, save for the thundering of her own heart and the slow drip of her blood in the sand, met her ears. Death surrounded her, infused with her dark, unnatural magic. She shuddered, and dropped her illusions, save for one.

It was that one she used to finish off her opponent.

Eliza summoned the illusion to her. It thundered across the sand, answering her call, and bounded straight into the last of her attackers.

He flew into the adjacent wall and did not get up.

She released a breath and cut the tie to her last illusion, sending it away to join the others in her head. Although she felt lighter, exhaustion filled her muscles, and she fell to the ground in a heap.

The carnage and destruction caused by her magic almost made her stomach empty. They might have been figments of her imagination, but they managed to cause more damage than she had ever thought possible.

This is what necromancy and Blood Magic can do. Bodies, broken and bent, littered the sand, crumpled against the ruins of Azula's city. Death and destruction. *That is all I am worth.*

Everyone—and everything—was dead. She could see the spirits of the assassins standing over their bodies.

She did that.

Stumbling to her feet, Eliza clutched her stomach as she limped towards the portal. She was going to be sick. *I did that. I killed them.* When she reached the portal, she closed her eyes and called out for the spirit guarding it, hoping it would answer her call.

Fresh air hit her wet cheeks. She sucked in deep breaths despite the heat that still radiated from the earth. She filled her lungs with it until she was sure she wouldn't be sick all over the sand.

Eliza opened her eyes. There was no one on the street, no one watching her. She spun in two circles to make sure there were no demons or shadow soldiers lingering in the shadows.

Nothing.

~

"Where the hell have you been?" Thorne asked when she finally stumbled through the front door of the house. He stood from his chair at a table, eyes wide, looking over her beaten body. "What happened?"

Eliza met his stare, then dropped it. "They found me."

"Who did?" Thorne walked up to her and grasped her shoulders firmly, forcing her to look him in the eye. "Eliza, who found you? Who did this?"

Behind him, Dorin stood with a mug gripped in his hands. Hair tousled, it looked as if he'd just awoken from an uncomfortable sleep. Seated at the table was his mother, and beside her, Celia, who looked even worse.

Finally, Eliza met Thorne's stare. "I found the portal, but there were assassins waiting for me when I got out."

"Why didn't you wait for me?" Thorne asked, voice harsh.

She closed her eyes and released a heavy breath, falling against his body. The weight of the magic she'd used, along with the fight and her lack of sleep left her empty, like she had no reserves left.

She craved sleep, but at the same time feared it.

"He's been down there, the prince," she murmured into his chest. Eliza breathed in his familiar scent, wrapping herself in it. "He isn't there now. But he was."

Thorne pulled away, just as Celia spoke. "You are bleeding. What did you do?"

Eliza looked down at her leg, at the blood that had slowly stopped spilling from her self-inflicted wound. "I did that to myself," she said, wincing as Thorne prodded it. "I was using Blood Magic."

"What?" Thorne hissed, stepping back.

Eliza shook her head and tried to ignore the way his actions made her stomach twist. "It was the only way. I lost my connection to natural magic, and I was running out of time. I needed to do something."

He shook his head. "You shouldn't have gone down there in the first place. You should have had someone with you!"

She flinched and limped towards a seat. "I don't need you to yell at me, Thorne. We are *so close* to completing this mission."

"You don't think I know that?" he asked, sitting down beside her.

Dorin's mother quietly left the room. Her son took her spot, his worried stare aimed at Eliza as well. He threw a cloth to her, and she wrapped it around her leg to stop the bleeding.

Thorne passed her a mug of water. "Tell us what happened."

"Alright," she sighed, taking a sip. "This is what I found out."

32

THE END OF TOMORROW

For the first time in weeks, Eliza's sleep was peaceful, undisturbed. She awoke the following morning feeling refreshed and vibrant, almost like the previous night hadn't happened. It had been a welcome change from the swaying bodies and the shadow creature. A welcome change from constantly dying in her sleep.

The water Thorne had given her the night before had been laced with a sedative, she was sure. Perhaps something he'd picked up in the last town. But she couldn't be mad, or blame him; for once, she felt ready to face whatever came at her, even if it was an army of shadow soldiers and demons.

"Where's Celia?" Eliza asked as Thorne entered her room—Dorin's room. He'd taken to one of the couches in his mother's sitting room, while Celia occupied the spare bedroom. Thorne, Eliza could tell, had slept in the hallway, either to keep watch or make sure she didn't sneak out again.

His voice was low when he said, "Resting. I didn't want to disturb her."

"You don't want her to know about this, do you?"

His eyes were sharp when they met hers. "No," he said, unflinchingly. "I don't. She doesn't need to be a part of this anymore. She isn't well enough."

"What's wrong with her?" Eliza asked, settling herself into the bed. Dorin's mother had provided Eliza with old clothing, including a thin nightgown Eliza wore to fend off the heat. She'd managed to unstick her hair from her skin and pull it back into a messy bun atop her head. "I... I know you two talked. About *a council* being mad about a deal..."

Eliza watched Thorne from the corner of her eye. In the dancing light of the Mesah sun, his skin looked golden, even glistening with sweat, she admitted. The strong line of his jaw was shadowed with dark stubble, the rise of his cheekbones reddened from the harsh sun. The slump of his shoulders revealed the muscles of his back and arms, the thin undershirt tight over his coiled muscles.

He did not have the same classical beauty of Dorin; when Eliza thought about Dorin, she imagined romance and a fluttering heart, of Disney princes and endless stars.

But then there was Thorne, who was rugged and broad and strong, who Eliza felt safe and comfortable with. There was a security about him, a peacefulness. But she couldn't escape the feeling that he expected more from her.

Heat rushed to her cheeks. He hadn't caught her staring—he was looking at his clasped hands, long lashes brushing his cheeks.

"The sickness..." He wavered and gave a stiff shake of his head. "It's not right. There's something wrong with the symptoms, but Celia won't listen to reason."

"Why not?"

Thorne's eyes were bright as he looked her over. "She's worried."

Eliza released a shaky breath. "About me? Or the promise she made to her sister?"

He stiffened. "What do you know about her sister?"

"Only that she died," Eliza said carefully, "at the hands of a... a shadow creature. That she tasked Celia with finding a way to destroy it."

Thorne nodded mutely, his attention elsewhere. "This whole mission has been hard on Celia. Seeing you, she imagines you're on the same path as *her*, and will end up the same way."

"Dead."

"Lost," he said quietly, meeting her stare. "That you will be lost to us."

Lost to us. Something in Eliza cracked, a fleeting memory— Thorne, tears wetting his eyes, Celia standing in the rain—clouded her mind for a quick moment before disappearing.

Eliza cleared her throat and pushed those emotions aside.

"We don't necessarily need to put Dorin into any more danger."

As she said the words, her heart raced.

"Exactly. Just you, and me." The way he said it brought up unfamiliar emotions. She hadn't realised just how much she had missed hearing those words, missed the feeling of it just being the two of them completing the mission. But it also meant keeping everyone around her safe—Dorin, Celia... it wasn't their fight, it wasn't Thorne's either, but he'd been there since the beginning.

Eliza closed her eyes briefly and released a sigh. "I killed those soldiers," she whispered. "I actually *killed* someone."

"You said they had black, red-rimmed eyes?" She nodded, confused. "If Henry Ivo is correct, and there is a chance that Blood Magic is involved, then those soldiers were being controlled by the Dark Master. They would have been forced into a sacrificial blood ritual. They were probably already dead."

Maybe Thorne was right; maybe they were dead, and their spirits had been holding on. Couldn't she have just found another way to get out, though? To save them?

For a necromancer, she thought, *I suck at dealing with the dead.*

"Stop feeling like you are to blame for their deaths. You had no choice; they would have taken you," Thorne said, forcing Eliza out of her thoughts. "You freed them from slavery, Eliza. If it *was* blood magic that bound them, then there would have been no other way. If anything, you freed them."

An emptiness yawned within her. "Still doesn't make it right."

Eliza didn't cry over them, though, and hated herself for it. Shouldn't she be grieving for the lives she'd taken? Wasn't that the right thing to do? She had used Blood Magic; forbidden, deadly magic. She'd used it to slaughter them. And she had enjoyed using it.

Amitel was right.

"It doesn't matter," Thorne said quietly, leaning in closer. Their faces were inches apart, so close that she could feel his breath fanning her lips. "You got out of there alive, and I am thankful for that."

She bit down on her bottom lip. "Even if I used Blood Magic to do so?"

He frowned. "Even if you used Blood Magic." Something dark flashed in his eyes, disappearing before Eliza could understand what it meant. "It is dangerous though, so I don't think you should do it again."

Eliza nodded. "It uses up too much power anyway. I held on to my illusions for only a couple of minutes. By that point I was exhausted and ready to throw up."

"How powerful were these illusions, again?" he asked, brows furrowed.

She shrugged; memories of the fight rose to the surface. "They were the ones that killed all the soldiers and demons. I created five monsters and made them disappear. I also made it seem like the tunnel was flooding."

Thorne looked away. "Although that would be helpful in battle, I wouldn't recommend delving into Blood Magic again unless it becomes absolutely *necessary*."

"Alright," she agreed. "No Blood Magic."

They sat in silence for several moments, listening to the bustling city beyond the walls. People shouted and carts rattled. Children laughed and screamed as they ran through the sandy streets. Dorin's mother could be heard cooking, while Celia occasionally coughed in the other room.

Peaceful, untouched normality. Something Eliza missed dearly. She missed New Orleans, the city that never slept. She missed her grandfather and Kay. She missed her life, her freedom.

Not long now, she thought.

"We still need a plan of action." She wrapped her arms around herself. "The tunnel is always being watched, mostly by demons."

"Fire usually wards them off." Thorne scratched his chin absentmindedly. "But if we want a chance of fighting them off, then you will need a lot more rest. We still don't know how far the tunnel leads out into the desert."

She pursed her lips. "The tunnel isn't high, like the ones we found in the south. The ceiling is probably just a head taller than you."

"Which means they won't be above us."

Eliza nodded, smiling triumphantly. "Exactly. Only problem is... the tunnel has corners, which means they could be hiding anywhere. I mean, we could flush them out. A wave of fire through the tunnel might scare them enough."

"But we'd lose the element of surprise," he said, meeting her stare.

"We already have." She released an exasperated breath. "They know we're coming. The Dark Master probably already knows I killed all those soldiers. He'll have twice the amount of men waiting now."

Thorne nodded. "I know. But now we know what he has, too. We know where he's been, and we know he wanted you. Alive."

Something about those words unsettled her. Her mind went straight back to her nightmares, about her two consecutive deaths. She imagined the person who killed her; first the figure, cloaked and mysterious who fell from the swaying bodies, then the shadow creature controlled by a man within. Neither time did it seem like she was wanted alive... Did he want to kill her himself, or was there something else he wanted?

Swallowing, Eliza supressed a shudder and hugged herself tighter.

"I think he wants something from me. That's why the soldiers were taking me alive." Voicing her thoughts sent her heart into her stomach, but she felt the need to tell Thorne, to have him reassure her.

His stare lingered, where the scar of her wound could be seen over the top of her nightgown. It stuck out against her tanned skin; shiny and red. It had almost completely healed, but there would be a scar, no matter how hard she tried to heal it, no matter how many salves and tonics were handed to her. It would always be there, a reminder of what her dreams could do to her.

Finally, Thorne's stare drifted up and he met her gaze. Emotions swirled in his stare, dark and anxious and passionate. "I will protect you with my life, Eliza," he said, voice rough.

She shook her head, ready to interject, but he continued, "It would be my duty, and my honour." Thorne leant over and kissed her forehead gingerly, lingering there for a heartbeat longer than necessary, before moving away.

Eliza felt a sudden coldness where his lips had been.

"Let's hope it doesn't have to end that way." Dorin stood in the doorway, his arms folded over his chest. Hair still a tousled mess, it looked as if he had just rolled off the couch. He wore no shoes, and his tunic hung at an odd angle over his lithe frame. The hems of his pants were rolled up, clearly too big for him. "I don't particularly want to see you die either." He smiled tightly at the two of them, then entered the room, his stare lingering on Eliza.

"I don't want to drag you into this," Eliza said, shaking her head, thinking about their secret moments. She couldn't let anything happen to him—he didn't deserve it. "I don't want to put you in any more danger then you're already in."

Dorin shrugged. "I like danger, actually. And last time I checked, you are *not* the boss of me. My mother is."

"You are such a child," Eliza replied, shaking her head. "Let me guess: she told you to get off your arse and come up here?"

He nodded proudly, a crooked smile on his face. "Of course." The softness disappeared from his face, suddenly replaced with a seriousness that Eliza wasn't accustomed to seeing in him. "I have magic. It isn't as strong or as powerful as yours, but I have some. It might be useful in those tunnels."

Her lips pursed as a memory buried deep in her mind came to the fore. A flash of light, but darkness quickly squashed it. She hadn't even suspected Dorin having magic. Hadn't sensed it.

Why?

Since the attack at the palace, and the deadly nightmare, she wasn't sure how strong she was anymore.

Eliza looked towards Thorne, who mulled it over. "I do not like the idea of putting other lives at risk," he said, meeting Eliza's stare before turning to Dorin, "but if you have something useful to offer, then I think the extra protection would be helpful. Someone to protect our front, another to protect our backs. Three would be enough to get us in there." He didn't sound particularly overjoyed, but the logic was there.

"You'd prefer an entire army, though, wouldn't you?" Eliza asked.

Thorne looked her square in the eye, unflinchingly. "Yes, I would. But I don't believe we have any soldiers to spare, especially so quickly."

"I should be there," Celia said from the doorway, a shawl covering her shaking body. "This is my fight too."

Both Thorne and Eliza shook their heads. "You aren't well enough," Thorne said, rising from the bed. "You can barely stand."

Celia locked eyes with Eliza, pleading. The rings around her eyes had darkened, and her cheeks were hollow. More weight had dropped from her already thin frame, leaving her looking like a twig. Her black hair hung limp over her shoulders.

"I'm sorry, Celia." Eliza started shaking her head. "But Thorne's right, you can barely stand." With her deteriorating health, she was a distraction. Although powerful, that power had disintegrated the moment she'd fallen ill, and if Eliza took the risk in taking her with them, then there was a chance she wouldn't return. Eliza couldn't let that happen, promise or not.

Celia looked down, shaking. "I can help."

"Then stay here and wait for us. Send word to the closest post of soldiers. Tell them where we are," Eliza reasoned.

As she went to walk away, Celia stumbled slightly and fell to the ground, body convulsing.

"Oh my Gods," Eliza whispered. Thorne rushed to Celia's side, pulling her body to his. "What's happening?"

Thorne placed two fingers to the base of her neck, where her pulse was. He stayed there for a moment before picking her up and carrying her to the bed. Eliza jumped up, allowing him to place Celia in her bed.

"I have a feeling she's only going to get worse. She's been completely cut off from her magic." Thorne crossed his arms, then uncrossed them, fidgeting profusely.

"Is there anything we can do?" Dorin asked from the other side of the room. He moved and stood beside Eliza. His hand brushed hers, and she took it, entwining their fingers. "I can go get a healer. There's a good one in the village."

Thorne shook his head. "No healer can help her now." Jaw clenched, he stood in silence for several moments, looking down at Celia before sighing. "I'll have to take her out of the city, travel south. It's the only thing I can think of."

"Will it help?" Eliza asked, voice shaking. She squeezed Dorin's hand, frustrated with how she couldn't do anything to help. Blood Magic and necromancy, with all their benefits, were useless now.

"I think it will. Her magic stems from her people," he said hesitantly, eyeing Eliza, almost like he wasn't sure if he could share that information. "She's gone too far from them, but I don't think that's it. They want her home for something."

Eliza furrowed her brows, something tugging at the corners of her mind. *A memory.* But was it her own? "That's... odd." She shook her head, but eyed Celia warily. "If you think it'll help, then go."

Thorne strode towards her. "That would mean holding off on going through the tunnels," he said. "I won't let you go down there. Not without me."

Eliza swallowed thickly, eyes flickering to Dorin. "If you aren't back by morning..." She looked back to the commander and noticed fear flicker in his eyes. "Then I think I'll have to. We've already waited too long. I don't think we can hold off."

His jaw clenched, and he looked away. "*I* should be going with you," he murmured.

Eliza shook her head. "You're the only one who can get Celia to safety. I'm sorry, Thorne. But if you aren't back by morning, Dorin and I will go down there alone."

By that point, Eliza was sure she'd have enough magic to get her through the tunnels and to the Dark Master. But would she be strong enough to do it all without him?

~

It had taken Thorne all of thirty minutes to gather the supplies he'd need to get Celia to a town past the desert where he thought she'd be safe. It was a farming town, he'd said, that traded with the people who lived in the desert. He'd mapped the route out quickly and efficiently, sure that he'd be back by the time Eliza was planning to leave.

But it was nearing morning, and Eliza wasn't sure if he *would* make it.

"He's running out of time," Dorin said, pouring Eliza a cup of tea. She took it without the intent of drinking it. "Will you really leave here without him?"

She shrugged. "I don't know. Maybe." She let her eyes flicker up to the man standing beside her, saw the utter faith glimmer in his eyes. Faith in her. She swallowed. "He could always come down after us if he gets here just after we leave. And he would, anyway. He wouldn't let me go down there alone." Eliza looked down at the green tea, the leaves swirling at the bottom of the white cup.

"He knows you can take care of yourself, right? Or is there something more between you?" Dorin asked cautiously.

Eliza looked up sharply, eyes narrowed. She hadn't missed the hint of jealousy in his voice. "There isn't," she said, standing.

She touched his cheek cautiously before bringing her mouth to his. The kiss was soft. He tasted like spice and the desert. Before she knew it, Dorin was moulded against her until she wasn't sure where she started, and he ended.

Before it could go any further—even though Eliza would have liked it to – all things considered, she pulled away. Her heart fluttered, and Dorin's eyes glazed over.

"Alright, I was just asking," he said, a goofy smile settling over his face.

She couldn't keep the smile off her own as she sipped her tea.

Butterflies took to her stomach in swarms, and anxiety pulled at her thoughts. What if they went down there, and there was nothing? Or what if she got Dorin or Thorne killed? Maybe the prince wasn't even down there; the guardian of the portal had told her that he came back and forth with his *master*.

The questions rushed through her, leaving her wanting certainty and answers. Half of her questioned how easy it was for them to get to this point. How had no one thought of the tunnels, or the desert? But she also wanted to cry at how long it had taken her to get to this point, and how it would forever change her life.

"Sun's coming up," Dorin said, audibly swallowing.

She knew she should stand, make to leave, but a tugging at her gut stopped her.

Dorin's mother entered the kitchen, a dish towel in her hands. Her silver-streaked hair was pulled back into a low bun, several strands hanging loose. Her eyes went to the blossoming sky.

"I suppose you will be leaving soon, yes?" she asked. The woman looked expectantly at Eliza.

Eliza turned her gaze to Dorin. That nagging feeling in her gut wouldn't subside.

Biting her lip, she took another sip of the tea, eyeing the brightening sky. "We should get going. Either he'll be there, or he won't. We can't wait any longer."

Dorin stood and offered his hand. The once goofy smile was now stiff on his lips. "Then lead the way."

33

SECRETS & LIES

Eliza was forced to cast away her connection to the land. The moment they entered the tunnels, the natural magic of Cadira fell away, leaving her defenceless. Instead, she focused on the magic that thrummed in her veins. It heightened her senses; gave her a kind of strength she'd never felt in New Orleans or when she'd first entered Cadira. The power she controlled from her blood was raw and real. She only had to rely on herself when it came down to Blood Magic.

She needed the elements, and her blood granted her that ability. A prick of her finger and blood welled at the point. Eliza used the blood to draw the alchemical symbol for *fire* on her chest, over her heart.

Her thoughts flickered to Thorne and the promise she made him, but she shoved the guilt aside. *No time for that.* It was better to ask forgiveness anyway.

Heat rushed through her veins and leapt from her fingertips.

Fire lit up the cavern and cast shadows over the decaying structures, giving light over the debris and the demons that skittered from the light, searching for darkness.

With both hands raised, she threw a ball of fire into a swarm of demons to her right, forcing them back with a sweep of her arms. Her next attack went towards a throng of demons behind them.

They weren't creatures she recognised; stumpy yet humanoid in figure, their long arms dragged across the floor while their unseeing eyes drilled into her. Their mouths opened to reveal fangs that dripped acidic saliva, while forked tongues slipped from open mouths to lick the air.

"We need to reposition ourselves," Eliza said, sweeping her arms around her, moving in a way a dancer would across the stage. She imagined her fire to be like ropes and swept them through the hordes of demons that surrounded them.

Behind her, Dorin grunted, a sword in one hand, and a flaming torch in the other. "I agree. Let's move."

They guarded each other's backs as they fought their way to higher ground—a mountain of rubble close to the centre of the abandoned city. It wasn't the highest point, but Eliza couldn't quite climb and fight at the same time, and she wasn't prepared to do so and risk tripping. She needed to get high enough to send fire outwards to scatter and kill the demons that cornered them and blocked them from the tunnel's entrance.

It's a good plan in theory, she thought, grunting as more demons broke through their defences, attacking with savage strength and unhinged jaws. *Now let's hope I can follow through with it.*

Without a word said between either of them, Dorin took Eliza's arm, wrapped his hand around her wrist, and jumped onto the mountain of rubble, pulling her along with him.

The demons surrounded their podium, clambering to the top. Dorin swung his sword around the base, forcing the humanoid creatures away.

"Are you ready?" he asked, wide eyes meeting hers. There was no fear in them, though, as if he were sure she'd be able to force them back.

She nodded tersely. Sucking in a deep breath, Eliza focused her energy; she imagined a spark igniting in her hands, felt the heat of that flame burst across her fingers. It spread up her arms until all she could feel was *power.*

Eliza released that same breath at once, sending the flame outwards in a spiralling circle. It hit the mass of demons and spread along the base of their mound, until the pair was surrounded by fire, and the demons were fully consumed by the orange-blue blaze.

Behind her, Eliza heard Dorin breathe out a sigh; she felt the rigidness of his chest pressed to her back as he released that breath, how it seemed to shudder through him in a sense of relief.

They waited for several moments as the rest of the demons burned. Being nothing more than conjured creatures from the depths of Cadira's hell, they returned to the earth as nothing more than ash.

Eliza shuddered. "I don't think I'll ever get used to that."

"Me either." Dorin shook his head and leapt to the ground, holding his hand out for Eliza to follow. With shaking knees, she took his hand, only a single thought rushing through her mind. *Where's Thorne?*

Dorin pressed his lips to her temple before starting towards the tunnel.

They walked amongst the ash and the upturned sand in silence. They stopped at the mouth, and Eliza raised a hand, sending a ball of fire through. "If any went in, they'll be scattered now."

Dorin nodded and held out his extinguished torch. She lit it with a wave of her hand.

"Where's Commander Thorne?"

Eliza spun, ready to attack. Her heart thundered in her chest, the sound filling her ears. She hadn't even heard anyone else in the cavern, but Amitel stood there, under the portal, arms crossed. A look of irritation crossed his sharp features as he took in Eliza and Dorin.

How did he know we were here?

"Where is he?" he repeated. His gold eyes bore into hers with an intensity of fiery anger that didn't quite suit his character.

Eliza swallowed thickly, extinguishing the flame that consumed her hand. "With Celia. She got sick."

"Does not explain why you are down here without him."

Beside her, Dorin snorted. "She doesn't need him to protect her." A sharpness had entered his voice, and Eliza wasn't sure if it was for her benefit or for his.

Amitel shook his head. "But the commander should be here. He is an adept fighter, and two people cannot go up against what might lay ahead."

"What else do you know?" Eliza asked, eyes narrowed.

"Not here. We should go back up and wait for the commander."

Eliza shook her head and took a step towards the tunnel. "I'm tired of waiting, and I am tired of being one step behind. I'm going in, with or without Thorne, with or without Dorin, and *especially*, with or without you." She released a heavy breath and shook out her hands. "So, if you want to help *protect me*, then by all means, come along for the ride. But if you want to wait around for Thorne and see if he shows up, give him my regards."

A moment of tense silence passed between Eliza and Amitel as they watched each other with narrowed eyes. Dorin bristled beside her, his hands clenching and unclenching as they brushed hers. She itched to take his hand.

Finally, Amitel gave a shallow nod. "Alright," he said, giving her a ferocious smile. "I will go with you for the added *protection*. But please do give me a moment to send through a message to the commander to let him know that we are all in one *piece* for now." His eyes briefly flickered to Dorin before he pulled a piece of parchment from his coat. A quill appeared a second later, and with a flick of his hand, the quill and parchment floated in mid-air, with a message being scrawled across the page.

The message then erupted into flames, the ash falling to the ground.

"Done. We should be off then, I suppose."

Eliza nodded, and she turned to the tunnel, Dorin to her right, and Amitel to her left. The former held out his torch for protection, while the latter claimed magic. Eliza wriggled her fingers in anticipation.

This is it. It's finally happening, she thought, and a smile twisted its way onto her face.

The three took a step into the tunnel and did not look back.

~

It took several hours of walking before they came across the first sign of life. Hidden behind a bend in the tunnel, a fire roared, and several shadow soldiers sat around it, weapons at the ready. They looked almost the same as those Eliza had fought off, and she felt a tug at her heart as she took them in. Was there a chance that she hadn't killed them?

The group of soldiers—five, in total—wore all black, hoods covering their ominous faces. They all wore bandanas over their mouths, too. Only their eyes could be seen, and even then, they made Eliza shiver. From where she stood, she saw only black, edged in red, the whites of their eyes gone.

These ones were different.

Any trace of Eliza, Dorin, and Amitel, had been magicked away earlier, a spell cast by Amitel to protect them. It acted as a shield; their footsteps were silent, their breaths a whisper. None could sense them. It was a kind of glamour, Amitel had explained to her quietly. It hid them enough to give them the element of surprise.

Amitel, Eliza, and Dorin retreated into the tunnel, far enough so their voices wouldn't carry.

"They will be twice as deadly as the ones you fought last time," Dorin murmured, one hand clutching the torch while the other hovered over the pommel of his sword. "They don't look right."

Eliza shook her head. "They definitely have a different *feel* to them. Any ideas on how they're different?"

Amitel rubbed a hand over his chin. "They have been experimented on with magic," he said as a matter of fact. "Meaning there is a chance that they have heightened *skills*, be less susceptible to certain types of magic. How did you get out last time?" He directed his question to Eliza, who swallowed thickly.

"Illusions, brought on through Blood Magic."

He shook his head. "They'll be immune to that now."

"How can you be immune to illusions?" she asked, brows furrowed. "That's powerful magic."

"Not powerful enough. Especially with the Dark Master. Unless you have any other tricks up your sleeves..." he trailed off, brows raised, as if waiting for her to confess some hidden power of hers.

Her lips parted, and she closed her eyes. Of course, she had a *secret power*.

Licking her lips, she said, "Just give me a minute. I'll be right back."

Creeping back towards the soldiers, she hugged the shadows to her body. It concealed her enough to get close to really *look* at them.

Perched on the shoulder of every shadow soldier was a shimmering light, usually associated with an out of body experience. Eliza followed the light with her eyes and saw the spirits of the soldiers surrounding the fire, faces twisted in pain.

For a moment, Eliza allowed the shadows to slip and caught the attention of one spirit: a young man, probably in his twenties. He looked up at her, eyes widening. His lips parted, and a look of relief seemed to cross his face.

Eliza raised a hand and beckoned him forward, hoping that the shadow soldiers he was attached to wouldn't feel the disappearance.

"You can see me," the spirit breathed as soon as they were alone, his voice low and bitter. "What are you doing here? How?"

"I don't have time to explain," Eliza whispered, constantly checking the group of assassins. "How much control do you have over your body?"

The spirit shook his head. "Only a small amount. Or at least, I *did*. But something changed, and now I just float beside it."

Eliza clenched her jaw. She'd tried once, to animate a body. Back in New Orleans, she'd watched a stranger die; it was a random man crossing the street, and he hadn't been watching where he was going. The car was too close to stop, and they collided.

Although the driver was fine, the man was not, and he had stood over his dead body with a look of remorse.

In that moment, Eliza had tried something different with her magic. *Reanimation*. She had pushed magic into the spirit with the intent of bringing him *back*, and although she had managed to give the spirit a second back in his body, the spell had failed. She'd never tried again. Later, she learned how dark and dangerous something like that could be. She was no Frankenstein, or a God. But she *was* a necromancer.

But Eliza had time, and she had the fact that the bodies were still *alive*. And all the spirits were still attached.

"Okay," she said, sucking in a breath. "I'm going to try something. You need to trust me, okay?"

He nodded hesitantly.

"Go back to your body. Tell the other spirits to be ready to fight for their control."

Eliza followed the spirit back to the circle of soldiers and watched as he stood behind his body once again. A new resolve had settled on his young face as he looked down at his own flesh.

Pulling her dagger from its sheath, Eliza cut open the palm of her hand. She let the blood hit the sand before she closed her eyes and opened her mind to the spirits before her.

Magic, far more powerful than she had ever felt before, burned in her veins. She called upon the forbidden Blood Magic, gave it her offering of spilt blood, and *felt* as it heeded her call and infused itself with her own dangerous magic.

Eliza focused her energy to the first spirit, giving him stability, and an opening. In her mind, she could see the line that tethered the spirit and the body, and she gave it a firm tug, forcing the spirit back into its body. She felt the collision of spirit and mind as if it were her own; the sensation of her magic reeled in the energy.

There was a sharp intake of breath as the spirit of the man took back control of his body.

Eliza fell back against the stone wall before deepening the wound in her hand. In her head, she could hear whispers. *Warnings*, against what she was doing. But she couldn't stop. It had worked the first time. She could do it again.

She managed to turn three of the soldiers before the other two caught on to the fact that something had changed. It was like a snap of reanimation for them too, like she hadn't been present until that moment.

One of the converted assassins struck before the other two could attack.

A blue-eyed soldier pulled a knife free and rushed forward, tackling a black-eyed man to the ground. They struggled in the sand, rolling over, before one fell limp atop the other.

The blue-eyed man rose, and the remaining black-eyed soldier swung viciously at the converted three.

"What the hell is going on?" Dorin came to stand beside her, his eyes wide as he took in the scene. Amitel followed and sent a blast of pure energy towards the black-eyed assailant, sending him to his knees. The last three finished him off in one sweep of a hand, removing his head from his shoulders.

Eliza winced, looking away. She quickly covered the blood that spilled from her hands.

"The spell is going to wear off," she said, catching the attention of the three she'd managed to pull through. "As soon as it does, you'll revert back to how you were. I'm sorry I can't make it permanent."

They looked between each other, sadness etching its way into their faces.

The one she had spoken to first stepped forward and offered her a smile, before bowing at the waist. "We are honoured that you gave us the chance to fight back. For your own safety, I would suggest ending our lives now, before we take yours."

A shuddering breath escaped Eliza's lips, and tears brimmed in her eyes. She couldn't take their lives, not intentionally, but he stood there, waiting. There was no fear or blame, only *hope*.

Eliza wanted to ask Thorne what to do, wanted his advice, but she settled for Amitel. She rested her eyes on him as he looked towards the men who stood before them.

He did not spare her a look. "I will make it painless," he promised.

Closing his eyes, Amitel raised both his arms and flicked his hands, snapping the necks of the three soldiers before them.

Eliza forced herself to watch as they fell to the ground, a single tear running the length of her face. She knew she could not have done that herself and sent Amitel a thankful look as she raised her hands, igniting the bodies. Amitel turned to her with sadness in his golden eyes.

Together, they watched the bodies burn.

~

The pounding of feet slowed their party to a halt. Since the soldiers, they had come across nothing else that would stop them in their search for the tunnel's end, though they had been forced to stop twice since.

The first had been because of Eliza, emptying her stomach in a crevice. She'd felt physically ill after watching the men die, and by the time they had walked another hour, she couldn't hold it in any longer. Following that was a dizzy spell, and Amitel had forced her to stop and rest. They had stayed there for all of twenty minutes before Eliza had stumbled to her feet and pushed onwards.

The second time they stopped, Eliza almost passed out. *Again.* The whispers in her head had grown louder, almost to the point of screaming, and she had planted herself in the sand with her head between her knees.

But this time...

Beyond the bend in the tunnel, Eliza noticed flickering light, much brighter than with the shadow soldiers. It sent a glow throughout the tunnel, though it didn't bend with the stone. Nor did it give off any heat.

"The mountain of Mesah will be your doom."

Eliza spun around. Behind them, the darkness had thickened, until there was absolutely nothing to be seen.

"What?" Dorin whispered, grabbing her arm. "What is it?"

She shook her head, biting down on the inside of her cheek, drawing blood. Her eyes flickered over the stone, and she searched the darkness.

Nothing.

She shook her head and turned back to the tunnel. "I thought I heard something." But that wasn't quite it, and she couldn't help but cast another glance over her shoulder.

The pounding footsteps were a steady sound; neither coming any closer, nor getting any further, almost like the people it belonged to were standing in one place. She could hear no real voices coming from the stomping stampede, but there were no other sounds either. Only the footsteps.

"Probably the Dark Master's army," Amitel said, rolling his wrists and cracking his neck. "Quite a few of them too, from the sounds of it."

Eliza nodded, and let her magic reach towards the army. It snaked across the sand, finding life and death entwined. Indeed, hundreds, *thousands,* of shadow soldiers. She shuddered. "I can feel them."

"How do we get through?" Dorin asked. He didn't sound worried, though, and Eliza met his stare.

"We don't," she said, furrowing her brows. Since the soldiers, Dorin had gathered his features into a constant *calmness*, not once breaking it. Eliza wasn't sure if it was because he was really *afraid*, or if it were for some other reason. Maybe for her benefit. But he hadn't taken her hand or touched her since. Was he afraid of her now?

"We'll wait for now." She directed her stare back to the opening.

She'd felt it an hour ago; a shift in the air, in the way Amitel and Dorin both held themselves. It had been subtle, but the whispers in her head had stopped as soon as it had happened.

Beware the sands, the voice had said in her head. *They lie.*

Since, Amitel had been more on guard, constantly checking to see if someone—or something—was behind them. Eliza had occasionally done the same, hoping Thorne had caught up to them, but no one had approached them from the darkness.

But Dorin... his entire demeanour had changed, though he had made a point to always check to see if she had been drinking water or eating even a morsel of food. His worry was genuine, she hoped.

The sands lie. Did her companions?

The footsteps stopped. Eliza craned her neck, hoping to catch something—anything—from where she stood, whether it be a shadow or a voice, but everything beyond the bend was silent. Ominous.

Threatening.

Amitel held a finger to his lips before bracing himself and casting an illusion around himself.

His illusions were different, Eliza had learnt. They weren't born of Blood Magic, but rather, elemental magic. It was the way he twisted the light that gave him the ability to seem invisible to the eye. It was interesting to watch.

Eliza counted the seconds—*one, two, three*—before he

reappeared. Eyes wide, lips parted in a silent scream, he tumbled to the ground in a heap.

"Amitel!" Eliza whispered, dropping down to the ground beside him. She shook his still form, panic rising in her throat. Behind her, Dorin said nothing.

The hairs on the back of her neck stood on end. Eliza didn't have a chance to brace herself as the darkness took her in its waiting grasp.

34

THE LOST PRINCE

She was in the courtyard of her home in New Orleans, standing by the main entrance. A cool, autumn breeze washed over her, and the smell of city fumes came with it. In the distance, Eliza heard the ever-constant chatter of the city that she had always loved, almost drowned out by soft jazz music that breezed through the open windows.

"Ah, I didn't think I'd see you this soon." Eliza directed her gaze to where Kay stood over a pot of delicate flowers, their petals dim and weathered. "But I suppose now is good."

The older woman looked up and smiled at Eliza, who couldn't help the tears that spilled down her cheeks.

"I'm scared," Eliza whispered, lip quivering. "I'm so scared."

Kay's smile dropped. The magic that brought them together seemed to dim slightly. Around her, Eliza could see dark-sand walls closing in on her.

"Eliza." Kay walked around to stand in front of the young witch. "Stay with me just a little longer, okay?" Her violet eyes were pleading. Eliza nodded hysterically, forcing her breathing to settle, for her heartbeat to steady. Slowly, the scene around her strengthened the longer she breathed. In. Out. In. Out. She repeated it to herself until a calmness settled over her, albeit uneasily.

"Good girl." Kay kissed the top of Eliza's head, spreading her warmth. "I am so very glad that you have come to see me."

Eliza sucked in a steady breath before meeting Kay's stare. "How did I get here?" Her voice still trembled slightly.

"I brought you here."

"Here?" Eliza's heart started thundering in her chest once again, but Kay's voice soothed her.

"I am in your dreams, Elizabeth. It is here that you—we—are safe."

Eliza shook her head hastily. "We aren't safe Kay; you need to go before he gets you, too!"

"He will not get me. Your mind is strong, as is your will."

Stepping away, Eliza ran her trembling hands over the flowers. She was home, back in New Orleans. She could taste cinnamon in the air and smell black coffee brewing in the kitchen behind her. There was a familiar sense to the landscape, but there was also a void, one that she wanted to—but could not—ignore. She had wanted so bad to go back there, and now that she was, she knew she couldn't stay.

"Have you found the prince?" Kay asked quietly, breaking the silence. "Are you with him? Are you two in danger?

Eliza shook her head. "I haven't found him yet... but I'm close. So close I can taste it, Kay. He's right here. I know he is."

"That doesn't answer my other question. Are you in danger?"

Eliza dropped her eyes to her feet, to the cracked cement below them. "I think I am, yes."

"I thought you were. I would not be here otherwise."

Eliza's head shot up at the sound of Celia's voice. The young woman stood beside Kay, still in her riding gear, her dark hair braided back. She smiled only slightly; there were dark circles beneath her eyes, and those untouched emotions swirled beneath the surface of her calm façade.

"How did you get here?" Eliza asked, looking between the two. "I thought you were with Thorne!"

Celia nodded sadly. "I was—am—with him. I think. When you were knocked unconscious, I was rendered so as well. I am in your thoughts, much like Kay."

Releasing a breath, Eliza asked, "Why are you here?"

"To protect you." She clasped her hands in front of her, back straightening. "And I am here to help you."

"How?"

"Your magic," Kay answered, smiling. "We will help you use your magic to release you from your restraints."

Eliza swallowed thickly and pushed a hand to her temple. Pain erupted there again, with the force of a sledgehammer, and it sent her stumbling to the ground.

"What?" Celia asked, rushing to her side. "What is it?"

Groaning, Eliza stood with Celia's help, and leaned against her for support. "I don't know." She squeezed her eyes shut as pain rocked through her again. "But whatever it is, it hurts like hell."

When she opened her eyes again, Kay had a look of quiet rage on her face; lips pursed, eyes narrowed, and hands on her hips. Eliza had seen that look a thousand times, especially directed at her. But there was a difference to this look, one that shook Eliza to the core. Fear. It seeped through the lines of her face, showed in the set of her brows. Kay had never been one to show fear, and yet... there it was, shining through the cracks.

"Okay," Eliza said, forcing a new kind of determination on to herself. "What do I need to do?"

Kay's eyes snapped to hers, and a flicker of relief appeared in her hardened eyes, softening her face. "We will teach you how to get out using a kind of magic that has been... settling, in your veins."

"You have always had this power," Celia said, wary, "but you have never been taught how to control it."

"Tell me," Eliza said, steeling herself.

Kay's lips thinned before she said, "Blood Magic."

Eliza's brows shot up and her eyes widened. "How did you know?" she trailed off when Kay's stare hardened again.

Her eyes dropped to her hands, to the shallow cut she had inflicted upon herself only hours before when she helped the shadow soldiers. She'd used Blood Magic. Despite promising Thorne, it had come so naturally to her that she hadn't thought twice about it.

"I'm a Blood Witch?" Eliza asked, voice cracking. "How?"

Kay swallowed. "I cannot give you the details, kid, but you need to trust the power that is flowing through your veins. You are far more powerful than you think. I know that, and most importantly, so do you. The Dark Master has been underestimating you. He thinks because of how you were raised you are no match for him. But that is not true. You and I both know that. So, prove him wrong."

This time, the determination that Eliza felt wasn't forced. It rippled through her, heating her blood. It gave way to that power she had been sitting on, power that belonged to her.

Pain shot through her head once again, a voice penetrating her dream.

*Wake up! it screamed. The words shuddered through her,
sending her to the ground again.*

Eliza looked up. "I'm waking up. You need to tell me what to do!"

*Kay and Celia shared a look. "Start delving into the magic that's
in your blood. That is all you need," Celia said, kneeling beside her.
"Use that power. And use that other power of yours, too. It will be
useful. Thorne is on his way. He should almost be there. Get to him,
okay?"*

*Eliza nodded, casting a glance over her home, before reality
struck her once again.*

Eliza awoke.

Darkness filled what she assumed was her cell; it was thick and
tense, filled with the sounds of rattling chains and the moans of the
dead. Dirt and rocks dropped from above, spilling to the ground
beneath her.

Eliza pulled at her arms, groaning as they strained against
shackles.

"You will die here," a voice whispered beside her. She jumped,
straining her arms again, grunting as skin broke at her wrists. "You
must get out."

A face appeared beside her. Shallow cheeks and hollow eyes, the
spirit watched her with a cocked head and a lipless frown. His bony
fingers swiped uselessly at her bonds.

"You want to help me?" she asked, quietly, releasing a breath. He
nodded. "What should I do?"

Fear crossed the spirit's face. "I have been here too long."

"Here?" Eliza pulled at her restraints again. Her energy was low,
leaving her dizzy. She could just *feel* the power in her blood, but
something was stopping it. It sent her stomach rolling. "Where are
we?"

"We are in the mountain of Mesah," he whispered, face
uncomfortably close once again. "In the caves. Where my people were
once enslaved with the Elves."

Her brows furrowed, and she tried again to break through her
restraints. She called upon the magic that lay dormant in her veins and
grunted when it didn't respond.

"If I don't get free, more will die too. You need to help me, so I can
help you."

The spirit looked down at his misshapen hands. But his head shot up and he disappeared, reappearing a moment later with a dull look in his translucent eyes. "It's too late," he moaned, head in his hands. "They're coming for you."

Eliza closed her eyes, feeling defeat begin to weigh down on her. The cell seemed almost emptier now, without the spirit or Celia and Kay helping her.

Light pierced through the darkness, blinding her. She ducked her head and squinted as three soldiers entered the cramped cave that served in holding her.

As her eye's adjusted, Eliza was able to take everything in; three soldiers stood over her, the shadows of demons flickering beyond the door. There were four skeletons across from her, and spiders covering every inch of the ceiling. The soldiers were dressed in black, cloth covering the mouths, leaving their red-ringed black eyes as the only feature Eliza could see. Every other inch of their bodies were covered in fabric, all of it black.

In the light, she could also see herself better, and noticed then that all her weapons and her satchel were missing from her body.

Eliza shuddered, and waited with narrowed eyes as the soldiers took their time in unshackling her from the restraints above her head.

She fell to the ground in a heap and held her wrists to herself. Sticky blood coated her fingers and stung with every touch. In her satchel, she had stored bandages and salve, but without knowing where any of that was...

The soldiers grabbed her arms and she hissed in pain as they shackled her once again. They pulled her arms behind her back and clamped the manacles down on her wrists, tighter than before. She was forced to her feet and pushed towards the door, amongst the horde of demons.

Two soldiers held her at all times, while another brought up the rear. Two more appeared before them, heading their party as they manoeuvred their way through the old slave tunnels.

The ceiling was high and dusted with cobwebs and hanging cells. Skeletons swayed in a forgotten breeze. A memory flashed behind Eliza's eyes, of her dream and the hanging bodies.

Around them were indents in the walls, where cells were located. With a press of a hand, a door would open. Old magic kept the cells closed. Old magic kept her restrained.

Sconces with lit torches scattered the walls, illuminating their way; the light danced off the red-dirt walls, giving them a bloody glow. The light only just reached the ceiling above them, where Eliza could still see the ancient dead. Demons watched from above, too, dancing between the bodies and the cells. There were over a hundred just above her, waiting for their next meal.

Eliza supressed a shudder.

The tunnel opened into a cave so big it put the Winter Palace to shame; the ceiling was twice as high as the tunnel, with stalactites hanging from above. More demons crowded around those, hanging from the dripping rock. Columns reached the sky, and the stone-floor fell into nothingness near the far wall. The walls were the same red rock; skeletons scattered the round walls, with the occasional torch bringing light to the spacious room.

A single man stood in the centre of the room, back to Eliza. A hood covered his head, and with his hands clasped behind his back, Eliza could feel the power that emanated from him.

The soldiers stopped her no more than ten feet away from the man and unshackled her.

"Thank you." Eliza recognised the low and demanding voice of the man in front of her. "Eliza, Eliza, Eliza." Though it had deepened, the way he said her name was the same.

Heart thundering, Eliza blanched as he turned and dropped his hood. The smile she'd grown so used to was the same; eyes a brilliant green in the dim light of the cavern. But the way he looked at her... that was what made her heart drop into the pit of her stomach.

This wasn't the same man she had watched the stars with or had kissed.

Eliza gave an angry shake of her head and looked away. "How could I have been so *naïve* and *stupid* as to trust you?" she whispered. "Everything was a lie, wasn't it?"

Dorin shrugged, head cocked. "Well, it wasn't *all* a lie."

"Why?" She shook her head, breath catching in her throat, panic seizing her. "Why do it?"

"Well, if you're asking why I *betrayed* you, then that's easy: I was never on your side."

Despite the assassins at her back and the warning in her blood, Eliza stepped towards him. "Who are you really?"

Dorin stepped up so that they were a breath apart. For a moment, she thought she saw remorse flicker in his eyes.

His voice was a whisper as he pressed closer, hot breath fanning her cheek. "Don't you get it, Eliza? *I'm* the lost prince."

35

POWER OF THE ECIX

Eliza closed her eyes as Dorin—*Alicsar's*—laugh pierced through the strange quiet of the cavern. Through his bouts of laughter, she could hear the thrumming of her own heart in her ears. It was enough to remind her who she was trapped with.

She wanted to curse herself for being so stupid, to allow her feelings for him to cloud her judgement. The fierce burn of her cheeks forced her to look him in the eye. "Was anything real? Or did you use magic?"

"Love potions aren't real," he said, "but compliancy ones are." Before she could step away, his lips were on hers, locking her into place. His hands gripped her forearms tight enough to make her gasp, his fingers digging into her flesh.

For a moment, she could almost forget the betrayal and the pain caused by his hands.

But there was no warmth in his kiss, not like there had been in those few days where she had believed in something *more*.

Suddenly, she remembered the masquerade, the dark magic that had hit her during the attack. Before it, she'd been worried about who Dorin was. But she had started to trust him.

No. She'd been spelled into trusting him.

Eliza pulled away first, shoving him back with what limited magic she had. Something flashed in his eyes as a smirk formed on his lips.

"You want to know how you couldn't tell." His voice dripped disdain. "You haven't figured it out, yet?"

Eliza's jaw clenched as she looked him over, the magic in her blood singing. Now that she could feel that raw connection, the pureness of her own power thrumming in her veins, she could see the lines of Blood Magic that snaked through him. "You were using Blood Magic this whole time, weren't you? You were using an illusion to hide yourself. No one ever saw the real you."

"Well," he murmured, devilish grin widening, "everyone but you. I just wanted to know if you would see what was standing right in front of you." Blood pounded in Eliza's ears as he circled her. She spied a sword strapped to his back, the knives along his chest. "I don't blame you for not recognising me, though." He grinned again. "I do take after my mother. However, I *did* use an illusion against you at the Winter Palace. Remember Duke Irvington?"

Eliza's stomach twisted.

Alicsar grinned. "Me."

She looked up with a shake of her head, meeting his stare. "What game are you playing, *Alicsar?*"

Behind her, Eliza felt a surge of power as spirits rose from their restless sleep. Her fingers curled with the magic in her blood.

Alicsar slipped behind her. "Oh, no game. I only want one thing: the throne."

Eliza didn't move. "You already have the throne." Irritation swelled within her, stopping the fear and panic from rising any further. "Do you have any idea as to how *long* King Bastian has been looking for you? He wants you back because he loves you. He has no other heirs, and he doesn't want anyone else. He wants *you* to take the throne when he steps down."

The lost prince circled her until he was before her again. Eliza watched every movement, aware that it wouldn't end well for her if she moved. There were still demons above her, shadow soldiers behind her, potentially an entire army at her feet.

"Why do you think I've been tracking you?" Eliza continued. "Not because I want to. I've seen the destruction caused by the Dark Master, and how it's affecting the king. He needs his *son.*"

The smile had disappeared from his face, but it reappeared as soon as she finished. "Bravo. You can act, I will give you that."

Eliza released an exasperated breath, clenching her jaw as he circled her again.

"Why do you think I want to be *given* anything? I can take the throne."

Finally, she threw her hands up. "Why? Because the *Dark Master* told you to?"

His face darkened, and he stepped up, eyes glancing her up and down. "You do not know anything about the war that is brewing. And you have no idea what your role is, either."

"I don't care," she said, her stare meeting his evenly. "I came to Cadira to do a job. If it happens to be a lost cause, then Bastian can't really blame me for that."

The prince smiled. "You know, I am the reason Celia fell ill."

Eliza's heart stopped in her chest before it started thundering. "Why?"

If she died... What would she do? The dark side of her wanted blood for the pain he caused her. She didn't recognise that side.

"Well, she was a threat for starters." Alicsar shrugged without remorse. "I knew she'd be able to see through the illusion eventually, being a Blood Witch and all. Oh, you didn't know that? Shame. Not to mention, if something were to happen to Commander Brandon Thorne's last link to his one true love, then I knew he would rush to *her* side, no matter how he feels about you."

Taking a step back, Eliza's hands trembled. She wanted to laugh at the absurdity. "What are you talking about?"

Cruelness marked his face in the twist of his lips. "You don't see it? Then again, I managed to get you all to myself in just a couple of hours. Too easy."

Frustrated tears burned behind Eliza's eyes. "Stop."

Alicsar laughed again. "The commander has been in love with you this entire time, and you threw that in his face by choosing *me*. Hopefully, that slows him down enough to give me what I want."

"He isn't—"

"Oh, but he is." Alicsar stopped in front of her and cupped her cheeks. She tried to pull away, but his grip was strong. "Why do you think he started turning away? He could see how you felt about me, and it killed him."

"What do you really want?" she asked.

Just a little longer.

Like Celia had told her, Eliza delved into the power that slumbered within her, stroking at it with hesitant fingers before grasping onto it.

Magic rushed through her, powering through the scrapes on her wrists, encircling her.

Alicsar's eyes crinkled, as if he were going to smile, but he snapped his fingers. Behind her, the sound of someone being dragged through the sand hit her, just as her fear snapped. Eliza's heart dropped into her stomach.

The prince gave her a wide smile. "I'd like you to meet my number one *spy* through all of this."

A body landed in the dirt behind her. Eliza turned.

"Amitel?" Her mouth went dry as she stared down at the blond-haired Warlock. Dark circles rimmed his eyes and blood dripped from his lips. In his stomach was a knife, blood spilling onto the sand.

Alicsar stepped up beside her and touched her cheek. She flinched. "Ah, yes, he was very faithful for some time. Led all my father's soldiers in all the wrong directions when they went looking for me."

Eliza dragged her eyes away from Amitel's bloody stomach and met the prince's devilish gaze. "Are you the Dark Master?"

He grinned. "Unfortunately, no. Nor do I know his true identity. Amitel doesn't either, before you ask."

With a nod from Alicsar, a soldier stepped forward and twisted the knife in Amitel's stomach.

The Warlock did not cry out, nor did he utter a sound. Eliza could see the pain in his eyes but couldn't see fear. Those beautiful eyes of his remained emotionless as he gazed up at her.

Eliza dropped to her knees in front of him as something inside her snapped, like a wick igniting. Her hands shook, and despite herself, she wanted to help him. Grimacing, Eliza met his stare, and pulled the knife from his body. She felt the blood stick to her fingers as she dropped it to the sand, keeping it in her line of sight. With her other hand, she quickly covered the wound, pressing down. Her fingers grew warm with the feel of his blood—and with the magic that started building in her veins.

Behind her, Alicsar growled in irritation, but she ignored him. Amitel had been right, *the sands lie.*

He'd said it to her, had left the warning for her. He had been the one urging her to use Blood magic. *He was preparing me.*

"You should not underestimate him." Amitel coughed, blood sputtering from his white lips.

Eliza cocked her head and with a calmness she did not feel, she said, "He should not underestimate me."

Soon, one of the spirits seemed to tell her. *Soon you will be saved.*

I no longer need saving, she replied. *I am my own saviour.*

The magic she harboured in her veins flared like electricity, filling her with a familiar warmth she relished in. That power she had once feared snapped at her fingertips, mingling with the blood that covered her hands.

"You have so much compassion for one who has lied to you." Alicsar shook his head in disdain.

She looked up at him with narrowed eyes. There it was again, that flash of emotion. Hurt? Eliza couldn't be sure. Did *he* feel betrayed knowing Eliza would help Amitel despite everything?

Eliza shrugged. "I have a hero complex, unfortunately. 'Everyone can be saved' and all that crap. Benefits of living in modern New Orleans."

Keeping the knife in her line of sight, Eliza stood. The prince crossed his arms over his chest, face pinched in disinterest.

"I've been told much about you. That power you have, the one you used to reanimate my soldiers? That's why you're here."

Heart pounding, Eliza straightened. "Finally, some answers."

"I need *you*, that power, to help me continue building my army." He spread his arm out towards the drop in the cavern. Eliza swallowed thickly and walked towards it, to see it with her own eyes.

Rows upon rows of masked soldiers filled the cavern below her, spanning in all directions. They were motionless, as if in a state of slumber.

Behind her, Alicsar continued, "They are neither dead, nor alive. I need *you* to give them life, give them purpose. I have used whatever Blood Magic I can to bring my own guard to life. Including all the ones you slaughtered."

Eliza shuddered; her illusions came to mind as they killed the shadow soldiers. *He* had set that up, with the hopes of dragging her to this exact spot for this reason. She had gotten away though, despite his best efforts. And he had tried to stop her again, by placing more guards in the tunnels. But she had stopped them too.

But there were *thousands* of soldiers lined up below her. Thousands of misplaced spirits, hovering above their own flesh.

An army that could surely go up against the King of Cadira, against the Fae and any who dared ally themselves with the kingdom.

Eliza swallowed back her bile and stepped away, head spinning.

"What does the Ecix have to do with any of this?" she asked softly.

"The Ecix is an ancient power that has belonged to the Blood Witches for thousands of years," he said. "It has started wars, and it has ended them."

"Why do you think I have this power?" Eliza walked back towards Amitel. She twisted her hand, hoping the energy would fall to him, would help him heal. She could still see the blood pouring from his stomach, mixing with the red sand.

Alicsar followed her back towards the centre of the cavern. His gait was calm, almost excited. He met her near Amitel, his face hard.

"The power of the Ecix grants one control over the dead. You can see spirits, converse with them, and you have the ability to animate the dead. You've managed to reanimate my soldiers with a little Blood Magic, and you have overpowered my own controls. But that won't happen again." There was a touch of... *desperation* in his voice as he listed off what she could supposedly do.

For as long as she could remember, her power had simply been known as necromancy, though the ability to bring the dead to life had just been beyond her reach. But what he had been saying was all *true*; she could speak with the dead, could animate bodies and push spirits back into their own flesh. Hell, she was sure there was *more* she could do if she experimented with her power.

Eliza raised her hand. *There is definitely more I can do.* The shadow soldiers had formed a line behind Alicsar, but they shook as she pushed her Blood Magic through them, forcing the dark magic from their veins. A ringing started in her ears, a sharp reminder that she wasn't as strong as she once had been.

But the dark soldiers dropped to their knees and bowed their heads, almost as if they were in prayer.

"What have you done?" the prince asked, watching her. Fear flashed behind those wide, green eyes.

The Blood Witch in her smiled. "I'm giving you what you want. The power of the Ecix."

Power rushed through her like nothing she had ever felt before; hot and cold, it filled her veins with an energy that robbed her of breath. It felt like lightning coursing through the sky. The power of the Blood Witches—of the *Ecix*—coursed through her, filling her with an endless magic that could not be stopped.

Eliza opened her eyes and saw the cavern in a new light; she could see every spirit tethered to the land, could feel the tendrils of the sloppy bindings of the soldiers. Her magic roamed the cavern and the mountains of Mesah, reaching and searching for death.

There was no fear in the way she controlled her power; like it had been when they had first entered the underground city, Eliza felt *right*, in control of the raw power untethered to the natural magic of Cadira.

Soldiers, under the control of Alicsar—under the control of the Dark Master—bent to her will; the brush of her magic was enough for spirits to find flesh, for bodies to be repossessed by their owners and rise to fight.

The magic didn't stop there; it reached out, extending her line of sight. It not only sought death, it touched life with careful, caressing fingers. She could feel what lived, and what would succumb to death.

The power brushed against Amitel's dying form. *Live*, it pleaded, caressing his blood-soaked face. *Live and fight.*

A growl, and the bite of steel in her arm caused Eliza's attention to snap back to the cavern, back to Alicsar and the soldiers that fought under her control. Demons dropped from the ceiling to protect their master as he circled her with palmed daggers.

She barely glanced down to the small, insignificant wound.

The prince's lips twisted up in a sardonic smile as they began their dance of death to the music of screeching and bloodshed.

Magic, raw and dark and engulfing, rushed from her being. The prince, with a shield of stolen magic, dropped to the ground and rolled, but the demons—black and twisted and starving—turned to ash. Where one fell, three appeared to take its place.

But she smiled nonetheless, sending out more feelers, reaching steadily for any that might join her cause.

Eliza slid the knife that had been by Amitel's dying form towards her. She released a soft breath as Alicsar attacked.

The prince threw a knife at her before swiping with his sword. Metal sang as it arced through the air, towards her neck.

The blade stopped inches from her flesh, giving her a moment to deflect the blow with the knife, and spin out of its reach.

Magic electrified the cavern. Somewhere overhead, she heard the mountain rumble in response. Eliza's power sang, and the echoes of the dead joined in her song.

Alicsar lunged, dragging her into the motions of a sword fight. She met every swing of his sword with magic, slicing carefully at him. She wanted to take her time, she decided with a slight twist of her lips. She wanted to drag him back to the king herself.

Their blades connected. Eliza smiled, and the prince fell back onto the sand.

Somewhere behind the fallen prince, the shadow soldiers—*her* soldiers—continued to fight, still tethered to the magic she possessed. When she looked a little further, she could feel Amitel, fighting. Demon hordes were falling, unable to protect their master.

Eliza's gaze fell on the now standing prince. He did not bother brushing himself off; red sand clung to his black pants and white tunic. It coated his skin, turning him somewhat demonic in the harsh light of the cavern. Blood speckled the tunic, crimson and bright.

"I'm growing sick of this." Alicsar swung again and missed Eliza.

Faster, she thought. She needed to be faster than him. Needed to think ahead. He wasn't just sick of their fight; he was growing tired. Although they both had enough stamina keep fighting, Alicsar had taken the offensive, constantly challenging Eliza, thinking she'd bend from exhaustion. The prince hadn't expected her to collect her magic so quickly.

And it worked quite well to her advantage.

"I'm not." She raised her free hand and threw a ball of fire, hitting him in the chest. It knocked him to the ground, singeing his tunic. Smoke rose from his clothing as he ripped his cloak off.

Eliza heard the cry of the raven before she saw it, perched on the shoulder of a skeleton on the wall. Beady gold eyes watched her carefully, and the way it danced across the skeleton gave away its anxiety. Eliza cast her eye over the hanging bodies—her dream flashed back to her, but she blinked it away.

The Knight was nowhere to be seen. Eliza hoped he wasn't too far.

Another knife flew at her, but she didn't duck. Instead, with a wave of her hand, she knocked it off course and back towards the prince.

It sailed into the palm of his hand. He let out a cry as he pulled it from his flesh, blood spraying onto the sand.

"You bitch," he growled, nostrils flared. He had dropped his sword. Eliza waved her hand and the weapon flew across the room, towards the raven. "You really think that'll stop me?" he spat.

He flew at her with a renewed vengeance, swinging at her with a sword made of darkness and shadow.

Thoughts of the shadow creature sprung to mind as she danced back. She remembered how it cut through her, slicing open her chest, leaving her to die slowly in that abandoned campsite.

Eliza imagined someone else there, crouching over her. She could feel their tears staining her face, their hands warming hers as the life slowly slipped out of her. She felt someone else's lips pressed against hers. She could see the darkness as it swept over the land.

"Eliza!"

Brought out of her thoughts, Eliza was thrown back into reality, with enough time to dive out of the way of Alicsar's sword.

He growled as he missed, his gaze flying towards where Thorne stood, sword clutched in his white hands.

Eliza followed the prince's stare and winced as she took in the commander; blood stained his shirt and sweat dripped from his face. His dark hair was tousled, and his chest heaved as he took her in.

She wondered, stupidly, what she looked like in his eyes. Did he see the scraped and bruised girl he'd first met? Or was he seeing a witch with power bleeding from her wounds?

The commander didn't hesitate; still standing at the cavern's entrance, he raised his sword. Fear and determination flashed across his face.

But it was for Thorne that she feared most, as the steel of a knife glinted from the corner of her eye.

Eliza screamed, and threw up a shield, just as Alicsar's blade left his hand.

It sung through the air, racing for Thorne's unprotected chest. The commander moved, but the blade rebounded off the wall of pure power she had thrown up to protect him.

With that moment of lost control, she dropped her soldiers, their spirits thrown suddenly from their bodies.

Alicsar grinned and snapped his fingers.

Thorne screamed for Eliza to drop the shield, but she couldn't. She focused on the soldiers, on the blood thrumming in her veins. She focused on seizing their spirits once more.

Whatever power she'd once had, whatever power that had been born out of her blood and the blood on her hands, was gone.

"It's too late for that," Alicsar said, voice all too loud in the cavern. "They won't bow to you again."

She had lost.

Eliza dove out of the way of the first soldier, rolling on the sand before clambering to her feet before sending a shock of electricity through his body, enough to stop his heart. He dropped to the ground, shuddering to a stop. The next attacker swung at her with his sword. She raised her dagger in time for the metal to sing at their collision, then pulled away with enough time to send a ball of fire into his chest. It knocked him to the next soldier.

Sweat dripped from Eliza's brow as she fought back. Exhaustion weighed heavily on her shoulders as she fought, both physically and magically. She knew that she couldn't keep fighting, not like she was. The Blood Witches whispered warnings in the back of her mind. But they didn't tell her to stop.

Thorne continued to shout at her, yelling for her to let him in. Every time she glanced over, all she could see was the blood, the worry in his eyes. Her head told her to let him fight, but her heart yearned to protect him.

Instead, she kept her attention focused only on the soldiers. Three down, six to go.

Eliza closed the part of her that wanted to care. They're basically dead, she thought, stomach churning. *They're lost to me. There's nothing I can do to help them.*

Two ran straight for her; she sheathed her dagger and reached for the power within her, sending bolts of electricity through the shadow soldiers. Both dropped to the ground, convulsing.

"Come on, Eliza," Alicsar taunted, standing back. She snarled. "You cannot keep this up."

Four left.

Breathing heavily, Eliza forced all four soldiers to their knees. With their energies locked between her hands, one twist of her wrist sent their heads to the sides, an audible *crack* resounding through the cavern.

Dead. All dead. She sucked in a shuddering breath and took in the chaos she had caused. Nine soldiers, dead by her hands. That didn't include the others she had helped murder.

I should feel more. Instead, she felt nothing. An emptiness yawned within her. The Blood Witches had stopped whispering their warnings.

The world spun. Her head filled with fog as she turned to meet Thorne's panicked stare.

But her gaze drifted from him and back to the cavern's opening. Standing in the shadow of the arch, silver-plated armour glinting in the flickering light, the Faery Knight raised his hand and pointed to a spot behind her. The gold eyes of the raven did not meet hers.

Eliza turned, breath caught in her throat, as Alicsar rushed towards her with his sword raised. He was close, almost within range of killing her where she stood.

Casting out a burst of pure energy and magic, Eliza's hands shot up in defence, and she watched in horror as her magic rebounded off of Alicsar's shadow sword. It hit the ceiling with a bang.

Alicsar's smug grin quickly turned into a frown as the cavern shook. Eliza dropped to her hands and knees, turning back to Thorne.

The shield dropped as the first stalactite fell to the ground.

"You won't get away," Alicsar whispered in her ear. He pulled her to her feet by her hair. She tried to pull away, flinching as a throwing knife pierced the flesh of her back.

Alicsar stepped away as Eliza collapsed to her knees. Around her, the cave's ceiling was crashing down, cutting her off from Alicsar behind her, and almost stopping Thorne from getting to her.

"We need to move." Thorne grabbed her and attempted to pull her with him.

She cried out. "I can't," she sobbed, breath catching in her throat. "You have to go." Reaching behind her, she struggled for the knife, crying out as she slid it from her back. Eliza tossed it into the growing rubble. The earth shook beneath her as the ceiling caved in.

Thorne dropped to his knees beside her and took her in her arms. "You have never been the type for self-sacrifice, Elizabeth Kindall."

Eliza searched his eyes. Fear pounded in her chest, that phantom voice urging her to protect the commander. With whatever power she had left, Eliza threw up a barrier to protect them as the cavern finally collapsed around them.

36

PRINCE OF LIES

The mountain shuddered around them; rocks tumbled to the ground, skeletons and stalactites dropping from the ceiling. "I can't stop it." Blood dripped from her lips, salty on her tongue. "I'm sorry."

"It's okay." Thorne bowed his head, until all she could see was him: not the crumbling cavern, or the ruins of the Dark Master's demonic army. "It's okay. Just breathe. You don't have anything to be sorry about... I've got you." His body covered hers as more rubble fell.

Beneath the rocks and sand, Alicsar was buried. The prince she had been sent to find, gone, like he'd never been there. Would she have to dig him up? What would she say to the king?

"I should have waited," she murmured. Now, she could feel the pain in her back, where Alicsar had stabbed her. It throbbed, slicing through her in agonising waves.

Thorne's hand was there, though, covering the wound. He was there, protecting her. Like he always had. *Like he always will*, a voice in her mind whispered.

"I shouldn't have left you alone," he replied, voice strained. "I should have put you first."

Eliza tried to shake her head, but the movement sent her spiralling towards the darkness that ebbed at the edges of her vision.

"Don't say that." She swallowed, still tasting blood. "Celia would have died."

He shook his head, but Eliza raised a hand and covered his mouth. "Don't." Pain shuddered through her. His eyes, glassy, watched her warily. "I'll heal. It'll be okay."

A laugh shuddered through him as he shook his head again. "You are unbelievable, you know that?"

Voices sounded from far away, near the entrance to the mountain. Shouts followed, and she could hear rubble being pushed to the side.

"Dorin betrayed us." She shifted, pain running up the length of her spine. "He was working with the Dark Master this entire time." She knew she needed to tell him first before anyone else. "He was the prince. I stupidly let myself get close to him and he betrayed us. Amitel betrayed us too, but not in the end."

Thorne clenched his jaw, eyes like a storm in darkness. He looked up towards the pile of debris from the cave-in. Eliza saw his throat bob as he swallowed.

"Amitel warned me. He wanted me to wait for you." Eliza felt the skin at her back tingle as the blood stopped flowing and began to stitch back together. "In the end, he was with us, and against Alicsar."

The voices steadily grew louder the farther in they climbed and the protective barrier Eliza had placed up around herself and Thorne slowly fell away as soldiers pulled at the rocks that covered them. Where there had been darkness, light slowly started to filter in.

We survived, she thought, smiling faintly as crumbling rock echoed in her ears. *I'm alive.*

But what about Alicsar? The dark thought popped into her head before she could push it away. *What about Amitel?* Her stomach twisted into knots.

She tried to send out feelers, to sense whether either of them had survived, but her magic recoiled. She was too weak physically for Blood Magic, not while she healed herself, and reaching for a connection to the land drained her.

"We're in here!" Thorne called out, voice stronger than before, resolute. His eyes lingered on Eliza for a moment, on her face, on the blood that covered her skin.

Light pierced through their small cave; soldiers stood around as Eliza's barrier finally fell away, revealing her and Thorne and the blood that covered their clothing. Grime and sand coated sun-tanned faces as she squinted up at them.

Eliza grunted as Thorne picked her up, holding her close before handing her off to one of the closest soldiers. The man carried her without fumbling, holding on as Thorne climbed out of the debris and took her back.

"You know I can stand, right?" she asked, wincing as the commander started climbing over the rocks. She tried not to think about Alicsar's taunting words.

At the mouth of the tunnel, several soldiers waited for them with a medic on hand.

A quick search of the collapsed cavern revealed nothing about the whereabouts of either Alicsar or Amitel. Eliza couldn't see their spirits either. Her magic still hid itself from her—Blood Magic and natural magic. She could only heal herself now. The raven and the Knight must have escaped before the cave-in and before the soldiers got to the mountain, Eliza realised, as she couldn't find them either.

Thorne stepped down from the rubble, jolting her as he did. She hissed, but she could feel the wound healing; torn muscle and scraped bone repairing effortlessly. She felt her skin knitting together as Thorne held her tightly to his body.

"You need to see a medic," Thorne said, voice soft as his arms tightened around her.

Eliza shook her head and waved off the oncoming medic. "I don't need to. I've pretty much healed on my own."

Brows furrowed, Thorne looked down at her in confusion. His fingers—calloused but soft—brushed the bloody skin of her back, sliding beneath her torn shirt. She winced involuntarily as his fingers brushed the healing wound but stopped when his hand rested atop it fully.

"Amazing."

Heat rushed to her cheeks, and she looked away. "Can we go sit somewhere quiet?" she asked, eyeing the soldiers warily. "I need to tell you what happened, and you can tell me why you arrived with an entire unit of soldiers."

Thorne carried her over to a quiet corner and sat her down carefully on a rock-mound caused by the cave-in. He stood in front of her, arms crossed over his chest as he leaned against the red rock wall.

"You first," she said quietly.

He cleared his throat. "I received Amitel's letter, telling me that you had already left. I was close to one of the barracks already, but I was afraid I was too late." His eyes, deep and soulful, bored into hers. "He said something about you being in imminent danger, but he could not give any details as to why. At the end of his messages, he said to bring an army into the tunnels and be at the mountain as quickly as possible."

Eliza released a heavy breath and closed her eyes. She ran her hands through her knotted hair, feeling the tangles pull at her scalp. Blood had dried at the ends, and sand coated her sweaty skin.

Finally, she opened her eyes. "They probably won't find anything here," she said. "The Dark Master had an entire army in the caverns below this one, and they disappeared pretty quickly."

"You said Dorin and Alicsar were... the same. That Dorin *was* the prince," Thorne said carefully, kneeling to match her height.

Eliza couldn't meet his stare. She had been the one to trust Dorin fully; she had stupidly cared for him, had let him kiss and touch her, had fallen for it all.

And he had never felt the same.

"Dorin—*Alicsar*, had fallen in with the Dark Master. They were working together to take the throne by force. Or at least Alicsar was. The Dark Master wanted my power," she said with a bitter laugh, angry tears forming in her eyes.

How stupid she had been.

"What do you mean?"

Eliza looked up at him and met his stare. "I have the power of the Ecix. The Dark Master wanted to use me to create an undead army."

Thorne took a step back. She saw it then, in his dark eyes: he'd known. He was aware of the power, of what it meant. She shouldn't be surprised, but...

In the blink of an eye Thorne punched the wall beside him.

"Oh my God!" Eliza jumped up and grabbed his hand, pulling him to her. She forgot about her own wound, focusing on his. She didn't have enough energy to help the healing process, but she could see the depth of his pain in the cuts and bruises on his knuckles.

"What was that for?" she asked, wrapping her hands over his. She had no clean cloth, and the medic was busy helping a soldier who had tripped in the rubble.

The commander shook his head and tried to pull away. Eliza held on though, despite his hiss as her hands tightened over his. He adverted his gaze, jaw clenched, but Eliza forced his eyes to hers.

"Why?" she asked quietly.

"I know how... *dangerous* the power of the Ecix is." Thorne's jaw ticked as he looked her over, eyes flashing with despair. "I've seen it kill people."

She stared at him for a moment. "How long have you known about my magic?"

"Since the moment I saw you," he murmured, unable to meet her stare. "I felt it *calling* to me. There was only one other person..." He shook his head. "I just know that it's dangerous, Eliza."

They stood in silence for several moments, listening to the soldiers as they worked through the rubble. Those final words hung between them in the tense silence, though neither one tried to pull away.

He was right, but at the same time, there had always been the chance that she would be dragged into this mess. She was a Blood Witch, after all. If anything, that made her just as much of a target.

"Commander Thorne!" a soldier shouted, dragging Eliza and Thorne out of their own thoughts. "We found a body!"

Eliza's eyes widened, and she met Thorne's confused stare. He let her stand from her perch on the rock, and together they watched as several soldiers carefully lifted a body from the rubble.

"Amitel?" Eliza whispered as she caught sight of blonde hair, but... something wasn't right about the way it sat upon his head. She couldn't see the leather tie that tied his hair together, couldn't see the full length of it. All she could see was blood mixed into the sand that coated his head. But hope still flared in her chest.

Eliza took several steps forward as the medic met with the soldiers. She stopped short as she took in Alicsar's body; blood splattered across his tunic, now stained red by the sand; his hair had taken on a red colour due to the sand and his blood, and his skin had taken on a sickly pallor. But his eyes fluttered, and the medic flashed a small smile when he checked Alicsar's pulse.

The commander in charge of the soldiers walked up to Eliza, eyes trained on Alicsar's unmoving body. "Who is this young man?" he asked, voice rough and wary. A look of recognition passed over his face as he took in Alicsar's body again.

Before Eliza could get a word in, the medic said, "My... is that?" He turned to Eliza for conformation. The look on her face must have said everything. "The Prince! The Prince has been found!"

37

MEMORIES BEST LEFT BURRIED

Sweat coated Eliza's body as she twisted and turned in her cot. The room she'd been given on the ship seemed to grow warmer. The blanket that had covered her now twisted about her ankles, tying her down as she was forced to relive her worst memories.

The cavern, being trapped with Alicsar as he waved his knowledge about like he had already won; the shadow soldiers, tied to her before being slaughtered; the raven and the cave-in; suffocating, her blood coating her...

A sob escaped her cracked lips as she pushed herself off the cot. Planting her feet on the wooden floor, she sucked in several deep breaths, forcing her heartbeat to slow to a calming pace. But all the blood, betrayal, and lies came back to her, assaulting her senses. She could still smell the copper of her blood. In the corner of her eyes she swore she could still see the sand of the desert, and the swaying skeletons that had watched her from above. The whispers of the spirits trapped in the mountain came to her so often she thought she was still there, trapped in a cell with her arms over her head.

Releasing a breath, Eliza shoved her feet into her boots. The minute they had made it to the barracks, and she had been handed clean clothes, she'd stripped down to nothing and had burnt her filthy clothing. She wanted nothing that reminded her of her time with Alicsar. Everything she had worn was covered in blood anyway or torn from the fight. There was nothing salvageable—not even her boots.

But the prince had been saved, pulled from the rubble like a messiah. She could still see the soldiers in her mind swarming him, begging him for answers, the medic's eyes on her as she confirmed that the man in the sand was—to her understanding—the lost prince of Cadira.

Prince Alicsar of Cadira had no memory of who he was, or who he had been.

It had taken them a couple of long hours to get to the soldier's outpost; the prince hadn't been able to move quickly, and the commander overseeing the soldiers had been too afraid of losing the newly found prince to make haste. But Eliza hadn't been able to bring herself to care, too numb to focus. She hadn't been able to sleep, and Thorne refused to answer any of her questions regarding Celia.

From the outpost, it was three days to Port Beewold. Waiting for them with a ship had been Captain Jed of the King's Guard, and Keeper Tyr, the white-haired portal keeper Eliza had met at the Winter Palace.

Both had seemed surprised to see Eliza, silent when the healers had carried Alicsar aboard, still unconscious despite their best efforts.

Eliza tried not to care.

Keeper Tyr had pulled Eliza aside to talk about the mission, about going back to the king.

But Eliza hadn't been able to answer and had merely walked away.

The thin, long-sleeved tunic she'd been wearing was slick with sweat. Pulling it over her head, she picked up a clean shirt and put it on, sighing as the cool material brushed against her hot skin.

She touched her cheeks, hot with the remnants of her nightmares. No longer did she dream about the swaying bodies above her head or the shadow creature slaying her in the abandoned camp. Instead, her dreams and thoughts were plagued with Alicsar.

The door to her cabin creaked, and the floorboards groaned as she stepped out. The only sounds were the snores of several guards, and the roaring of the ocean. She rocked back and forth on her feet for a moment as she gathered the courage to leave the small corridor. Across from her was Thorne's room, and to her right, in the medical bay, was Alicsar. Both rooms were unnaturally silent.

Shaking her head, Eliza walked out onto the deck of the ship. One man watched the waves from the crows-nest; he looked down at her when she stepped out but directed his stare elsewhere just as quickly.

Two more people wandered the ship aimlessly, keeping watch in case of a threat.

Eliza stopped; breath stuck in her throat.

Standing by the railings, dressed only in a thin, cotton undershirt and rolled up pants, Alicsar gazed out over rolling ocean.

A floorboard groaned under her weight as she stepped back, intent on returning to her room. Alicsar's face flashed in the back of her mind; a ferocious smile and a sword made of shadows. Her blood coating his hands.

Eliza spun around but stopped at the sound of his voice. "Wait." He didn't sound the same. There was a softness, an innocence in his voice that she could only associate with a child. Uncertainty lingered beneath the single word, causing her to look back. He almost sounded like the boy she had met in the capital, who had found her wandering the corridors and had gazed up at the stars with her.

She couldn't bring herself to focus on his face, though. In the last couple of days, he had grown the shadow of a beard that changed his face drastically; it aged him but contradicted the youth shimmering in his eyes.

"I knew you, didn't I?" The question came out almost hopeful.

Eliza turned around fully and crossed her arms over her chest. Sweat still clung to her, and she hated it. She hated how nice it felt to be outside because it was cooling her off. She hated how she enjoyed the night air, despite Alicsar being only a few feet away.

She gave a simple nod, untrusting of her words. She was sure if she spoke, her voice would crack and she'd scream. She'd beg for the time before his betrayal, before the entire mission.

"I hurt you." It wasn't a question. Maybe it was the look in her eyes, or the fact that she kept scratching at her sides with blunt nails. But those three, simple words, resonated within her. Because *he* hadn't—not the man in front of her. She didn't know him, didn't recognise him. It was the man he was before that hurt her.

Eliza pursed her lips, unsure of how to answer. Suspicion rose in the pit of her stomach, but she wasn't sure what to make of him.

"I'm sorry," he said, voice carrying. She could hear the sincerity in his words, but she couldn't bring herself to accept his apology. How could she when he'd attempted to kill her on more than one occasion?

With a nod in his direction, Eliza hugged her arms to herself, and walked back to her cabin.

~

Alicsar hadn't made an attempt to speak with Eliza again before they docked. But she hadn't made any attempt to go anywhere near him either.

Her nightmares grew worse the longer they travelled. From the port, she knew they had only a day's ride before reaching the capital and the king, and the closer they got, the more she dreaded it.

Her future was in the king's hands, whether she liked it or not. *Was it too late to run away?* she wondered, taking in their escort as they began their journey back. There had been no word from the king since the barracks—he hadn't sent a message or a letter asking about their progress, though she doubted she'd hear anything about it if he did; the leader of their escort took care of *everything*. She welcomed the ignorant bliss she could live in, even if just for a day.

The escort used the cover of night to smuggle the prince into the palace; Eliza had watched his face carefully for any sign of recognition or change in his demeanour. But when he saw the towers and spires that jutted into the clouds above them, a look of wonder and fascination had danced across his face. His eyes danced over the turrets and the gargoyles, the stone balconies with their detailed-railings, and the walls of vines that gave the palace its ancient feeling.

Their party didn't use the main entrance, but rather circled the wall of the palace and entered through a private tunnel that took them directly to the guards' barracks.

Eliza dismounted quickly. She grabbed her bag and landed off her horse before rushing into the gardens.

Despite the cool, night air, she still felt like she was suffocating, like she was still in the cavern, sticky with blood and coated in sand, being buried alive by rubble and ancient skeletons.

"You took off," Thorne said, catching up to her by the hedges. He touched her shoulder lightly, but she brushed him off. "Are you okay?"

She released a shuddering breath. "I just can't *stand* it. I can't stand the silence or any of this."

He cocked his head, eyes softening. "You should not be going through this alone."

"But I am," she said, sucking in a breath. "I have to, because now Bastian has my life in his hands." Eliza wrapped her arms around herself, shaking. She looked at him then, voice breaking. "I don't want any of this."

Jed, called over to them, beckoning the two to join the group as they headed towards the palace. His crooked fingers hooked around the pommel of his sword, and his inky-black hair shone in the dim gaslight outside of the barracks. A look of impatience crossed his features, but Eliza wasn't in any hurry.

Thorne placed a hand on her back. "You can talk to me, whenever you are ready."

Eliza remained silent as they met with the group. The moon sat still in the sky, occasionally obscured by clouds. Nearing midnight, barely a soul littered the gardens, save for the spirits only Eliza could see. Guards who patrolled the grounds were as quiet as death.

"Elizabeth."

Her head shot up, heart racing. Standing in a flood of golden light, dressed in black-slacks, leather shoes, and a simple grey, button-down dress-shirt, her grandfather smiled warmly down at her.

Eliza pushed through the party and ran towards Davis, throwing herself in his arms. He smelt like exhaust fumes and powdered sugar and *home*.

"I missed you," she murmured, hugging him close. "Gods, I missed you."

She could feel his laughter as his chest vibrated and his arms closed around her. "I missed you too, my little witch."

~

In twenty minutes, you'll meet with the king.

It wasn't enough time for her to properly prepare, but her grandfather had guided her to his bedroom, handed her a set of clean, fresh clothing, and told her to get ready.

Exactly twenty minutes later, she paced outside the king's office dressed in a simple white blouse and a pair of her favourite jeans from New Orleans. Her breath sounded ragged in her ears, and it took all her will not to just turn around and walk away.

The door to the study opened, and Eliza was beckoned inside.

Sitting behind a dark-oak desk, the king watched her critically as she took a seat before him. At Bastian's side was Jed, ink-black hair swept back, and sitting beside Eliza was Alicsar, looking just as grim as she felt.

Eliza's heart plummeted, stomach churning. She tried not to flinch.

"I am glad to see you both in one piece." His dark eyes roamed her face; she noticed how he refused to look towards where his son sat. Shouldn't they be celebrating?

Something in her gut twisted. Had Alicsar's memories come back? Had he mentioned... *no*. If he had said something, he—or *she*—would likely be in chains.

Eliza shifted in her seat warily, aware of the king's eyes on her. She lifted her gaze to meet his.

"I would like to know why my son has no memory."

The bluntness of his question startled her, but did it surprise her? Of course he wanted to know why his son had no memory of his capture and sudden rescue. Eliza wanted to chide herself but refrained from making any movement.

But she could feel the prince's eyes on her, like a weight that could not be lifted. She could imagine the question in them:

What did this strange girl know?

Eliza swallowed. "All I know is that upon the cave-in, Prince Alicsar lost all his memories."

King Bastian sat back in his chair, dark brows rising. "You must understand, Elizabeth, that I find it hard to believe that he lost his memories upon being rescued. What happened?"

Eliza clenched her jaw, her gaze finding Alicsar's. Mouth going dry, Eliza wasn't sure what to say to him; hope flashed in his bright eyes, taking her by surprise. It coiled around her heart, stopping her breath in her throat. It was her chance, she realised, to tell the truth, to reveal to King Bastian that his son had been working with the Dark Master.

Then what was stopping her?

"Elizabeth?" the king prompted, sitting forward.

Shaking her head, Eliza swallowed back the words that would guarantee her as a traitor. Why wouldn't it? The king wanted a beacon of hope, and if Eliza threatened that, then not only would she be arrested—then likely executed on the grounds of having necromancy—but her whole family would be in danger too.

Not just her grandfather or Kay, but Thorne and Celia too.

"I made it to the mountain alone," she said, the lie tasting bitter on her tongue. "When I arrived, I was taken by the Dark Master's soldiers and thrown into a cell. After a while, they came back for me and took me to the main chamber. That's where I found your son, but no Dark Master. There was a fight; the prince was knocked out, and I used my... *magic* to free us. That's when Commander Thorne found us and the cave-in happened. I was too far from the prince to help him, and I was injured."

The king removed his gaze from Eliza's and looked up to his captain of the guard. "We will send soldiers back to Mesah."

Eliza released her breath in a huff, her heart rate slowing only a fraction. "I could go back to the desert," she offered. *Anything to get out of this room.* "I can—"

The king shook his head. "No. You are needed here. I have called upon the Blood Witches to aid in unlocking his memories."

Eliza's blood ran cold. She could almost hear them now in her head, whispering, warning. She swallowed that fear of not knowing what they would do to her. Would they claim her as their own? Punish her for using their forbidden magic?

Eliza didn't want to find out.

Captain Jed said, "We're sending Commander Thorne to Mesah with a battalion to better comb the rubble, those cells, and see if they can come up with anything about the whereabouts of this army you saw."

Thorne will be gone. He was leaving, going back, and she was what? Remaining at the palace?

A feeling of entrapment settled over her, squeezing at her insides.

She knew then she would find no freedom yet.

38

CREATED

Breathe. Eliza's heart hammered in her chest as she smoothed down her blouse for the fourth time since entering the council hall. The corridor, illuminated by gaslights and candles, looked too bright to her, too white. The high-arching windows were open, letting in a soft, frigid breeze, the smell of rot and lavender carrying on the wind.

"Relax." Her grandfather rested a hand on the small of her back, and she tried not to flinch.

"It would have been nice to have Thorne here." But he had been forced to take a team back to Mesah, to the tunnels. He'd been forced to leave her. Again.

Eliza sucked in a deep breath and released it through her nose, closing her eyes. A headache bloomed behind her eyes, the white light not helping. Only an hour ago, she'd received word that the Blood Witches were on their way.

Were they claiming me? Eliza shuddered at the thought. This had been what she'd wanted, right? Answers to the accumulating questions that muddled her mind? But standing before the door to the king's court, nausea rose in her stomach. It wasn't fear; Eliza had more to fear than them, she understood. But it didn't make it any easier, to be standing there, left bare.

"I know you and Commander Thorne are friends," Davis said, "but you need to remember that this meeting is about *you* and learning more about what happened with the prince's memories."

The door to the meeting room opened with a flourish as a butler stood with his arm spread as a sign to enter. The man's moustache twitched as he took her in, but his bright eyes quickly averted.

Swallowing thickly, Eliza entered the room first, with Davis at her heels. The door clicked behind them, and the room was silenced.

Eliza took in the hall in one quick sweep; one entire wall was made of glass, broken up by winding iron to create a magical scene of a garden, a marble floor, a gilded throne perched on a raised dais before the stained-glass.

King Bastian's throne was empty, the king himself nowhere in sight. Several guards lined the walls, Captain Jed amongst them. Then Eliza's gaze found *them*. Women in blood-red robes.

"Eliza!" Celia rushed forward, dropping the hood of her cloak. She pulled Eliza into a hug. Stilted—and confused—Eliza wrapped her arms around the older girl, closing her eyes and sucking in a breath.

Eliza pulled back first; brow creased. "What are you doing here?"

Celia stepped away. It was then that Eliza noticed the blood-red cloaks made of heavy linen draped over their shoulders. Beneath the cloaks, Eliza could see that they wore riding gear: thick trousers and tunics, leather vests and knee-high, laced boots. They all had weapons strapped to their bodies, and belts full of magic potions.

"I am a Blood Witch." Celia watched her with dark eyes.

Eliza's heart hammered, and she remembered Alicsar's words beneath the mountain, and the dream that had seemed so real, yet unbelievable after what had happened. "Like me?"

The Blood Witches behind Celia did not answer.

"Yes." Celia cleared her throat, chest heaving. "In another life, you were my sister."

Eliza felt the blood drain from her face. *That* was their connection? Somehow, it clicked in Eliza's mind; why Celia wanted her to turn back, why she stuck by Eliza's side and how she knew Thorne.

But that doesn't make any sense, she thought. *In another life...*

Stepping back, Eliza ran a hand over her face. Her hands shook. She wasn't sure she could meet Celia's stare, or anyone's for that matter. She could feel her grandfather's presence behind her, warm and protective, but she stepped away from him and Celia.

"I don't understand." Eliza shook her head, desperation filling her.

Celia's jaw clenched. "I know," she said, voice cracking. "But I will explain, over time..."

"Over time?" Eliza laughed incredulously and shook her head

again. "I want to know everything."

Lips pursed, Celia looked back to the other women. One with golden hair and a hardened smile stepped forward and lowered her hood. Eliza could just make out a scar that slashed over her left eye, blinding her.

"My name is Idgeth. I am your Athir."

Eliza's brows furrowed. Somewhere, in the back of her mind, she thought she recognised the woman, the word. But she shook her head, the memory disappearing. "I don't know what that means."

"Athir," Celia clarified, "is like a mother, of sorts. You were born into the tribe without a mother."

"Without a mother?" Eliza met the stare of the woman; no, they would not have been related. They didn't have the same tanned complexion or green eyes. Idgeth was shorter, thin, while Eliza had curves and was taller. Idgeth only looked twenty-five, at least.

"Ecix's do not have mothers," Idgeth said, brows drawn in a line. "They are born of blood and magic."

Eliza took another step back. Disgust welled deep in her stomach. She swallowed back bile. "So, I was *created*."

"In a way." Celia reached a hand out in an attempt to comfort her, but Eliza stepped back again, shaking her head. "This is why I did not want to tell you all of this at once."

"I deserved to know," Eliza snapped. Tears burned behind her eyes, and her mouth dried. "None of this should have been kept from me!"

"The Dark Master attacked our village, searching for you. He has caused the death of the Ecix on more than one occasion." Idgeth, with her hard eyes and distant demeanour, seemed to sadden at that. "He sent riders for you, and in the fight, he killed many Witches. Including your Athirian sister."

A dream. She had thought it was nothing more than a dream—a nightmare, about a girl who was taken, who watched on as another girl was killed in the process. Celia was the Athirian sister of Eliza's past life. The life connected to Thorne. Finally, it was starting to make sense.

"I remember that," Eliza whispered. She felt the blood rush from her face, and her knees quivered. *Too much. This is too much.* "She was shot with an arrow."

Idgeth nodded solemnly, jaw clenched as she looked away.

So many dead... because of me.

"How is an *Ecix* created? Can it be stopped?"

Standing besides Idgeth, one of the other women hissed. "You cannot just stop a power like that."

"Why not?" Eliza demanded. She stepped forward and spread her arms wide. "I hate it. I hate having this power and not knowing what to do with it. It causes more trouble than what it's worth, and if it were destroyed, then maybe we could stop the Dark Master."

The same woman dropped her hood, revealing ink-black hair and obsidian eyes. She was frightening, but Eliza held her ground. "The power of the Ecix is sacred, it cannot be merely... *taken away.*"

Eliza choked on a laugh. "Seeing dead people is one thing, but not being able to help them is another. I can't do *anything* but stand there and watch."

Eliza sucked in a long breath, heart thundering in her chest. Her cheeks felt warm; she could feel the heat radiating from her face.

"The Blood Witches have spent too long protecting—"

"Protecting?" Eliza couldn't help but laugh, the sound bitter in her ears. "You've been *using* it for your own gains, haven't you? This power... it doesn't help anyone. The reason the Dark Master wanted me was because he had an army to build. I was going to be a *pawn* in some sick and twisted game, and I *hate that.*"

Celia stepped up to her and cupped her cheeks, forcing their eyes to meet. "Since the death of my Athirian sister, an Ecix, just like you, I vowed to find a way to remove the Dark Master from this world. If you want me to make this same promise to you, to find a way to destroy this power, then I will."

Her bright eyes bored into Eliza's, and it was in that moment that Eliza knew she could trust the other girl, with her life and the promise she had just made.

Drowning out the protests from the other Blood Witches, Eliza nodded.

"Good," Celia said, smiling. She took a step back and straightened. "Then I will help you, sister, because I would do anything to know that you will not die before your time."

Even though Celia wasn't her blood sister—or the sister she'd been raised with—there was still an undeniable bond between them, that linked them through time. Eliza couldn't forget the way she'd felt when she'd first met Celia, or the dreams that had followed. *Memories* of the life they'd shared. Eliza couldn't deny that Celia still saw her own sister in Eliza, but Eliza needed a friend, someone to help her with the Dark Master and the festering nightmares that continued to plague her.

She couldn't help the smile that touched her lips. "I'm not worried about dying because of it. I'm worried about *others* dying. It brings more harm than good."

"That depends," the last woman said, "on who wields it. Several centuries ago, a woman with the power of the Ecix used its magic to bring forth an army of the dead to destroy the land. She succeeded in bringing plague and famine and destruction to Cadira."

Eliza swallowed thickly.

The woman continued, "But the one who inherited the power after her, a saviour in her own right, rebuilt this kingdom—this world—with that same power."

Eliza went numb with the overwhelming dread that shuddered through her. "How much power do I have?"

"That is something we need to find out," Celia replied, lips thin. "It is not something to worry about at this time."

The great doors opened and the butler stood aside so the king and several guards could enter. Behind the party, Prince Alicsar walked slower, his gait heavy with wariness.

"I do believe we must try and find out if my son is a true amnesiac or not," Bastian said, settling onto his throne. "I want to know what he remembers. This lack of cohesive memory worries me."

Eliza pursed her lips. Without Thorne there to back her up, she wasn't sure what she should say in the event that the Blood Witches found his memories, revealing that he was working with the Dark Master instead of against him. Eliza still couldn't even look Alicsar in the eye, let alone stand with him. Seeing him... it brought back every memory of under the mountain, of the tunnels and the soldiers she had to kill in order to find *him*.

It brought back other memories too, but Eliza locked them away.

A guard moved a single chair into the middle of the room. Everyone watched with bated breath as the prince slowly approached it, his eyes on the king, who looked as if he was mildly put-out by what was about to happen.

Eliza had managed to avoid Alicsar after their meeting the night before, but now, as he entered the room looking almost like the boy she'd fallen for, those memories and feelings she had locked away came flooding back in.

"Your Highness," Idgeth said, bowing her head. Celia and the other Blood Witches did the same. "We will be looking for any sign of your lost memories, and we will be bringing them to the surface."

Eyeing Alicsar, Eliza noticed how... *unaffected* he looked about having someone delve into his mind. He nodded wordlessly to Idgeth, giving his consent. His eyes conveyed absolutely nothing—no fear, no guilt, no worry.

"Eliza and I will be the ones to delve into your mind and find your memories," Celia said, continuing from Idgeth.

Eliza sent Celia a confused look, ready to shake her head and hand the job over to one of the other Witches. There were others who should have done it. Why her? Hadn't she done enough?

"Trust me," Celia murmured, offering Eliza an encouraging smile. "You need to know."

Finally, Eliza nodded stiffly, and followed Celia to the chair.

Alicsar took a seat, hands in his lap. From behind, Eliza could see his knuckles; tight from holding his hands together. Someone had clearly attempted to brush his sun-streaked hair back and out of his face, but it looked as if he'd ran his hands through his hair a dozen times since then.

The room fell into a tense silence as Celia and Eliza moved to stand behind the prince. They each placed a hand on his shoulders; Eliza hesitated slightly before settling her left hand warily on his shoulder. She raised the other hand and closed her eyes, just as Celia did the same.

Eliza had never done a spell like this before; the intensity of it stumped her, and she knew that one wrong move would turn Alicsar into a living vegetable. She wasn't even sure why Celia had dragged her over to help, but curiosity got the better of her, and it won out over the fear she'd felt when he had walked into the room.

Celia began a low, whispered chant; Eliza remained quiet and waited. Almost like instinct took over, Eliza was moving, turning so that she now stood beside the prince, across from Celia.

Warmth spread through her, the naturalness of the spell unfolding within her. Almost like another person had taken control of her, Eliza felt at ease with what she was doing.

Their hands reached over the top of him, and clasped.

Light flared behind Eliza's eyes as she was thrown into Alicsar's mind.

Flashes of memory sped past Eliza, but she could barely make anything out; blond hair curled around a baby's fist, a crown atop a man's dark hair, a splash of crimson, then... fog.

Everything from then on was covered in a mist, caved in and indistinguishable. However hard she tried, she couldn't see *anything*.

Maybe his memories really were gone.

She caught a glimpse of one thing; a figure covered in their own blood. She could feel the remorse from him, felt his desperation. He did not want to hurt this person, and yet he was.

Light flared again, and she was gone.

Opening her eyes, it took Eliza a moment to orientate herself.

She wasn't in Alicsar's mind, but rather a room with people she knew.

Eliza sucked in a breath and released it slowly, before stepping away from Celia and he prince.

"What did you see?" the king asked impatiently.

Celia cleared her throat. "The prince's memories truly *are* gone, Your Majesty. He remembers nothing of his time with the Dark Master."

39

LONG LIVE THE PRINCE

The room Eliza was in wasn't hers, but it was supposed to be. It didn't have her movie posters, or wall-hanging plants, or the polaroid mural of her life. The room wasn't bare brick with a splash of paint. Odin wasn't sleeping on his chair in the corner of the room, and the Cadiran constellations did not shine bright on the ceiling.

It was hers, but it wasn't.

Much bigger than the last room she had while in the palace, Eliza had been given an upper-floor chamber, with its own private balcony, a sitting room with a fireplace, a bathing room and walk-in wardrobe that rivalled the size of her bedroom in New Orleans.

The bedroom itself was large, with the bed taking up a third of the space. Gold and blood-red pillows scattered the thick duvet, and there were at least three different throw blankets carefully folded at the end of the bed. A four-poster with a canopy above, it seemed fit for a real princess, not herself. But she couldn't help but admire the red gauze-like material that had been woven along the beams of the bed; that same material fell so that it gave the bed some privacy, though the curtains were pushed back, giving Eliza a full view of it.

She released a heavy sigh.

"You don't like it?" her grandfather asked, following her into the bedroom. He prodded at the mattress before smiling. "I like it. It is very... *you.*"

Eliza shook her head. "It's nice, but it isn't home."

Davis' eyes softened. "Of course not. But you can make it your home."

I have to stay. Eliza had little choice in the matter; not only did King Bastian want her to stay at the palace, but so did the Blood Witches. To *keep an eye on her*, though they would never admit it. She was a flight risk, a threat.

"I don't have much of a choice now," she murmured, dropping her bag onto the bed. She eyed the ottoman at the end, where a large box sat. She nodded towards it. "What's in there?"

"Oh." Davis stepped away from it with a smile. "I brought it with me. I received a message from the king almost immediately after you found the prince, to come back here, and knowing you would be staying, I brought this with me."

Eliza swallowed thickly. Since finding the prince, a heavy feeling of foreboding had settled within her. It tore at her thoughts and filled her mind with doubts and uneasy questions.

"Open it," Davis said, placing a hand on her shoulder and guiding her to the box.

The cardboard flaps pulled open easily, and revealed, first and foremost, a pillow. Eliza laughed, and tears pricked at her eyes. The knitted cover, made by an old neighbour of theirs in New Orleans, had been given to her when she'd first arrived in the foreign city. She'd been young, but she would never forget the older woman hobbling up to them, weathered face pulled into a smile. The pillow had been Eliza's first gift in New Orleans, and she couldn't imagine facing Cadira without it.

She grabbed it and hugged it to her chest, breathing in heavily. The smells of home hit her; Kay's lavender perfume, her own coffee-scented candles, Davis' musky aftershave, and the smell of New Orleans itself.

"I thought you'd like that," he said. "It always made you feel safe."

Eliza nodded and sniffed, forcing the tears back. She carefully placed the pillow on the bed, and began rifling through the rest of the box; her books, including a dusty, dog-eared copy of *Harry Potter*, and an even more worn edition of *The Curious Case of Benjamin Button*, a set of battery operated fairy-lights still in their box, at least three candles, photos of herself and her family, and her favourite shirts.

"I couldn't bring too much, of course," Davis said, voice soft. "But I thought I might bring you some things to make this large, expensive room feel more like you."

She smiled and nodded, but something tugged within her.

"Why was I taken to you? As a child, I mean. Why not here at the palace, or the Courts of Light? Or even the Fae Territories? Why New Orleans?"

Davis sighed and took a seat on the ottoman, setting the box on the floor and patting the seat beside him. "You were brought to me for protection. It was the only way to make sure you—and that power you possess—did not fall into the wrong hands."

"Like the Dark Master's."

He nodded slowly. "Yes, like his."

"Why was I taken from the Blood Witches? They would have been able to protect me, right?" she asked, heart thundering in her chest. Did they really give her up because of the Dark Master? Or was there another reason? Although a large part of her didn't really want to know, another part of her yearned to know about her past, about her heritage.

"It is..." Davis trailed off with a sigh.

"Complicated?" Eliza said, huffing. "It can't be that complicated!"

Lips drawn in a thin line, Davis sent her a look of irritation, though she thought she saw a hint of a smile. "If you are determined to interrupt me and assume you know all, then by all means, you tell *me* what happened."

"Alright," she muttered, crossing her arms. "I'll shut up now."

A tap sounded at the door, and an older woman stepped into the bedroom. Her dark eyes surveyed the white-marble walls and gold accents, and her blonde hair glowed in the white light streaming through the open windows.

"Miss Elizabeth," the woman said, straightening. A polite smile crossed her face. "I will be helping you prepare for the upcoming celebrations."

Eliza turned to her grandfather. "Celebrations? What celebrations?"

"The King has been... preparing since your last meeting. Nobody knows what is happening, but there will be an announcement about the prince's return today."

Groaning, Eliza ran her hands through her hair in frustration. "And why do I have to be there?"

Davis leant down and kissed her forehead. "Because you found the prince, silly girl. I do believe His Majesty will be *rewarding* you today as well."

"The king requires you to be at his side," the woman said. Eliza eyed her warily. "Celebrations begin in three hours."

~

There were no clouds marring the beautiful blue sky of Cadira. The sun produced a warmth that left Eliza sweating slightly as she waited for the king and his son by the carriage. Both were, of course, late, but she stood with her back straight, and tried to keep her anxiety from showing.

Davis touched her shoulder lightly before giving it a squeeze, offering her a soft, encouraging smile. "You will be fine. Everything will be fine."

She opened her mouth to reply, only to find her throat close up. Would she, though? Would she be fine? She didn't even know what was *happening*. How could she be *fine* if she wasn't even sure what she should be worried about?

The doors to the palace opened. Eliza's heart stopped in her chest as she took in the approaching king and his son, both dressed in their finest. While King Bastian's dark hair was swept back beneath a heavy gold crown encrusted with rubies and diamonds, Alicsar looked modest with his untidy hair, unadorned by any crown. The golden lapels of both their jackets glinted in the bright light of the day.

Her grandfather dropped into a bow, and Eliza followed, curtseying hesitantly.

Eliza's dress, at least, was a thick material that managed to ward off the chills of winter. The high collar protected her throat, long sleeves covering her arms. Eliza couldn't help but miss Mesah. The bottle-green gown had pockets, which Eliza shoved her hands into as soon as she could.

"Are we ready?" King Bastian stepped off the marble staircase. A valet draped a golden cloak around his shoulders.

Davis and Eliza straightened. "Of course, Majesty." The valet opened the door to the carriage for the king and bowed at the waist again. Eliza waited until the king was seated, before taking her grandfather's offered hand and entering the carriage. Behind her, Alicsar hesitated before following, taking the seat beside her.

The look Davis offered her seemed to say '*I'll be following you*' before closing the carriage door, locking her inside with her previous attempted murderer and the man who spawned it.

Eliza swallowed and winced as the carriage began moving.

"You look lovely," Alicsar said, clearing his throat. He offered her a wry smile, his eyes bright. Red burned along his cheeks as he clasped his hands tightly in his lap.

She grimaced in return. He looked like the boy she had kissed, and not the one who had tried to kill her. It unsettled her. "Thank you, Your Royal Highness."

The prince's smile wavered slightly, but he nodded his head and looked away.

The king, on the other hand, seemed to beam.

Silence ensued as their carriage took them to a large, open amphitheatre on the other side of the capital. Eliza hadn't seen it on either of her trips into the city, but her new maid had pointed it out to her that morning, barely touched by the brightening rays of morning sunlight.

The chatter of people steadily grew louder the longer they rode. Beside her, Alicsar continued to hold his hands tightly, and whatever smile that had been on his face earlier had slipped away into a grim line of unease.

Some part of Eliza wanted to comfort him, but a stronger part of her kept her hands—and words—to herself.

When the carriage rolled to a stop, all the breath left Eliza in a single sigh. *Here we go.*

~

People of all ages, stations, and gender filled the amphitheatre; some were seated along the grand, sweeping staircases that lined the entire stadium, while others loitered on the ground in the front. At the top were huge boxes used by the nobility of Cadira, who were all present for the celebration.

Eliza sat with the king and Alicsar at the very front of the mass on a giant platform that looked out over the still growing crowd.

A whistle sounded and the crowd hushed. Her heart skipped a beat as all eyes drifted to them.

"Thank you, people of Cadira, for standing witness to a historic event!"

Absolute panic washed through her; Eliza wasn't one for getting up in front of large crowds. She didn't do theatre or public speaking.

She had been home-schooled. No crowds save the dead—but they didn't count.

Whatever it was that the king had planned for her, she was now certain that it couldn't be good. Not when her stomach clenched, and she found a worried Celia standing in the crowd.

"We are gathered today to give thanks to a witch who set out to find the son who had been taken from me."

Eyes snapped to Eliza, and when they had their fill, their eyes drifted to Alicsar, and lingered.

The prince didn't look like his father. Though they both had similar heights and builds, Alicsar took after his mother; thick, sandy hair that brushed his chin and complimented his emerald eyes, classical features and a smile that could win a crowd over. His father had dark features and eyes that conveyed power, that held the audience in the palm of his hand.

King Bastian stood, indicating for Alicsar to do the same. His son, sitting to his right, graciously stepped forward and gave the people of Cadira that winning smile, before offering Eliza a hand.

She hesitated for a heartbeat, but felt her grandfather's steady presence behind her, felt him urge her forward. She wanted Thorne to be there, though. She wanted him to be by her side. She hadn't done it alone, hadn't *been* alone during the hunt.

Sucking in a breath, Eliza took Alicsar's hand and stepped up with him.

The crowd erupted into applause, cheers spreading throughout the amphitheatre. Eliza stood there in rapt wonder as the people cried over the return of their lost prince, or as others chanted his name. She could just make out the faces of several little girls, all pointing to her with light dancing in their innocent eyes.

Eliza's gaze went back to Celia, who stood amongst the thicket of people on the ground. No emotion danced across her face, and instead she eyed Alicsar, and then the king beside them.

Three women stood with Celia: blood-red cloaks drawn over their young faces. Eliza knew who they were—the women from the meeting with the king. Ones who claimed to know her. Was the king going to hand her over to the Blood Witches? Let her go with them to the Labyrinth Mountains? Looks of displeasure crossed their faces as they looked up at the king and Alicsar—at *her*.

Eliza dragged her eyes away from the circle of women, redirecting her gaze into the crowd.

"I would like to announce that my son will be my one and only heir to the throne!"

Alicsar's hand tightened around hers as cheers continued to echo through the amphitheatre. She couldn't blame him; her heart thundered in her chest at the same speed as the claps, and blood pounded in her ears.

The king paused for effect before the whistle sounded again, forcing the crowd into silence. "There will also be a royal wedding, to celebrate my son's return, and to thank the witch who brought him back to his rightful home!"

Eliza's heart dropped into her stomach, and the blood rushed from her face. *A wedding.*

Oh, Gods. Oh, Gods. She wasn't being granted amnesty, or the chance to leave with the Blood Witches. She wasn't even going back to New Orleans. Eliza had thought perhaps her reward would be her freedom. Her *life.* But this?

"To Alicsar and Elizabeth, may their union bring peace and hope," King Bastian finished.

She wanted to pass out, or to run. *Running sounds like a good idea.* Her eyes slid to the prince, who looked as stunned and unprepared as she did.

Shocked murmurs and excited cheers rippled through the crowd. Eliza's stare instinctively went back to the circle of women and Celia, who looked far more displeased then before. Celia met Eliza's stare.

But three others had joined the circle with Celia. Three men that Eliza had seen before in passing.

Eliza pressed her lips into a thin line and forced a smile onto her face. The men that Thorne had met with when they had first arrived in the city. Who wouldn't give him information because of their oaths.

Their oaths, Eliza knew, to the Blood Witches.

A shiver ran down Eliza's spine as the eyes of the Brotherhood and the witches fell on her. With hooded gazes, they watched her with a wariness she could feel in her bones. Like they were judging her for being up there.

The applause faded into a low hum of excitement. Eliza could hear the exclamations of surprise.

"A royal wedding!" an older woman towards the front of the mass murmured, voice loud enough for Eliza to hear. "How grand!"

Another man to her left huffed. "A witch for our queen? I don't care if she saved the prince."

The voiced opinions went on; some, Eliza could hear, didn't care if she took to the throne or not—they were just excited for the celebrations that would follow. Others looked at her with disgust. Although Eliza's features didn't scream her heritage, the point to her ears gave away that she wasn't *quite* human. But neither were half the audience. There were Witches and Warlocks spread throughout the standing mass, the sitting, and the boxes above. Fae-bred Halflings were spread thin throughout the crowd, too. But those who looked down on her for being different.

Eliza wanted to disappear, but she stood there anyway, with her head held high.

From the corner of her eye, the raven watched her with its head cocked. It stood on the shoulders of a tall man—the Knight, though if it was, she couldn't tell with the large cloak and hood that covered his face.

Alicsar led Eliza back to the dais and offered his hand as she took her seat beside him. She went through the motions without complaint. King Bastian had put her in a position that left her unable to refuse.

"With this union, we will bridge the abyss that has separated our people since that horrific night! With this union, hope will be brought back into your lives—and mine. And with this union, we will strike back at the creature that dared go against me!"

Clenching her jaw, Eliza adverted her eyes from the king, who now stood from his throne. The crowd roared in agreement. They wanted to strike back.

She felt sick.

Eliza searched the boxes above, trying to look anywhere but at the king or the frantic crowd at her feet. She noticed the nobility she had dined with at the Winter Palace.

Henry Ivo watched on with a blank look, lined face eerily unemotional. His arms were crossed over his robed chest, his shadowed eyes dancing over the crowd. What was he thinking about? Eliza wondered, catching his eye as they drifted over to her.

Henry offered her a tight-lipped smile.

Eliza reciprocated the gesture.

While the king continued his speech about what he wanted to accomplish with the wedding, the crowd had begun humming with fervour, with the need to fight back. She could *feel* it bleeding from the crowd. It gave strength to the spirits that lingered along the edges.

Eliza spotted the little girl from the Winter Palace, her body translucent in the sun. She stood hand in hand with the two other children from the port, who had led Eliza to the demons in the alley. She offered the girl a smile, but she looked away.

Following the path of her stare, Eliza's smile dropped from her face.

Standing in the shadows, nearly completely hidden by the crowds, stood Amitel.

Something inside of her urged her to go to him, to ask if he was okay after the cave-in, if he knew anything about what had happened to Alicsar or the Dark Master.

But in the blink of an eye, he was gone. Suddenly Eliza felt very alone.

40

ANOTHER LIFE

The portal opened and Eliza caught her first whiff of home.

Diesel fumes and pollution hit her nose, an utter contrast to the clean crisp air of Cadira. Eliza could almost taste the bayou and the heavy whisky that stuck to the air. She sucked in a deep breath, smiling as her grandfather stepped towards the portal, his hand held out to her.

"Are you ready?" he asked, smiling.

Tears sprung in her eyes, and she did nothing to stop them from falling. She'd been ready since she got back from Mesah, when her grandfather had dragged a box of her belongings into her new bedroom at the palace. She'd been ready since Kay had warned her in her dreams while locked in the cell, when she'd seen her home again after the weeks of searching.

Eliza nodded and stepped up beside him, taking his hand. Beyond the portal, she could see nothing but darkness. Barely distinguishable was the white marble of the temple, and the eternal flame that continued to burn.

But even with the distance between herself and the portal, she felt so much closer to home, to freedom. Her whole life, she had wanted to be a part of Cadira, but standing by the portal, she wanted nothing more than to be back in New Orleans, with a coffee in one hand and a book of spells in the other, sitting with Kay at a corner coffee shop, watching the tourists wander through the old streets she called home.

That isn't your life anymore. She pushed those thoughts aside.

Less than three months, and she'd be married to the crown Prince of Cadira. In less than three months, she'd be one step closer to losing her freedom entirely.

"Let's go," she said, nodding furiously. Eliza could almost hear Kay calling her name.

Behind them, the king stood with his son, watching. Although the thought of home pulled at her heart, she could clearly feel the absence of Thorne, still in Mesah investigating the tunnels and cavern. She had sent him a letter, telling him that she was on her way back to New Orleans, but she had heard nothing from him in return.

She hadn't mentioned the wedding and she wasn't sure if news would have yet reached Mesah. But she wanted nothing more than to speak to him in person, to explain to him her fears about the whole situation. She wanted to know his thoughts.

But he wasn't there. He was in the desert, investigating the Dark Master.

Eliza spared a single look over her shoulder, taking in the imposing figure of the dark-haired king and the lithe, uncertain body of the once lost prince. Henry Ivo, dressed completely in white, watched with a straight back from the other side of their official party.

A light breeze carved through the forest clearing, leaves made of emerald and glass twinkling in response. The treetops buzzed with nymphs and sprites and pixies, alight with a happiness Eliza hadn't noticed when she stepped through the portal the first time.

Where there had been snaking darkness, light was slowly weaving its way back into the land.

She couldn't help but smile as she took her grandfather's hand and went home.

~

Eliza couldn't see any difference to the home she had always known; it still stood three storeys high, with large windows and ivy growing up the brick walls. Old lamp posts still lined her street, and behind her she could hear the cemetery and its spirits whispering to her, calling out her name in delight.

The streets of New Orleans were still loud and boisterous and full of tourists; the back-seat of the beat-up BMW still smelt like its peppermint air-freshener, and the sky, dazzled with stars, looked down on her with a familiarity that brought tears to her eyes.

She was home.

The doors that led to the courtyard of her childhood home opened to reveal Kay—dressed in torn denim jeans, paired with a white shirt and wearing an oversized cardigan of all different colours—she rushed by the wrought iron and opened her arms.

Tears slipped down Eliza's cheeks as she dropped her bag and ran into Kay's waiting arms.

"I missed you," Eliza sobbed, tears staining the cardigan. "I missed you so much."

"I am so glad to see that you're okay," Kay murmured, voice thick with tears.

Eliza's bones turned to stone as relief rushed her. Standing there, wrapped in Kay's arms with her grandfather only an arms-length away, gave her a sense of security she hadn't felt since leaving home.

Eliza's smile faltered; she wasn't sure what she would have done if she didn't have the support network she had.

"Let's go inside and have some cake," Davis said from behind her, breaking her out of her thoughts.

Eliza stood back as her grandfather and Kay headed into the courtyard, where she could see bright yellow balloons and blue streamers waiting for her.

The smile on her face dropped, and she turned to the street.

Sitting in a tree, watching her, was the raven, and beneath it, the Knight.

Eliza offered them both a smile and waved. And before she turned back around, she swore she'd seen the Knight wave back.

Despite the questions that still hung in the back of her mind, itching to be answered, she locked away the ones concerning the raven and the Knight. They were a problem for another day.

The courtyard looked exactly the same, save for a new outdoor seating arrangement Kay must have bought, and the flowers in bloom. Balloons littered the stone floor, some tied to the vines that still grew up the walls and around the balcony. Streamers ran from one side of the balcony to the other, crossing in an overhead lattice of blue, green, and yellow. Eliza could almost imagine the magic and frustration put into it.

At the centre of the courtyard, Kay had set up a table full of food; bowls of chips, cupcakes, a confectionary of skittles, gummy-bears, and sour-worms. A home-made chocolate cake sat in the centre of the table, towering over the rest of the food. Eliza spotted croissants and pastries from a bakery down the street, and she stopped, realising how much she *missed* junk food.

"Expecting more visitors?" Eliza asked, laughing. She picked up a plastic cup and took a swig of Sprite, wincing at the fizziness after such a long time of only drinking water and ale.

"Well," a voice behind her said, "I believe most of that is for you, though I think your family wanted us to try *chocolate croissants* and *gummy bears* while we were here."

Eliza spun around and dropped her cup before rushing into Thorne's waiting arms. "You're here," she breathed, feeling the tears stinging at her eyes again. She pulled away, then crumpled into Celia's waiting embrace. "What are you doing here?"

The smile dropped from his face. "Aren't you happy to see us?"

"Yes! But..." Eliza trailed off; lips pursed. "I thought you were still in Mesah, in the caverns. I didn't think I'd see you again until I went back to Cadira. Either of you."

"We thought we would surprise you," Celia said, eyes bright. A smile twitched at her lips. "After all, we did decide to work together."

"We already found the prince." Mention of the wedding, of her *reward* buzzed in the back of her mind. "And I have to go back for training now and then there's..." She couldn't finish the sentence.

"But we haven't found the Dark Master," he murmured. His eyes darkened, and Celia nodded in agreement.

Eliza stepped away from them and lifted her chin. *Leave it.* "I'm going to find him," she promised, whether for their benefit or hers. "And I *will* stop him."

Thorne smiled. "Then I guess we will be doing that together."

"Agreed," Celia said with a grin.

Her heart leapt, and she couldn't help the smile that twisted at her lips. *Together.*

ABOUT THE AUTHOR

Stephanie Anne grew up in different parts of Australia before her parents settled down in a small beachside town in northern New South Wales when she was twelve. There, she developed her love of reading, and began penning *The Lost Prince Of Cadira*, amongst other books.

Currently, she is in her second year of Griffith University, completing her Bachelor of Arts in Creative Writing and Literary Studies. She lives with her two roommates and little sister on the Gold Coast, and can usually be found hiding in her office, watching Criminal Minds, or drinking too much coffee.

https://www.stephanieanneauthor.com/

ACKNOWLEDGMENTS

First and foremost, I want to thank you for reading this book! Without the continued support of so many people, I would *not* be publishing this book now. Since I sat down to write my first book, I've wanted to be an author. I immediately knew that's all I could ever be, all I ever *wanted* to be, and without the amazing support from my mum, Jenny, and close friends and family, I wouldn't be writing this.

I need to thank my mum, Jennifer, most of all. Without her, I wouldn't be a writer. She is the reason why I am here today. My sister, Emily. She's been a little helpful but mostly just there (she's going to kill me if she reads this). But she deserves a huge thanks for proofreading this book, because I wouldn't have finished without her!

My beautiful friends: Jess C., Jess P., Jess W. (there's a couple of them), Carlie, Kim, and Ally. They became my home away from home, my family, and without their continued help and support I wouldn't have had the confidence to push through my doubts to get to this stage.

While writing and developing this book, I need to thank, my co-writer, best friend, beta reader, the person I go to with every idea—Dee. She read the very first draft of this book, way back when we were both writers on Wattpad. She's helped me since, and I wouldn't be here without her. We've got a long road ahead of us, and I can't wait to have her on every next step.

To my critique partner, Caitlin. I don't think you realise just how much you helped me with this book! The hours spent talking on the phone, the messages, the pep talks and brainstorming did so much to push me.

Also to my beta readers, Jennifer, Leeva, Ashley, Dee, Jenny, Eme, Dani, Marika, Lauren, and Karla—who all read previous drafts, and were instrumental in these final beta rounds and edits. You were all beyond helpful, and this wouldn't be finished without you.

My editor, Chloe Hodge, who has been so great and supportive since I booked with her in 2019. She did an amazing job with the copy-edits of this book, and I am so grateful to have gotten the chance to work with her.

And finally, my beautiful cover designer, Celin. She created such a *beautiful* set of covers for this book. Getting to work with her has been such a blessing, and she has become such an amazing support for this book! I cannot wait to continue our friendship and journey together.

I can't leave without thanking you, the reader. Your support is instrumental. You will keep me writing.

I hope everyone has enjoyed the beginning of Eliza's journey. 2021 will bring you the next book in her story. The Shadowland Saga has only just begun.

SIGN UP FOR THE MONTHLY NEWSLETTER

FOR EXCLUSIVE ACCESS TO NEW MATERIAL, SPECIAL OFFERS, DISCOUTS, SHORT STORIES, UPDATES, AND INFO ON NEW RELEASES FROM THE AUTHOR:

WWW.STEPHANIEANNEAUTHOR.COM

Lightning Source UK Ltd.
Milton Keynes UK
UKHW040708010221
378044UK00003B/632